I0618478

Sword of Allah

By

James Marinero

Also by James Marinero

Fiction:

Gate of Tears
Sicilian Channel (The Maghreb Trilogy Book 1)

Non Fiction:

Susan's Brother

Image Credits

Cover Images: fotolia.com
Artwork: projectpdq.com

A *Wavecrest* Story

Published by Wavecrest Publications
3 Murray Street, Llanelli
Carmarthenshire, SA15 1AQ, UK
www.wavecrestpublications.com

Sword of Allah

First Edition 2016

Copyright © James Marinero, 2016

ISBN-13: 978-0-9568426-9-5

The moral right of the author has been asserted.

All rights reserved
Without limiting the rights under copyright reserved above, no part of this publication may be reproduced, stored in or introduced into a retrieval system, or transmitted, in any form or by any means including electronic, telepathic, mechanical, photocopying, scanning, recording or otherwise, without the prior written permission of both the copyright owner and the above publisher of this book.

With the exception of certain historical figures, events, scientific papers and news items for which references have been provided, all persons, organisations and events in this novel are fictitious, and any resemblance to actual persons, organisations or events is purely coincidental.

The paperback version is printed on paper which accords with UK: Forest Stewardship Council™ (FSC®) Mixed Credit.
FSC® C084699

Contents

ACRONYMS (These are <u>not</u> fictional entities)

AQIM - Al Qua'eda in the Islamic Maghreb

AISI - Agenzia Informazioni e Sicurezza Interna (Italian internal information and security agency)

AISE - Agenzia Informazioni e Sicurezza Externa (Italian external information and security agency)

CISR - Comitato interministeriale per la sicurezza della Repubblica (Italian Interministerial Committee for the security of the Republic)

DIS - Dipartimento delle Informazioni per la Sicurezza (Italian security information department)

DRS - Département du Renseignement et de la Sécurité or Department of Intelligence and Security – the Algerian Secret Police

HMG - Her/His Majesty's Government (UK Government)

ISIL (so called) Islamic State of Iraq and the Levant (aka ISIS - Islamic State of Syria and the Levant)

NAJA - Law Enforcement Force of Islamic Republic of Iran

PAVA - Iranian Intelligence and Public Security Police, part of NAJA

QUDS - The Quds Force - a special forces unit of Iran's Revolutionary Guards responsible for extraterritorial operations

TOR - The Onion Router – an internet mechanism for anonymising communication. TOR routes internet traffic through a free, worldwide, volunteer network consisting of more than seven thousand relays

*'Submit to Islam and be safe. Or agree to the payment of
the Jizya (tax), and you and your people will be under
our protection, else you will have only yourself to blame
for the consequences, for I bring the men who desire
death as ardently as you desire life.'*

- Khalid ibn al-Walid, 'Sword of Allah'
(b. 585 A.D, d. 642 A.D.)

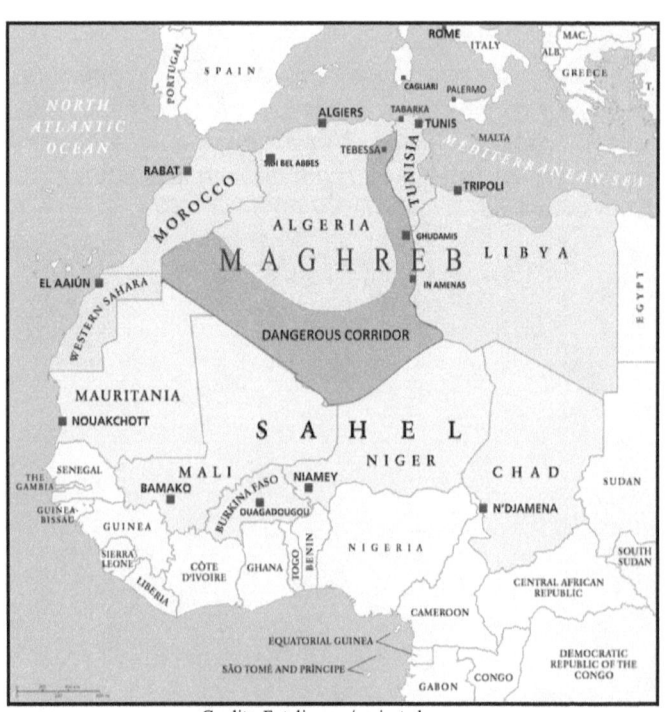

Credits: Fotolia.com/projectpdq.com

Prologue

Maruška Pavkovic was slowly lowering herself to the floor after her ninety third push-up when she felt the familiar pain between her shoulders. She collapsed onto the marble and screamed. She waited for the next pulse. It didn't come. She opened a bottle of water and speed dialled Wan Chuntao on the new phone, after it confirmed her fingerprint and retina pattern.

Under the Guoanbu building in Hainan, it was early morning. Six floors above, there was snow on the ground and the temperature was well below zero. In Room 5, Wan Chuntao had lost track of night and day. The work had been frantic, unceasing and had produced little in the way of results until now.

The message from Wan Chuntao was detailed – the target had been identified and speed of action was essential. Then there was an unequivocal: 'Move Now!"

The line dropped and Maruška was packing her bag when she heard someone shout *Hariq! Hariq!* from the street below. She didn't understand the word and looked out of the window. She saw and recognised Jacob just as the pension's fire alarm went off. He saw her at the window, and she reacted.

She rummaged in her bag and withdrew the small device, then peeled the back off the sticky pad on the back of the charge. She stuck it to the wall behind the door and tested the adhesion gently. Then she carefully pulled out the trigger cord and tied it to the door handle, then pressed the arm button. She threw her sports bag out on to the landing and started to close the door taking once quick glance around the room. Shit, her phone! There on the bedside table. Four seconds of ten. She crossed the room and picked up her phone, six seconds. Back to the door, eight seconds. She held her breath as she closed the door gently. Nine, ten seconds. Armed. She let out her breath gently and picked up her bag. Once the tension changed on the cord then the 500 grams of high explosive would do their work.

Moving towards the stairway to the roof solarium, she heard footsteps on the stairs below, but was not seen as she moved up to the roof. Moving across to the parapet she prepared for the leap across the alley to the next roof.

She climbed up and looked across. In her peripheral vision she could see a couple in a clinch below. She jumped, just as the man raised a Browning Hi-Power towards her, too late. No shot, just a shout as she landed awkwardly, sprawling across the other parapet. Her mind had not been focused on the landing, it had been drawn to the face, trying to place it.

Behind her, in the *pension,* Aaron Rainsford and Elias Stone approached her room. She could hear the two-tone siren of the local *pompiers* approaching - they would certainly have a fire to deal with.

Rainsford tried the door handle, slowly and gently. He turned to Stone and shook his head, then stood back and balanced as he raised his right foot and kicked the door beneath the lock.

Then she had it, the face clicked. Baldwin! How the hell had he found her? She sprinted for the next parapet, following her prepared escape route.

The sound of the explosion did not cause a change in her stride as she reached the street and crossed it, heading for the steps down to the marina. She heard a shout behind her and pushed some German tourists aside, taking the steps three at a time.

The charge inside her room had taken out a section of the thin wall – and the door. Aaron Rainsford had been flattened against the solid stone wall across the narrow corridor. He was beyond help – the door handle and lock assembly together with his sternum, was embedded in his heart. Elias Stone was completely untouched physically, apart from a temporary loss of hearing. He quickly checked Rainsford for vital signs – there were none then looked inside the wrecked room. It was clear that there was no other body and the bathroom was empty. He ran for the stairs.

Halfway down the steps to the marina, Maruška turned and snapped off a shot. There was a scream from the tourists but

Baldwin kept on coming – and behind him another two faces she recognised from her captivity in Malta.

*

The Beginning

The plume of smoke over Grand Harbour was spreading with the wind, carrying the smell of burning oil, plastics and flesh.

The bomb attack on the Cunard cruise liner *Queen Katherine* had been an outstanding success and debris was still falling as the motor yacht 'Meltemi' - a middle-aged Fairline 45, accelerated out through the southern entrance to Grand Harbour, its twin 220 horsepower Caterpillar turbodiesels driving it easily up on to the plane on the flat sea. As it reached the top of its bow wave it levelled and accelerated further as Anwar adjusted the trim tabs.

The patrol boats of the Malta Defence Force were based in Marsamxett Creek, over on the other side of Valetta, up towards Pieta and the Gozo ferry berth, right under the vertical northern bastions of Valetta itself. The ugly, apparently ungainly patrol boats were aging now – they had been bought from Australia twenty years before, but they still posed a threat.

They would surely have been scrambled by now and would soon be coming through the north narrow entrance under St Elmo's Fort, where the old storm gates used to be – if they could squeeze under the footbridge. No matter, he was well on his way. Anwar knew the planned course, and turned to starboard to head down past Marsascala.

Abu ben-Zhair smiled. Naval activity had ramped up in the years since the immigrant crisis which started in 2014, but he did not anticipate being challenged. Not today, not now.

All the signs were that the attack had achieved its objectives. His presence up until the last few minutes had been only to encourage his team, to keep them steadfast and remind them of the glory of the act that they were performing, to say their prayers with them, and to remind them that their place in heaven was assured. So much for the rhetoric, he thought. It sounded good, but the real benefit was that his grip on the organisation would be stronger and he would be able to get rid of the dead wood – and carry out the next two operations, each bigger that the previous one and on a scale far beyond that of 9/11 and the Twin Towers.

Besides, a great leader had to be seen on the front line.

Ten minutes later they passed the entrance to the shallow bay of Marsascala and on down past the fish farms to pass the Freeport. Looking over the starboard quarter he could see the plume of black smoke, already several hundred feet into the air over Malta, drifting slowly west from the carnage at Grand Harbour. Success, so sweet. *Allahu Akbar*.

It hadn't been necessary for him to use the mobile phone bomb trigger - the heroes had done as ordered and driven the fishing trawler *Marie-Anne* right in between the stern of the *Queen Katherine* and the quay wall, detonating their cargo. It was a sign of his skill at managing his team that they had not faltered. He looked at the mobile phone in his hand and threw it over the stern into the boiling wake of the boat on which he was escaping.

It had been a tiring journey, with several legs to make tracking him difficult – if indeed he was being tracked. He had no reason to suppose so. For years, ever since he had been student in Moscow and learned the black arts, he had moved carefully using multiple identities. After that he had spent time in Beijing and taken on a new affiliation. Beijing knew about his time in Moscow – but the Russians knew nothing of his Beijing links. It was a dangerous game.

Just twelve hours go he had arrived on the ferry from Catania after checking preparations for the next operation, the Sword of Allah. That had been almost two years in the planning, the most complex operation by far. Complexity meant risk and high probability of failure, but he was as sure that he could be that all risks were properly controlled. And. in the event that the operation failed there was a backup operation which would take place almost simultaneously. If both succeeded that would be wonderful – but it only needed one to succeed for the apparently outrageous and as yet unpublished claim to be validated. That announcement would be made worldwide in just a few short weeks. The text was ready and had been agreed by the Inner Council of the Islamic Caliphate in the Maghreb.

He smiled to himself. 'The Inner Council' – what a notion! He controlled them, the plans and project concepts were his alone. The Council were incapable of turning vision into reality. They did his bidding and those that refused – well, they had early appointments with Allah.

In a couple of hours the videos of the martyrs would be published on Al Jazheera and would be going viral on the web, as millions of people clicked to watch it on their smartphones and head-up displays, and then share it with their friends, gawping at death and disaster filmed from the drones his team were controlling over Grand Harbour and the wreckage. Or, if they were true Muslims, he thought, they would be glorying in the strike against the hated city of the Crusaders.

By that time, he would have cleared Malta and the Italian Island of Pantellaria would be to the south of them. That island had served him well in getting his team into Italy for the next project.

Within a dozen hours they would pass through the western end of the Sicilian Channel, past Cape Bon in Tunisia, turn west by south outside Tunisian waters and then follow the coast for over a hundred miles. Then they would be in Algerian waters. Home – wherever that was, safe where risks were minimal, if only for a short time. Next week he would be in Rabat in Morocco, discussing progress on the preparations for the following operation – still a year away - but already many years in the planning. Beautifully simple in concept, with the huge impact on Western nations, 'The Cause of All Causes' would be his swansong – provided that the 'Sword of Allah' did its work first. The bid test was now less than six months away.

*

To fanatical Muslims (or people who called themselves such), the Crusades represent a massive bloodstain on the history of their religion.

The most appalling acts of terror and genocide in history have been caused by religious bigotry, and it still continues. There are no good sides and bad sides. Genghis Khan, the Romans, even the British, French and Spanish killed millions of native Americans, north and south, and treated Africans as savages and animals. The twentieth century had seen Stalin, Pol Pot, Mao Tse-Tung and Hitler, though the latter had plumbed new depths of sickness. The list is endless and grows even today.

But for Muslims – or Islamists as the most extreme are now identified – the Crusades are still a painful collective memory in their consciousness.

He turned to the helmsman, a trusted jihadi.

"Today, Anwar, we have struck a glorious blow for Allah – may He be praised - against the Infidels, the Crusaders, and the British. It will go down in history next to the destruction of those towers of filthy American commerce on 9/11."

Anwar turned and smiled,

"*Allahu Akbar*".

"*Allahu Akbar*" acknowledged Abu ben-Zhair as he passed Anwar a bottle of fruit juice.

He didn't take any himself. His stomach could cope with mass murder, but a gentle swell was its limit at sea. He consoled himself with the thought that fasting was a religious commitment.

He smiled grimly. They were fools, blowing themselves up for the promise of a few virgins in heaven. But useful fools.

It is power that matters, power to do what I have done today, power to bend others to my will.

He could talk the talk, and today he Abu ben-Zhair had walked the walk - but he was under no illusions about those above him in the chain of command. They too harboured no illusions, either about Islam or about power. They would watch him and he would watch them - and then he would climb over them. He had controlled first the GIA, then the Salafists and now the Islamic Caliphate in the Maghreb - his Maghreb.

Then there would be more to come as he took control of IC itself, and built an empire of a size never before seen. He did not think of his ambitions as madness – his aims could be achieved a lot more easily using new weapons with total ruthlessness. Protracted wars would be consigned to history.

*

The Maghreb traditionally encompasses the area of North Africa ranging through the modern-day countries of Libya, Tunisia, Algeria and Morocco, almost from the Suez Canal, through the Straits of Gibraltar and down the Atlantic coast to the country known as Mauritania.

Maghrebi Arabic (Maghrebi Darija) is the principal spoken language in the Maghreb and the ethnicity of the people is Berber (hence the term 'Barbary Coast').

Libya and Algeria are very wealthy countries with large reserves of oil and natural gas, but Tunisia is less so, with Morocco being the least wealthy (and, conversely, most stable politically). The history of the Maghreb is long and bloody.

*

Ben-Zhair planned to go ashore just to the east of Cape Rose in Algeria. There was a sandy beach there in the Golfe de Canier, about 20 miles to the east of Annaba (or Bone as the French had known it), a major port. Bone had once been a small fishing port and a base of the Barbary corsairs – fast pirate craft that preyed on merchant shipping, even as far away as the English Channel. Merciless and cruel, they captured seamen, fishermen, passengers and even soldiers and sold them as slaves to the Dey (ruler) of Algiers, under whose patronage they operated. They were fearsome and cunning cut-throats who were not averse even to attacking naval vessels with their fast and manoeuvrable craft which used both sails and oars to great effect in the fickle winds of the Mediterranean Sea.

The beach at Cape Rose was no more than six miles from the Tunisian border, and 'Meltemi' would stay well offshore until they had crossed into Algerian territorial waters – this area was heavily patrolled by both sides and there was a narrow 'corridor' into Annaba which vessels had to use.

"Anwar, our orders are to go to Annaba."

"*Aiwa.* We have fuel for more than 500 miles – I have prepared as instructed."

"Good, we must be at Annaba early tomorrow morning, when the patrols are sleepy. Ensure we stay at least 50 kilometres off the Tunisian coast until we are off the coast of Algeria – I do not want to see any Tunisian patrol boats. Change that flag at the back to a Moroccan flag. We are now a Moroccan boat, and I am a wealthy Moroccan businessman returning from a visit to Sicily. Is that clear?"

"*Aiwa.* We have talked about this before, and I remember all the details. Everything is ready."

"Good, I will give you new papers when we get nearer to Annaba. Let me know when we are off Cape Bon. I am going to sleep now – it has been a long night, and a wonderful morning."

"It shall be. In five hours we will be off Cape Bon. I will call you then. *Allahu Akbar.*"

"*Allahu Akbar.*"

Ben-Zhair's real plan had some crucial differences, but Anwar did not need to know that. The real events would be different too, but even Ben-Zhair could not know that. Plans rarely survive first contact with the enemy and this would be no exception.

*

On January 6, 2016, North Korea announced a fourth nuclear weapons test, described as a miniaturised hydrogen bomb test.

There was little doubt in the West (or China) that the underground test had taken place at Punggye-ri, but the claim that it was a fusion bomb was belittled. Hydrogen bombs have a much bigger bang than fission bombs (a fission bomb is actually used as the trigger in a fusion bomb – at least in the 'conventional' design).

The explosion was measured as being about 5.1 on the Richter Scale (as used for measuring earthquakes) which is typically produced by a device in the range of 8-10 kilotons (read 8-10 thousand tons of TNT equivalent). A fusion bomb would typically yield 100 kilotons – 15 to 20 larger than the typical fission bomb.

However the very smallest conventional fission bomb – such as the US *Davy Crockett* tactical warhead or the MK54 nuclear artillery round back in the early 1950s - could have a yield as low 0.01 kilotons - 10 tons of TNT equivalent. This contrasts with the estimated 25 tons of actual TNT used in the British Lochnagar mine in the Battle of the Somme in 1916.

One area of concern in the West was the claim that this latest fusion device was miniaturised – a key requirement if the weapon is to be used on the tip of a missile. In a double-whammy, North Korea had also successfully tested a submarine-based ballistic missile launch system a month before, in December 2015. Then, in early February 2016, North Korean successfully tested an intercontinental ballistic missile – the Kwangmyongsong - placing a satellite in orbit.

And it got worse, the bad news just kept on coming.

In July 2016, IHS Jane's Defence Weekly reported that it had analysed images which showed that North Korea was building two 490ft shelters at its Mayang-do base. These would accommodate much larger submarines than North Korea's then current Romeo-class vessels which were only 250ft long. There was little doubt that North Korea was planning to build much bigger missile submarines to provide a platform for its tested submarine-launched missiles.

It is said that Dim Pong-un, the Supreme Leader of North Korea, was fulsome in his unpublished praise to the head of the weapons test programme for several reasons unknown to Western, Russian or even Chinese intelligence agencies.

This was because North Korea had in fact extended the bounds of an existing fusion research avenue directed towards peaceful use in clean power generation. They had developed a pumped laser fusion device ('PLFD'). Although not yet capable of miniaturisation, its low fusion yield could make it practical as a battlefield weapon - and posed a significant threat to South Korea. It was also relatively 'clean' in a radiation sense – useful if you are bombing your neighbour and don't want to get the fallout brought back to you on the wind from next door.

*

Late in the year after the announcement of another successful North Korean H Bomb test, *Chong Ryon San,* a general cargo freighter of about 7,500 tons, left the North Korean port of Chongjin bound for Bandar Abbas in Iran. This was the 234th voyage in the life of the tired freighter. Although it was a regular trade run, it was closely monitored by US and other intelligence agencies concerned about the ongoing ballistic missile cooperation between Iran and North Korea (for which the US had imposed sanctions in January 2016).

Two days later, from Bandar Abbas, the *Chong Ryon San* routed around Saudi Arabia and the Yemen, through Bab el Mandeb (The Gate of Tears), up through the Red Sea, the Suez Canal and west through the Sicilian Channel to Annaba in Algeria (Algeria is one of North Korea's largest trading partners). Two days later, the ship headed back through the Suez Canal to Bandar Abbas and then on to Chongjin in North Korea.

In Langley, Virginia, the CIA had flagged the voyage as an anomaly but there was little intelligence to supplement the facts or increase suspicion (which was always present in copious amounts). Satellite images showed little other than regular cargo containers (each of which could admittedly contain a 40 foot missile stage). More detailed image analysis (paint scrape patterns, dents and the like) yielded the fact that twelve containers unloaded at Annaba had been loaded a Chongjin. This was to be expected in the normal course of trade.

The CIA had no people on the ground so their humint capability was very low in Annaba (a very sensitive port) and almost non-existent in Bandar Abbas. What little they did know came from friendly seamen in bars - and there was precious little of that. The little information available from Karachi gave no cause for suspicion. The British fared little better but the French sources in Annaba mentioned military convoy activity in the port during the visit of the *Chong Ryon San.* It was several months before this information found its way onto Langley's database and no satellite imagery was available for the period in question.

Langley never became aware that the critical cargo had left the ship at Bandar Abbas on the outward voyage and was transported by road to Yazd in the central mountain region of Iran.

*

Abu ben-Zhair

His family had a proud history. In 1956 his father was a young boy of six years and had escaped south into the Tassili N'Ajjer area on a camel with his grandfather. They had spent the winter there, man and son, at a concealed base where his father had become a young man.

In the early 1950s, Algeria was in revolt, as was the French Foreign Legion. The plan to cede Algeria to its Nationalist party – the front for the terrorists or freedom fighters, depending on one's perspective – had caused military rebellion in France. The OAS (Organisation de l'Armée Secrete) featured in the headlines daily.

Many French soldiers had been born and raised in Algeria and were of mixed – even pure – Arabic parentage. They considered themselves thoroughly French. Generally, the idea that France should give up a part of itself to terrorists was anathema and the OAS had been born. It was less than secret, founded and run by disaffected French Army Officers and able to mobilise many men as well as strong opinions in France and Algeria. France had just dis-engaged from Vietnam after the disaster at Dien Bien Phu in 1954, effectively ending French colonialism.

As with some other European countries, colonialism had left a bitter aftertaste and even today the Algerian Arabic ghettoes in France are places of hopelessness and raise xenophobic and racist feelings in some French people.

The multitude of problems is both complex and extensive, and the outcomes dreadful as terrorist atrocities continue across France today.

In Algeria itself, a whole generation grew up with a legacy that stimulated many to associate themselves with groups such as Al Qua'eda and ISIS - and to try to re-establish Shariah Law and a return to the old ways.

*

The six years-old boy had woken to the sound of shouting and his mother's wailing. He could hear the rough wooden door being smashed down and then heard shouts in French. He recognised the language as that of legionnaires, but he understood little. There was commotion and the sound of breaking furniture. He heard men on the flat roof above him. Then the door to the room in which he slept was thrown open and two legionnaires burst in, with torches.

'Il n'est pas ici' one said as they turned his bed over and scattered his possessions, trampling the rug and dragging him out into the family room where a legionnaire had broken a paraffin lamp over the wrecked table with a rug thrown on it. The trooper took out an old brass cigarette lighter which reflected the flame as he struck it in the dark room and set the fire.

His mother was outside, wailing as the soldiers removed her clothes, exposing her shame. There was no sign of anyone else beyond the legionnaires. The village remained almost silent bar the roaring and spitting as the flames took hold and he heard the dry wood of the poor furniture crackling wickedly. The air pockets expanded and burst the cellulose fibres, feeding the eager fire and sending sparks up through the fallen roof. He was tied to a camel.

The fire was now roaring but would soon run out of fuel and die. Spitting and groaning the roof timbers were surrendering their load and falling inward. There was another crack, louder than the noise of the fire, and a legionnaire fell to the ground.

'Merde' uttered one of the troopers. The squad did not panic, they fell to the ground almost as one man, rolling, seeking cover and trying to locate the source of the shot. They were exceptionally well drilled and their MAS-49 rifle shots cracked systematically. Capitaine Moitessier shouted to the sergeant, ordering cease fire.

A further order was given quietly and one of the legionnaires broke cover to run to the next building, across the stony track which ran between the homes. Their injured comrade – not a true compatriot as the squad comprised many nationalities – was groaning as the medic hauled him into the shadows cast by the waning moon. In his pain he had fallen back on his native tongue, though none of his squad understood the Gaelic prayers. It was well after midnight as they watched and waited silently and patiently. The bait offered by the trooper crossing the open ground to the next building was without effect, no further shot was taken at them, no fire was drawn.

For weeks they had been trying to locate this one man. Tonight they had information that the young boy's father knew the identity of the 'Spectre' as he was known. One shot, one death – and so it had been for three months in this area. One or two legionnaires were picked off every week. Morale was falling.

A few minutes later, Moitessier was told that the injured trooper was gut-shot and bleeding heavily, with little chance of recovery. He walked across and shot the man through the temple. Life was hard out here and those of the squad who still thought that there was a god – or were just regularly superstitious – crossed themselves. Every one of them would have made the same choice in the circumstances.

They loaded their dead comrade onto a camel and after a quick headcount set off for their base.

Abu ben-Zhair's father had learned to fight, to shoot and had received a modicum of education. He had skirmished with the Foreign Legion and learned to stay cool in the heat of a firefight.

Now, as a man, Abu ben-Zhair's legacy was to fight on a much larger scale than that of his father. He was not fighting for the liberation of Algeria. He was fighting for the Muslim religion itself on a world-wide scale. He was not a 'spectre' as his father and grandfather had been; his name was publicly known now since the bombing of the *Queen Katherine* cruise liner in Grand Harbour, Malta, earlier in the year.

That was the legend, that was the plan.

*

Larger in land area than the major countries of Europe, Algeria is a country rich in natural resources including oil, gas and minerals. It extends from the Mediterranean Sea southwards into the heart of the continent of Africa, and includes much of the Sahara Desert. The official name (in English) of the political entity which we know as Algeria is 'People's Democratic Republic of Algeria'.

With a population of over 40 million people, and a nominal GDP of $181 Billion, it is a powerful country, and, because of its natural wealth it has no need to encourage tourism. In contrast, North Korea, which aspires to sit at the top table of nuclear powers – those which acknowledge possession of nuclear weapons – has a population of 25 million people and a GDP of $16 Billion. North Korea encourages tourism – but few people want to visit.

Ancient Algeria has had many invaders over the centuries, including the Phoenicians, Carthaginians, Romans, Vandals, Byzantines, Ottomans and of course, latterly, the French. Berbers are considered to be the indigenous people of Algeria and despite widespread use of the French language, the official languages of the country are Arabic and Berber. Berber, is of course, the language which was used by the Barbary Pirates. French and English are considered by the CIA to be *lingua francas* of the country.

Algeria is at the core of the region known as The Maghreb and is a member of the modern-day Maghreb Union, which it founded, and although most Algerians are Berber in origin, most identify themselves as Arabs.

*

Ghudamis is a town in Libya near the conjunction of the Libyan, Tunisian and Algerian borders. Today the N53 route which heads south for Tassili N'Ajjer National Park, a World Heritage site, becomes the N1 onwards to Tamanrasset. This is classical French Foreign Legion country. To the south lies the Aïr Country of Fort Zinderneuf where Algeria meets Niger and Mali - the setting for the novel Beau Geste.

The people of this region are Tuareg – an ancient nomadic tribe who inhabit central Africa and pay little heed to borders.

They are classified as a Berber tribe and their DNA extends across much of North Africa. Tough and warlike, many were hired by Muammar Gadhafi to form his elite 'presidential guard' in Libya.

Just south of Ghudamis lies the village of Deb Deb.

The night that Le Capitaine Moitessier and his platoon visited Deb Deb is not forgotten there, even more than seventy years later. The legacy of that night in that poor village lived on in the emotions of Abu ben-Zhair, in the stories his father had told him and in his very genes.

*

Under the burned out house, the air in the soft rock tunnel cooled as the young boy's father shimmied away from the seat of the fire. He could hear nothing, and when he emerged from a home further down the track the squad had already left the village.

The officer had decided that losing one man was enough – there would be no search of the village this night. The men would take it out on the woman. As for the boy, they had lost him. In the confusion, although tied to the camel, he had urged it out of the village at a trot. Too late. The shots were aimless - he had escaped and the spent bullets fell uselessly into the sand.

Two hours later, the boy met his father a mile away from the still-cooling embers of what had been their home. The man spoke in Arabic and there was no reaction. He tried French and the camel dropped onto its knees. The boy remained silent as the man cut the boy's bindings. Then he mounted the camel and made his son comfortable on his lap. With gentle urging in the man's limited French, the camel set off.

They did not speak of the boy's mother as they located their water reserve hidden in a nearby cave. They quietly loaded the goatskins and headed south towards Tassili N'Ajjer. Abdel Zhair was proud of his son and grieved silently for his wife – he had no illusions that she would be dead by the time the sun was above the horizon. Although they did not know it, the wife and mother was already dead and had given nothing away before she died. She knew about the tunnel but little about his activities. Knowing even that was too much and did not save her.

*

Ben Zhair's father was noted for his cunning and intelligence. Commanders marked him out for further education – the new Algeria would need sound and capable men to run the new, independent country.

Within the family (and other circles) he was legendary. Together with Saleem Malik who had been known as 'Le Spectre' they had made a formidable duo in the building of the new Algeria.

Abu ben-Zhair was in many ways like his father and grandfather, but the need for more change in Algeria was driving him in his own way. He had enjoyed the privileged education as a child of a senior government official, including attending university overseas in Moscow. Later he had spent time as a graduate student in Beijing when China was starting to turn outwards and see the world as a pool of resources for its use – and Africa was ripe for development. In Algeria, the Islamists in the form of the GIA had been causing problems within major terrorist acts against tourists and the government alike. Eventually, a form of co-existence was established between the Government and the extremists. This continued through the so-called Arab Spring which had led to the liberalisation of Tunisia and Egypt, and major civil war in Syria.

*

Iran Rolls Over

The infighting at the top of the Iranian hierarchy continued unabated after it signed the nuclear arms agreement in early 2016. Supreme Leader Ruhollah Sistani struggled to contain the strife between the factions of his government.

After the nuclear deal with the so called P5 +1 (the UN Security Council Members plus Germany), the Iranian Government was in turmoil. No one was happy with the deal – and that extended to the P5+1, Israel and others as well.

As part of the agreement, Iran had transferred 10 tons of atomic fuel to Russia, mothballed 12,000 centrifuges (used to enrich uranium ore), and poured concrete into a plutonium reactor.

In exchange, the White House lifted sanctions, allowing Iran access to $100 billion in frozen assets.

U.N. weapons inspectors would be on the ground to watch whether Iran tried to cheat on the deal.

Israel's Prime Minister, Binyamin Netanyahu, denounced the historic deal on Iran's nuclear programme. Netanyahu said the agreement was a "capitulation" and a mistake of historic proportions:

"Iran is going to receive a sure path to nuclear weapons" *(sic)*

*

Good deals were Win/Win, but there were many in both Iran and the West who thought that the symmetry had not been there in the 2016 nuclear arms deal.

Of particular concern was the ultra-hard right in Iran, some of whom had been involved in managing the funding of Hezbollah (for example, some sources cite the provision of over 10,000 missiles) and other more extreme organisations - particularly those engaged in fighting the Saudi-sponsored IC in Syria – and elsewhere. There was direct involvement too with the Quds Force - a special forces unit of Iran's

Revolutionary Guards responsible for their extraterritorial operations. The Force reports directly to the Supreme Leader of Iran. Shrouded in secrecy, its size was estimated at 15,000 troops (2007). The United States has designated the Quds Force a supporter of terrorism since 2007.

In order to stabilise the government and protect Iran's security, Ruhollah Sistani stressed – in high secrecy and to a very small audience of less than six people – that there were ways around this deal which could not be detected by the UN Weapons Inspectors whose presence was permanent and mandatory as part of the deal. North Korea had proved to be a reliable ally and would continue to be so. Indeed, they were offering to share new technology.

The project had been given the name 'The Great Answer' - پاسخ بزرگ – in Farsi.

Those briefed were satisfied with Ruhollah Sistani's stance but were nevertheless concerned about the perception in the wider Muslim world that Iran had rolled over for the 'American Devil'. They would continue their public opposition but refrain from going so far as to de-stabilise Sistani's government.

In fact, the circumvention of the deal was well under way at the time of that briefing, with planning having begun way back in 2014.

Following the unloading of the ship *Chong Ryon San* at Bandar Abbas the programme had accelerated, and a prototype PLFD was being assembled using the North Korean design and components. This work was taking place at a new underground site at Yazd which had not been declared to the UN – and crucially, had not been detected by US satellites. Yazd is the site of a uranium mine and also has a low power particle accelerator 'engaged in geophysical research to analyse the mineral deposits surrounding the city'. Iran was hiding the new facility in plain view – if you want to hide a tree, what better place than a forest?

It was anticipated that the prototype would be available for testing within a year after the nuclear research deal was signed. In support of that, another visit by the *Chong Ryon San* brought sufficient plutonium 'sweetener' to be used in the prototype.

Although technical projects of this scale and complexity often slip due to unforeseen technical research issues, this development was an exception. The North Koreans' own successful prototype had worked well and although some refinement was necessary, the Iranian copy would take substantially less than a year to bring up to test readiness.

Additionally, immediately after the signing of the nuclear research deal with the P5+1 countries, work was put underway to move Iranian assets so that they could not be frozen in future by the P5 and wider international community. There were still many countries friendly to Iran.

This was all part of 'The Great Answer'.

*

Green Seas

The swell gradually subsided as they left the Gulf of Tunis astern and the hot afternoon burned down. Anwar had noticed some cloud from the northwest earlier that day, but his father's weather lore had long been forgotten. The easterly swell had died completely as they passed over the north end of Banco Estafette and the waters began to deepen into the Western Mediterranean Basin. The sea was from the northwest now, and building, with the wind.

Anwar could no longer doze. Though his weather knowledge was scant, he was uneasy about the prospects ahead. He reduced speed by a few knots to try and make the ride more comfortable – the boat was beginning to pound now and he was glad of the padded seat.

Just after four pm, ben-Zhair reappeared. He did not look too good – there was a green tinge to his face, and he looked clammy. He held tightly to the grabrail in the deck saloon, trying to adjust to the motion of the boat.

"How long will this continue, Anwar?"

Anwar shrugged. "Only Allah knows – may he be praised" he replied, "but at our present speed we have another 10 hours of this – at least."

There was some contempt in ben-Zhair's expression at this news, but he stayed silent.

"I can reduce speed some more if you wish."

"No, no, it is important that we keep to the plan."

"As you wish, but I think it will get worse."

They felt the bang through the deck of the boat. She slewed to starboard across the sea and an unhealthy banging continued from under the stern.

Anwar swore.

"What is that?"

"I think we hit something. We may be damaged."

Anwar checked the instrument panel and could see that the revolutions on the starboard propeller shaft were falling. He shut the starboard engine down.

"I will go and check in the engine room."

Just then there was shrill alarm and a red light came on. The legend beneath it said "Bilge Water Level."

He switched on both engine room bilge pumps on the panel, then after resetting the autopilot and reducing the power on the port engine, he went down through the hatch into the engine room.

By the time he returned, ben-Zhair had been sick into the galley sink. Anwar did not feel too well himself, and the sight of ben-Zhair's half-digested lunch made him gag.

"We have damaged the starboard shaft and propeller. We must have hit something. The stern tube is leaking but I have tightened the gland and wrapped packing around it. We are safe for the moment, the pumps can cope. We should make for the nearest harbour."

"Where is that?"

"Bizerte. It is about 25 miles to the South."

"But that is in Tunisia."

"Yes, but Annaba is another almost 100 miles further, and the weather is getting worse. We have the night ahead."

"We are not going to Tunisia as long as we can make progress towards Annaba."

Anwar looked unhappy.

"Very well. You are the leader. The coast is dangerous in this weather and there is only really one other harbour – Tabarka. But that too is in Tunisia – just. Even Tabarka is 70 miles."

"As you said, I am the leader of this mission. If the boat is in no immediate danger then we continue towards Annaba. Tabarka remains an option, though that is so close to Algeria as to make no difference. Except of course for the border."

"It shall be" Anwar said as he turned to the galley, shaking his head. He found a plastic pan in one of the cupboards and handed it to ben-Zhair.

"For you" he said. "I will clean up. You will find some anti-seasickness tablets in the first aid box – there." He pointed to the bulkhead just as the 'Meltemi' hit a big sea and ben-Zhair retched into the pan, just managing to hold on to the grabrail.

Anwar checked the radar and Automatic Identification System. They were a little south of the main shipping tracks, but he could detect at least eight ships within 20 miles. AIS gave the details of the ships as he moved the AIS cursor around and it passed over each ship's symbol. There was an oil tanker header to Gulfport in the US, two grain carriers, a deep sea tug and all the general cargo ships that make up a typical day on this busy route to and from the Suez Canal.

The cursor passed over one target which showed the data of a ship called the *Chong Ryon San* with a speed of 17 knots on a heading 270 degrees true, with a mixed cargo, non-hazardous, headed for Annaba in Algeria and an ETA three hours later. Anwar would never know its significance.

Two hours later ben-Zhair felt better though a little sleepy as a result of the pills. In the heads compartment he struggled against the motion of the boat as he cleaned himself up. He knew that he had made history, but the prospect of even greater glory was tantalisingly close. Then he headed up to the bridgedeck. The spray was flying but the wind had shifted and they were now making more than 12 knots under the one engine.

"OK Anwar, we will divert to Tabarka, but only until the weather forecast improves."

"It's better already, but there may be worse to come."

The worst of the weather held off and a little over eight hours later they passed inside the ancient Genovese fort at Tabarka. Anwar stopped the boat just inside the marina and prepared the mooring lines. As he belayed the stern line on the cleat ready docking, Ben-Zhair cursed his earlier seasickness. He had forgotten to change the vessel's ensign to a Tunisian flag, and the self-adhesive registration numbers for the bow were in his cabin. He had three sets of ships papers, but now he would have to stick with the Maltese version.

Next would be the bureaucracy and the bribes for the officials. He sighed in resignation – Anwar could sort all that out. After that he would be needed no more.

China Stirs

In musical terms, the attack of a note is the shape of its initial rising edge. The attack of a note is a characteristic of the instrument generating it – one reason why a given note sounds different on a violin to a piano. Earth tremors (such as occur after earthquakes or nuclear tests) are analogous to sound waves and their shape can provide useful information.

Further analysis of the Chinese seismograph data collected at the time of the North Korean test had shown an anomalous 'attack' in the compression waves at the very first instant. This peculiar effect was only present in the data from one seismograph station – just inside the Chinese border at Hyesan and less than 60 mile from the North Korean test site. Other stations – including those in other countries - were not able to observe this anomaly on account of the phenomenon known as dispersion – basically, the way that waves tend to spread out with distance. The 'attack' of the seismic data suggested a two-stage explosion with a gap of less than hundredth of a microsecond between the stages – this gap was at the extreme resolution of the seismograph.

The air samples that the People's Republic of China had collected near the site of North Korea's claimed hydrogen bomb test had been analysed when the radiation had finally percolated out of the ground after a few weeks. While the samples did not provide absolute proof of a hydrogen bomb test, when taken in conjunction with the seismograph data the probability of the truth of North Korea's claim was seen as too high to treat lightly.

This data had been collated into a report and included 'Conclusions' and 'Recommended Actions'. It was printed on paper – one copy only – and was marked 'General Secretary - Eyes Only'. It was hand delivered to the General Secretary (who was also the President) in person by the head of the Guoanbu.

Within hours a special task force had been set up within the Guoanbu. China's technical intelligence resources were vast, but not infinite, and the quantum computing facilities in the Decryption Agency of the Guoanbu were re-prioritized so that more computing power could be dedicated to real-time analysis of North Korean communications. Additional agents were inserted across the border and sleepers were activated.

The General Secretary knew that if the West got hold of this information then hostile action would be very likely – right on China's doorstep. China, as a putative friend of North Korea, would be between a rock and a hard place. The country was powerful enough not to have any military concern, but commercial impacts could be painful – and disturb the people.

*

It has long been recognized that the Chinese are masters of strategy, and although they are not thought to have invented chess, they did invent 'GO' sometime around 2500 BC. It is an apparently simple game but is much more complex than chess, with the number of possible games well in excess of the number of atoms in the universe. Strategy is everything in Go. And so it is in Chinese politics, economic policy and diplomacy.

Back in the 1960s, Mao Tse-tung was building Chinese power in the international arena. Historically, China had always been inward looking but since the days of Mao their stance has gradually changed and their economy is now the second largest in the world. They have a serious blue water naval capability, a growing carrier fleet and a huge nuclear weapons program. They have put men in space.

They have a vast intelligence network and huge cyberwarfare capability headed up by the Guoanbu. These are the aspects that are apparent in everyday news broadcasts. Mao's strategy lives on, although it has flexed to meet progress.

Mao Tse-tung started his days as a revolutionary, and as part of his strategy China funded terrorism and fomented revolution. The dictum 'Keep your friends close and your enemies closer' led to the concept of controlling terrorism. It was seen as better to fund and direct terrorism, even if some of its acts were against one's own state. Future leaders could be identified and developed, their policy influenced and controlled – and their efforts turned against other countries. Robert Mugabe in Zimbabwe had been one such terrorist leader.

Many countries follow such a policy, if only in a minor way. Some, such as Russia, have been enthusiastic, callous and visible followers of such policies. On a larger scale, proxy wars are useful for testing new weapons and tactics, and developing one's own future military leaders through active combat experience – as 'military advisors'. Since Vietnam, China has been more circumspect, but the clues are there for those who look hard enough.

*

Preparations

The purchase of the property had finally been completed after months of bureaucracy and sweeteners. Construction work in this sensitive heritage area had been approved and the work on the new commercial bank started. At the outset the weapons technology to be used had not been settled on and it was only by good fortune – and the will of Allah – that had led ben-Zhair to meet with an Iranian – a Sunni Iranian in reality, but a practising Shia to his colleagues and the world in general. It seemed that the Iranian establishment was peppered with closet Sunni Muslims in positions of power. From that link had come the tie-in with Hashemi Firouzabadi – a politician looking for revenge and revolution. He in turn had led to Jafa Sharifi, the technical team he had hand-picked – and the weapon which ben-Zhair had named 'The Sword of Allah'.

That was the moment when it seemed that the workings of Allah were revealed to ben-Zhair and the technology to be used in the bank building was finally defined. From then on it was just a matter of careful planning. Of course ben-Zhair did not believe that it was the plan of Allah – it was his own ability to take advantage of information, to be persuasive and ruthless and to build on the vision he had established, that of a powerful weapon in the heart of an infidel city.

Firouzabadi had been a fool and was sure to compromise the operation given enough time. He had made it to the ship, but his voyage ended at sea, with a bullet from Hamadani. That decision had helped Jafa Sharifi and his technical specialists understand that there would be no turning back.

Since the sanctions on Iran had been lifted in early 2016, pent-up Iranian investment capital had flowed freely as the need properly to re-establish Iran as a world trading economy had required. Those close to the project believed that it was to be a new branch of an Iranian bank, although there was nothing in writing to support his - the apparent property owner was an established private Italian company. Investigation of the ultimate owners of the company would have proved difficult and time-consuming, had anyone bothered to do so.

It was pure coincidence that the lead construction company engaged for the development was one of the companies which had been controlled by the now dead Tumino brothers, who had been linked to Charles Tobin's gold extraction project.

There was little publicity about the building project, and those who asked – if they could find anyone to ask – were told that the new bank would be open the following year. And no, no name could be given as the client wished to remain anonymous at this time.

*

Morning turned into afternoon as the 'Meltemi' thundered on past Pantellaria and towards Cape Bon. It was over a year since the building project had started. Malta and the still smouldering wreck of the *Queen Katherine* was a hundred miles astern. After they had eaten, ben-Zhair said he was going back to his cabin to make some phone calls – Anwar had seen the small satellite phone earlier. He thought that they were dangerous – everyone knew that the Americans could track them. They did.

The call went through to a number in Marseilles, France. It was not answered. One minute later ben-Zhair called again. It was unanswered. Then, after the third attempt the call-back came, as arranged, from a fresh number on a clean, unused phone.

"*Bonjour* Jean-Claude, it is good to speak to you at last."

"*Bonjour* Charles, I have been waiting for your call."

"Is all well with the family?"

"Yes."

"Then the birthday celebration will go ahead."

"That is good."

"Alas, I cannot be there but I have sent money as a gift."

"Thank you, we have received it. We saw the family news. It was a great event, *oui*?"

"*Certainement.*"

29

"I will contact you again, a week before the celebration."
"I will look forward to that."
"A bientot."
"A bientot."

Aabis Tawfiq walked to the Café Rouge on the Boulevard de Paris in Marseilles and confirmed the next shipment. He was enthused – the bombing in Malta was a great boost to morale and the team planned to celebrate on Friday evening.

The following day Tariq Saqqaf would leave Marseilles with a small parcel mixed in with other assorted packages on the inter-city groupage truck for *La Poste*, the French postal service. It was a daily run to Paris with parcels, more than eight hours by truck. Up one day, back the next. The overall risk of transporting one kilo of Libyan semtex twice a week to Paris was lower than transporting half a ton in one journey. It was safer too, and this would be the final consignment.

Aabis Tawfiq would return to Paris in his old but reliable Citroen car.

In the US NSA's data archives, the details of the satellite call – the metadata (including the approximate location) and full transcript - were stored. The only flag was against the source location – near the Algerian coast. The analysis system at that time had no way of recognizing that the source phone had not been used before – such an analytical ability would have raised another flag. Most terrorist calls were from land based phones, and they were wise to monitoring.

*

Less than a week later and less than twenty minutes after the extraction of the Chinese agent Pavkovic from the warehouse in Grand Harbour, the panel van stopped outside the stone-pillared gates to the villa. It was really an old farmhouse - between Zabbar and Zeitun, near Luqa airport in Malta. It had been easy to find – Bryan knew the vineyard which was on the side of the Freeport road.

There were no lights on and the padlocked gate yielded easily to Bryan's jemmy. In its day it had been the centre of a small vineyard, but now the land was owned by the Marsovin wine company. The farmhouse itself had been gentrified and was on long lease to the British High Commission. They drove up the track to the main building. It would do for a few hours.

Bryan quickly broke a rear window and unlocked the patio doors. There was no alarm system as far as they could tell – unless it was silent.

Bryan helped Tobin stagger in, walking very awkwardly.

"Put him on that couch there."

Steve dragged Maruška into the kitchen. Kicking her feet from under her he put cable ties around her feet, shackling them together.

"There's no need for that – I am here voluntarily, although I should be going to Tunis."

"Don't kid yourself."

Helena looked across. "What's that about Tunis?"

Maruška looked at Helena and tried to shrug. "That is for negotiation."

Steve tightened the ties a couple of notches. "You are in no position to negotiate."

"You'd better check that first with your lady boss."

Helena's phone vibrated and she left the room as Bryan spoke.

"What do I do about Tobin? He needs a doctor."

"Treat him for shock. He has a broken hand and a missing testicle. He will live. He didn't get to learn my full repertoire of tricks."

"Like you showed Tom Brown?"

"Brown? I don't remember – there have been so many men in my life."

"Djibouti."

"Ah yes, I remember now. That was good. He died slowly, crying like a baby. He told me everything."

"How's the ear?" Steve twisted her left ear, hard.

Maruška's reply was cut off as Steve wrapped the duct tape tightly round her ears, mouth and over her nose. She struggled and tried to kick. He found a kitchen knife and cut two small holes for her nostrils, just as her kicking was starting to slow.

He saw her breathe hard and fast, although there was no fear in her eyes.

"Steve, in here."

He walked through into a salon area where Helena was looking at her phone.

She turned and looked at him. "London. Fan, shit etcetera. We've got to release her. It's ok. I'll explain later."

"What the..."

She held up her hand. "It's cool – just. I can't say any more in the present company. A couple of cars are on the way over with the cavalry, plus a doctor for Tobin."

"But she's killed our people – your people, the firm's people."

"I know, but we need her. This goes way, way over Tobin – and it's not the technology. Or techies have cracked the Chinese comms and the chip. There's a technical team on a plane from Northolt right now – with a very senior person. ETA two a.m. Tobin is nothing – we're into a whole new operation – and it seems that she's our key."

"Tunis?"

"We think so – there are links to the *Queen Katherine* bombing, but this is much bigger. We're talking international crisis. Black One. You know Tunisia, right?

There was a call from the kitchen. "Tea anyone?"

"Yes thanks – two and strong."

"I'll make some for Tobin too."

When it came, the tea was flavoured with brandy.

"It's good Bryan."

"We all need a pic-me-up I reckon. That brandy was a lucky find."

"Bryan - we're expecting visitors, friendly. How's Tobin?"

"Still got one spare of each, but his hand's pretty badly mangled – he says she used a hammer on him."

"Believe me, he was lucky. She puts Dr Mengele in the shade."

"Mengele?"

"Never mind Bryan, long story, World War Two."

Helena went to talk to Tobin just as headlights came up the track from the road.

The extraction of the Chinese agent – a female Serbian assassin known variously as Andjela Karanovic, Marie Broussard and usually as Maruška Pavkovic – had gone more or less according to plan.

*

The team of four entered the house in pairs. They were followed by a fifth man. They were in plain clothes underneath body armour, and carrying H&K MP5s and Browning sidearms.

Helena stood ready, hands visible.

"I'm Dave. I'm in charge here."

"No, you are not" said Helena. "I am."

"On what authority?"

"Black Swan."

"White Egret. Ok, acknowledged."

"Acknowledged."

"Why is everyone called Dave?"

"Don't know Ma'am. That's just what I'm known as."

The two troopers moved smoothly into the other rooms.

"Clear."

"Clear."

The calls came progressively as each room was checked.

"One casualty."

"OK."

Two more armed men appeared from other rooms. They had not come in through the kitchen.

"Steve, Bryan – all clear now."

Steve and Bryan came in through the kitchen door to the surprised looks of the SAS troop. No weapons visible.

"They are my guys."

Another man came in, behind them, weapon raised.

"Set a perimeter."

Four troopers left the kitchen.

"Can't be too careful Ma'am. I have been ordered to secure this site and all personnel. Within that constraint, what are your orders?"

Helena pointed to Maruška. "She is to be held here pending further orders. Extreme caution advised. The casualty needs first aid urgently and then secure medical attention - and I mean secure. He is a British National, captive under the Counter-Terrorism and Security Act 2015, but not hostile. He has been tortured – not by us – by her." She nodded in Maruška's direction.

"She removed one of his testicles."

He winced. "Ouch. OK, there's a chopper *en route* from *Bulwark* with more backup, though they're only marines. We'll ship him back there – they have a hospital aboard." He touched his throat mike. "Get the doc in here now Jim."

The sound grew quickly and then a red light went on in the paddock at the rear of the villa followed by illumination from the Merlin helicopter at it descended and hovered while two fire teams of Royal Marines dropped and deployed.

There was some headshaking in the troop.

"Now the fucking marines. That's all we need."

"Shut it Shane. We've got to work with these guys."

Then the Merlin touched down and the RM Lieutenant and 'Dave' exchanged professional courtesies. Handshakes were brief and formal - the inter-service rivalry was obvious. After a short pissing contest about authority, Dave pulled rank and gave the orders for deployment – and for responsibility.

Two medics ran in to the villa with a stretcher. The doctor briefed them quickly and within three minutes Tobin was sedated and airborne, headed for *HMS Bulwark*.

Steve turned to Helena. "What now?"

"We wait. Our Middle East Head of Station is flying out right now with the technical team."

"You'd better put the kettle on then, Bryan."

"And I'd better charge my phone. Steve – where are those phones from the warehouse – they are important?"

Fifteen minutes later, Helena's phone pinged and she disappeared into another room.

"So, Steve what's the story with the girl?" Dave said, nodding at Maruška.

"It's enough to say that she's a match for any of your guys – plus. She just killed two of her own team."

"A black widow, eh?"

Steve nodded.

"I'd better brief the lads then."

*

Abu ben-Zhair had worked his way up through the GIA ranks, and after identifying a few like-minded and disaffected comrades, they had set up the Algerian Islamic Front, an organisation bent on achieving a fully Islamic State, under Shariah Law, in Algeria. As political spectra go, they were well out on the left, where it merged again with the right, just as Hitler had merged with 'socialism'.

Over a half dozen years, they had operated carefully, rarely getting too close to the actual torture and beheadings of tourists, diplomats and Western-inclined prominent Algerians whose demise they had planned and instigated.

Year by year the volume and audacity of the attacks had increased.

The biggest operation that he had planned would shortly shock the world, and make *all* governments take notice – and treat IC as a state, not a 'so-called' Islamic State, but a true Caliphate. Ben-Zhair had cemented his control of the ICIM after he had demonstrated his ability for running the mission, leading from the front against the *Queen Katherine*. Next, after the 'Sword of Allah' attack he would carry out a purge of the Inner Council and move from being Chairman to the ultimate public position of 'Caliph of the Maghreb'.

Then there would be one final mission and he would go down in history as the greatest fighter for Islam, a supreme jihadi in the 'Cause of All Causes'. He would surpass even Khalid ibn al-Walid, the original 'Sword of Allah'.

He was not mad; he was just a supreme visionary and planner – two traits which are rarely combined – and above all, a leader with tremendous self-belief and power of persuasion – and with a generous view of his own capabilities.

The ICIM was not yet in complete control of Libya and access to certain matériel in the region still required cooperation with aligned but not yet subordinate forces in that country. Delicate negotiations had taken place deep in the Sahara between disaffected Libyan revolutionaries and ICIM intermediaries. One tonne of Semtex had been required and it had to be well within its 'sell-by date' and available for shipment at Annaba. There, it was subdivided and shipped in several batches at various times by sea to Oran in western Algeria, thence by ferry to Alicante in Spain and on to Marseilles in France by road. It was a long and tortuous journey designed to cover trails and allay suspicions – and, as with drug smuggling – on the assumption that some would be discovered but without jeopardising the overall operation.

*

Malta was still in chaos after the recent bombing of the British cruise liner, but this was insignificant compared to the Pandora's box which the Islamic Caliphate in the Maghreb was opening and to which Maruška Pavkovic held a key.

The Head of the North African Desk of the SIS and an accompanying team from London had landed in Luqa at 02:00 and had been driven straight to the British High Commission Villa outside Zeitun, just ten minutes away.

The most versatile agents tended to blend in, but Ogilvy certainly didn't. His hair was now shot through with grey and his heavily lined face betrayed years of stress, though his pale blue eyes were still clear and his look would cut ice. With a firm, square jaw and penetrating gaze, he commanded attention, but the surprise came when he spoke. His voice was gentle and quiet, but backed by the sharpest of intellects.

"Those are the terms – Marie, Andjela, Maruška or whatever your name is tonight. Let me emphasize that we understand how you are being controlled through a nanochip implant in your C Six vertebra. It's basic but effective – as you know. We can reduce the effects of that with a jammer and possibly with drugs, but you have to agree. Once this mission is over then we will remove the nanochip. You will be free of the Chinese – and us. I assume that you will want to disappear then. Given your record, I think we are being extremely generous with these terms. I could lock you up for the rest of your life - or just end it here, without a problem or any questions."

Maruška jerked in her chair as Helena cocked her Glock. The movement of the slide was only 2 millimetres, but Maruška knew that the 'safe action' Glock was anything but if you were at the wrong end. The emphasis was clear.

"You need me; you want the knowledge I have. Anyway, how can I be sure of all this? How can I trust you?"

"You can't. But why are you here? You contacted us, remember? In case you doubt that we understand the technology…" Ogilvy turned to the techie. "Jacob, please." Jacob touched an icon on the tablet. Maruška jerked silently, her lips pressed hard together, then relaxed slowly as the pulse stopped. She started breathing deeply.

"Sorry about that – a bit too strong I think. But I'm sure you'll agree we've nearly got the hang of it. I'm certain we'll get better at it. So, do we have deal?"

Maruška nodded, her eyes closed.

"Jacob, please fit the sensors."

Pavkovic was tied to a chair in the dining room of the villa, bound with cable ties. Helena Williams leaned against an ornate Maltese sideboard, a Glock pistol in her hand.

"I'm not having any sensors on me!"

Ogilvy stared at her and said, gently "We need to make sure that you are telling the truth and also track any pain levels – for example if your Chinese controller sends a pulse through. That will help us help you."

Jacob, the senior communications specialist, fitted a fingertip sensor to Pavkovic's right index finger and a sensor patch to her temple. He adjusted the camera and started the live data feed to London. "We're good to go, Sir." Ogilvy nodded and the debrief started.

Despite the intercepts of the Chinese communications with Pavkovic, there were still many gaps in Ogilvy's knowledge of the Chinese operation. It always helped to compare stories from different sources and try to fill those gaps, to look for weaknesses to probe and to find inconsistencies.

After two hours, the primary debrief had been completed, and the supplementary questions asked. It was very sketchy, focusing on the key immediate information needs, with a few cross-checks thrown in. Then the second pass took place. A full debrief with data checks and file follows would take months, but the pressure was considerable – the risks and rewards unlike anything typical of peacetime operations.

"Right, this is what happens next." Ogilvy spoke slowly and checked, step by step, that her understanding was clear.

*

By now it was 4 a.m., and two black Range Rovers were passing through the outskirts of Tarxien, one turning left towards Marsascala, headed for the back of the villa while the other continuing down to Birżebbuġa to meet two crewmen off a Chinese container ship which was berthed at the Freeport. They had left the Chinese restaurant in Hamrun, a small town outside Valletta. Time was tight if they were to meet the deadline. Such operations were rarely carried out at short notice, but the orders had come from the highest authority.

At that moment, Ogilvy shook the techie awake.

"A problem, Jacob, and I need a quick solution. I've just seen the latest intercept. The Chinese are going to change Maruška's phone in Tunis – and they're taking back the old one."

"So, that compromises both the hardware and software I put in there, and also our control link and tracking, Sir?"

"Exactly. We need a solution."

Upstairs, Baldwin was pacing quietly, while Bryan Elliot and Helena Williams were dozing in a bedroom, Maruška had been re-bound to a chair in another bedroom pending her transport to Zabbar before she joined the ferry. Her doctored phone and laptop sat ready to go in a plastic carrier bag – a reminder that she was completely under control.

It was a quiet night – the storm had passed to the north - and the threat level was now considered low. The SAS troops had left and the villa was secured by the Royal Marines.

Inside the villa, there was a knock at the dining room door. "Come". Ogilvy raised his eyes from the latest decoded intercept. It was the marine lieutenant.

"Sir, we have orders to return to Bulwark. The helo is on its way."

"What? You're not withdrawing until I say it's OK. I'll get this sorted with London, now."

"Very well Sir. You have about ten minutes."

Fifteen minutes later, Baldwin and Helena Williams stood across the table from Ogilvy.

"They had their orders. I couldn't get them changed – 'C' was unavailable."

"Shit."

"Yes Baldwin, exactly. I think that the situation is low-threat, but we'd better be prepared."

Then the lights went out.

A flat sputting sound and suppressed flash, followed by another, then a grunt – a man's grunt, the sound of a body falling to the floor.

Steve eased himself round the end of the table. He snapped off two shots, the unsuppressed Glock delivering flashes and bangs like the worst of a Malta thunderstorm.

He thought he heard a groan from outside, but his eyes were still recovering from the gun flash.

"OK?"

There was a whispered "OK" from Helena and a groan from Ogilvy.

Another shadow crossed the open doors and disappeared. Then, there were two shots from the kitchen and the sound of feet on the stairs and going into the bedroom overhead – Maruška's room.

"Stay here. I think Ogilvy's hit."

Baldwin moved out into the hallway and to the bottom of the stairs. His eyes were readjusting to the low light from the pre-dawn that was brightening by the minute.

Then, a shadow in front of him.

He pushed the pistol against the neck of the man, holding it at arm's length.

"Don't think about."

He felt the body stiffen, the whisper was urgent.

"Steve?"

"Fucking hell Bryan, you'd be dead if it wasn't for that disgusting aftershave!"

*

"Jacob's in the kitchen, he's ok I think. I got two off. No hits."

"I think Ogilvy's taken one, condition unknown. I clipped one – legs, so could still be a threat. Outside."

"How many?"

"Four, five?"

There were two shots from outside, unsuppressed.

Helena, Steve realised, and he was torn, torn by the natural protective instinct when a woman was in a fire team. He fought the instinct.

"Up. Maruška's room. You take left."

They eased up the stairs in the semi darkness and turned.

"Clear."

They edged along the landing. The door to Maruška's room was closed. Steve nodded and stood aside as Bryan charged it. It was heavy, it was walnut, it was Maltese – and a chair had been propped against it.

Bryan groaned and bounced back.

Another two shots outside.

"They've gone out through the window – they wouldn't fight their way downstairs."

Steve turned and ran into the next bedroom, over to the window. He threw it open. The light was stronger now, the sky was clear and a fine autumn day was promising itself.

He could see Helena behind a wall and Maruška running with three men across a field, turning into a road. A fourth man was trailing them. Helena was moving and firing, but her aim was well off. Steve realised that she would not want to hit Maruška.

The drop from the window was on to paving slabs – and about ten feet. As Steve rolled aside Bryan landed next to him - both intact. There was blood on the patio next to the French doors and it trailed across the driveway. Steve could see Jacob tending Ogilvy in the dining room.

They sprinted across the driveway and lawn, into the field – to meet Helena on her way back.

"They got away."

"Even the wounded one?"

"Yes, two Range Rovers. It suits us."

"Suits us?"

"Yes, we thought it might pan out this way. The Chinese will have no suspicions about Maruška."

"Is that why the Marines were withdrawn?"

"I honestly don't know, but I do know that Ogilvy was trying to stop it."

"Bloody hell – isn't that just typical?"

"It's just one of those things Steve, just one of those things."

Then, suddenly, the shooting was rapid and continuous Helene and Baldwin dropped as one to the floor, scuttling for the cover of bushes.

"Shotguns. What the fuck? Where? They're all around us."

Bryan was strolling towards them, laughing.

"Get down Bryan for Christ's sake!"

"It's ok, it's just for the birds."

"The birds?"

"Yes, the Maltese love to shoot small songbirds at dawn - with shotguns. There are stone hides all across the fields here." Bryan waved his arms.

As the sun was coming over the horizon, they could make out the hides in the fields beyond the vines. And they could hear the Maltese indulging in their very strange tradition.

Two hours later the secure call finally came through to Ogilvy's cellphone, from Sir William Gore – 'C', Director of MI6.

"We've just been attacked and Pavkovic has gone. Why the hell were the marines withdrawn - SIR!"

Sir William ignored the question.

"Casualties?"

"Me. Shot in the thigh, superficial. We found one Chinese dead in the orchard. No ID. Williams got him."

"Unfortunate. You should really be more careful. You've cleaned up?"

"Yes Sir."

"Good. It worked out more or less as planned and Pavkovic retains credibility. Now, I don't have much time for chat. This latest intercept - are you sure of our source?"

"Absolutely – but we are reliant on GCHQ. We only have to consider whether it's genuine or not."

"Your view?"

"Solid gold."

"I agree."

Condescending bugger, Ogilvy thought, wincing at the pain in his thigh.

"Her cover is that of a French journalist, Cherif Hatoui?"

"Yes, but she's too smart to be obvious about that."

"Understood. I have to call the PM now. She's called a Cobra meeting at ten a.m. our time."

The line went dead and Ogilvy swore.

*

"Steve, this could be the most important thing you have ever done for you country."

"How many times have I heard that before – and got stitched up? No way am I going to Tunisia!"

"Keep your voice down Steve."

They were in one of the bedrooms of the villa.

"I don't bloody care who hears me."

"Just hear me out, please. If you can't respect basic security then I'll have you arrested."

"You wouldn't do that."

"Try me – you are still subject to the Official Secrets Act. There's a lot at stake here – a world war could start."

"Pull the other one."

"And if I said that a terrorist group had a nuclear bomb?"

"I wouldn't believe you."

"Good, because I didn't say it. We think that the *Queen Katherine* bombing was just a start. Look at it this way – you and me on Adèle as cover. Tourists. You did tell me you'd like to see the country."

"Why not use the SAS or some of your regular fucking secret agents?"

"The SAS are hard men, not intelligence agents. They will be there for us to call on. As to our regulars, we don't have anyone with the right profile who we can put in-in time."

"I'm not a bloody intelligence agent."

"No, you are an all-round star – with the right profile. You proved that. And you speak Arabic and French. And – the clincher – you want Maruška. She is a part of this operation."

"What?"

"Yes. That's what Tunis was about. We know a bit about what the Chinese are doing and what they want her to do. As I said downstairs, we're monitoring their comms with her. Mostly it's good for us. We just let her carry out her mission – and watch her of course. Make sure there's no double-dealing.

We know that the Chinese have re-tasked a satellite to monitor the Libya-Tunisia-Algeria region.

The thinking is we head for Tabarka in Adèle and moor there. It's lower profile than Tunis and gives us a good cover story. Bryan will take the car ferry over and meet us over there."

"Is Bryan up to this?"

"What do you think?"

"He's done OK so far. A bit of a plodder."

"That's how he's meant to look on this job – he's playing a part."

"Nursemaid you mean."

"Monitoring is just a part of his role. He's versatile and his record is very good. Believe me, there's much more than meets the eye. I've known him for a few years and worked with him before. Anyway, it's not a plan yet, but it's a start." She raised her eyebrows. "Comments?"

"It sounds ok but I'd need to check on Tabarka. I guess it's a couple of hundred miles, but with this wind we can probably do it in 36 hours. And we have no idea what Maruška will be up to."

"That's where you are wrong – and that's why we have techies here."

"Why not go straight to Tunis? That would make much more sense – and it's nearer too."

"Because we don't think that's where the action will be. She has been given the name –Abu ben-Zhair. Remember, there's credible intel that he was behind the *Queen Katherine* bombing and that he's got an even bigger atrocity planned. We think Maruška's headed ultimately for Algeria – Annaba looks to be the likely destination. Tabarka is only six miles from the Algerian border and less than eighty from Annaba."

"Jesus, Algeria - that's a whole new ball game."

"But you've been there too, so you're qualified."

"Only out in the desert - a natural gas plant at In Amenas when there was a terrorist attack. Bloody dodgy place. In and out by helo. Never again. We'd stand out a mile in Algeria – no tourists and police everywhere."

"Maybe it will not come to that."

"She'd be mad go in to Algeria and we'd be mad to follow. I might pull it off, but you? No way."

"Let's take it one step at a time, be flexible. Is Adèle ready?"

"We just need some fuel, water, food."

"HMG will pick up the tab. And I can promise you a good bonus."

She winked, but he shook his head. "I've heard that before too. I just can't believe it. To think that a few weeks ago I thought you were just a pretty Greek waitress. I must be a real schmuck."

"I am *very* good at my work."

There was a knock at the door. "Come in. Yes Dave, what is it?"

"Sorry Ma'am, but I've orders to head back to base once the people arrive from the airport – they're on the way now and should be here in a few minutes. We'll leave you with the Jollies."

"Jollies?"

"The *Royal Marines*. Nickname" said Steve.

"Good luck."

"Thanks Dave."

*

Later, at the guest house in Zabbar, Maruška was fully expecting awkward questions about her recent location from Wan Chuntao, who would undoubtedly have tracked her nanochip. She had her story ready.

She logged on. The briefing was in her inbox. When the decrypt was complete, she sat back on the bed, hardly believing the details. Ben-Zhair – 'find him and we will let you retire'. She could see why he was so important, but couldn't believe it.

Capture him and hold him until a team arrives to interrogate him - clear enough. She had never been involved in such a project. But the interrogation by a team? It was always straight termination – well, except for Tobin – but that was specific information. They were giving her a Geiger counter. How did that connect to ben-Zhair.? Maruška was intrigued.

She had arranged the passage to Tunis, but avoiding the security difficulties of a flight meant two ferry trips as there was no direct route. Then she fell back on the bed, exhausted. She fell asleep thinking about the previous twenty four hours. Two dead to add to her lifetime tally, although they were her team, so it didn't really count did it? Anyway, she had long ago lost track of her professional tally, though all the details of her private tally were still vivid.

An hour later she awoke with a start and searing pain. Wan Chuntao. Fuck that woman. So much for British promises.

Her smartphone vibrated on the table beside the bed. She waited, quickly running over her story, then picked up.

"What now?"

"Aren't you going to thank me?"

"For what?"

"For getting you out of that Villa."

"I would have got out myself anyway. The British are fools."

"But they knew about Tobin?"

"Obviously, but I don't know how. They killed two of my team."

"I know, we found the bodies in the warehouse."

"How did they capture you?"

"Gas."

"Gas?"

"Yes, they had gas masks on. Mansur and Yasmine were shot and I held a gun to Tobin's head but passed out. Your people should have got there earlier."

"We had difficulty locating you – there were problems with your signal and GPS coordinates."

"I thought that Chinese technology never failed."

"I will ignore that. Now, about your cover story. They gave you the documents? You have a new passport and a pass for Agence France Presse?"

"Yes, a journalist, no problem. Can you provide weapons?"

"Yes. We'll send a car to meet you in Tunis. There will be other equipment as well, including a Geiger counter."

"Isn't that for radiation?"

"Yes. There will be a new phone too, as you seem to be having problems with your old one. Give it to the courier. Don't miss your ferry – you have 4 hours to get to the terminal." The line dropped.

At least her story had held – so far. Double dealing was a dangerous game, but danger was what she lived for.

*

46

Rage in Teheran

The Supreme Leader of Iran, Ruhollah Sistani, was incandescent with rage.

"Missing?"

The call had come directly from Brigadier Hossein Ashtari's cellphone.

Ashtari, head of the NAJA, the Persian law enforcement agency, was also head of PAVA – the Iranian intelligence agency. He was one of the few who had been briefed on the secret of the Great Answer and was essential to maintaining the overall secrecy of the project. He was a loyal and trusted ally of Ruhollah Sistani.

"Yes, Supreme Leader. Missing."

There was a long pause. Sistani's colour deepened – he was a very pale man and spent very little time in direct sunlight, preferring to spend his time studying the Quoran through thick spectacles. His face reddened and then that colour took on a blueish component, making it almost purple in colour.

He began to speak very slowly, obviously having difficulty controlling himself.

"What exactly is missing?"

"I am told that it is called the '*hohlraum*'."

"Do we have another one?"

"Yes, the original we bought from North Korea. We made three copies. I am told that it is made of gold and holds the fuel pellet. I have been told that two fuel pellets and what they call the 'plutonium sparkplug' is also unaccounted for. These may be replaceable quickly by our friends in North Korea."

"They will not be our friends much longer if they hear about this. We paid them almost twenty billion dollars for this technology and the radioactive fuel pellets. They will want much more next time. We cannot be made to look like fools."

"But only the North Koreans will know about the loss."

"Are you stupid Ashtari? That doesn't matter. They will think us idiots. They may not even provide what we need if we cannot be trusted with their technology."

"The plutonium sparkplug was made from our own plutonium which we had hidden from the nuclear weapons inspectors. That will now be difficult to replace – or so I have been told."

"By the Prophet, this is a disaster. Surely such a weapon must be difficult to conceal and transport?"

"I thought that too, Supreme Leader, but it is apparently not the case. The missing items can be transported in a large truck, or so I have been told. However, much more is required to build a working bomb."

"Why does that not make me happy? How much more is needed to build a bomb?"

"I have been told that many lasers and a large power feed are required. The North Korean design required a building to house it. However, as you know, we have highly inventive people and we have reduced its size beyond what the North Koreans achieved. Perhaps we can use that knowledge in our bargaining?"

There was a long pause on the line, and Ashtari felt sweat running freely down his back and shifted uncomfortably in the seat of his official car. He desperately wanted to stand under a cold shower.

"Ashtari, do not remind me that we have clever people – we invented chess and calculus centuries ago. I know we have great minds, minds so great that they can lose a nuclear bomb! Kindly explain to me how these key components of The Great Answer have gone missing. Who is responsible for this catastrophe?"

"We do not yet know for certain, Supreme Leader', but we suspect that Hashemi Firouzabadi is responsible."

"On what do you base this statement?"

"He is also missing, Supreme Leader. He and his family were in Dizin, last weekend. "

"Skiing?"

"Yes, but we have tracked them to Chalus. We think he had arranged a boat – maybe to Turkmenistan or up as far as Baku."

"Armenia?"

"Yes."

"Then that dog could be anywhere. Why have you not been monitoring him?"

"Priorities which you – yourself - set, Supreme Leader."

There followed a string of the most base expletives known in the Farsi language, totally atypical of the pious cleric. Although he was using a cellphone, Ashtari's face drained of colour. He had never before heard Sistani use such unholy language.

"What are you doing about it?"

"I have agents in Baku who are trying to find the boat – a fishing boat. Also along the coast in Turkmenistan, but that is more difficult."

"How can this all go missing – the technology, the people? Our new site at Yazd is the most secure and secret installation in Iran – and you are responsible for overall security."

"The components were being transported from Yazd to the test site in the earthquake zone at Kerman. As you know, we planned to disguise the test as an earthquake. The Saberin Takavar Battalion of the Army Special Forces were responsible for security during the transportation phase. Major General Qasem Hamadani was in command. There is other bad news too, Supreme Leader."

"By all that is Holy, can it really be worse?"

"Perhaps. Hamadani is missing, as are the Chief Technical Designer, Jafa Sharifi who was reported missing this morning, along with four of his technical team."

"Let me be clear. Am I right in saying that our prototype weapon, along with our team of head technicians is missing?"

"That is my understanding, yes. As you know, they were all Sunni Muslims. There was one Russian also. That may have been a risk."

"Perhaps, but they were the best brains we could put on the project. I thought that you had them under control?"

"Yes, they gave every indication of being truly faithful Iranians. At the moment we are trying to discover if they have left the country."

"Do you smell the involvement of the House of Saud in this?"

"No, but one can never be sure of such things. The Saudis are cunning and the sons of camels, but we have no evidence of any such links."

"You do camels a dis-service. The sooner that monarchy is destroyed then the better it will be for all Muslims – and we can at last start sending our faithful on Haj again."

"One more thing, Supreme Leader - the design files are safe – I am told we have multiple secure backups, although we should assume that copies have been taken. All personnel involved are being been isolated for interrogation. The reasons for NAJA actions will not be disclosed."

"Is that really all?"

"Yes Supreme Leader, that is all."

"By the Beard of the Prophet – may He be praised – this cannot get worse. Could the Israelis be behind this then?"

"Perhaps. Mossad is very powerful and far reaching, but how would they know about it? They have outstanding technology as you know – their Stuxnet virus set our uranium enrichment programme back by years. I do not believe that our high level communications are being intercepted - we continue to test with misinformation and there is no reaction. I am sure that they have no agents here – if one can ever be sure about such things. In any case, would Hashemi Firouzabadi work with the Israelis?"

"Hashemi would do anything for political advantage. The man is a dog. And Qasem Hamadani – he commanded Quds at one time – so he has strong connections with our revolutionaries in Afghanistan, Syria and Libya – even worldwide. But he would not work with the Israelis. He would use the bomb against them if he had the chance. Perhaps that is his plan?"

"If so, why not wait until it is ready and take control then?"

"Impossible. He would have to engineer a coup. I could never let him win in an election, and anyway he is not a politician. He thinks like a monkey."

"Could the secret have been leaked to the Israelis by North Korea?"

"Why? I think we all know that is the least likely answer. There would be no reason for it that I can see. If it was Israel, they would have attacked us by now, not stolen the weapon. The chain of probabilities is too long. No, Israel cannot be involved. I believe that this is internal, here, in our own government."

"Then this is a threat to the Revolution, to us all. With such a weapon..."

"...they have to do nothing. Just possession of the knowledge is enough. This is a very dangerous situation. The more I think about it, the worse it gets."

"But Hashemi Firouzabadi did not know about the Great Answer?"

"Somebody has told him. You must detain all those present at the briefing I gave."

"The arrests are already in hand and all related passports have been revoked. They are being taken to Gohardasht gaol as I speak."

"Good, just the name of that place will make them talk." Sistani pictured the gaol as he spoke, with vivid memories of his own visits there. Gohardasht, one of the harshest political prisons in Iran, some 20 kilometres northwest of the city, was noted for the brutality of its regime, with a torrid history of rape, torture and execution of opponents of the Revolution. As a young Sistani, he had presided over many summary trials and passed many death sentences. His conscience was clear; all the deaths had been under the guidance of Allah. Still, it was a name to strike fear into the hardest of hearts. The breeze wafted in the scent of oleander from the courtyard, refreshing the air in the room, and he shivered.

"I want you here at the Palace for a meeting with General Jamshidi, Commander of Quds, this afternoon, before prayers. The Quds has operational links to all the foreign groups who could be interested in this theft. Who was responsible for close security of the Great Answer at Yazd?"

"Takavars from the 23rd Division of the Saberin Battalion."

"Ah yes, you told me, and the Commander is missing. So, bring in Major General Hamadami's second in command as well - we will see him after Jamshidi. Be in my office within the hour so that we can prepare for the meetings."

"I am on my way, Supreme Leader."

Ruhollah Sistani broke the connection. At the other end, despite the air conditioning it was stifling in the car. Ashtari mopped his brow as he issued his orders. He knew that his meeting with the Supreme Leader would be more than a planning session. He asked the driver to stop the car and buy him some fruit juice. It gave him enough time to take out his clean cellphone and call home. The shower would have to wait.

He would take his wife for an early birthday surprise holiday break on the Gulf, the coming weekend. He would not use their real passports. It would be easy to get a dhow across to Dubai. During their nineteen years of mostly happy marriage they had adjusted to the sadness of childlessness, but at that moment Ashtari thanked Allah for not having been blessed with offspring.

In the meantime, he would double-check that the flash drive had arrived safely with his lawyers in New York. Only last week had he completed the operation to obtain video footage of the Supreme Leader enjoying his personal and highly illegal sexual predilection. That flash drive contained his ultimate protection against the machinations of the Supreme Leader, and one week should have been long enough for his personal courier to deliver it via the Iranian Diplomatic Baggage to Iran's Embassy in Washington – and onwards to New York.

In his office, Ruhollah Sistani stopped pacing and sat down in his chair. He considered the list of those who had known enough to plan this theft and remembered that Ashtari was the one who knew most. Even greater care would be necessary. Who could he trust? Only last week Ashtari had attempted to entrap him. He unlocked his safe and checked – yes, the flash drive was still there. Tonight it would roast in the charcoal of his barbeque, and the lamb would be especially good. That score with Ashtari was yet to be settled. He shut the safe door and spun the tumblers, then called in his Chief of Staff.

Al-Quds is the modern Arabic name for Jerusalem, after which the Quds Force is named.

The Quds (Jerusalem) Force of the Iranian Revolutionary Guard Corps (IRGC) is responsible for operations outside Iran, including terrorist operations. The Force's national headquarters are in the southwestern city of Ahvaz with current force strength estimated at 15,000. Quds is the Government of Iran's primary foreign action arm for executing its policy of training and supporting terrorist organizations and extremist groups around the world, including the Middle East, North Africa and even South America.

It provides training, logistical assistance, matériel and financial support to militants and terrorist groups, including the Taliban, Lebanese Hezbollah, Hamas, Palestinian Islamic Jihad and the Popular Front for the Liberation of Palestine.

Members of these and similar organizations from Tunisia, Libya, Egypt and Sudan receive military training at a 'Guardians of the Revolution' camp outside Teheran. It is said that training courses include marine as well as terrestrial operations.

Quds is also involved in financial and economic terrorism, for example by issuing counterfeit US dollars and other securities with the aim of destabilizing Western economies.

A typical Quds operation was identified publicly on 11 October 2011, when the Obama Administration alleged that the Quds Force was involved with the plot to assassinate Saudi Arabia's Ambassador to the United States, Adel al-Jubeir. The Iranians planned to employ Mexican drug traffickers to kill Jubeir with a bomb as he ate at a restaurant, simultaneously with plans to bomb the Israeli and Saudi embassies located in Washington, D.C.

Because of the schism between Shia and Sunni Muslims, Quds has been actively involved in actions against the so-called Islamic State which is absolutely Sunni Muslim in religious orientation, specifically the Wahhabi flavour – as followed by the controlling organs of Saudi Arabian State.

The great majority (upwards of 85%) of the world's more than 1.5 billion Muslims are Sunni. In the Middle East, Sunnis make up 90% or more of the populations of Egypt, Jordan and Saudi Arabia.

However, the population of Iran is 83% Shia Muslim, making it unique in the Muslim world – and an arch enemy of Saudi Arabia which is the region's most powerful Muslim state, both economically and militarily.

The Commander of the Quds Force reports directly to the Supreme Leader of Iran.

*

In Teheran, the security review started an hour later and went on well into the night, with the interrogations continuing, as they would do for several days.

It had been determined that the stolen equipment was being transported in a shielded shipping container. It could not easily be transported as airfreight although the largest component was less than one cubic metre in size. The radioactive items were also small – although requiring very heavy shielding. The deuterium-tritium fuel pellets were plastic spheres holding the radioactive elements. Smaller than marbles, they had to be maintained at temperature close to absolute zero in high vacuum conditions. This required specialized vacuum and refrigeration equipment plus a supply of liquid helium. Potentially, this requirement would make the search easier.

By the end of the week, Ruhollah Sistani and Dim Pong-un were engaged directly in negotiations for more tritium-deuterium fuel pellets and plutonium to manufacture a 'sparkplug', plus other specialized materials. The price extracted was punitive. Dim Pong-un had been outraged by the fact that the designs had been stolen. He very quickly understood that it could be used to wider advantage, but he didn't explain that to Sistani - he just doubled the price.

Not one of the missing personnel had been traced or captured. Their families had been imprisoned and were being questioned, which in Iran was the euphemism for 'tortured'.

Iran had a long history of a brutal secret police force, with skills honed and passed down from SAVAK, the much feared organisation set up in 1957 by Iran's Mohammad Reza Shah (the 'Shah of Persia') with the help of the United States' Central Intelligence Agency – and Israel.

*

Khalid ibn al-Walid

Abu ben-Zhair had named the weapon 'The Sword of Allah' in recognition of one of the greatest Islamic warriors, Khalid ibn al-Walid (خالد بن الوليد) who was the first person to be so known. Not indeed a sword, but a man revered in the world of Islamist war, a man buried in a mosque named for him, in the city of Homs in Syria – still a country of turmoil.

Since his death there have been several jihadis who have deigned to use this title, but none can even begin to achieve the military feats of Khalid ibn al-Walid.

His exact year of birth seems to be uncertain, but was between 585 and 592 C.E. (A.D.). He was born in the city of Mecca into noble Arabic blood and given the name Abū Sulaymān Khālid ibn al-Walīd ibn al-Mughīrah al-Makhzūmī. He was not a Muslim by birth, and his father, a Sheikh of one of the clans of the Arab tribe of Quraysh, was vociferously anti-Muslim. Khalid was converted to Islam at the age of 44 in the house of Muhammad himself.

Up until this time he had actively fought Muslims on the battlefield and emerged as a brave and capable front line soldier, but it was after his conversion, during the Battle of Mu'tah where he really made his mark as a leader when three commanders above him were killed and he took control. His heavily outnumbered Muslim army of 3,000 men held together against an army of 10,000 of the Byzantine Empire and Ghassanid Arabs. Using guile and psychological warfare techniques he staged a successful retreat, saving his heavily outnumbered army. He is said to have broken nine swords during the battle and it was after this outstanding military achievement that he was given the title 'Sword of Allah'.

During his life of about fifty years, he fought the Byzantines, the Romans and the Muslims, invaded the Persian and the Byzantine Empires and was the first military commander of a united Arabia.

One reason for Khalid's success as a commander was his melding of the individual skills of Arab Bedouin warriors into coherent fighting units known as the Mubarizun ("champions"). These were highly trained and skilled swordsmen, and Khalid deployed them effectively in an almost gladiatorial way to target and slay enemy officers in personal combat. This tactic seriously damaged enemy morale. Before Khalid's time, the Arabs were raiders and skirmishers, typical of tribal peoples. Battles were broken down to a set of simultaneous unit skirmishes and coherent command of enemy forces usually fell apart. Khalid was ruthless and slaughtered his enemies without mercy, in huge numbers.

He was eventually dismissed from military service because a personality cult was developing around him, and his Caliph at that time, Umar, wanted to make it clear that the victories were those of Allah, not Khalid. He died in his bed in 642 after being the victorious commander in more than fifty significant battles.

A study of the life and campaigns of Khalid serves only to illustrate the tribal and religious complexities of this whole region and why it is so difficult – even impossible – to arrive at a durable and persistent political settlement even today. Of course the region – both in political and religious terms – expanded through the influence mainly of the Ottoman Empire, even into southern Spain. The whole of North Africa is now Muslim – including the Maghreb and stretching down well in Saharan Africa and down the west coast as far as Mauritania.

Khalid only ever fought at times and in locations of his own choosing, and always with a clear line of retreat – usually back into Arabia. Much of this is classic 'Art of War' doctrine as defined centuries before in China, by Sun Tzu - but of course unread by Khalid ibn al-Walid.

Ben-Zhair's objectives were much more ambitious than those of Khalid, whose objectives were essentially defined by the whims of his political masters. Ben-Zhair was focused on political power achieved through humbling western society – not through defeating tribal elements in the Arabic world – and along the way gaining revenge for the Crusades as a media-worthy by-line.

Abu ben-Zhair had studied the strategy and tactics of Khalid, but there was little that applied to his 'Sword of Allah' plan which involved stealth and secrecy with supreme weapons in the heart of enemy cities. Indeed, ben-Zhair's strategy was more akin to that of the Viet Cong during the war in Vietnam in the 1960's, with troops embedded within the enemy population – and notional tunnels provided by the flow of emigrants and refugees into Europe.

*

The Suez Crisis

In the years of political chaos in the Middle East and North Africa during and following the Arab Spring in 2010, many dictators (or firm rulers depending on your viewpoint) had disappeared, died or been deposed, even jailed – Gadhafi of Libya, Mubarak of Egypt, Ben Ali of Tunisia. Assad had fought a bitter civil war in Syria and all but destroyed a proud country. Iraq had descended again into civil war and Bahrain had seen civil unrest.

Only the monarchies of Jordan, Morocco and Saudi Arabia, together with the Gulf States, seemed to be able firmly to keep the lid on their populations.

The power vacuum had been filled by the Islamic State (so called), which recognized no territorial boundaries – all land and people in the region were there to be taken. In general it was a self-funding operation – more land meant more oil. Western economies were desperately developing energy security policies and reducing their dependence on oil and gas from the region.

Worse, a second Suez Crisis was in the making. The Suez Canal cut 4,700 nautical miles off the oil supply line to Britain from the Gulf States and Persia.

In 1956, Great Britain and France had dropped paratroops into Egypt in support of Israel as the UK Prime Minister, Anthony Eden, sought to retain control of the Suez Canal in the face of Abdel Nasser's sudden nationalization of the waterway. Great Britain, France and Israel found no support amongst their allies and an embarrassing withdrawal was the result, leaving years of bitterness.

The importance of the Suez Canal grew as the Chinese economy fed Western appetites for cheap electronics, industrial good, steel products, clothing and household goods. That was all in addition to the huge increase in world trade in the two generations since the first Suez Crisis. The Suez Canal cut more than 3,000 nautical miles (23%) off the route from China to Rotterdam, reducing cost and improving responsiveness to market demand.

Since that British foreign policy fiasco in 1956 the Canal has been widened and deepened several times, and was, by 2016 taking ships of 200,000 tons deadweight, known as the *Suezmax* size.

There were brief – and for the international markets, terrifying – interruptions of service during the Arab-Israeli *Six Day War* in 1967 and the *Yom Kippur* war in 1973, but after the Canal had been cleared of the sunken ships and mines, service resumed as normal.

Today, the arms of the Islamic State were reaching to encircle the Canal and put a stranglehold on international commerce. Not a fatal stranglehold – ships could still carry their cargoes around the Cape of Good Hope – but sufficient to cause trade disruption in the short term and possibly even induce a trade recession.

Western governments seemed to have been slow to react to this threat. They were slow to bolster the emerging government in Libya and help Egypt to gain full control of its population. They had been frightened by the aftermath of their ill-advised adventures in Iraq and Afghanistan. The difficulty was that the only way to achieve stability in these regions was by means of a dictatorship – ruthless or benevolent – and this ran counter to Western sensibilities of democracy.

*

Abu ben-Zhair had read most of the strategic analyses of the Suez Canal issue, and he saw it as being, for him, no more than a diversion. It was always possible that the West would have a change of heart and once again start to support ruthless regimes in the region – but it was, by now, too late for that. There was a ruthless regime, and it was called the Islamic Caliphate. He was pragmatic enough to know that it could not survive for even a century or two, but it was time enough for him.

He was taking the war into enemy territory. No Western country was safe – he had warriors waiting with new forms of weapon – chemical, biological and even nuclear. And beyond those forms, he was defining a new one, one of global scale.

But first, The Sword of Allah.

*

Wan Chuntao

As she walked down the corridor in answer to the summons of her superior, Wan Chuntao was thinking about her recent conversation with one of her agents, Maruška Pavkovic. Perhaps the time for termination was approaching? A recent operation against Charles Tobin, a gold market manipulator and genetics entrepreneur had gone badly wrong and she was trying to pick up the pieces using Pavkovic, who was in Malta, now freed from British captivity but having lost Tobin.

Tobin still held critical knowledge relating to the extraction of metals from seawater. Chinese researchers had been unable to unlock the full genetic code for a key bacterium that Tobin had developed. Extracting gold from seawater was no longer the issue. MOFCOM (the Chinese Finance and Commerce Ministry) had lost control of the original gold extraction project when it became clear that metals such as tantalum and even, potentially, plutonium, could be extracted using Tobin's technology, but amounts would be small and the locations very specific and obvious to governments – but very valuable nevertheless. Specifically, Tobin at that very moment still held the DNA mutation sequence details for a piece of supposedly 'junk' DNA which was capable of enabling extraction of these exotic metals.

He had encrypted this information and despite the efforts of the Guoanbu's code breakers and all the quantum computing power available within the department, the encryption had been unbreakable so far. The cryptographers were dubious about the code being broken within a practical timescale unless they were lucky. Despite the superstitious nature of the Chinese people, Chuntao knew that luck was not considered a factor in foreign or domestic policy. Tobin's interrogation – with considerable malice - in Malta by the Chinese agent Maruška Pavkovic had been messy and unproductive. He was a very tough nut to crack.

British agents who were obviously very keen to prevent Tobin's knowledge being acquired by other countries – and by China in particular – were believed to be tracking Pavkovic.

Was this the reason for Wan Chuntao's summons? Was she being sent to a farm on the steppes?

Her career had progressed well and she was now a senior intelligence operations controller in the Guoanbu. Her rise had really started when she was given responsibility for running a new agent – Pavkovic - as her first assignment in her new position as an intelligence operations supervisor.

The agent had been introduced to the agency by an existing operative, a German national (run by an experienced desk officer in the Guoanbu), who had carried out a number of assassinations of dissident overseas Chinese citizens, criminal Chinese businessmen and double agents in Western Europe. He also had a number of private contracts, and Chuntao knew that he had, indirectly, worked for Tobin though probably without the direct knowledge of the entrepreneur.

The secret war with Taiwanese agents had intensified and there was pressure on the Guoanbu's resources. 'Wet work' was not officially within its remit – that was usually undertaken by the Ministry of State Security. However, its informal remit now included such work where necessary within its overall remit of economic espionage and intelligence gathering. Results mattered, and with the raised suspicions of Chinese intentions by the women leaders of the US, the UK and Germany, she had been given more latitude to achieve results.

Although the Guoanbu had an extensive network of Chinese nationals capable of this work, it suited the Guoanbu to keep these particular operations separate from its existing native networks. 'Foreigners' working against Chinese nationals would play better in the media should one of these black operations ever come to light. The Guoanbu ran teams all over the world – in fact pretty much anywhere that Chinese food was enjoyed and cheap goods were available in bazaars.

Wan Chuntao knocked the door of her manager's office and entered. The office was barely two metres square, and there was a man she did not recognise sitting in the spare chair. Her manager, Mao Mingli, spoke.

"Wan Chuntao, you are being placed on special assignment."

Her pulse quickened but her face betrayed no emotion.

"Please go with this man. Your personal items from your work area will be sent to you. You are not to discuss this with anyone."

She nodded her head deeply.

"I understand."

She stood aside as the stranger got up from the chair and led her out of the office.

As they walked they identified themselves at two body chip scanners, entered an elevator and descended six floors below ground level. At room number S623 they identified themselves to the ID scanner. By now Wan Chuntao was terrified, although externally she appeared to be a picture of inscrutability.

The stranger knocked on the door and they entered. Another desk, another stranger. The man at her side left the room and she was invited to sit down.

"Wan Chuntao. You are being placed on special assignment. I do not know what it is, but you are to report to building 4, room S27 in 30 minutes. Your ID is being reprogrammed now. It will enable you to move to that building and permit you access."

"Honourable comrade, please permit me to know the reasons for being moved."

"Chuntao, it is not your place to ask such questions, only to serve the People in whatever way you can do best. However I do know that you are not being punished. You will be escorted. Go now."

The door opened and a security guard entered.

Thirty minutes later Wan Chuntao was seated around a conference table in Building 4, along with two other women and four men. They did not speak. Each had been given numbered tags. Wan Chuntao's said Northern Wind Five. A fifth man entered and stood at the head of table. By his demeanour and dress he was obviously very senior. He started to speak.

"Welcome. You are now members of the 'Northern Wind' project team. This is a highly classified project which only the President and six other people know about – besides yourselves. I am the head of the project and I am to be known as Northern Wind One.

This project is a matter of the highest priority to our country and you have all been selected for the special skills you bring to the team. Failure cannot be countenanced and success will bring you great professional credit – although you will never be able to talk about it.

A very great threat to our country has been discovered. We must neutralise that threat. You will each be assigned specific tasks. You must complete them with great diligence and speed. This is the only time you will meet with each other and you must not discuss the details of your work except with your direct superiors - either Northern Wind Two or Three. You will each be assigned an office.

If there is anything – and I mean anything – that you require to complete your task then ask your superior. You will not leave this building until this project achieves its objectives. That should not take more than two weeks. This floor of Building 4 is dedicated to this project. Now go to work – you must succeed."

Two men entered the room from a side door. They introduced themselves as Northern Wind Two and Northern Wind Three. Wan Chuntao and two others were taken to individual offices. Wan Chuntao entered room number 5 after her ID chip scan. Her few personal possessions were already in place, together with the latest versions of the terminal she had used in her previous role. There were tea facilities and a small washroom, together with a small desk, two chairs, a pull-down bunk bed and a large screen display. "It's almost better than home" she thought.

She tried to log on and found that her credential still worked. There was a voicemail from Maruška. She could not access it – it had been tagged as 'Closed'. That could mean anything.

Her inbox was empty bar one message from Northern Wind Three – 'Make tea and wait for me. I will brief you shortly.' So much for the revolution.

There was a knock and she tried to open the door. It was locked. She scanned her ID tag and the door opened. She bowed slightly as Northern Wind 3 entered.

He sat down. He was about thirty years old, dressed in a good quality western suit and an open necked shirt. He smiled briefly and then started to speak.

*

Wan Chuntao scrolled down the screen, reading the file to which she had just been given access. A man, an Algerian, had been fitted with one of the first production nanochips, almost twenty years previously when he had been a graduate student in Beijing. At that time the design was very basic – it was far from being a nanochip in size and was embedded in a heart pacemaker. The first batch of one hundred had been produced and implanted in a cohort of foreign students over a period of two years. The implantations had taken placed when they had been hospitalized following regular health checks which had uncovered seemingly irregular heart rhythms. The students were very happy to have first class treatment at one of China's leading hospitals, and most eventually forgot that they carried one.

The microchip embedded in the pacemaker had been relatively simple, able to detect a mobile phone network and send a location signal, date and transmission number. There was no GPS functionality and the 'prod' – the nerve impulse connection – had not been developed at that time.

The later generations of the design had been shrunk in size and were embedded near the spine and invisible to almost all scanning technology at airports and in hospitals. Over a thousand had been successfully implanted over a period of ten years, such as in the case of Maruška Pavkovic with which Wan Chuntao was very familiar.

Ben-Zhair's file contained a link to a datastream which had been very intermittent. The signal serial numbers showed that only about 10% of transmissions had got through, if sent at all. The last year of data had a couple of hundred records with position signals from a wide range of places including Kabul, London, Aleppo, Karachi, Beijing, Jerusalem, Paris, Cairo, Rome, Jeddah, Malta, Dubai, Tunisia, Morocco, and Algeria. Chuntao clicked a link to a mapping function, entered a timeframe – the last 12 months - and pressed the 'animate' button.

The map slowly built up the tracks ben-Zhair had followed. The data was incomplete, although there was no knowing if the data was complete. The most recent signals had been from Paris, Kabul, Rome, London, Malta, Tunisia and Algeria.

He had to be stopped.

*

Behnavaz

Three weeks after voyage #234 of the *Chong Ryon San*, another ship - the Iranian container ship *Behnavaz*, 54,851 gross registered tons, docked in Annaba, Algeria. Her current voyage had started in Yan, in China and *en route* she had called in Mumbai, India, then Pakistan where she had spent 24 hours moored at the East Wharf in Karachi harbour to take on more cargo. Then she headed west for Iran, arriving in Bandar Abbas 650 miles and thirty six hours later.

From Bandar Abbas, Iran, she crossed the Gulf to Jebel Ali, the freeport in the Emirate of Dubai, before passing back out through the Straits of Hormuz, down the Gulf of Aden. The she Passed through the Gate of Tears (Bab el Mandeb) up, the Red Sea, through the Suez Canal and Eastern Mediterranean before arriving in Annaba. One container in particular – one of a specific pair – was unloaded in Jebel Ali, later to be loaded on to a small local coaster for transhipment to Yanbu in Saudi Arabia. The other container continued on to Annaba.

Of the 3,631 shipping containers aboard when *Behnavaz* arrived in Annaba, 273 were unloaded and 14 loaded. Over the next few days the arriving containers were loaded on to trucks and railway wagons and distributed through eastern Algeria in the normal way. Customs paperwork was in order and no containers were opened by the customs police although a random sample was checked externally with sniffer dogs. As arranged, the dogs were kept away from the four containers of Japanese whisky.

One container in particular was shown on the cargo manifest as containing farm machinery. It was checked by the dogs but radioactivity had not been part of their training - though had it been they would certainly have been able to detect it - even at low levels – because it generated ionized gases. The Customs dog-handlers did not think it strange that farm machinery should be in a refrigerated container.

After about 48 hours in the customs enclosure the container was loaded onto a flatbed trailer and taken south by truck to the town of Souk Aras, there to be parked in the barn of a farmhouse. This town was near the edge of the area now controlled by elements of the Islamic Caliphate. Military presence was limited – neither the legitimate Algerian Government nor the Islamic Caliphate could have presence in strength along the huge Algerian border almost 4,000 miles in length.

The container waited there, in a warehouse, for ten days, within twenty miles of the Tunisian border, under unobtrusive guard. During that time it was repainted and new serial numbers were attached. It was then transported further south to Tebessa, deeper into the region which is considered dangerous for foreigners – a corridor 50 miles wide which extends south along the Tunisian border, then along the Libyan border. Just south of the town of In Amenas, this notional dangerous corridor widens to 150 miles as it turns west along the borders of Niger and Mali, across the heart of the Sahara Desert.

The danger to foreigners is not because of the desert – which is very unforgiving – but comes from the presence of fundamentalist Islamic terrorists – and ICIM.

*

In Iran, Hashemi Firouzabadi, his associates and the technical staff were still unaccounted for. Sistani and Hossein Ashtari had agreed that this theft must have required considerable internal help to succeed and that this put Iran in serious danger – politically, commercially and militarily.

There had been no trace of the missing components and materials. Despite extensive interrogation resulting in four deaths, there was still no explanation of how they had been removed from the underground facility at Yazd. There were several theories but none stood up to close examination.

Sistani had personally selected and assigned a small team to watch and investigate Ashtari, and then five days after the theft of the *hohlraum* from Yazd, Ashtari and his wife were not in a smuggler's dhow to Dubai as they had planned. Their bodies were at the bottom of a flooded marble quarry near the city of

Ahvaz. Ashtari had protested his innocence throughout a brutal interrogation which included having to watch the torture of his wife. He had finally agreed to a confession which bore no resemblance to the facts of his innocence, simply to be able to die quickly, after his wife.

The story in the Iranian press of their abduction by thieves demanding ransom – and subsequent murder - was noted by analysts in the Pentagon, but his file was kept open. He and his wife had no other family. Who would pay a ransom? No the Iranian Government surely? Then the DIA's computers (tasked primarily with military intelligence) started linking other stories and intelligence about several Iranian military and political personnel whose communications traffic had changed in nature. Lexical analysis suggested that the content was not created by the supposed originators. In Langley, a special team was formed to research further into the anomaly.

The agents in the UN Weapons Inspection team reported no unusual activity at any of the research sites – the increase in security activity was not apparent as their own activities were anyway subject to the most rigorous and intrusive security. The team did not usually check uranium mines – yellowcake mining was low technology – so the secret installation deep underground at Yazd stayed secret – even from the satellites - and the construction spoil had been hidden underground in those areas of the mines which had been exhausted.

Although the Iranian Armed Forces readiness was stepped up very discreetly, the changes were noted in Washington, London, Moscow, Beijing and particularly in Tel Aviv. Diplomatic and other intelligence resources sought to understand the motivation, but all that Teheran would say was that it was a routine re-organisation and 'stretching of muscles'.

*

London, September

"Right everyone, please sit and we'll start" said the Prime Minister.

The tension was beyond electric – no one present could ever remember a Cobra meeting being held in the bunker complex below Downing Street.

This was also the first Cobra since the huge reorganisation of the Security Services following the ICIM attack on the *Queen Katherine* earlier that year. There had been a major turf war in Whitehall with the result that 'C', the head of MI6, now reported directly to the Prime Minister on the crisis. The change had resulted in the resignation of the Foreign Secretary and his replacement by Shami Munchetty. She was seen by many as the best of a weak list of candidates and change was expected during the next reshuffle in the spring. The Home Secretary had fought hard to retain control of MI5 and had succeeded – just.

"This is a formal meeting of Cobra to update us on progress in the follow up to the atrocious attack on the *Queen Katherine*, but there is one more item we will cover at the end. It may take some time and is the reason that we are in this room. Sir William, if you please."

All eyes turned to Sir William Gore, head of SIS. He had a commanding presence as one might expect, but clearly the stress of recent events was taking its toll. His eyes were heavy and his face pallid and damp with sweat. As he opened his presentation it was clear that he was extremely tired.

"Thank you, Prime Minister. The information we have assembled at present indicates that the planning for the attack on the *Queen Katherine* took place in Algeria. Information from our colleagues at the DGSE on Quai D'Orsay indicates that the leader of the operation is likely to have been one of three people - Mansour Bouyali, Abdelkhader Maliani or Abu ben-Zhair. We are seeking to confirm this through other channels. We believe that ben-Zhair was in Malta – actually in

Grand Harbour – at the time of the attack. There is mobile phone evidence to support this, although it is only probable – not definite.

We believe he travelled immediately after the attack by small boat to Tabarka in Tunisia. This comes from satellite imagery and Malta radar data – this part of the Mediterranean has seen a lot of migrant trafficking, as you know. From there we know no more but assume that he has travelled back into Algeria where he has strong family, political and business ties. He is an Algerian national and was closely associated with the now defunct GIA terrorist group which has morphed into something called the ICIM – Islamic Caliphate in the Maghreb.

We have diverted additional intelligence resources and are liaising with the Director of Special Services.

I have nothing more to add today. Questions?"

There were none. It was as silent as the lying in state of a monarch – except that Westminster Abbey would not have air conditioning purring in the background.

The PM turned to General Mike Rushby GCB, CBE, ADC, the current Chief of the Defence Staff.

"Prime Minister, we have deployed an additional battalion of the Prince of Wales's Royal Regiment to Malta to assist with clearing up operations after the atrocity. One squadron of the SAS has been deployed, and a squadron of the SBS is standing by on HMS *Bulwark* off the Algerian coast. Our flagship *HMS Queen Elizabeth* is on patrol in the central Mediterranean with full fleet support, and of course a full complement of F35s. This is the exactly the type of situation for which she was conceived, if I may say so – even though I'm an Army man." He stared across at the Chancellor of the Exchequer, who responded tartly "What? Fight an asymmetric war with an aircraft carrier? I think not. This is about intelligence and covert operations, surely?"

"The Islamic Caliphate is a *de facto* state, with a huge military budget, sophisticated command and control which we have difficulty breaking, and superbly trained – and need I add, highly committed soldiers…"

"…and control of large areas of sand" the Chancellor persisted.

The Prime Minister rapped the table sharply with her Swarovski glass paperweight – one of her few affectations - other than kitten heels which had been sold on eBay for charity.

"Gentlemen, we are not here to score points. General, please keep to your report."

"Very well Prime Minister. Informally the Pentagon has asked why we have suddenly changed our fleet plans – they seem to doubt that the bombing of our cruise liner is sufficient reason to deploy a carrier task force which we have done following your instructions. Planning is well underway for a range of tactical options.

We are working closely with the Foreign Office to ensure that the message is consistent across all fronts – both the Pentagon and the State Department. Thank you Prime Minister."

"Thank you, General."

"Prime Minister, may I ask why we are deploying a carrier taskforce?"

"Certainly, Minister. It is because we need to be prepared for all eventualities. No more questions - we shall move on. We come to the additional item. It is not related to the Malta attack. I shall be unable to attend tomorrow's meeting of Cobra. It will be chaired by the Deputy Prime Minister."

The Chancellor nodded.

"I will be attending what is to be a secret session of the UN Security Council – the 'P5' as the press has dubbed it. It has been called because of information which has come to light about the latest North Korean underground nuclear test. Sir William, once again if you will."

There was an audible intake of breath by most of those present and the sense of excitement in the briefing room was even more palpable as eyes once again turned to Sir William.

"Thank you again Prime Minister. This matter carries the rather unfortunate code name 'Blue Angel' – a random computer selection I might say. We have information both from our own sources and the United States about the latest North

Korean atomic weapon test. The radionuclide residues which have finally percolated through the subsoil and into the atmosphere have a radioactivity signature which is typical of a fusion bomb – that is, a hydrogen bomb."

There was a gasp around the table.

"Beyond that, there is little in the sample data which is typical of a fission bomb – the usual trigger of a hydrogen bomb. I am advised that there is no way that the test – which measured five point one on the Richter scale could have been a fusion bomb – at least with the technology as we understand it. However, the radioactivity data would definitely appear to support the claim that North Korea made about a fusion device – with qualification. I stress the phrase – 'the technology as we understand it'. The nature of the radionuclide signature is unique – it has never been seen before. Now, we have Jonathan Tweedy on secure video link. He is the Technical Director of the Atomic Weapons Establishment at Aldermaston. It is a briefing and he will not be taking questions."

Sir William touched an icon on the screen before him. Each Cobra member had a touch screen in front of them. The screens switched on and showed a grey haired man, about forty years old, clean shaven with very intense dark eyes. He was completely at ease even though he was about to speak before the country's top politicians on a matter of the greatest gravity.

"Good morning Director, you are online to the Cobra meeting. Could you please give us the brief technical overview of Blue Angel as you and I discussed early this morning?"

"Er...certainly, Sir William. Prime Minister, Ladies and Gentlemen, I believe that Sir William has provided some context. I will erm...try to keep this briefing as non-technical as possible."

Although the burr of his voice betrayed a Northern background modified by years in Cambridge and some time spent in the US, no-one in that room noticed – their focus on his content was total. His delivery was fractured in a way typical of academics whose minds are running ahead of their mouths. The silence was absolute bar the slight whirring of a faulty air conditioning fan.

"The conventional hydrogen aka fusion bomb requires a fission – aka an atom bomb - as its trigger to generate the high temperatures necessary to enable atoms to fuse (classically these are deuterium and tritium which are forms of hydrogen). In the process huge amounts of energy are released.

In contrast, peaceful fusion research has been geared towards maintaining a high temperature plasma of deuterium and tritium in a relatively steady non-critical state. This requires continuous high energy input and the output must be controllable and continuous - an atom bomb is clearly out of the question! The energy output must also be usefully greater than the input for it to make economic sense for power generation. Present experiments are achieving the holy grail of 'net energy gain', but only for microseconds."

His delivery was improving as he got into his technical stride - he was comfortable with the content, but less so with the audience.

"There are many technical issues – it is a far more complex process than making a bomb. Indeed, for the last sixty years, fusion power has always been 'at least fifty years away', whereas the first hydrogen bomb was tested in 1952.

Some avenues of current fusion power research involve the use of high-energy 'pumped' lasers to produce the high temperatures required and also need a lot of electrical power to hold the hot plasma stable in an electromagnetic 'doughnut' – the so-called *tokomak* – a Russian word. This is a complex configuration in which to maintain the stability of a very hot plasma. The United States and, we assume, other countries have been exploring alternative methods. Of course we have one ourselves.

If the energy output is not required to be continuous as for power generation but just one big pulse - as in a bomb - then high energy input needs only to be for the briefest of intervals and the challenges of maintaining plasma stability are greatly simplified. A special fuel pellet is used in the US test configuration – for peaceful purposes of course." There was snigger or two at this statement, but he carried on regardless. "It is a mixture of deuterium and tritium – forms of hydrogen, held in a small plastic pellet. The pellet is located in a small gold canister known as a '*hohlraum*' – the German word for space – smaller than a sewing thimble, although the term is also used in the physically larger context of a conventional nuclear bomb. Then, more than a hundred lasers pump out huge quantities of energy in less than a billionth of a second with the energy focused on the fuel pellet in the *hohlraum*. This has been demonstrated in fusion power research at the Lawrence Livermore lab in the US – supposedly for peaceful purposes as I said although the prime directive of the Lawrence Livermore Laboratory is to enhance US national security. Of course, many would argue that energy security – and therefore peaceful nuclear power research – falls within this definition. I digress, sorry. Here is a picture of a *hohlraum*."

Tweedy clicked on the link

http://cdn.phys.org/newman/gfx/news/hires/2014/hohlraum_cut_away_with_capsule.jpg

and then continued with is explanation.

"These are big lasers and many of them are required for just one *hohlraum* - delivering one point nine megajoules of energy in slightly more than a nanosecond, the lasers are rated at five hundred terawatts – that's five hundred trillion watts. That's equivalent to well over twenty thousand times the output of Dungeness nuclear power station in Kent. But it's only for a nanosecond. I know, too much information – but please don't lose my thread."

"We're trying very hard to stay with you, Director."

"Yes, sorry, Prime Minister. One of the difficulties for a 'rogue state' or terrorist group in building a *conventional* atomic or fusion weapon is that some components - for example very fast-acting electrical switches for detonation - cannot easily be bought on the open market and are subject to very strict export controls – and they are not easy to make at home. And that's the least of the difficulties. Plutonium – or enriched uranium – is required. This is not easy to obtain. Then, miniaturization to produce a suitcase-size fission bomb is practically impossible for any entity other than a major state.

But with a pumped laser fusion device - 'PLFD' for short - these scarce, tightly controlled components would not be needed. The components that we envisage would be required are much more freely available, although still specialist – for example high power lasers. This would simplify the construction process. Nevertheless, some exotic materials *are* required but deuterium and tritium are relatively easy to obtain through university research laboratories. We believe that these weapons are feasible – I'll say no more on that – but nevertheless, the reality of a practical weaponized PLFD had been thought to be several years away.

One further and critical advantage of the PLFD is that fissile material - usually uranium 235 or plutonium - would only be required in very small - that is sub-critical amounts - to enhance the performance of such a device. Or even not at all. So, a little goes a long way – at least in theory. And, uranium 235 is much more easily obtainable than plutonium.

Another aspect of the PLFD is that it would create minimal fallout. This would make it more useful when targets are nearer to home and does not create long term radioactive no-go areas – unless it is doped with, say, cobalt. I cannot see any way that such a device could be miniaturized, but, within limits, it could be a relatively simple route to constructing a true fusion bomb, and could of course avoid the use of plutonium or enriched uranium which are difficult to produce and relatively easy to track – unless of course they obtained some from a country friendly to the terrorists..

I have a team of technical analysts still working on the sampling data from the test. We are also trying to work out if North Korea could have 'hoaxed' us by falsifying a specific radioactive signature as part of a conventional atomic weapon test. We think that this would be very difficult to achieve and is very unlikely given also the seismographic data. That is all I am able to say at present, apart from the fact that apart from the North Korean aspect there's nothing secret here – this design is all in the public domain. Sorry if I got a bit enthusiastic there – it's a very interesting development. Thank you."

"A development we could well do without, thank you, Director, you've said more than enough."

Sir William cut the link.

"Jesus Christ."

All eyes turned to the Chief of the Defence Staff.

"Sorry, Prime Minister."

"General, I'm sure that we share your sentiments though we might use more acceptable language – and address your comments through the Chair."

There was a lot of nodding and some chatter started but the PM again tapped the table with her paperweight. "Sir William, please continue."

He nodded to the PM.

"We are proceeding on the basis that this is a viable device. In 2015, North Korea was believed to have enough fissile material for five or six conventional atomic bombs - typically six kilos of plutonium per conventional atomic bomb. We know that their stock has increased since then as their breeder reactor continues operation. As the AWE Director indicated, in the PLFD scenario a little could go a very long way – although miniaturisation for a warhead seems improbable. They have already demonstrated that they have mastered the submarine ballistic missile launch technology, and the missiles. We believe that they are in the process of productionizing the weapon – that is, making multiple warheads with a standardized production process. It is not a simple task. We expect them to have an operational submarine-launched ballistic missile capability within two years, on new, larger submarines to be based in their new submarine shelters at the Mayang-do naval base. Their existing submarine fleet is generally old and unsafe for its seamen, but that should not make us complacent.

Whilst we can track purchases of components for conventional atomic weapons, without any clear idea of the design of a putative PLFD we can only guess at what components they might be using. Clearly, we do not even know if they are using lasers – that remains a working assumption. As the Director of AWE said, some exotic materials which may be trackable would surely be required. The problem is that we don't know what they are – we have to guess. We have a team working on this supply chain analysis now and we're also looking at precursors to the exotics.

Acquiring any sort of humint from within North Korea is hugely difficult and most analysis is based on sigint and elint or is inferential.

Informal contact with Moscow and also the Chinese Government indicates that their data is broadly similar. We assume that their analysis is likewise so. Thank you, Prime Minister."

There was a pulse of excited chatter but it stopped as the PM tapped the table, once again and rather harder. "Sir William is not taking questions on this today." She turned to the Chief of the Defence Staff.

The large screen displays flickered into life again, showing a satellite image of the region.

"General Rushby."

"Thank you Prime Minister. I'll keep this very brief, although it is highly significant in the context of what we have just heard. Three Divisions of the Chinese Republican Guard are currently moving towards the border with North Korea. Russia also has a short – eleven miles – land border with North Korea, west of Vladivostok, and is moving infantry forces in division strength to the border region. We believe that a Russian naval battle group is preparing to sail from Vladivostok.

The United States is beefing up support for South Korea, sending two wings of land-based F35 fighter bombers, plus the newly updated A10 Tankbusters and other assorted air support to reinforce South Korean defence forces.

Additional US Army advisors are being deployed together with five US Marine Corps detachments.

The US Pacific Fleet Command is sending a 7th Fleet battle group into the Sea of Japan. We have no doubt that the US has nuclear weapons in-theatre although they do not admit that even to us.

Military activity in the region has increased significantly and the risks of an incident are now extremely concerning. At present we are making no significant military preparations in that region, other than through our intelligence resources, although we do have hunter-killer submarine assets close by on routine patrol. Thank you, Prime Minister."

The PM nodded again.

"Foreign Secretary."

"Yes Prime Minister. There has been a lot of sabre-rattling over the Chinese annexation of the Spratly Islands and the decision in favour of the Philippines. This latest news from North Korea is ratcheting up the tension even more.

On the diplomatic front this is all being kept extremely quiet at the moment although activity is intense. North Korea has close links with Iran and we are concerned that if the Israelis get wind of this test data then they will take precipitate action, even though North Korea is outside their direct sphere of influence. We don't believe the Israelis have the capability to extend their forces that far east in any strength but there is always the possibility that it might suit the US to use them as a proxy – and provide assistance, of course.

There are public calls in Japan for their defence-only treaties to be torn up and the US has gone on record as guaranteeing Taiwan its territorial integrity – Beijing has made no comment about this.

I shall of course be flying to New York with you. There is a news blackout on our travel; I have forty-eight hour flu for the media. Thank you."

"Thank you, Foreign Secretary. As you all will have gathered, this is about as serious as it gets. The WMD data which triggered the Iraq invasion was flimsy and sexed up. Here we have raw scientific data of probable new and tested fusion bomb technology and seemingly a P5 consensus about that data. It doesn't bear thinking about that this technology may be in the hands of Dim Pong-un. Finally, although the Home Secretary is not here for this meeting, he is being kept fully informed as there is a possibility of some anti-war demonstration activity around the country when this leaks out -

as it surely will. The Press is already on to the Russian and Chinese troop movements, and US deployments."

A hand went up at the far end of the table and the PM dismissed it with a wave. "Sorry Minister, no questions. We will have a long session on this in two days' time and there will be plenty of opportunity for questions then. I don't need to remind you all of the need for absolute secrecy. This is not to be discussed outside the confines of a Cobra meeting. Thank you all. Meeting closed at 11.37 am. And will somebody get that damned aircon fan fixed!" The PM tapped the table with her glass paperweight and quickly left the room.

*

Malta Briefing

"Steve, this could be the most important thing you have ever done for you country."

"How many times have I heard that before – and got stitched up? No way am I going to Tunisia!"

"Keep your voice down Steve."

They were in one of the bedrooms of the villa.

"I don't bloody care who hears me."

"Just hear me out, please. If you can't respect basic security then I'll have you arrested."

"You wouldn't do that."

"Try me – you are still subject to the Official Secrets Act. There's a lot at stake here – a world war could start."

"Pull the other one."

"And if I said that a terrorist group had a nuclear bomb?"

"I wouldn't believe you."

"Good, because I didn't say it. We think that the *Queen Katherine* bombing was just a start. Look at it this way – you and me on Adèle as cover. Tourists. You did tell me you'd like to see the country."

"Why not use the SAS or some of your regular fucking secret agents?"

"The SAS are hard men, not intelligence agents. They will be there for us to call on. As to our regulars, we don't have anyone with the right profile who we can put in immediately."

"I'm not a bloody intelligence agent."

"No, you are an all-round star – with the right profile. You proved that. And you speak Arabic and French. And – the clincher – you want Maruška. She is a part of this operation."

"What?"

"Yes. That's what Tunis was about. We know a bit about what the Chinese are doing and what they want her to do. As I said downstairs, we're monitoring their comms with her. Mostly it's good for us. We just let her carry out her mission – and watch her of course. Make sure there's no double-dealing.

We know that the Chinese have re-tasked a satellite to monitor the Libya-Tunisia-Algeria region.

The thinking is we head for Tabarka in Adèle and moor there. It's lower profile than Tunis and gives us a good cover story. Bryan will take the car ferry over and meet us over there."

"Is Bryan up to this?"

"What do you think?"

"He's done OK so far. A bit of a plodder."

"That's how he's meant to look on this job – he's playing a part."

"Nursemaid you mean."

"Monitoring is just a part of his role. He's versatile and his record is very good. Believe me, there's much more than meets the eye. I've known him for a few years and worked with him before. Anyway, it's not a plan yet, but it's a start." She raised her eyebrows. "Comments?"

"It sounds ok but I'd need to check on Tabarka. I guess it's a couple of hundred miles, but with this wind we can probably do it in 36 hours. And we have no idea what Maruška will be up to."

"That's where you are wrong – and that's why we have techies here."

"Why not go straight to Tunis? That would make much more sense – and it's nearer too."

"Because we don't think that's where the action will be. She has been given the name –Abu ben-Zhair. Remember, there's credible intel that he was behind the *Queen Katherine* bombing and that he's got an even bigger atrocity planned. We think Maruška's headed ultimately for Algeria – Annaba looks to be the likely destination. Tabarka is only six miles from the Algerian border and less than eighty from Annaba."

"Jesus, Algeria - that's a whole new ball game."

"But you've been there too, so you're qualified."

"Only out in the desert - a natural gas plant at In Amenas when there was a terrorist attack. Bloody dodgy place. In and out by helo. Never again. We'd stand out a mile in Algeria – no tourists and police everywhere."

"Maybe it will not come to that."

"She'd be mad go in to Algeria and we'd be mad to follow. I might pull it off, but you? No way."

"Let's take it one step at a time, be flexible. Is Adèle ready?"

"We just need some fuel, water, food."

"HMG will pick up the tab. And I can promise you a good bonus."

She winked, but he shook his head. "I've heard that before too. I just can't believe it. To think that a few weeks ago I thought you were just a pretty Greek waitress. I must be a real schmuck."

"I am *very* good at my work."

There was a knock at the door. "Come in. Yes Dave, what is it?"

"Sorry Ma'am, but I've orders to head back to base once the people arrive from the airport – they're on the way now and should be here in a few minutes. We'll leave you with the Jollies."

"Jollies?"

"The *Royal Marines*. Nickname" said Steve.

"Oh. How's the prisoner?"

"Making eyes at my lads – that's about all she can do the way she's trussed up."

"Keep it that way."

"Yes, Ma'am."

*

84

Building Work

"Why does a commercial bank want such a bloody big electrical power supply?"

The site foreman was talking to the supervisor from the electrical company carrying out the installation of the supply. They were sitting in a café enjoying café americanos. The sun was well up and it was going to be another hot late summer day. Humidity was climbing and the threat of thunder was in the air.

The tourists were out in force, with bare midriffs and short skirts much in evidence.

"I don't know – what they want is more than enough for ten banks."

"How's progress on the vault?"

"A few problems but we should be ready for you by the end of the week."

"That's good. They have some strange requirements for the power to the vault – and some unusual equipment scheduled. It will be a bitch to set up."

"Everything's strange about this job. Bloody Arabs."

"I heard they were Iranians."

"Iranians, Palestinians, Algerians - same difference isn't it? And a bank at that. They're taking us over."

"Well our contract ends once the vault is in. We only ever see parts of the architect's drawings – just enough for the job."

"I know it's a bank, but talk about secrecy! And I've never seen so many firms on one job. A bit here, a bit there. It's only the client's project manager who has the big picture – and he's another Arab. Or an Iranian. They all look the same to me.

The world is going crazy. 'No elevators' - to save energy they said. 'Keeps the staff fit walking up and down the stairs', they said. And that weird energy recovery system in the elevator shaft – I've never seen so much stainless steel piping. I'm buggered if I can understand how that might work. It's a madcap design if you ask me."

The foreman whistled and nodded to his colleague as the girl turned her head, barely taking her eyes off her smartphone.

"I'd love to pinch her arse."

"Swedish?"

"No, I think German."

"Maybe, but a real blonde I'll bet."

"Yes, it's a pity we don't have more of our own. I'm getting tired of black holes – a bit like this bank project."

*

James Marinero

Chinese Policy in Africa

After Algeria regained its independence from France, both China and Russia – started taking even more interest. Of course, Egypt had been aligned for years with the Soviet Union, as the USSR set to counter US Middle East influence exercised through Israel. The USSR sponsored Libya as well, but Russia, as it later became, lost influence as the Arab Spring spread through the region. Russia was reduced to propping up Assad in Syria as the Islamic Caliphate spread.

China starting taking an interest in Africa many years before that – not only because of its vast natural resources, but because of its instability and proximity to Europe. China bought up large tracts of farmland, invested in mineral extraction, power infrastructure and people.

In Algeria, the GIA – the Armed Islamic Group of Algeria – had become the Salafist Group for Preaching and Combat over the period 1999-2003, when they announced support for Al Qua'eda. This group eventually morphed into Al Qua'eda in the Islamic Maghreb (AQIM).

Since the days of the GIA in the 1990s, funds had been provided indirectly from Beijing, and control exerted delicately. Potential leaders were identified and developed – discreetly, some even without realizing that they were puppets and proxies, although ben-Zhair was under no illusions about his Chinese sponsorship when a student in Beijing. Data was collated, promising individuals were tracked, missions suggested, monitored and even, occasionally, deliberately compromised to protect agents or manage events for political advantage.

The organisation known as ICIM evolved from the disparate collection of Algerian terrorist organisations, falling into line with the so-called Islamic Caliphate, IC as it, too, evolved.

The Sword of Islam Announcement had been outside the scope of Beijing's knowledge and caused consternation in

Beijing. The search for the weapon had stalled and the race to retrieve it became even more critical.

The Announcement caused much deliberation and argument for two days at the highest levels between the various Chinese intelligence agencies. The argument had been about turf and responsibility in the search for the Sword of Islam. The Guoanbu was tasked primarily with economic and technical intelligence gathering, not control and direction of terrorist networks. However, obtaining the weapons technology that North Korea had delivered to Iran was seen as well within the remit of the Guoanbu.

The final decision was made by the General Secretary in consultation with the President. Within hours, a list of names was delivered to the man known as Northern Wind One, six floors below ground in the Guoanbu building in Hainan province. On the list were three names of the individuals who were identified as possible leaders of ICIM.

Three members of the Northern Wind Team were each given a name to research. Unprecedented access was granted to other systems within the Chinese intelligence community, ordered directly by the General Secretary without a reason being given. Full cooperation was guaranteed.

Northern Wind Five - Wan Chuntao - was given the name Abu ben-Zhair. He was thought to be the most likely candidate, having been linked to the recent Malta atrocity. His file in Beijing indicated a 'high degree of strategic vision and extreme levels of personal ambition, supported by outstanding leadership capability."

Northern Wind Four was given the name Mansour Bouyali and an agent based at the Embassy in Alger (Algiers) was briefed. The name Abdelkhader Maliani was provided to Northern Wind Six who briefed an agent based in a shipping company in Oran. These latter terrorist leaders were seen as being tactically capable and charismatic, but tended to involve themselves in 'token gestures of terrorism' - or so the analyst had recorded in their files.

Four countries each had three names. The US was behind the curve, learning several days later of the names through the Homeland Security reading of the French DGSE comms traffic.

*

Dangerous Corridor

Just 15 miles from the Tunisian border, located within the so-called 'dangerous corridor' is Tebessa - a large city of more than 600,000 people and famous for its Algerian carpets.

The location ben-Zhair had chosen was a farm that had been acquired several years before and used as a college for very select groups of committed Islamist *jihadis*. It was in a shallow valley and sheltered within a ring of tall palm trees, well within the area that was now part of the Islamic Caliphate in the Maghreb, the rogue area outside of the control of the legitimate Algerian government – a government which was governing a rapidly decreasing area.

The palm trees were mature and provided some shade from the fierce summer sun which regularly raised temperatures to more than 45 degrees Celsius. The solid stone of the main farm building – parts of which dated back to Roman times – helped to provide some coolness which encouraged a very gentle breeze to waft through the house in the mornings, before the air-conditioning became necessary.

A variety of contractors had been used during the refurbishment of the farmhouse, so that no one – other than ben-Zhair - had the complete picture. The contractors were used to dealing with secretive wealthy Algerians, so they did not question the hi-tech 'clean room', airlocks and air-filtration systems which were installed and, unknown to them, were a duplicate of another installation elsewhere in Europe.

The farmhouse itself had all modern conveniences with plentiful power from a large generator with several months fuel supply – enough for the assembly and mobilization phase. Similarly, food supplies had been brought in for which large refrigerators had been installed. Supplies were sufficient for twenty men for the duration. The farm had a deep water borehole, and additional bottled supplies had been brought in. There was no alcohol permitted at the farmhouse on pain of death, but it was not an issue. All the men on site were devout

Muslims, although their interpretation of the Quoran was beyond extreme.

Women were not permitted at the farm. This had been an issue at first and the solution had been to obtain wives for them from Mali – kidnapped schoolgirls. The girls were assigned husbands and kept together under guard in another farm. There were tribal differences as well as the focus brought by the international search for the girls and the arrangement was not a happy one. It did, however, keep the stress levels down amongst the *jihadis.*

The men – or warriors – as they preferred to be called – slept four to a room. These warriors included technicians and guards. The 'officers' slept in individual rooms, as did the Technical Director, Jafa Sharifi. The Mission Leader – Abu ben-Zhair - had assigned himself the 'owner's suite'. Although the working language of the technical staff was Farsi, while the guards and management spoke mainly Arabic, this posed few problems as the key technical specialists were capably bilingual.

One other room contained a video suite and another was used as a prayer room. Under the farmhouse were two large cellars which had been used for grain, dates and vegetable storage from Roman times. One of them now housed the latest in cryogenic technology - a small unit capable of cooling its contents to 18 degrees Kelvin – that is, considerably colder than the dark side of the moon and just slightly warmer than deep space at 2.7 degrees Kelvin - or in layman's terms, minus 270 degrees Celsius. The farmhouse had been carefully chosen and once the team were in place, it was completely isolated from the outside world, in lockdown. There was no satellite communications link, no electrical grid link and no mobile phones on site.

*

The Ruling Council

Ben-Zhair had, as a matter of good sense, kept the Ruling Council of the Islamic Caliphate broadly aware of his plans. Details of the Sword of Allah had been as closely guarded as efficiency permitted. The Council was generally thought to comprise ten members, but in reality only three people made the decisions – they were the Inner Council and ben-Zhair as he was known to them, was the Chairman.

He had ruthlessly rooted out and disposed of any waverers or those he perceived as being a risk to security.

This small coterie had access to liquid funds approaching $3 billion for the purposes of their operations – and most of it would be required to complete these projects. However, there was plenty more funding available.

At first there had been a lot of argument. 'The future was cyberwar'. That was the mantra he was tired of hearing. The main thrust of the argument went roughly as follows:

"Why do big states have big weapons?"

"Because that is how war and weaponry has evolved. We do not need big weapons now. Cyberwar enables us to compete on a level playing field with the biggest nations."

"Not so. Real cyberwar needs huge investment and technology – for example in quantum computing."

"But market pressure will deliver that power to us."

"When? Much of it is secret and will never be available to us. They read our communications, control the satellites and – don't forget – they can use cyberwar against our own infrastructure."

"We can have access to big weapons now and sit at the top table. We will be able to control most of Africa, much of Europe, the Levant and even the Far East where Islam is strengthening by the day. And with that power you can have your cyberwarfare as well."

His arguments had found the support he needed. A weapon named 'The Sword of Allah' had a ring about it and the title pushed the right buttons in those Islamists who mattered, although it had never really become public. With such a name it was not difficult to obtain backing – and funding - from unlikely sources.

Wealthy beyond what most people could conceive of, Sheikh Khalifa was a distant cousin of the Saudi royal family. His closest family were more than usually devout Sunni Muslims of the Wahhabi sect, more observant of Shariah law than was usual in the higher echelons of Saudi society. Most of the Saudi ruling clan were, in common with the rest of the human race – or at least those who professed to being religious - hypocritical when it came to religion. Alcohol was enjoyed in secret, but sexual vices were less the norm amongst males – after all, the faith permitted polygamy.

As far as the common man was concerned, Shariah law was strictly enforced and in Saudi Arabia with 157 beheadings in 2015. Amputations as a punishment for theft were everyday occurrences, and stoning women to death for adultery was far from unusual.

The Saudi prince with dollars to burn by the billion was not interested in business. Money had little value in his eyes – other than as a tool to enable him to achieve those things which he thought were important in the world – and those revolved mainly around religion. That included the war against Satan in whatever form he took, whether as the United States, the Shia State of Iran or tyrants such as Assad in Syria. The prince had even provided very discreet support to Osama bin-Laden and the Taliban, and latterly to a range of terrorist organisations which were aligned with the Sunni interpretation of Islam.

The major Western countries knew about Saudi support for Islamist terrorists and that they had provided huge funds to IS in its war against Assad in Syria. The problem was that Saudi buying power in the arms - and other lucrative markets – was huge. They controlled vast amounts of oil reserves and at a blink they could seriously damage the Western economic model. The West bought the oil, Saudi Arabia spent the petrodollars on arms and consumer goods, on building huge leisure complexes to attract tourists and take more western money. And so the money continued to go round and round, with a small but very useful percentage finding its way to Islamist terrorists. After all, Saudi Arabia was the guardian of Mecca – it had responsibilities to Islam and to the legacy of Muhammad.

And so, the Saudi prince amused himself funding wars and projects which took his fancy. He circumvented the problems of money laundering and funds transfer by making use of the *hawala* money transfer mechanism. To prime the process and prevent the obvious imbalance he had a personal yacht built, as did all Saudi princes. This yacht was not conspicuously large when compared to those of his cousins, but it was large enough to occasionally transport a ton or two of gold from Saudi Arabia to other countries where it would percolate out through soukhs and other outlets and so fund his projects. This method was below the radar of the Western security services and impossible to track.

Sheikh Khalifa was not the only such patron of Islamist terrorism in Saudi Arabia, but he was the one who had enabled ben-Zhair to acquire the Sword of Allah

The beauty of it was that the Sword of Allah had been stolen from the Shia Muslim Republic of Iran to further the Sunni Muslim cause – but only the Inner Council of the ICIM - and a Saudi prince - knew that. And Iran would get the blame.

*

Tunis

Two days later, the team tracked Maruška off the ferry, through passport control and customs. Tunisia was now a dangerous place since IC had all but taken control of Libya and started fomenting problems across the Tunisian border. Europeans were rarely seen these days and the tourist trade had been virtually dead since the fatal shooting of 38 tourists on the beach at Sousse in 2015.

The ferry journey had taken almost three days, with a leg from Malta to Catania and then a train from there to Palermo to catch the Tunis ferry. When Maruška got off the ferry in Tunis she saw her car as expected, but did not expect the Chinese driver. It had been a very tiring journey and her patience was little more than a veneer. They exchanged non-duress passwords and the car moved away from the kerb.

"We are being followed."

"To be expected. Drive me to an underground car park."

"Okay. Check the Adidas bag at your feet."

She looked inside.

"Good."

"The new phone is an upgrade – it works with both satellite and terrestrial networks. Leave your old one in the car – in the Nike sports bag on the rear seat, along with the tablet. There is a wristwatch which contains a radiation counter. You know the protocol for a new country. New equipment, numbers, email addresses…"

"You think I am stupid? You are just a fucking Chinese driver, so drive!"

Charles Tye, a supposed trade attaché at the British Embassy in Tunis, was parked outside the ferry port in a non-descript and cheap rental 4x4. He watched Maruška walk out and meet a Tunisian who led her to another equally bland white Nissan saloon. As they drove off he started to move. Bryan and Jacob drove out of the ferry port in their Malta SUV and joined the traffic a few cars behind Tye. He heard Jacob's voice in his earpiece.

"Whisky One, here. Whisky Two, let's hear you."

"OK. Whisky Two here. I'm two cars ahead of you in a white Peugeot 4x4."

"OK I see you. The brief is to keep on her tail until she's split from the pickup car. She's a passenger in the white Nissan – it's a Hertz rental." He recited the Nissan's registration tag – the numbers used were in western form. "Ignore the Arabic script in the middle of the numbers – that just translates as 'Tunisia'."

"Understood."

The followers were mixed discreetly with the vehicles disgorged from the ferry travelling along the Route de la Goulette towards central Tunis. This road was built on a causeway, bordered on the north by the very shallow Lac de Tunis and on the south by the ship channel which led to the docks in the city. The light wind was from the north east, and the shallow water of the saline lake glittered in the late afternoon sun.

The white Nissan turned on to the A1 road and within a couple of minutes left the autoroute, turning into the Montplaisir district and then down into an underground car park on the Rue de Japon.

"Whisky Two, I'm following down."

"Whisky One, our vehicle is too obvious although she'll know we're following. We'll wait on the street, cover the exit."

"Roger that."

"Extreme care advised."

"OK."

Bryan double parked the Toyota 4x4 on the street above, opposite the exit.

As they drove down into the car park Maruška moved some of the other items into the Nike bag. When they had parked they shut the doors carefully and walked away towards separate exits. She dialled a number on her phone and received an acknowledging beep. Then, as the white Peugeot 4x4 drove towards her she fingered the Czech CZ75 in her holdall.

"Whisky One, I'm on the second level down, just stopping. I think she has seen me."

"Get out of there now" Bryan shouted.

"She's out of the car and walking towar…"

There was a grunt.

"Whisky Two come in. Come in Whisky Two. Tap the mike if you cannot speak."

There was no reply.

Bryan u-turned the 4x4 and headed down the ramp. He easily found Tye's SUV on the second level, which was about half full of cars. There were two holes in the windscreen. Tye was obviously dead. Bryan found Tye's weapons under the driver's seat as Jacob called the Embassy emergency Six number. Bryan glanced at the other car - it was empty. A quick search revealed nothing.

Jacob looked across at him. "Her tracking signal has gone. The phone appears to be dead."

"Shit."

"I'll run up the pedestrian exit after her."

"Waste of time, we don't know if she took the elevator or the stairs. And there's the driver as well. He may be covering her rear."

Bryan accelerated, following the exit signs then came to the barrier. He swore. It might be ok in films he thought, but the 4x4 with was too obvious to run through the barrier and would be on camera. It would take at least 5 minutes to pay - he did not have Tunisian dinars.

"Hang on." Jacob climbed out of SUV and walked around to the barrier control pillar. He waved a scanner past the ticket slot and the barrier went up. Bryan drove through.

"We'll never find her now. I'm calling Ms. Williams."

*

Alex Ogilvy had just arrived back at his desk in London when the call came through – Helena had conferenced him in.

"One down and we've lost the target."

"OK, I can see the location on the tracking screen. Now let's check that Pavkovic responds to a prompting. Continue with the arrangements as planned, but first check the car she used – carefully – before the police get there – someone may have called it in. I'll call you back. I need to liaise with Head of Tunis Station."

Bryan drove the 4x4 back to the car park, and down the ramp.

"Jacob, take the 4x4 up to the entrance barrier and buzz me when you see the local police or anyone remotely official. I'll check out the other car. We'll have to be quick."

"Will do."

Jacob drove off and Bryan walked up to the hire car. There was a Nike sportsbag on the rear seat. He tried the door – it was open. Bryan looked carefully at the bag. His instinct told him it was too easy, told him to back off.

"Bryan, black Mercedes just coming in - fast. Four guys. I'm driving out now. See you topside at the pedestrian exit."

"Roger that." Bryan heard the tyres squealing as the Mercedes raced round the level above him. He looked across at the pedestrian exit and reckoned he had just enough time. He reached for the bag.

Just then the black Mercedes 300 reached his level and screeched off the ramp in a fast left handed turn. Bryan looked up just as the gravity switch triggered.

The half a kilo of Semtex took Bryan apart. Blast and pieces of bodywork killed the driver and front passenger of the Mercedes which then swerved and ran into the burning wreckage. The two men in the rear got out just before the Mercedes was engulfed in flame.

Jacob was parked near the pedestrian exit and did not notice the tremor in the heavy 4x4, but he heard a cacophony of car alarms. A minute later he saw smoke rising through the exit. There was no reply when he called Bryan. He waited a few minutes and when there was no sign of Bryan he moved off just as two police cars came down the road. After driving back on to the A1 autoroute, he took the N9 turnoff and then, to avoid possible road cameras, he turned off again onto local roads and headed northeast for ten minutes, past the ruins of Carthage, skirting the President's Palace, and on through the suburb of Sidi Bou Said. He needed to dump the car – quickly.

At the Carrefour supermarket a couple of miles away in La Corniche he parked the SUV in a corner. After wiping it down carefully he walked away although he doubted that he had removed all his – and Bryan's - bio traces. The rental company at the port would have details – but only of his current false ID. He found a seat on the Corniche, looking out over the Gulf of Tunis towards Cape Bon. In the dusk he could see the regular flash of the lighthouse on Ile de Zembra, though his conscious mind did not realise it. His thoughts were elsewhere.

Jacob was a technical specialist in SIS and although he had passed all the required training courses, until now he had only been involved in relatively minor operations. The action at the villa in Malta was the first one that had directly involved him in the cruel reality of his profession and now he had lost a partner. The adrenaline was wearing off and the feeling was not good as he started to tremble. He glanced around. There were few people about – the late autumn northeast wind was cold and rain was threatening as he called London. Was he really cut out for this?

*

Less than twelve hours later Maruška's driver had crossed the border back in to Algeria and re-joined the team of Chinese consultants. They were helping Algeria set up a vast 10 gigawatt solar panel farm in the Sahara. It would supply much of Algeria's electrical power needs for the next twenty five years, in return for supplies of oil and gas. He was just another of the Guoanbu's worldwide network of 100,000 agents and a miniscule part of China's huge investment in Africa.

Meanwhile, in Tunis, Maruška had rented a car and gone to ground.

*

Three hours later after using buses and avoiding taxis and the train, Jacob walked past the safe house on the outskirts of Tunis and after another circuit found the rear entrance in the dark. The electronic lock on the door clicked open when his smartphone NFC transmitted the correct code. Half an hour later he was joined by Simon Cruickshank –'Mago' - from Tunis Station. He swept the top floor apartment with his smartphone and turned on a radio. Safe houses were not always safe – and bug sweeping software was not infallible.

The next call to London took longer.
"Mago? Clear to talk?"
Cruickshank, Deputy Head of Tunis Station confirmed that he and Jacob were online and clear to talk. Mago, his codename, was that of one of Hannibal's younger brothers.
"Good. Jay, talk us through exactly what happened this afternoon – everything you can remember, every detail."
After Jacob's detailed account, Ogilvy updated them.
"There has been no response from the target. Her Chinese mobile appears to be dead. Despite repeated prompting through the nanochip, there has been no response and we now assumed that it is inoperative – at least to us."
"It is possible that they knew we had doctored it. Perhaps they changed a frequency?"
"Maybe, we're looking into it. We know that she has a new mobile provided by their embassy in Tunis. But she is not the focus – we have to find out why she was headed to Annaba, but told to wait in Tunis. She's been tasked with nailing ben-Zhair."
"It could be a feint by the Chinese, Sir. Perhaps Tunis is the real objective. Anyway, GCHQ should be able to find her if she is in Tunis, just as they did in Malta – by hacking the phone network servers."

"We think she may have moved to a satellite phone, but GCHQ are already on the case. It should be easier now they have data signatures they can match, however we don't have a known phone call – either a time or a number that would make it quicker to pin her new phone down – if of course she has one. We know her cover story, though she's not showing up on any hotel registers under her cover name. She's much too smart to be trackable through hotels, credit cards or transport.

But why Tunis? That's what's bothering me. The only angle we can come up with is that it is a ferry port. They run ferries from there to Spain, France and Italy. Security tends to be less intense in Tunisia than in Algeria."

They debated the matter for several more minutes. It was agreed that in the absence of further information, Helena would not be diverted from Tabarka to Tunis. Algeria was still the likely objective. Jacob would sit tight – for now.

*

Tebessa

At the converted farm outside Tebessa, ben-Zhair had the only phone and he kept it with battery removed, buried in a steel box. When he used it he left the compound and drove into Annaba to make his calls. All his other communication with ICIM high command was face to face and took place at remote locations. He and Sharifi occasionally travelled to the master control centre in western Algeria, outside the city of Sidi Bel Abbès. In a small farm, the telemetry from the weapons components was monitored using satellite channels carrying the encrypted sensor data from the assembly laboratory in Tebessa and the storage container in Yanbu, Saudi Arabia. The farm at Sidi Bel Abbès was currently a 'lights out' telemetry centre which would play its full part as the Cause of All Causes came to fruition.

Those working at the farmhouse in Tebessa never visited the city, never left the compound, other than to visit their wives once a week. The core of the team worked under the direction of Sharifi and his four senior technical specialists from Iran who trained them. They had been radical Islamist physics or chemistry students in one of the Algerian universities, recruited by ben-Zhair's quartermaster. Promised wives and a major role in the ICIM, they were making history. Their days were long and tiring, working in the mock-up office building, software lab and clean room readying the power control system, trigger software and other systems.

Then, on a clear mid-August morning, a team of four left the compound to collect the trucks from Souk Arras. This was the hottest time of the year, but it did not slow down progress. An intense period of work started as the equipment was checked and assembled, the whole process being recorded on video. The laser-combining mirrors were checked and polished. The miniature '*hohlraum*' – where laser power and the fuel pellet would ultimately be united nanoseconds before nuclear fusion - had been precision-machined from solid gold in Yazd, duplicating the North Korean prototype which had been purchased. Several copies were made – gold was cheap and plentiful, but plutonium was another matter. The sparkplug had been machined and a very small portion was to be used to provide a post-explosion radioactive fingerprint. This would demonstrate the capability and resources of ICIM. The *hohlraum* copies were carefully checked, as were the myriad of other weapon components. It was then dis-assembled and reassembled – with no component sequence errors. Finally it was disassembled, re-crated and repacked into the container in the correct re-build sequence. Then, one Wednesday evening in early November, the first container left the compound for its long cross-border drive to the ferry terminal at Tunis.

It took two days to build the cryogenic unit into the remaining space in a second container. During the third week of November, Abu ben-Zhair arrived in a small refrigerated truck with three guards.

Jafa Sharifi, although a native Farsi speaker, spoke in Arabic.

"Salaam Alaikum."

"Alaikum Salaam."

They shook hands. "All is ready?"

"Yes, the container has arrived at the target and the equipment has been unloaded in the sequence you specified. It is in the vault."

"That is good, Almahdi. Then we are ready to transfer the fuel pellet."

"We have maintained the temperature within the parameters you specified. Please check the temperature data log to be sure."

The journey with the pellet and cobalt-60 had been arduous, having come out of Iran on a large refrigerated trawler to the Freeport at Jebel Ali in the Persian Gulf, and then by sea again to Tripoli. Sea containers with integral refrigeration for transporting fish were commonplace. The deuterium-tritium pellet was physically and metaphorically the central component in the plan.

"I am downloading the data now."

They were in the mission control laboratory – alone – and they waited until Jafa's laptop beeped.

"The satellite telemetry is working well. The temperature log is within tolerance limits as you said. The alpha particle emission record is good too. As expected. The pellet is ready for use. I will supervise the transfer of the pellet to the container."

"You are sure that it cannot be detected with scanning equipment?"

"Certain, *Insha'Allah*. It will be housed in the supercooled container within the lead sphere – just as it was in your truck. You had no problems?"

"None, although the boxes of fish are now rotting."

"And what about the plutonium 'sweetener' and cobalt-60?"

"You advised that it is probably the most easy to detect, so to lower the risk to the mission we have sent it separately. It will be here in two days, along with the cobalt-60."

"Good. The device will work without the plutonium – I have planned for that. I have removed a small portion of the sparkplug to provide some contamination as you requested. Once that is done, then we will begin. I will install it myself."

"This change to the plutonium sparkplug must not affect the next stage?"

"It will not. We will still have enough to triple the yield for the next device."

"Good. We still have three stages to complete."

Jafa nodded. "And eight weeks. We are on schedule."

"The cobalt-60 is required for other purposes and will be transported elsewhere. You do not need to know more at present – all will become clear in Allah's time."

"I understand, Leader"

"You know the timing of our message is critical. The first announcement will be made next week – and you must stop calling me Leader now that we will be moving in public places. Just call me Almahdi."

"Of course, Lead...er...Almahdi. That is a good name – 'the guided one'.

"Yes, Jafa. I think that it is appropriate."

"Do you think that the infidels will agree to our demands?"

"Certainly not. This bomb will have to work to convince them. That is why the plutonium trace is important. Also, the cobalt will provide the large scale contamination."

"This will not be a full-scale cobalt bomb, Almahdi, although the resulting cobalt-60 contamination has a half-life of five years – if the design works."

"I know, Jafa, but five years is enough."

"It will work, *Insha'Allah*."

"*Insha'Allah.*"

Jafa gave the order for the forklift truck to being the transfer. Soon they would be at Ground Zero.

Three nights later the container left the compound and was moved across the border and on to Tunis along the usual trucking route. Two cars and five others also left separately for Tunis. Jafa Sharifi had his four lead technicians with him, covering construction, laser systems and triggering. Ben-Zhair was in the other car – his three guards would follow on later.

Customs officials at the border enjoyed a healthy income from smugglers and this container was just part of the regular night's business. No questions asked, no inspections. The next morning, in the ferryport marshalling area of Tunis, the trailer was unhitched ready for loading on to the ferry. The paperwork (and money) was approved by customs.

The truck – without trailer - headed back to the compound in Algeria. It never arrived. Ben-Zhair's team also cleaned up the compound, burying the bodies and demolishing the building with C4.

Abu ben-Zhair believed in tight security – this historic mission demanded it, the emerging new worldwide order demanded it.

*

Cobra Stirs

There was a hubbub in the briefing room.

"Order please! Let's get on with it. I've come straight from Northolt, I'm knackered and need to get some sleep."

The Prime Minister started her report.

"First, the latest P5 session at the US airbase in Terceira in the Azores – mid Atlantic. Very secure and out of sight of the media. There is a consensus in the P5 that North Korea has very probably got a miniaturised fusion device. By miniaturized we seem to agree that it is not a suitcase, but needing several trucks at the smallest. So, it's not *yet* a practical proposition as a missile warhead. This information comes from the Chinese who probably know a lot more than they are letting on.

The Chinese did say that they have seismographic data from one site that supports the theory. They shared it with us.

All P5 members are pulling out all stops to pressurize the North Koreans.

Now, this is completely unprecedented: we are *jointly* working on a plan for disarming North Korea. The Chinese have volunteered to invade and replace Dim Pong-un. Not all members were happy about that – the Chinese would obviously have access to the technology – not that they need it – we're all up to our necks in H bombs already. However, the plan does have the attractive elements of simplicity and low cost – to us that is.

Politically it keeps us clean, though we'd have to make a show about condemning Chinese aggression and so on, for public consumption, but that's understood by the P5. And China will insist on the new North Korean regime being Communist – in their own image. We can live with that. Japan might have an issue though, but the US would have to manage them. There would be some sabre-rattling from Tokyo. Of course, this would all be orchestrated in advance."

If such a thing were possible, the silence intensified in the briefing room.

"That is the good news. When I was in the plane on the way back, Sir William called me. It gets worse. Much worse. Sir William, please update the committee."

He nodded.

"Prime Minister, ladies and gentlemen. In the last 24 hours we have discovered that North Korea has shared the new fusion technology with Iran. It seems that Iran has developed a new weapons research establishment at Yazd, unknown to us or the UN Weapons Inspectors until now. Iran has been building a prototype of the new device for the last several months in an effort to circumvent the nuclear arms treaty which they signed two years ago.

Even more disturbingly, we believe that Iran has lost control of the prototype, and we have further reason to believe that it is now outside Iran. I have high confidence in this intelligence and this information is certainly not being sexed up. Naturally I cannot discuss our sources of this information.

As you would expect, we are deploying all our resources – and I do mean all – towards determining the full facts and the location of the missing nuclear technology."

He nodded to the Prime Minister who held up her hands and waved to attempt to silence the eruption of noise around the table..

"Thank you Sir William. I cannot go into sources and reasons, but we believe that the Chinese know about this nuclear technology leakage. We very much doubt that other members of the P5 do. For the moment we are not sharing this with the United States – there is simply too much risk that Tel Aviv will hear about it and then, well…you can imagine.

I'm not taking questions now, but would remind you that this is Ultra Secret. I want you to think about policy implications so far as it impacts your individual responsibilities. No discussion anywhere but here. Nothing in writing and no documents on your systems. It's not to be discussed with *any* of your staff, not even your Permanent Secretary. Don't clear your diaries – that would raise questions. Just cry off the appointments as necessary. We will reconvene at three pm. Meeting closed. Sir William, please wait behind."

Six members of the Blue Angel quorum left the meeting.

The door was closed.

"Right, let's have it. I want you to run through again what you told me about earlier."

"Well PM, in addition to what I just told the meeting, we believe that the prototype device is in North Africa – probably Algeria - and under the control of ICIM – that is 'IC in the Maghreb'.

"Good God! This is an unholy situation."

"Quite, Prime Minister."

"Algeria. We can't brief them in on this although the Foreign Secretary might want to. They've lost control of half their country."

"Agreed. It is absolutely vital that this intelligence does not leak. We cannot let anyone know that we have sources of this quality. We have certain knowledge which indicates that at least one Chinese agent is tracking the device and is tasked to take out the mastermind behind it. We have assets close to the agent – very close. We expect other Chinese agents to be inserted in the next day or so.

It is very likely that the Chinese are leaning heavily on Iran. There are indications of increased diplomatic activity and signals traffic, but we know no more than that."

"I thought we could read some of the Chinese traffic."

"We could until recently, but the cryptographic war is never ending. They are continuously upgrading encryption – and decryption - technology."

"Then how do we know all this about Blue Angel?"

"If you don't mind Prime Minister, I'd prefer not to comment. It's better that you don't know at this time."

The PM's eyebrows arched and her lips pursed – rather sexily thought 'C'. "Very well, I understand – but if this proves to be more sexed-up intelligence data then…"

"I fully understand Prime Minister. I have the highest confidence in the source."

"And you are sure we are not being fed a line here?"

"As certain as it is possible to be. You have heard what the other P5 members have to say."

"Nevertheless... Very well, please go on."

"We believe that ICIM intends to use the device, although we have no idea of the target. Of course, they could just use it as a threat, but that is not their usual style. In our favour is the fact that this device, although said to be miniaturized, is thought to require at least two large trucks to transport the components.

We have a team in pursuit and our special forces are ready at hand.

The British 'Protector M' drone had flown off the carrier *HMS Queen Elizabeth* in the Gulf of Sirte soon after midnight, and headed across Tunisia and into Algeria. When the target site had been identified, shortly before dawn, it launched a five-strong drone swarm and went into a holding pattern ready to relay the datastream up to a satellite. At the same time, its high definition camera and ground radar were relaying data to the swarm controllers in RAF Command in High Wycombe, to help them direct the drones.

In Vauxhall Cross, the displays were split into six panels, with a camera feed from the Protector and individual data feeds from the drone swarm. There was an audio commentary from the swarm controllers.

"Protector IR shows possible burial site. Location tagged."

"Drone Two radioactivity count slightly above background level, moving towards source. Confirm radiation twenty five to thirty counts per minute. Location tagged."

The high level video view confirmed the earlier satellite pictures – the site had been levelled by high explosives.

"Alright, I've seen enough".

"Director?"

"Yes, 'C'"

"That's a go on the troop. We need radioactivity samples and a complete site check-out asap."

"Understood. I'm online to Hereford and committing assets now, as planned. It will take about eight hours for insertion and extraction. The lab on *Queen Elizabeth* will do the analysis."

The SAS troop was already airborne and inbound from *Bulwark*, 20 miles northwest of Annaba, Algeria, on a Merlin helo, hugging the ground in stealth mode.

It had been a long night, and an even longer day lay ahead. The Director of UK Special Forces picked up his whisky. Talisker - his particular favourite for special occasions. The peaty flavour took him back to a holiday on Skye when he had been younger and carefree, just before joining the Army. That first taste had been the best.

In Algeria, the drones turned away from the target and at their individual pre-programmed safe locations they landed. Their self-destruct programs were triggered, their classified components were dissolved by acid and then half an ounce of C4 distributed the rest. Meanwhile, the Protector mother drone turned back for *HMS Queen Elizabeth*.

Later that morning in the Blue Angel ops room, Vauxhall Cross, 'C' addressed the team.

"I'll summarize the situation as I see it.

One – we have a target list and dates, based on religious – that is Christian - associations and dates, with Christmas Day most likely.

Two – this is not a suitcase bomb – we're ninety percent probable on it being in a building.

Three – we have a name - Abu ben-Zhair, as the possible operational leader or even the planner. We believe he was in Malta at the time of the attack on the *Queen Katherine*. His trail leads into Tunisia through Tabarka – very close to the Algerian border.

Four – The technology trail led us to Tebessa in Algeria. We're fairly confident that components passed through a farm near there, subject to the samples we should have analysed by lunchtime. These include pieces of what we think are NBC protective suits and breathing gear. The team also found the graves of about eight men – who were contaminated with radioactivity. There was a pit containing tons of rotting fish. We need to join the dots from Algeria to – where?"

He looked around at the exhausted faces.

"Now go and get some sleep and dream about how we make sense of the data. Reconvene here at seven a.m. There's a long way to go and we don't have much time."

*

"Tunis, Annaba, Algiers and Oran. Those are the places we have to focus on. The Chinese have despatched at least one agent to Tunis. We have equipment trails leading to Annaba and Algiers. Let's have your input."

Ogilvy looked around the table at the Blue Angel team. Afya Hossein broke the silence.

"We know that there is a terrorist controlled corridor inland between Tunisia and Algeria – more than that – it's almost a rogue state in the south. It would offer a secure location to prepare the equipment. From there it would be relatively easy to access the Mediterranean ports – we know that the border between Tunisia and Algeria is porous." Afya stood up at the wallscreen and pointed to the region.

"Good thinking, Afya, but it's a huge area. How would we home in on any location? I'll check, but I'm pretty sure that any radioactivity would not be detectable from a satellite. They would have to shield it to stay alive. It's much too big an area to search by any other means. But it could also be in Libya too. They are much closer to IC. They practically run the country."

"If ben-Zhair is on the up and up he would not go to Libya to make his mark. Too much interference. Algeria is his home ground and all his history is there. And let's not forget Algeria's wealth – it's got much more oil and gas than Libya. What help could we get from the Algerian Government?"

"I don't know, but I'm not involving them yet."

"Sir, what about satellite terrain images, before and after. The CIA would have access to those."

"IC are wise to all that. Even back in the time of the IRA training in Libya they knew the times of the satellite passes and went indoors. But, fair enough, the US does watch that corridor closely- they might have picked up something. I'll take that up with them immediately – but I'll need a credible reason without giving too much away. Any other ideas?"

"Transport, Sir. We know the dates that the pumps, lasers and cryogenic units arrived in Annaba and Tunis."

"That's a mammoth task even if the records exist, but I'll get the French onto it. You never know, they might turn up something. Whether they will share is another matter."

"Frighten them. Tell them we have intel that Paris is a target."

"That's a bit devious."

Afya shrugged. "So?"

Ogilvy nodded. "Yes, why not? Your idea – so, you come up with a story to tell them. I'm going to call Langley and check the satellite idea."

Twenty four hours later, a satellite had been re-tasked by the NGA controllers in Fort Belvoir, Maryland. More than 15,000 square miles of border territory had been imaged and compared by computer with a previous pass six weeks earlier. More than two hundred significant differences were noted and tagged for closer examination by satellite within a further six hours. The data was piped real-time from Fort Belvoir to GCHQ.

Six hours after that the analysis was ready and 'C' called the Secretary of Homeland Security. It was just before 10 p.m.in West Virginia.

"Good evening, Dick."

"Sir John, good morning. I'm at dinner – I'll have to go out and take this in my car. Five minutes. I'll call you."

A few minutes later the call re-started. By then the Secretary knew from his own analysts what 'C' was about to tell him.

"Sorry about the time and your dinner. Thank you for agreeing to re-task the satellite."

"Congratulations on your appointment, and before we start I want to make it clear that you owe me big time, Sir John – it's my wife's birthday celebration."

"Understood, how about this - we have something concrete from your data. I have a team on the ground now."

"On the ground?" Now that was news. Dick Langella hated surprises - someone on his team would get a kicking later. "What have you found?"

"A flattened villa with several burned bodies in shallow graves – some with a radioactivity count almost ten times background levels. We also found pieces of what we think were NBC protection suits, breathers and tools. They were hot. There was also quite a lot of radioactive shielding. We have samples on the way back for analysis."

Langella cursed. The Brits had been quick, very quick.

"Sorry, Dick what did you say?"

"Nothing, just a piece of chicken stuck in my throat. Sounds like you guys did a great job."

"I'll let you get back to your dinner. We'll speak tomorrow when the analysis is in. We should be able to identify the source reactor. You'll get the report as soon as I do."

"Okay. Let us have the data as soon as you can – and any samples too."

"We don't have much left after testing. I'll see if we can get some on a plane to you."

Pigs may fly, thought Langella.

"Great, thanks."

"Thank you for the assist with the satellite and please give your wife my best birthday wishes."

"You're welcome – and you still owe me. Till tomorrow, Sir John."

The line dropped.

'C' shook his head - this was not a propitious start to his tenure. He would have to work hard on Langella – maybe some flowers for Langella's wife? Yes, that might work. He made a note to organise it.

He muttered to himself then smiled.

"You're welcome, too, Dick, you're welcome too."

In Washington, Langella left the party and shouted for his driver. He was pretty certain that the source reactor was North Korean – and that indigestion would ruin his sleep.

Chinese Developments

After the fourth nuclear test China increased political pressure on North Korea to stop their H-bomb research and development programme. They were ignored. Dim Pong-un knew he held the upper hand.

Communications traffic metadata analysis and eventual decryption had indicated increasing cooperation between North Korea and Iran. Then, three weeks too late, China uncovered details of the provision of technical support and fusion bomb components to Iran.

The Chinese were masters of long-term strategy and diplomatically, China had always played 'the long game'. Now events were overtaking them. The General Secretary of the Chinese Communist Party (and also the President of the People's Republic, a dual role) – the highest-ranking official within China - tasked the Ministry of State Security with revising an old planning scenario involving a 'true' people's revolution in North Korea. This plan had been designed originally to remove Dim Pong-il, but had never been implemented, although it had been updated during the time of his son Dim Pong-un.

While the quantum computing facilities of the Guoanbu were doubling every six months, they were still inadequate for the task at hand. Encryption technology was being hardened and what had been a three week backlog of data to be decrypted was increasing. Within days of the discovery of the shipment to Iran, several computing projects (including 'Divine Lotus' – which involved Charles Tobin) had been put on hold to free up more system capacity. 50 petaflops of quantum computing power were now devoted to decryption, but still the backlog stuck stubbornly at more than two weeks, so they shelved a week's data and jumped forward a week, hoping to back-fill the gaps.

Worse was to come. Through a highly-placed agent in Pyonyang (now executed), China learned of the theft of the

Iranian nuclear components. This was confirmed a week later by the latest signals decryption. The Ministry of State Security was instructed to start active planning for the revolution in North Korea, and People's Republican Army units at the border were gradually reinforced.

The troop movements were not missed by the United States or by Russia – and both those countries started to ramp up their own forces in the region.

*

In London, Ogilvy was walking towards his office when his phone vibrated. He looked at the code number and the icon. It was the Deputy Director of GCHQ, Robert Grey who was responsible for Blue Angel in Cheltenham.

"Robert, what have you got?"

"We're just picked up the data signature for that nanochip on the *Tunisiana* mobile network. We got the number it wormed through and then picked up a call from that number. We're running it through decryption now, but it may take some time. Looks like the encryption has been upgraded."

"Where was the call to?"

"The Antarctic."

"You're kidding."

"No. It went to the Chinese Zhongshan Antarctic research station through the regular international network via the Iridium network and then up to one of their own satellites."

"Bugger!"

"No really – it's good news. If it had gone direct to satellite we'd have no chance. Anyway, we've got the coordinates of the call origination in Tunisia. It's coming through on your Blue Angel status screen as we speak. But there is a problem."

"What?"

"We monitor their satellite aerial direction at that research station. I think it was one of their newest Mozi quantum communications satellites."

"Shit!"

"Exactly. Her new phone is using quantum encryption. We cannot yet crack it – if ever. All we can work with now is the location data."

"At least we will still know if she's using the phone, won't we?"

"Only if we can pick up the signal. If she's using a directional aerial then we're completely in the dark."

"OK. Let's park that for now."

Ogilvy looked at his tablet and clicked the icon from Grey, opening up a satellite image. He clicked on the map pin and brought up the street view.

"Got it, excellent, Bob."

"The call was made about twenty minutes ago. The cellphone appears to be switched off now, but we're still seeing it handshaking with the network masts. The location is being updated continuously on the Blue Angel tracking screen."

"Great Bob, thanks."

"I'll let you know when we've got a decrypt. I'm assigning all our quantum decryption power to this until we've cracked the new encryption."

"You can't give me a time estimate?"

"Sorry, Alex, impossible."

"Ok, speak later - I've got to move on this. 'Bye"

"'Bye"

Ogilvy called 'C' and explained that the Tunis hostile asset was being tracked again, then clicked the icon for Ellie Williams.

*

On the Trail of Maruška

Steve was in a bar – yet again – overlooking the marina at Tabarka in Tunisia. Another marina, another bar. Both the bar and the harbour had seen better days.

The pilot books called it a marina. The locals called it a marina. At least, the locals who had any pretence to be tourist-minded did. It might have been a marina. Once.

Now it was a very faded, very tired harbour, with a fleet of fishing boats. The marina was surrounded – almost hemmed in it seemed - by tourist hotels and bars, with peeling sky blue paint trimming the whitewashed walls. Even before the Arab spring, when a spark in small Tunisian coastal resort, to the south – had been caught and fanned by the wind of change, it was dilapidated. And despite the new government and all the hope and plans, it was still dilapidated now, many years later.

That little spark, that little defiance by a teenage boy who had been told that he needed a licence – a corrupt licence - to sell goods on the street to support his family had grown into a conflagration which engulfed Tunisia and spread. The outcome had been a Middle East more screwed up than it was before, and it would be screwed up for generations to come.

Yachtsmen who had visited these Tunisian ports had been frustrated by graft, by having to pay exorbitant prices for second class facilities, had been exasperated by being asked for gifts by the customs officials and port police. Certainly, the average family struggled and was short of money, but Tunisia was a wealthy country, with plenty of oil and gas reserves. Nevertheless, corruption had been endemic. Anyone in a position of authority had a licence to extort. Since the revolution that had changed, but only to a degree – graft was part of the culture. Steve's difficult and dangerous passage earlier in the year through the Suez Canal had been blighted by requests for *bakhsheesh* despite the change of government in Egypt. "When in Rome..." seemed like a good idea, but it did grate on him.

Some traditions take generations to die. Without greasing, the wheels of bureaucracy could grind very slowly, and quite legitimately. But efficiency – well, that required backhanders. Then after the struggle to check in with the bureaucrats, there were the facilities to deal with. Not that there was much in the way of facilities.

Electricity was available on the quay, but you had to hot wire the connection box. 'Water at the tap' he read in his pilot book – 'yes' said the harbour manager. Firstly though, Steve had to find which tap worked, then string three hosepipes together after borrowing two. Along the quay there were some tourist boats, made up to look like Barbary Pirate ships. It was all part of the fun and charm of cruising in Tunisia.

But the pirates were still there in Tunisia – and the Islamist terrorists too, as had been brought painfully into focus by the mass murder of tourists in 2015.

Baldwin had asked someone why everything was painted white and sky blue, and the answer had been "a law was passed many years ago." It seemed that popular tourist destinations in Tunisia had to follow this painting scheme. Bizarre, that's how it seemed to him. It would have been better if they'd fixed the power and water and cut out the graft. Now the walls were being painted with blood.

A north easterly wind had made the trip from Malta relatively easy – he and Helena had sailed across in less than 30 hours, keeping up to schedule with use of the engine when the wind fell light.

The decision to cross on Adèle had been easy – hiding small arms and other equipment was straightforward and certainly easier than using a car ferry to Tunis.

Despite the bribery and crumbling infrastructure which he had expected, he'd been pleasantly surprised at Tabarka - there was a good boat hoist and fabrication facilities, though getting hold of chandlery was difficult.

The town was off the beaten track, although there was a tourist development a few miles to the east. Most people were pleasant and interested in tourists, even proud of their country, and the food was acceptable though not always of the best quality. French-style supermarkets could still be found and alcohol was available at reasonable prices – if you knew where to look – and wine had been made here since the time of the Romans. Unfortunately, outlets for alcohol were becoming increasingly secretive as the Islamist pressure increased.

Tabarka itself had a certain charm, and Steve thought that staying here for the winter was a distinct possibility. He had no intention of visiting Algeria - whatever Helena said.

Tabarka would be his last stop before the six day direct voyage to Gibraltar, unless he wanted to head up to Sardinia, across to Majorca and coast down the Costa Blanca. That route had no appeal for him – he'd seen enough of the yacht charter brigade in the Ionian, the harbours were usually busy and there were few all-weather anchorages. Yes, a winter in Tabarka was a possibility, he thought, a distinct possibility. But first there was the matter in hand. Maruška, yet again. She was like a severe case of toothache, but could be fatal.

He'd had a morning run along the isthmus which the Genovese had built to join the Ile de Tabarka to the mainland, when they had built their fort atop the small island. The climb up through the trees along the winding road was steep enough to get his heart working hard. The view from the fort at the top was magnificent – the Algerian border was six miles to the west and across the bay to the southeast the huge sand dunes stretched eastward for miles, though backed by some unpleasantly large hotel developments.

A couple of hundred feet almost vertically below he could see the boatyard, and outside the harbour wall the coral covered rock bottom through the azure sea. Steve had stopped at the summit for water after his ascent. The curator of the fort had not arrived for work, and the fort was closed. Then, a few sets of push-ups and stomach crunches followed by a gentle trot back down the hill set him up for some of the excellent local bread and coffee. The French influence was still strong, and the baguettes readily available.

As he broke the bread he thought of his father, and the 'Jenny C' all those years ago, fishing out of Portsmouth. Fishing was certainly easier here in Tunisia – at least the weather was more benign and there were no tides to worry about. But then again it came down to the availability of fish – the Med had been overfished, as had the English Channel.

Here he was, still doing dirty work but at least the money kept him going. He cursed. If it wasn't for his skill with Arabic and his missions in Libya and Algeria he would be free and heading for Gibraltar. Then again, he might have called here anyway. Maybe there were other reasons too. Maruška had really got under his skin. He thought of Tom's death in Djibouti and what she had said. It was unfinished business. What really bothered him though was that he had professional respect for her, no matter how disgusting her behaviour. She got results.

And then there was the strange sexual effect she had on him, almost animal. She knew it and had needled him about it. Helena just didn't have that same effect – with her it was quite different – the difference between selfish sex and making love - caring deeply for the other's enjoyment. Still, he hesitated to think of Helena in terms of love. The concept felt alien and was something he didn't think he'd felt at any time in his marriage.

Love required trust, and thought that Helena still had a long way to go on that score. She always trotted out the Official Secrets Act when he tried to delve too deeply. During the week that they had spent sailing together in Crete, she had told him about her background, but given that she had pretended to be a waitress when they first met, he had found it difficult to believe.

She had told him that a degree in History at Oxford had led to a career in the Civil Service. He remembered her words clearly.

"I did stretch the truth a bit about my parents. My father worked in the British Embassy in Athens when he met my mother – she was a secretary in the Embassy. It was her father – my grandfather - who was the fisherman. So, I had a Greek upbringing but my passport is British."

She had caught his eye as a waitress in a taverna, but as an upper middle class English woman she would have been far too classy for his usual taste. He would usually steer clear of such women – and most of them would steer clear of him. One woman had told him that she didn't like men who 'held a table knife like a paintbrush', but Helena hadn't seemed bothered. That now seemed so long ago, before the *Queen Katherine* bombing, yet it was only a matter of weeks.

He knew that she was a spook – that much had become clear in Malta the previous week during the operation to capture Maruška, reinforced when Ogilvy, a very senior player from MI6, had come out to debrief the Chinese agent. He could see that the ability to act, to play a role, was a skill she possessed in abundance – and she was very capable under fire too. He still wondered what role she was playing with him – and he still hadn't figured out why she had been there in that Greek taverna. And then there had been that other spook – Cassidy – on the island. They obviously knew each other. There were a lot of unanswered questions.

Had that been part of the act in the anchorage in Fodele Bay in Crete, when she's had him do things to her that even a hooker in Portsmouth would think twice about? And it had not been at his request, but at hers. Her sexual tastes bordered on the *very* exotic – and required a lot of trust on her part and maybe that was indicative of her real feelings towards him? It was a thought, although his sexual tastes were much more mundane. He felt an erection growing and cursed as he adjusted his position on the chair.

She was like the weather – you never quite knew what was coming next – and at that very moment she walked in and he snapped out of his reverie.

"What's up? Ants in your pants?"

"Nothing really, hard chair, blood supply, you know."

"Hmm. You're well into the beers then" she said, eyeing the empty bottles on the table. "Where's mine?"

"I drank it – thought you'd run off."

"I did run, then found the phone shop and got a couple of sims. Cost me a lot – they wanted to see my passport."

"Bloody police state." Steve kept his voice low. "Don't fit them here. Too many eyes."

"Do you take me for an idiot?" she hissed.

Steve held his hands up. "Ok, ok sorry."

"How was your morning anyway?"

"I went for a run and did a recce of the place. There are one or two guys who seem to be wandering around aimlessly, just smoking. Tunisian secret police I guess. The black leather jackets are like a uniform."

"I had one keeping an eye on me all morning, he wasn't bothered about being seen. I lost him during the run!"

"The local police are back and forth quite a bit too. They are on edge – I guess it's the Malta bombing." Steve pointed to the local paper. "The headlines. Word is out about an Algerian terror cell linked to ICIM. Things are bound to be a bit tight here, so close to the Algerian border."

"I'm glad you can read that."

"That's why HMG is paying me so well and I'm on a bonus from you."

"You had that last night."

"First instalment wasn't it?"

"We'll see. It could be the way things are going. I haven't decided yet. Anyway it worked well - I slept like a baby afterwards." She whispered "I'll have to get some proper handcuffs."

"The last woman who lay on that bunk was Maruška Pavkovic – with cable ties on her."

"You're kidding me?"

"No. I had her there in Djibouti, and I don't mean in the Biblical sense. I should have finished her off, there and then."

"Why didn't you?"

"Orders."

"Whose?"

"Booth."

"Booth? That makes sense. He's been airbrushed out from our history."

"Why?"

"I can't discuss that."

"Don't tell me, Official Secrets Act. I signed it too, you know."

"His name is not mentioned any more. Anyway, enough history."

"Yes, back to last night. I woke about two a.m. – I thought I heard some shouting from that big stinkie moored behind us."

"What's a stinkie?"

"It's what sailors call a gin palace or flashy powerboat. Stinkie people call us sailors 'raggies'. Anyway, the guy aboard acts like crew – he's certainly not the owner. Maltese flag too. Odd. I thought they usually went to the flashy places like Monastir or Hammamet. The boat's called 'Meltemi'. Seems out of place here.

"Did you say 'Meltemi' - as in the name of a wind in the Aegean Sea?"

"I think so – you were in Crete. You should know, your father being a Greek fishermen and all at the Embassy in Athens."

"Ok, ok, point taken, no need for sarcasm. He was a fisher of men." The comment was lost on Steve.

"Anyway, the boat's there, on the quay right astern of us."

"That rings a bell. I'm not fully briefed in on the *Queen Katherine* operation, but I seem to recall a link with Tabarka. I'll mention it to London."

Steve looked at her.

"I knew it. Here we go again."

"What do you mean?"

"Forget it for now. What do you really think Maruška's up to?"

"Just waiting – or so London told me earlier. She's had some contact with the Chinese but they seem to have lost track. I don't think London are telling me everything though."

"Nothing new there then. They treat us like mushrooms. Bryan should be ok as long as he keeps well away from her."

"It's just a watching brief."

"Bloody hell Ellie! Even that's dangerous. We should keep our distance. We've got her number haven't we?"

"She might be using a satphone now."

"OK, but she's not an idiot - she'll know he's on her – she's expecting it anyway."

She looked hard at him- he only called her Ellie when he was angry with her.

"Ok, chill out Steve. Bryan is no fool either. She knows we've got her on a short leash."

"She's a total psycho, she enjoys torturing and killing people. I lost a mate to her. You saw what she did to Tobin and her own team too. She might do Bryan in just for fun. Pull him back. She's unpredictable and takes chances for entertainment."

"I hear you. It's above me. Come on, let's head back to Adèle."

*

As they walked out her phone vibrated.

"Hang on Steve, it's London."

"I'll get another beer then – I guess you are going to the Ladies?"

She nodded and headed to the toilets.

A few minutes later Steve watched her return to the table. Her lips were pursed and her eyes dark and almost moist. She looked very serious as she sat down. He felt a flutter in his chest.

"Get me a brandy."

"A bit early isn't it?"

"Fuck that. You may want one too."

"I don't hear you swear very often. What's happened?"

Steve called across to Younis behind the bar and she waited silently while he ordered a brandy and another beer.

"Maruška has gone off the grid."

"What do you mean?"

"She's taken out Bryan and one of the guys from Tunis Station, and she's disappeared."

"What the fuck!" Steve shook his head. "The fucking bitch. I knew this would happen! Bryan was an alright guy. I am going to nail that fucking psycho."

Although the bar was empty, Younis looked across at them again. A lovers tiff?

"Keep it down Steve. Maybe. At least it was quick – a car bomb - not her usual style – she had company."

"What about London – I thought that they could prod that nanochip she has? 'Puppet on a string' is what Ogilvy said."

"No response. They don't know where she is."

"But it just doesn't make sense. First she wants to be pulled out by us, she offs two of her own people, and now she's taking out our people."

"I know. London has no idea what's happening. They looked at all the mobile calls at the underground car park where and when she took out Bryan. There was one call from a phone there just before the bomb. The phone had not been used in Tunisia before that call. They think she was arming the bomb. So they had her number. Turns out it was a throwaway phone."

"When did this happen?"

"Yesterday."

"Yesterday? What the hell. Why didn't they tell us sooner?"

"Need to know."

"Fucking need to know will kill us all. I am going to get that bitch."

"Join the queue."

"No way I'm staying here. I'm getting a car and heading for Tunis."

"She may not be there now. Our people are trying to pick up her trail."

"There's no chance of that, she's too good for them."

"So why go to Tunis?"

"That's where she was last seen."

"At least wait until London has more info. I've been ordered to stay here pending further orders. That includes you. We still think she's headed for Algeria."

Steve scowled and picked up his glass.

"And the cavalry?"

"*Bulwark* is west of Malta with an SBS squadron ready less than 2 hours by helo from here. There are other major assets being put into place. I have no details – need to know."

He nodded. "Need to fucking know. Don't you wonder why they have *Bulwark* and the cavalry out there for one woman? You must be right about Algeria."

"How do you think this is going to play out?"

"NFI."

"What?"

"Sorry, 'no fucking idea'. Apart from 'waiting for orders – that's the soldier's lot - plus a heap of shit coming down the chute, for sure. Tommy this, Tommy that."

"Kipling."

"Yeh, that's right. Plus ça change…"

"That's Jean-Baptiste Alphonse Karr."

"Whatever."

"Come on, cheer up you miserable bugger."

"How can I – we just lost a great guy?"

"Well let's get even then shall we?" Helena nodded towards the dock, across to where Adèle was moored, near 'Meltemi'. "What's with the police and that 'stinkie' as you call it?"

"Didn't you notice the smell when you left the boat this morning?"

"No, I went the other way for a run along the beach. The long way around. Why?"

"Something very ripe. I put it down to the fishing boats. I should have realised."

"Shit, I meant to check with London. I'll do it now. What was that name again?"

"Meltemi, Fairline 45, Maltese Flag."

Helena fired off the email as Steve finished his beer.

"I've marked it urgent."

"Another brandy? A beer?"

"No thanks, but you go ahead."

Her email chimed quietly. "Oh, Oh – here we go again. London says 'Meltemi' is on the Maltese registry of vessels. She was berthed in Grand Harbour, Malta – and – wait for it – she checked out the night before the *Queen Katherine* was bombed. But it seems she was still there when marina staff did their midnight and six a.m. patrols."

Then her phone vibrated and she stood up. "London – urgent. I'm going to the 'Ladies'."

Steve finished his beer and waited. He saw an ambulance arrive and then a body bag being carried off the Meltemi. The police were by now wearing protective suits, their faces covered with masks.

Helena returned.

"Come on, let's see if we can find out what's happening. I'll fill you in as we go."

Steve gulped his beer, dropped some coins on the table and they strolled out, to all appearances a couple of carefree tourists – except for their very serious faces.

"London still says there's a clear link to ICIM – they claimed responsibility for the Malta bombing, but London are not telling me anything more right now. London is hooking in with the French DGSE who are tight with the Tunisians and still have links with the Algerians."

As they approached Adèle picking their way over power cables, mooring lines and hosepipes, they were stopped and questioned briefly by two plain clothes policemen. One asked for their papers and after checking those they said that they wanted to inspect the Adèle. Steve agreed – he knew that his two Sig-Sauer pistols were almost impossible to find, with Helena's Glock safely alongside them inside a drum of used engine oil.

After the police had left, apparently satisfied, Steve got some cushions out and they sat under the sun awning in the cockpit of Adèle eating a simple lunch of cheese, bread and olives, with a light local Tunisian white wine. They were perfectly positioned to watch events on the 'Meltemi'. The police had left one guard to sweat in the sun, and a string of police tape.

Helena stretched luxuriously. "This waiting around is killing me. I've read your file – you excelled when you joined the Royal Marines and your career after that was outstanding, although you rejected the opportunity to take on officer training. I'd love to know more about your childhood – what made you who you are."

"I don't talk about that Ellie, drop it."

They settled back in the hot sun, the harbour quiet at this time of day.

Helena's interest had brought back the memories and Steve thought of his father who had been a fisherman, running his trawler out of the Camber – the dock in Old Portsmouth right at the entrance to Portsmouth Harbour. What would his Dad have made of this, his undercover work in Tunisia – and this remarkable woman – and lover – next to him? Steve had been born and brought up as an only child in Portsmouth, but there had been rumours of other siblings as a result of his father's dalliances. The family home had been a council flat near Fratton, a mile or so from the docks. Social housing they called it, but Steve's socialization had been tough.

His father made a living at fishing, just, but when the catch was poor then he would come home after a skinful at The Bridge – a pub on East Street hard by the Camber - and give Steve's mother a beating. When the catch was good Mike, his father, would celebrate with a skinful, then come home and give his mother a beating. Steve started fighting at school on a regular basis (and out of school too for that matter) and this came to the attention of the educational psychologists.

By the time he was 13, Steve had started stepping in-between his parents during their nightly battles and getting a hiding for his trouble, but as he matured and grew he started giving almost as good as he got, and his father became more wary. Nevertheless his parents had split up by the time he was 16. Steve still saw his father occasionally – his father had taught him beach fishing at 6 years of age, and by the time he was 10 was helping out regularly on the trawler at weekends. By that time, he lived with his mother and worked weekends with his father – their relationship was pretty good now that his mother was safe; his father had shacked up with another woman down in Southsea, but Steve knew nothing else about that side of his father's life.

He had been far from a star pupil in school at the Priory Comprehensive, but he'd stabilised after his parents had split up, and was able enough, though not academic. The fighting was in the past – he'd gained his spurs. He skipped a day from school occasionally and took his gear down to the beach at Southsea to do some fishing.

Adept at faking illness notes to the school, his mother was never fined by the authorities for his truancy. Once, his mother received a phone call from the school as he had missed two Mondays in succession. It was one of the rare occasions when his mother actually contacted his father, and he got a belting – or at least, that's the story that his mother heard. His father was more understanding, but still kept back a weekend's pay from him.

'It'd better to hurt your pocket than your body' is what he had said. 'Besides, you're getting too big for it.'

He had watched the ships – tankers, warships, cruise liners and more – entering and leaving the Solent, and his horizons widened as he matured.

Then he'd started thinking about joining the forces. The Royal Navy appealed, but after a discussion at the recruiting office in the city he wondered if there would be enough action. Yes there was travel, yes there was the sea, but he was unsure. He'd talked to his father about it, but his father was keen for him to go into partnership with him on the trawler. Then one evening over a beer in The Bridge, after a good day with the nets, his father suggested he think about the Royal Marines.

"Steve, get it out of your system", he said, "do a few years, sow your wild oats, and come back to the trawler. We'll buy a new boat when you return and you can take over."

He had been non-committal, but by the end of the week Steve had taken the first step and committed to the entrance assessment. A visit to the Royal Marines museum across the road from the beach at Southsea had cemented his resolve.

"Right, what shall we do this afternoon? A siesta?" Helena winked at Steve. Then her phone vibrated again.

"I spoke too soon."

She went down below to take the call. Five minutes later she re-joined Steve in the cockpit. "We need to move – we've got a break. London says that there was a dead body on the boat – that's from the French DGSE who are well connected here."

"Tell me something I don't know."

"Ok ok. They're hearing that it was natural causes."

Steve raised his eyebrows and looked dubiously at her.

"I told you I heard shouting in the night. Didn't mention it to the police though – just keeping it simple."

"I told London. The French say it was apparently a heart problem, nothing sinister but there were signs of a struggle. The Tunisians printed the boat. Two recent sets. One unknown – the dead guy - but, get this – they circulated the prints to the Algerians. One set matches an Algerian with known terrorist associations. He was linked to the GIA and they are linked to ICIM. Real name Abu ben-Zhair. Bingo. Cross check!

The name that the Chinese gave to Maruška to track. Algerian terrorist background, came up through the GIA, then the Salafists and now linked we think with ICIM. It's all very sketchy – there's not a lot more. His father was a big mover and shaker in the Algerian Government, but little Abu took the left hand path. The French are sending us what they have - supposedly. There should be a photo of their passports in the police office in town, but the French intel says that no photocopy was made as the copier was out of order when they checked in."

"Didn't the police hold the passports?"

"Did they hold ours?"

"No. Point taken. They prefer Euros."

"Exactly. They think he's probably slipped back into Algeria. The Algerian DRS – their very heavy secret police – are on the case."

"Then that's where Maruška is headed. We should have moved yesterday."

"We don't have orders yet. London is still trying to get a handle on the next steps. We know that the Chinese sent Maruška to Tunis to find ben-Zhair."

"Bollocks. It doesn't sound right to me. We're not getting the full story. If it really was that guy ben-Zhair and he's behind the Malta job then he's too smart if there's a file as long as your arm on him. He'd be covering his tracks. That wasn't natural causes on the gin palace."

"And the prints?"

"Careless maybe."

"You just said he was careful."

"Strange things happen at sea. Why would they take prints if it was natural causes? Obviously the French have their suspicions. And don't forget, we're hearing this fourth hand – the Tunisians –the Algerians, the French – your bosses in London - all with their own agendas."

*

"'C', we need to talk now, in a quiet room. Number 3 is free."

"Fine. Five minutes, room 3"

They sat down and waited for the 'Secure' sign to illuminate. "Fire away Alex."

"GCHQ have found the Chinese viral code on the *Tunisiana* Telecom mobile network servers. They've loaded an analyser which will report any re-directs. The redirect numbers are not stored – they are held in the call metadata. So, we have to wait for a call to go through before we can grab the number and triangulate from the masts. Then we will have Maruška on the leash again. Of course they may have other agents on that network too."

"And if she's not using the satphone network."

"Of course."

"What about email addresses?"

"Still unknown, Sir."

"Let's keep her in the dark for now – it may be better that she doesn't know that we've got her on the leash again. Just monitor her locations and comms."

"In hand, Sir."

"Anything more on ben-Zhair?"

"Not yet. The French are working on it."

"Very well, at least I can tell the PM that we are closing in, working both ends."

"Cautiously, Sir, this is all very tentative."

"To hell with caution, we need to make things happen. We're faced with a catastrophe. You do your job Alex, and I'll do mine!"

*

Steve and Helena were in a hired Suzuki and heading for Tunis, seemingly a couple of tourists to any casual observer. It was late afternoon and they were on the P7 road headed through wooded country towards Nefza – it was a round-about route as there was no direct highway to Tunis. There had been overnight snow on the higher mountains to the southwest but the P7 road was clear. Rain was threatening rain from the north east – and the heavy clouds presaged more snow in the mountains.

"I didn't bring any warm clothing."

"There's no heater in this off-road – a bad choice, sorry – my fault. There should be a fleece in my bag. This country gets bloody cold at night. Even in the desert."

"Got it, thanks."

"I've never been into a real desert, but I know you have."

"Yes. Too many times – The Dead Quarter in the Yemen, Libya, the Sahara. Places I'm not supposed to talk about."

"I'm sure I'd be cleared to hear it. Come on, we've got a few hours to kill. Tell me all about it. We can't go all the way to Tunis whispering sweet nothings."

*

2011, late August, and Tripoli had fallen to the rebels. The National Transition Council had installed itself in the capital, but Gadhafi was still on the loose – defiant statements from him had been broadcast on Syrian Radio where Assad himself was buckling and massacring his own people. The Arab world was in turmoil.

Gadhafi's son Khamis had supposedly been killed by a rocket from a NATO helicopter hitting his armoured Toyota Landcruiser, but these reports were regular and many originated from Khamis himself as he tried to lose his pursuers. Gadhafi's wife Safia, his daughter Ayesha and several of his seven sons had been given refuge in Algeria.

On 30th August, Sky News had been reporting that Gadhafi was on the run south into the Libyan hinterland. There had been persistent earlier reports that he was retreating to his home town of Sirte for a last stand, but these reports were thought to be carefully placed feints. Ultimately, the time-worn truth that bullies are cowards was being borne out, and the Sky News reports were accurate. Or were they?

As Winston Churchill had said, "truth is the first casualty of war." There had been several feints from the Gadhafi family.

That day, Steve Baldwin and three colleagues from 41 Marine Commando were in a small convoy of three Nissan Patrols trucks, heading south into the desert in pursuit of Gadhafi. They were 'advisers and mentors' to a team of rebel special forces. This Libyan team were experienced professionals originally from Gadhafi's army – not his elite special forces, but the best otherwise available.

Steve had landed in Libya with his colleagues several weeks earlier from *HMS Manchester*. This hadn't been an SAS job – all the UK's elite special forces were fully committed elsewhere in Iraq, Afghanistan and other undisclosed countries including Pakistan and Iran. There were still two squadrons in Hereford - these were inviolable and on hand should an emergency occur in the UK. Hence the Royal Marines were taking on many more missions, and Steve was heading south towards the Sahara, breathing the baking hot late summer sand. Steve, Dave and Windy, with Rick as the team leader, had spent the previous eight weeks with the rebels in their push west from Benghazi, keeping away from front line news cameras as from incoming fire.

Then in mid-August, they had been pulled out late one night at short notice. After a briefing they had been dropped from a Chinook west of the city of Zawyah to join the push eastward towards Tripoli. In Zawyah they met up with their current Libyan squad, tasked to capture Gadhafi. There was plenty of intelligence as to Gadhafi's location, but the analysts were having great difficulty sorting the wheat from the considerable chaff of misinformation.

Steve's unit had been one of the first squads into Gadhafi's compound, and knew for certain that he had escaped south across the city using his vast network of escape tunnels. Whilst the media and rebels were focused on Sirte and the final battle to come, the tyrant was heading south. The analysts had correctly gamed this scenario, and two imported English springer spaniels with the squad had tracked Gadhafi's scent through the tunnels. Progress through the network had been slow as two other dogs checked for booby traps. The exit was an innocuous garage under a block of flats in south Tripoli.

The best estimate was that Gadhafi had a start of twelve hours. The worst estimate was thirty hours.

Informed opinion was that the Sirte story was a bluff and that Gadhafi would head south and then swing west towards Ghudamis, the nearest Libyan town to Algeria, known as 'The Pearl of the Sahara'. This would mean that he would circumvent Tunisia, and a wise move as the Tunisians would be only too happy to capture him and turn him over to the new Libyan government for a 'fair trial'. A narrow 'tongue' of Tunisian land, about 60 miles wide, extended southwards and closed to a point just north of Ghudamis where the borders of Libya, Tunisia and Algeria met at a point in the Sahara. Of course, he might take a chance and cross the Tunisian border twice, south of the Libyan town of Nalut, near where the tongue of Tunisia came to a point to meet Algeria and Libya. This was deemed too risky as border patrols had been strengthened following NATO pressure on the young Tunisian government.

Then there was Ait Nahad, south of Tripoli - a stronghold of Gadhafi's supporters, so it was thought. But, assuming he was a coward, would he really go into the centre of Libya and make a last stand there? Would he want to be found as Saddam

Hussein had been in his country of Iraq, hiding in a hole in the ground like a fox? Was he that cunning? Or more like a rat?

If he headed south, then he would certainly have half a dozen options, and could branch into one of several countries from which escape by air to a receptive country would be much easier. Tunisia was crossed off the analysts' (and presumably Gadhafi's own) list of options, as was Egypt. Niger and Chad remained, with Mali as a more distant possibility.

The analysts had identified several possibilities. Psychologists had factored a model of Gadhafi's likely behaviour in relation to the options. They couldn't predict the method, but the Ghudamis route was gamed at 62% probable. No other options came close.

The hunt had gone on, and in early September, 'undisclosed sources in Niger' had said that three Libyan trucks carrying senior Libyan army personnel (including generals) had crossed the border into the country. This was a credible report, but the analysts knew that there was no way Gadhafi would travel with his generals. He could no longer trust them, not with a tasty reward in the balance. They would sell him out as soon as look at him.

Ghudamis remained the most probable option.

Before the rebellion in Libya had flared up, Gadhafi had been accompanied by a series of young and attractive nurses, the latest being Oksana Balinskaya. They were not Arabic and could not speak the language – an obvious security precaution. Balinskaya was Ukrainian and an obvious beacon to his whereabouts, but she had not been seen for months.

It had been many years since Gadhafi had done any serious ground-level travelling in the desert. It was a journey of almost four hundred miles to Ghudamis and staying on the main tracks was a bit obvious. Using a helicopter too would be asking for trouble, and NATO had total air dominance anyway.

What the analysts had not predicted, and Steve's squad therefore didn't know, was that the ex-leader had escaped in a concealed armoured Landcruiser. This was one of three which had been driven, each into one of three apparently dilapidated, but armoured, hi-tech cargo containers, heading south into the

Libyan heartland. Just another cargo delivery to Ghudamis, just another dictator and his goons.

Given the probable route, a Chinook helo had picked up Steve and his team from Tripoli, and dropped them in the hills near Ghudamis.

Gadhafi's following in these hills was not strong – they were from different tribal areas, and the feuds stretched back for many generations despite all being Berbers. Although the Great Leader's reign had erased many of the brightest potential leaders, some had survived. These were the people that had formed the core of the group leading the rapid advance into Tripoli in the final week of August 2011.

Borders meant little in these areas, tribal and family ties meant everything – as did blood feuds. Gadhafi knew that there was a $1m reward out for him, and it was certain that he was matching that to each of his guards, most of whom were Central African mercenaries. They were generally thought to be more reliable than even his own tribesmen, especially when a new Libya was being formed. Libyan nationals would want to return to Libya, provided of course that they did not have any major crimes hanging over their heads.

Outside Ghudamis, Steve's squad had met up with two local contacts of the National Transition Council, but there was no new information. They had left their Supacat reconnaissance vehicles a mile away in a wadi, with Will keeping watch and monitoring comms and satellite data. Their group was the modern day equivalent of the Long-range desert group which later become the SAS.

"Right lads, we're pushing on further, across the border. Just remember that we got lost – that's the story ok? We're going as far as a place called Deb Deb.

It's about fourteen miles into Algeria, and we've got 3 hours to yomp there before dawn when we'll hole up. The Tuareg locals are smart and tough – we'll be hard pushed to stay unseen. If we do meet them, any talking will be done by The Rash – with Baldy as his backup - but our aim is to leave no traces unless we find the target."

Rashid Younis was from Bolton and he uttered a quiet 'Aye, boss' in response.

"We'll use the road and when Will gets a target we'll split right and left on my signal. When we're a mile from the border we'll head off road and cross about a mile from road. Anything new from the satellite Will?"

"No, boss. Images show two small huts at the border, intel says no traffic at night and we're not seeing anything in IR. Watch out for camels and local smugglers that's the gen, but we should see them first on IR. No update on the three trucks they picked up earlier, we've lost them."

"OK guys, six miles to the border. No info about minefields here – the sands drift so much that we shouldn't expect any problems. I'll take point, Baldy, stay 50 yards behind."

"Rightie-ho Dick'" said Steve to the lieutenant, known to all as Dickwick.

Twenty miles over a desert track in 3 hours was simple in theory – if the track had not drifted over, but at least there was no wind driving the sand. It was cold and the air was dense, making breathing easier. The moon was just past full and would provide enough light until dawn and make the going easier. It would also make them easier to be seen by others.

"Target, 2 miles ahead. Moving across the track."

Dickwick slowed their speed and at one mile the target had stopped, just off to the south of the road. He signalled them to stop.

"What's the score Will?"

"Hard to say. Thermal signature looks organic when I can see it."

"OK, we'll send Chas and The Rash to recce."

Within a couple of minutes The Rash had crossed the road from the other Supacat and set off with Chas.

Fifteen minutes later, Will said "They're on the move." Dick's headset beeped quietly as the recorder switched on and Chas's voice came through.

"Fucking camels, Boss. No sign of any men – reckon they are wild or escaped - no ropes or anything we could see. Reckon they got our scent and headed off pronto."

"OK get back guys. I'm not impressed by your technique though – letting those camels get your scent. Camels can't smell for shit."

"Yes Boss, but we need a shower." They'd lost half an hour and still had to cross the border, with daylight approaching.

"Steve, look out!"

The steering wheel bucked violently in his hands as the horn of the truck blasted them and the goats scattered in alarm as the 4 x 4 ploughed into the rough stones at the side of the road, stopping just at the edge of a steep drop of several hundred feet into the valley below. "Jesus Christ, that was close. Where were you Steve? I thought we were going over. Get out! I'll drive the rest of the way- there's only about twenty miles to go anyway. But first I need to answer a call after that, that..."

"Near miss."

"Yeh, near miss, that's it. Too fucking near, Steve, much too near."

"Sorry Ellie, my mind was elsewhere."

"I don't want to know. Let's just get to Tunis in one piece. You can finish your story another time, I want to stay alive."

"There wasn't much more to tell – and you asked to hear about it. News came in about Gadhafi being found, beaten and shot in Sirte. We were pulled out a couple of hours later."

"Bugger that, Gadhafi's long dead! Let's just concentrate on staying alive ourselves - for now, right?"

*

Sidi Bou Said

Ehsam Bourguiba, a clerk in Tunisian Police Headquarters, was responsible for collating all the passport data of non-Tunisian visitors. All visitors' passports were scanned at their point of entry and the details transmitted to his section. There the passport image was filed along with the visitor's movement and hotel registration data. Systems were still not fully integrated and his section was kept busy. It was a sensitive position and he supplemented his income by occasionally providing data to a person who he knew only as Atlas. Atlas paid very well, so he got the best service. The French were mean and he made them wait, as a matter of policy.

A variety of 'flags' were used to identify persons of interest. Fifteen sets of records had been flagged that week – including data relating to a Maltese national, Joseph Baldacchino, and another set relating to an Algerian national Anwar Zaman. The flags had been added because of an enquiry from the French DGSE, and the death of Anwar Zaman. They had entered Tunisia together.

That particular morning, he had found a note in his letterbox and was happy to oblige. Ehsam Bourguiba provided the data and photographs that had come in from the Tabarka police station that week, to Mago. The data included Baldacchino and Zawan. There had been no flags against the names of Baldwin, a British man, and a Greek national, Helena Antonakis. Baldacchino had apparently left Tunisia on a ferry to Palermo and Anwar Zaman was now deceased and in a morgue. The copy of the death certificate indicated 'natural causes'.

*

After a quick scan on tripadvisor.com, Maruška had selected a *pension* in the tourist resort of Sidi Bou Said, ten miles north east of Tunis city centre and booked online for two weeks, though she might well move elsewhere during that time.

Although the tourists were far fewer these days, there was still a plethora of foreign faces for her to hide amongst while she waited for orders.

Large hotels were to be avoided and anonymity was much easier here, but as a precaution she did not use her new French passport to register. She explained in French to the proprietor that she was trying to hide from her violent husband who worked in the police force and would be able to trace her. A hundred euros and a doubled room-rate bought her anonymity. Cash payment in euros was always welcomed as the Tunisian *dinar* was very weak.

Her room was comfortable and after the proprietor had shown her the lounger area on the roof – apparently a necessity for German tourists she switched on the television. *Télévision Tunisienne 1* was reporting a shooting and car bombing in Tunis that afternoon, killing four people and injuring one other. Two of the dead were believed to be policemen. She smiled as she added their notches to her notional 'bedpost'. She had lost the accurate count a few years ago at about one hundred and twenty deaths, including the private pleasure killings. Now, she just kept a rough points tally and awarded herself extra 'points' for the policemen.

As she did floor exercises the news droned on. She reflected on Tobin's offer during his interrogation in Malta. $20 million dollars had been attractive, but she already had much more than that salted away from the various smuggling jobs and rackets back in the days of the Bosnian war and its aftermath. On top of that the Chinese had paid her well. Besides cash and gold bullion, she owned high-grade property in London, Paris, Geneva and Monaco.

Still, she mused, if those English bastards had not interfered she could have taken Tobin for much, much more. What she had told Tobin was the truth - money did not interest her, but Tobin had been astute in understanding that for her money was a means to an end – although she had yet to figure out what that end might be.

As she went through her physical routine she looked across at her Chinese phone and the unused local throwaway phones she had bought that afternoon. Since leaving Malta she had not felt any pain, and wondered whether the new phone was the reason. She knew that the British would never remove her implant. They would use her just as the Chinese did. The challenge of playing one against the other would have been fun and not without pain, but now, however, she knew more about the technology they used – and the location of the implant near the C6 vertebra. One of the very best Swiss clinics would surely be able to remove the nanochip. Then she could retire in comfort and have some fun, maybe find a girlfriend with similar interests.

After two days being stuck in the *pension,* the waiting was becoming unbearable. Her upbringing had bred a deep bigotry and she did not enjoy being surrounded by Muslims, even if they spoke French. She had walked the shops, bought some fresh clothes, clean underwear and new training shoes. She had watched CNN with interest and caught up on the latest news about the Malta bombing atrocity. She wondered how she might be fitting – if at all – into that overall picture.

*

She was slowly lowering herself to the floor after her ninety third push-up when she felt the familiar pain between her shoulders. She collapsed onto the marble and screamed. She waited for the next pulse. It didn't come. So, it was not the British. She opened a bottle of water and speed dialled Wan Chuntao on the new phone, after it confirmed her fingerprint and retina pattern.

Under the Guoanbu building in Hainan, it was early morning. Six floors above, there was snow on the ground and the temperature was well below zero. In Room 5, Wan Chuntao had lost track of night and day. The work had been frantic, unceasing and had produced little in the way of results until now.

The Northern Wind team had hacked umpteen commercial systems, waited while firewalls were breached, encryption systems broken and waded through terabytes of data. They had tracked measurement equipment, raw materials, precision machine tools, remote handling equipment, protective equipment and all the plethora of consumables and supplies that were required to run an atomic weapons assembly workshop.

They knew that the British, Americans and French were following a similar process – their footprints had been detected in the penetrated systems. Each team was setting traps for other teams and several companies found that their data had disappeared or systems had shut down unexpectedly.

"I thought I'd lost you, Chuntao. Did you get the voicemail with Tobin's key? I left it for you four days ago."

"I have more important priorities."

"Well, I want my payment for the Tobin operation. It was a success."

"Noted."

"Is that all you have to say?"

"Be quiet and listen."

"Not until I get paid."

"I will see that the transfer is made."

"Then we will talk when I see the confirmation of the payment."

Maruška jerked as the pain spasmed in her spine. She began to regret the impulsive act of breaking the link with SIS and the promise of escape from this Chinese puppetry.

"We talk now. You will get your payment."

She groaned in resignation.

"Go ahead."

"We have not yet located the target Abu ben-Zhair, and we know that the British are also trying to find him. They have moved more people in to Tunis."

"I terminated at least one of them today."

"Yes, we had the report from your driver. That was unnecessary. There will be a discount taken from your money. Now listen very carefully to what I have to say."

*

As Ogilvy headed back to his office in Vauxhall Cross, his phone vibrated. He looked at the number and the icon. It was the Deputy Director of GCHQ, Robert Grey.

"Robert, what have you got?"

"We're just picked up the data signature for that nanochip on the 'Tunisiana' mobile network. We got the number it wormed through and then picked up a call from that number. We're running it through decryption now, but it may take some time. Looks like the encryption has been upgraded."

"Where was the call to?"

"The Antarctic."

"You're kidding."

"No. It went to the Chinese Zhongshan Antarctic research station through the regular international network via the Iridium network and then – well we don't know where. Probably up to one of their own satellites."

"Shit."

"The good news is we've got the coordinates of the call origination in Tunisia. It's coming through on your status screen as we speak."

Ogilvy looked at his tablet and clicked the icon from Grey, opening up a satellite image. He clicked on the map pin and brought up Streetview.

"Got it, excellent, Bob."

"The call was made about twenty minutes ago. The cellphone appears to be switched off now, but we're still seeing it handshaking with the network masts. The location is being updated continuously on your tracking screen."

"Great Bob, thanks."

"I'll let you know when we've got a decrypt. I'm assigning all our quantum CPU power to this until we've cracked the new encryption."

"Good. It's of the utmost priority. You can't give me a time estimate?"

"Sorry, Alex, impossible."

"Ok, speak later - I've got to move on this. 'Bye"

"'Bye"

Ogilvy called 'C' and explained that the Tunis hostile asset was being tracked again, then clicked the icon for Helena Williams on his screen.

*

It was almost lunchtime. Steve and Helena had checked in to the Hotel L'Acropole in Tunis the previous evening after the long drive from Tabarka. Dinner in a Lebanese restaurant had been followed by a night in a proper bed as a proper couple. They were starting to spark off one another.

"Last night was great."

"Plus one – maybe even plus five to that! You are quite a package."

"I've been saving it up for a sailor."

"Hm! Seems like you've known a few sailors – or marines. Your recent repertoire raises a few questions."

"Only one marine – you – and my repertoire comes from reading, not experience. But I am a quick learner."

"But I'm no teacher."

"Well, we seem to be doing ok together."

"Maybe yesterday's near death experience on the road spiced it up for us?"

"I don't know, but I don't want to try that again. It was too close."

"Yes, you seemed to really panic yesterday and yet I've seen you under fire and you've been as cool as a cucumber."

"Women are from Venus."

Steve looked at her vacantly.

"Never mind, it's a chick lit thing."

"Ah, I see – I think I understand."

Helena laughed.

"Steve, it's pretty clear that you don't understand, but never mind, we'll save it for another day."

"OK. I didn't get a classical education like you. Anyway, should we really being doing this? I mean, it's frowned on in the Forces. No skin off my nose, mind, though other parts might wear out if you keep up that pace."

"That's one way of putting it. I call it team work."

"Ok, Boss. I'll follow orders then. They say that sex is better when the end of the world is nigh. There might be more to come."

"Less of the 'end of the world' stuff please."

"And more of the other?"

They laughed together as they strolled easily from the hotel L'Acropole and turned left off the Rue Loch Ness along the Rue du Lac Windermere, towards the British Embassy overlooking Lac Tunis.

"These are bloody bizarre street names."

"Yes, strange. Have you ever been to the Lake District, Steve?"

"Where, in England you mean?"

"Yes. North of Watford."

"No, never. Too far north for me."

"I'll take you there one day."

"You don't need to rush it for me - I prefer the coast. Beats me why they named this road after Windermere."

"There must be a story behind it. I'd understand if it was named after a French Lake.

"Maybe Lady Windermere's Fanny?"

"You berk! I didn't know you read Wilde?"

"I'll read anything at sea. It was free on Kindle."

They laughed.

"Still, there is a lake. Probably very salty. Reminds me of something else, but I'll save that for later."

Steve smacked her bottom.

"Hey, you get jailed for doing that here."

"I think not, woman. You are a second class citizen here. In fact you should be walking three paces behind me!"

"Fuck off you misogynist!"

"What's that?"

"I'll tell you later."

"Can't wait."

Helena stopped and took out her phone. She looked at Steve, mouthed "London" and he stepped away. She looked around as she answered. Apart from two heavily armed policemen on patrol – in fact loitering in the shade - about a hundred metres away, there was no one else nearby – at least, no-one visible on the road - but the buildings around would certainly have their quota of spooks as they were in the Diplomatic quarter of Tunis.

She said nothing other than "Yes" during the call and started retracing their steps as the call continued. Steve fell in behind her.as she put the phone back in her pocket.

"They have a handle on Maruška – she's about ten miles away in a place called Sidi Bou Said. The brief is to watch and wait. She thinks she has cut loose from us, but we're tracking her again – can't read her traffic though. The Chinese have picked up ben-Zhair's trail and we're right behind."

"So how did London find her again?"

"Same way as in Malta – your idea – and GCHQ sweating the details. We still don't know why she came over to us and then cut us out."

"We might never know. Her sort likes taking risks. It's all about the game, not about money. Her game is risk, sadism and murder."

"We can use people like that."

"What a fucking business. I don't know why I'm doing this."

Helena looked at him and smiled. "I think you do."

"And you can tell that to the marines, again."

"I just did. Come on, let's move it - we're meeting someone from Tunis Station in a café in thirty minutes."

*

Steve took her hand "We need to play the part." Helena smiled back as they crossed Avenue Principalé and found the Café Afrique on Rue Lac Victoria. They walked past the café on the other side of the road and walked back to it, pausing to look in a real estate agent's window.

"Pricey."

"To be expected. It is the *Quartier Diplomatique.*"

"It looks ok to me."

"Let's get a coffee then."

They were surprised to see Jacob seated at a corner table. He nodded at them. The lunch crowd had more or less cleared and there were few people in the café. Steve held the chair for Helena as Jacob stood up and they shook hands.

"Good to see you both."

"Yes, what a surprise."

"When did you get in?"

"Last night, we plan to take in some of the sights. What do you recommend?"

"I'm new here myself, but the Great Mosque of Kairouan is not to be missed – so they say."

Protocol had been observed, the all clear given. It was down to business.

They chatted while the waiter took their order for coffee. Jacob pointed to the newspaper on the table in front of him. "Interesting story in there, about Tabarka. Illegal immigrants. They're usually going the other way."

"Can I borrow it?"

"Be my guest. I've finished reading it."

"Thanks. I look forward to reading it later."

Jacob's cellphone was on the table and Helena placed hers alongside it. An LED flashed green on each and then stopped.

"If you are looking for somewhere to stay I can recommend a good *pension* in Sidi Bou Said, just up the road. I have a friend staying there. In fact there's an ad in the paper. 'La Mer d'Or' it's called."

"Did you just say what I thought you said?"

"No, it's my poor French. It's 'The Sea of Gold', not 'The Golden...' well, you know what I mean. It just sounds the same."

"That's a relief. Thanks, we'll check it out. It would make a change from an anonymous hotel."

"We heard that Bryan took a turn for the worse."

"Yes - hell of a thing. Not far from here in fact. Could have been me – we were together until a couple of minutes before it happened. Car accidents are like that – very nasty. Anyway, I have to get back. Nice to bump into you – maybe we can do a beer sometime?"

"Yes, let's. I'll call you."

"I look forward to it."

Jacob stood up and strolled out trying very hard to look nonchalant but failing. Just then their coffees arrived. The waiter looked at Jacob as he left and Steve spoke *"Il ne sent pas bien."* The waiter shrugged and moved to another table - tourists were a strange breed.

"Awkward conversation. He was nervous – and he really did look ill."

"He's young and supposedly a techie. He's been thrown in at the deep end. There's only one way to get experience, and he's learning fast."

After the coffee Helena put the newspaper in her shoulder bag and they strolled back to the hotel *L'Acropole*. As Steve put the keycard in the slot, Helena tapped his arm and put her fingers to her lips.

Steve opened the door and noticed a carryall in the room.

"Ah, they sent my bag up, that's good." She switched the television on and threw a towel over it. "I don't want anyone watching us when we are in bed." She winked.

He looked bemused as she opened the LaCoste carryall and took out towels and pyjamas. Then she pulled out a toilet bag and opened it. She took what looked like smartphone from the bag and turned it on, placing it on the coffee table. It blinked red continuously.

She put her finger to her lips again and he nodded.

Steve just caught the other toilet bag. "This is for you big boy." He looked at the Browning Hi Power, then another device. "What's this?"

"One of my toys."

"OK, I see the label now. Bloody hell, I've used one before, years ago during training for…well… I didn't know you were into that sort of kinky stuff."

He winked back. It was a Terra-P compact Geiger counter.

"I'll try anything once."

"I can't wait…"

The smartphone LED changed to a continuous green colour.

"OK, we're all clear. No emissions in the room – and don't say it, I know what you're thinking!"

The sportsbag was nearly empty - she checked the magazine and the action of the Beretta Model 38 SMG pistol and Steve checked the bulky Hi-Power.

The final item in the carryall was a new tablet pc.

Helena took the newspaper out and found the ad for the *pension* 'La Mer d'Or', ringed in ink. Between the pages was a scribbled note 'His photo is on your smartphone'.

"Check the view from the window, Steve."

He knew that it was a nice way of telling him to mind his own business. She fired up the tablet and placed her phone alongside. Fingerprint and retina scans completed, she entered two passwords and brought up the Blue Angel status screen. After checking her inbox she closed the tablet down.

"OK, we have a picture of the man we think is Abu ben-Zhair. It seems that his passport was scanned by the police in Tabarka. He left the country last week, travelling as a Maltese national, Joseph Balducchino. He was on a Grimaldi Lines ferry to Palermo and disembarked there. GCHQ has hacked the ferry terminal camera data and passenger info. Balducchino didn't leave Palermo on the same ferry. They have a partial facial match with someone who boarded another ferry there and went on to Civitavecchia – that's near Rome. Match was only partial – spectacles and hat in the way. 60% probability. Travelling as Giuseppe Baldacci. Italian passport."

"That has to be him. He switched ID."

"London certainly thinks so, but the match is only at the possible level, not probable."

"What about Maruška?"

"The Embassy are dealing with her."

"That spells disaster."

"It's not ours to question why, etcetera…"

"Not yours you mean."

"Let it go, Steve. You took the Queen's shilling."

"Yes, the Queen. But she's gone now. It's a King – and he hasn't paid me yet."

"He will."

"Maybe, but I'll have to take it in instalments. How about an *aperitif* and an early dinner?"

"On the King I suppose?"

"Instalments, as I said."

"Where?"

"Sidi Bou Said?"

"Jesus, you never give up. Okay, but no funny business right? We can go straight to the airport after that."

He winked. "That's one advantage of travelling light."

Then the penny dropped.

"Airport? What's going on?"

"Sorry, forgot to tell you. We're flying to Rome, tonight. Orders."

"Bloody hell, Ellie, stop keeping me out of the loop. It's not good for trust!"

"I honestly forgot Steve – I only had the orders an hour ago when you were in the shower."

His jaw was firm, his look was grim. It had been a genuine oversight. Maybe.

*

Steve parked the Suzuki near the railways station in Sidi Bou Said, and they walked up the steep hill into the cobbled tourist area, still busy in the early evening as visitors dithered over trinkets and artwork. They were a couple of hundred feet above the sea and below them was a steep stairway cut in the cliff, heading down to a car park with food kiosks and the yacht marina. In the grey evening they could see clear across the Gulf of Tunis. To the right of the marina, they could see the Presidential Palace and its own private dock, just to the south.

"What are those ruins there, by the white wall?"

"I think that's Carthage – you know, the Greeks, Carthaginians, Phoenicians, Romans, – they all lived there at one time or another. Wiped each other out in turn. Did you do Latin in school – the Punic wars and all that?"

"You must be kidding. Not in Portsmouth's Priory Comprehensive School. No way."

"I think the Vandals came, killed off the Romans and wrecked the place."

"As in vandalized, you mean."

"That's right. They were Germans."

"Probably supported Bayern Munich then."

"What are you talking about?"

"Never mind, let's find that *pension.*"

Helena shook her head and checked the map on her smartphone.

"This way."

They climbed some steps and turned left into an alleyway.

Jacob was standing in a doorway reading a newspaper. He noticed them and jumped with surprise.

Helena and Steve were equally surprised and turned quickly into a bar. They sat at a table, as Jacob came in and looked around. He joined them.

Steve got the first word in.

"What the hell are you doing here?"

"On an op. A takedown. You shouldn't be here."

"Did you check your life insurance."

"What? I'm a clean skin, so they wanted me on the job."

"How many in the team?"

"Four of us. She took out Bryan yesterday. I wanted in on this."

"What's the plan?"

"One of the team is throwing a smoke grenade on to the flat roof in…"Jacob looked at his watch "…four minutes. I'm phoning the landlady to tell the place is on fire, to clear out the guests. Then we take her as she comes out. Got to be taken alive."

"Exits?"

"Front only. Old building with a high back wall, un-scalable."

"You think."

"We checked."

"Are you carrying?"

"What?"

"Jesus." Steve hissed "Are you fucking armed?"

"Yes."

"You'd better get back to the job then. Expect the unexpected."

Jacob nodded and touched his ear piece.

"Roger three minutes. I'm on my way."

"Jesus, Steve, what do they teach them these days? I know we've been recruiting like crazy but this is ridiculous. He's a techie. He shouldn't be out here doing this."

"We were all young once." He checked his watch. "Three minutes. Let's take a quick look at your map. Got Streetview?

"Yes if there's a signal."

"She'll have checked it already and will not do the obvious."

Steve looked at the overhead satellite shot from Google Earth, then Streetview.

"Ninety seconds, if my watch is right."

The waiter approached. Steve stood up.

"No thanks, we'll come back later for a beer."

He took Helena's hand and they crossed the road from the bar, heading uphill in a narrow alley. A minute later they were in position in a doorway across from the side of the *pension*'s high wall. Steve put his arms around her whispered in her ear. "We've got to play the part, remember?"

Helena heard the slide engage as Steve checked his Browning under the rear of her leather jacket, chambering a round, safety off. The kiss lasted rather more than a minute and as they broke for air they heard a shout and as an old man outside the bar pointed at the roof of the *pension*. A fire alarm sounded. They did not see Jacob and his colleagues move into position.

Maruška was slowly lowering herself to the floor after her ninety third push-up when she felt the familiar pain between her shoulders. She collapsed onto the marble and screamed. She waited for the next pulse. It didn't come. She opened a bottle of water and speed dialled Wan Chuntao on the new phone, after it confirmed her fingerprint and retina pattern.

Under the Guoanbu building in Hainan, it was early morning. Six floors above, there was snow on the ground and the temperature was well below zero. In Room 5, Wan Chuntao had lost track of night and day. The work had been frantic, unceasing and had produced little in the way of results until now.

The message from Wan Chuntao was detailed – the target had been identified and speed of action was essential. Then there was an unequivocal: 'Move Now!"

The line dropped and Maruška was packing her bag when she heard someone shout *Hariq! Hariq!* from the street below. She didn't understand the word and looked out of the window. She saw and recognised Jacob just as the pension's fire alarm went off. He saw her at the window, and she reacted.

She rummaged in her bag and withdrew the small device, then peeled the back off the sticky pad on the back of the charge. She stuck it to the wall behind the door and tested the adhesion gently. Then she carefully pulled out the trigger cord and tied it to the door handle, then pressed the arm button. She threw her sports bag out on to the landing and started to close the door taking once quick glance around the room. Shit, her phone! There on the bedside table. Four seconds of ten. She crossed the room and picked up her phone, six seconds. Back to the door, eight seconds. She held her breath as she closed the door gently. Nine, ten seconds. Armed. She let out her breath gently and picked up her bag. Once the tension changed on the cord then the 500 grams of high explosive would do their work.

Moving towards the stairway to the roof solarium, she heard footsteps on the stairs below, but was not seen as she moved up to the roof. Moving across to the parapet she prepared for the leap across the alley to the next roof.

She climbed up and looked across. In her peripheral vision she could see a couple in a clinch below. She jumped, just as the man raised a Browning Hi-Power towards her, too late. No shot, just a shout as she landed awkwardly, sprawling across the other parapet. Her mind had not been focused on the landing, it had been drawn to the face, trying to place it.

Behind her, in the *pension,* Aaron Rainsford and Elias Stone approached her room. She could hear the two-tone siren of the local *pompiers* approaching - they would certainly have a fire to deal with.

Rainsford tried the door handle, slowly and gently. He turned to Stone and shook his head, then stood back and balanced as he raised his right foot and kicked the door beneath the lock.

Then she had it, the face clicked. Baldwin! How the hell had he found her? She sprinted for the next parapet, following her prepared escape route.

The sound of the explosion did not cause a change in her stride as she reached the street and crossed it, heading for the steps down to the marina. She heard a shout behind her and pushed some German tourists aside, taking the steps three at a time.

The charge inside her room had taken out a section of the thin wall – and the door. Aaron Rainsford had been flattened against the solid stone wall across the narrow corridor. He was beyond help – the door handle and lock assembly together with his sternum, was embedded in his heart. Elias Stone was completely untouched physically, apart from a temporary loss of hearing. He quickly checked Rainsford for vital signs – there were none then looked inside the wrecked room. It was clear that there was no other body and the bathroom was empty. He ran for the stairs.

*

Maruška had a rucksack on her back when she appeared on the parapet of the roof area, surrounded by white smoke and billowing bedsheets on a washing line. She jumped across the narrow alley above them, to the adjacent property, scrambling to get a hold. When she was safely on the roof she peered over the parapet in surprise. Her swearing was inaudible to them as she recognized Steve, then disappeared.

"Come on Ellie, follow me" he shouted and started running down the cobbled hill. Helena looked back and saw Maruška come out a side alley and cross the road, headed for a flight of steps. Jacob, watching the southern perimeter saw Maruška cross the street and started running. Two of the takedown team had disappeared inside.

"Steve where are you going – oh fuck…" Helena looked at Jacob, looked at Steve and ran after Jacob. Just then she heard and explosion somewhere behind her.

The steps were very steep and half way down there was a short rope and plank bridge over a ravine, then the steps continued down through rough brush. There were a few tourists who had been on the steps but had been pushed aside by Maruška and were sprawled at the sides of the path which was strewn with all manner of rubbish. The smell was rank.

Helena didn't count the steps but she could see that Jacob was gaining on her – and on Maruška. At the bottom of the steps, Maruška stopped, turned and fired in one smooth movement. A double tap, but Jacob had seen her turn and dived into the bushes at the side. Another two shots went into the bushes and then fire was returned.

"We need her alive Jacob."

Maruška raised her pistol higher and Helena was lucky to take just a nick in the shoulder of her jacket as she threw herself sideways, the bullet ending up in the leg of Francois Martin, a sailor from La Rochelle, carrying a framed picture from one of the art shops. His wife screamed. Then, Maruška was away and into her rental car, driving away by the time Jacob reached the bottom of the steps and snapped a pic of the car's rear. He ran on, with Helena behind him.

The road from the marina was broad and curved slowly round the hill and up into the town. Maruška took the corner accelerating hard, and changing into fourth gear, when she saw a white Suzuki 4x4 slew across the road in front of her with the only choice to stick or twist. She twisted too late and ran off the road into the trees at the side of the hill. The airbags exploded as the car ran into a solid old olive tree.

She shook her head and threw the door open, dazed, her weapon already in her hand. Steve slammed the door hard, knocking her arm into the air and breaking her wrist as her gunshot went high. She made no sound, burying pain as she had when first raped as a young girl in Serbia. Steve's Browning hit the back of her head.

"I've got you again you fucking bitch."

Jacob and Helena puffed to a stop. "Let's get her in the 4x4, quickly. Jacob - there – her weapon on the floor. Anything else?"

"Ok I've got her rucksack."

"Move, move, move!"

They could here sirens sounding and floodlights came on in the Presidential Palace across the ravine.

"Where are we going?"

"Fuck knows. Jacob, hit her with your pistol if there is any sign of her waking up. Hard."

"She's well out, bleeding freely from the scalp."

"Check her eyes."

"Yes, she's definitely out."

"Check her arms – I might have broken one of them."

"One of her wrists looks bent, it's very bruised. No bones protruding, but I'm no doctor – just the basic field first aid course."

"That's probably good enough for now."

Steve slowed as they passed the railway station and two police cars shot the lights and headed down towards the marina. Two more were headed up the hill in the direction of the *pension*.

"The Embassy has a safe house on the other side of the city."

"How far?"

"Three or four miles I guess."

"Too far this time of day through a city. This SUV is hot. Jacob, what did you come in?"

"A rental, but I don't have the keys. The Malta SUV is up the road in Carrefour. At least it was. I dumped it yesterday."

"So hot or very hot. We'll stick with this, but we need to get off this road."

Just then Jacob's smartphone navigator started voicing directions.

"We'll head out into the sticks – there's a forested area."

"Good thinking."

Steve filtered on to the Nationale 10 highway.

"You're welcome. This should take us around the back of the airport and keep us away from the city and heavy traffic. It's still a few miles."

"Are you okay Helena?"

"Fine, nearly caught one from her, went through my jacket, grazed my arm. Nothing to worry about. Anyway how come you stopped her?"

"Once I saw Streetview it was obvious where her car would be. It's all pedestrianized. It had to be at the nearest point – down in the marina car park, but there's only one way out of there."

"Up the hill."

"Exactly. She thinks like a soldier, but her choices were limited."

"Strange she didn't try to lose herself in the town. At least you guessed right."

"Intuition."

"Experience."

"Whatever."

There was a groan from the rear seat followed by a wet sounding thud.

"That's for Bryan, you cow."

"He's learning."

"Too right. She blew the *pension*."

"I heard the bang. I'm not surprised."

"How much time have we got?"

"About three hours before the flight."

"Security will be tight at the airport."

"We need to lose this 4x4 quickly. Jacob, you'd better call this in to your great leader."

"It's Mago."

"Whatever."

"The rest of the *pension* team are off the net. I'm calling Mago direct."

"Ok, Mago suggests the car park near the Café Nahli in Parc Urbain Ennahli, north of the airport. The café itself should be closed and the park quiet this time of day. It's about ten minutes for us. I'll get us directions."

They parked in a corner, then sat and waited.

There was a groan as Maruška stirred again, the another thud.

"That's for Aaron Rainsford."

"Steady on Jacob, we need her alive. Use your belt to lash her wrists."

"I'm with you on this Jacob."

"Shut up, Steve."

They had to wait almost an hour before Mago arrived in the darkness in a rental car along with cold rain, closely followed by two other men in a beat-up panel van with ladders on the roof and the words 'All your building problems Solved – call Us now!' in French on the sides.

Helena and Mago exchanged security introductions while Maruška, still apparently unconscious, was being watched by Jacob.

Maruška was bundled into the beat-up builders van. One man climbed in, checked her vital signs and examined the wounds on her head.

"Is she ok Eli?"

"Yes, but concussed I think. A couple of deep scalp wounds, hit on the head I'd say. I don't think there's any skull damage..."

"She was resisting" Jacob piped in, rather anxiously. "I think she's got a broken wrist as well."

"...so I'll sedate her properly, OK?"

Mago nodded. "OK Eli, get rid of the 4x4." He looked at Helena.

"There's a flight booked for you Williams – and him - with these new passports. The last flight into Rome Christmas Eve." He didn't look at Steve. They're British – seemed easiest all round despite the need for visas. Give me the others – the searches at the airport are *very* thorough and they'll be tied to that 4x4 rental and your entry. We'll send them on to Rome with a suitable exit stamp. Charlie here will take you to the airport tomorrow - and you'd better leave your weapons with him. Jacob and Eli have a ferry to catch."

Helena spoke quietly. "Thanks. She's all yours now. I don't know what your orders are, but I was instructed that we want her very much alive. She has embedded technology. She must be kept sedated or the technology could be used to kill her – from a long way away."

"That's what I was told." He looked at Steve. "We lost a good man in that explosion and Elias was lucky to get away. I'd heard you were trouble wherever you go. Now you've given me a big problem with that Serbian woman - if that's what she is. Don't come back – that's my advice. It could be awkward."

"Listen, Mago or whoever you are, I didn't fucking ask for this. You send raw people out against the best and I've got to sort out the mess. I get stitched up time and again by your lot. The *pension* was your disaster, not mine. Fuck you, pal." He pointed at the disappearing van. "And if I ever see her again, I will fucking kill her whatever the orders are. I've lost two good mates because of her. She's death. Keep her well under, or you will lose more people – I guarantee it. And I'll definitely be back – my boat is in Tabarka."

"Calm down Steve. Mago, it's been a tough few weeks. Steve is understandably pissed off. You've got her now, and without our help you would be up a creek. So, get real. Mission achieved – with collateral damage. And I'll be claiming for a new jacket on *your* expenses - I can't wear it through security. Here – this is very important."

Helena handed Maruška's rucksack to Mago.

"Don't lose her phone – it's in there. London needs it. More vital technology. Jacob is the expert."

"It needs to go into the metal tool box. Did you bring it?"

"It should be in the van."

"But the van's gone."

"Shit."

"That's a great start, Mago, you twat."

"Shut up Steve. Let's go and get some rest and prepare for Rome."

*

Ogilvy listened as 'C' spoke. I'm on my way to see the PM. What's the latest on that Serbian woman we've been using – the one that the Chinese are running?"

"Damaged goods. Had a set-to with one of our people in Tunis. She's hospitalized under guard on *Bulwark* – she'll be back here in our clinic in a couple of days."

"Christ, how did you get her out of Tunis? No, on second thoughts I don't want to know. How will the Chinese play this – do they know we have her?"

"I can't say. She should be immune to any interference through her nanochip – we know how to isolate that now – but they must suspect something's up. It is possible they might assume it's equipment failure, but I'd expect them to cover all bases anyway."

"Thanks. I'm just going into the elevator to the bunker. I'll call you later."

"Before you go, there's just one more thing. We have been debriefing Charles Tobin on *HMS Bulwark*."

"What's he got to do with Blue Angel?"

"He has been working on a new bacterium to extract plutonium from seawater."

*

"Are you serious?"

"Never more so, Prime Minister."

'C' had been surprised to find that he was alone in the Cobra bunker with the PM. The Cobra meeting had been rescheduled.

"Go on, 'C'."

"Yes, well, he was tortured and the Chinese now have the complete DNA sequence for the bacterium – and they know how to overcome the challenges of the radioactivity when cultivating it. Gold we knew about after that fiasco in the Red Sea. We suspected precious metals as well, but never plutonium."

"Good God!"

"Quite."

"Now we have it."

It was a statement, not a question.

"No Prime Minister, I am afraid not. Tobin is resisting disclosure."

"I assume he wants a deal?"

'C' nodded. "Yes Prime Minister."

"Very well, send me your proposals for me to review. I assume that there is no leverage we can use?"

"None, he holds a very strong hand. He has taken precautions to make the details available to Russia in the event of his demise or disappearance. Not public. Just Russia. There is a timescale, and I have to say that not even persuasion – I use the word advisedly – is possible."

"OK, thank you, 'C', I'll wait for your proposals on Tobin. You'd best get back to Vauxhall."

"Before I leave, you should know that we are hearing whispers – 'chatter' is too strong a word – about a weapon called 'The Sword of Allah'. At present we have no evidence to link that name to the missing device."

"Good God man, I just hope that it stays that way. It's just the kind of name that would draw the faithful and the madmen together. We'll keep this from Cobra for the moment. I want pre-briefings on all developments so that I can decide on the Cobra agendas."

"Very well, Prime Minister."

The PM's Chief of Staff entered and 'C' left the briefing room, thinking about the PM's reputation for attention to detail – or was it micromanagement?

The PM sat alone in silence for another 15 minutes and then took the elevator directly back to her office.

*

The Announcement

ANNOUNCEMENT

Issued by: Islamic Caliphate Operations Command
Dated: 24 Safar1440 A.H., 06:00 hours, Mecca time.

The IC today advises the infidel states of the world that it has miniaturised nuclear weapons in place in several major infidel cities. These weapons – the Sword of Allah - are ready to use.

We have a list of demands which we expect to be met unconditionally by the appropriate countries and organisations if use of the Sword is to be avoided. These demands must all be met by 20 Rabi al-Awwal 1440 A.H. (20th December this year). There will be No negotiation, No agreement, No truce, No dialogue. All diplomatic channels – and backchannels - are closed.

Our demands are:

1. Formal recognition of the Islamic Caliphate by the US, EU, China, Russian Federation and all other members of the G20.
2. ICIM Membership of the United Nations
3. Freeing of all IC prisoners worldwide
4. Withdrawal of all infidel forces from IC territories in the Levant and Maghreb
5. Abolition of the so-called State of Israel and transfer of the government to IC control

Signed: IC Operations Command

End

The announcement became public simultaneously on Al Jazeera, YouTube, Vimeo and 47 other websites. It took the form of a text slideshow with no audio. There was one picture included in the deck of slides – that of a '*hohlraum*' – the small but central component in a new design of nuclear fusion device originally developed in the Lawrence Livermore Laboratory, just east of San Francisco.

*

"Shit, that's bloody impossible, Ellie. The West will never agree to terms like those. It must be a bluff."

"What choice do we have, Steve? Bluffing usually involves negotiation and counter-bidding. There is no communication at all. So, we have to find the device. We think the weapon – at least one - may be – or was - in Algeria."

"Is it credible – ICIM having a nuke?"

"In a word, yes. We think North Korea provided the technology to Iran and a weapon somehow got into ICIM's hands."

"Holy Mother! I can't begin to get my head around that."

"Precisely. It's a wonder we're not at war yet. Things are bound to be very tight here, so close to the Algerian border."

"So that's why HMG is paying me so well"

"It's not a joking matter. The way things are going it could be the last if the US attacks North Korea and Israel goes for Iran. And then there's China to contend with."

"Just gallows humour. You need it when things get really tough."

*

Vauxhall Cross

Ogilvy sat at the meeting room table, but now with a new 'C' on the other side. It was well after 3 a.m. and none of the team had gone home for days.

"This is a hellish situation, Alex. We're up against the possibility of at least one nuke in a western city, maybe even Moscow. The P5 need to work together but each wants to get their hands on the new device and keep the technology to themselves."

"Working together is a pipe dream, Sir, and frankly, not many people here would be disappointed if it was Moscow."

"We're unlikely to find it by looking at building plans for Christ's sake. We and the Cousins – and even the French – are working more or less together, but when any one of us sees the hare then the race will start and all bets are off. It's a desperate situation but I'm not sharing everything from our sources, particularly the Chinese link with your asset in Tunis. That's a gem." He nodded at the large screen display. "Anyway, it looks like we've got the feed now. Call the rest of the team in."

*

Cobra, Black Friday

It was the last Friday in November, the day after Thanksgiving now known almost worldwide as Black Friday. The name originated as the day when US retailers' net revenue notionally moves from the red into the black as the Christmas shopping season starts.

In the bunker deep below Downing Street, those around the table were shocked by the Prime Minister's appearance. She had not slept and her pallor was grey even under the makeup. The bags under her eyes were pronounced as she opened the meeting.

"Ladies and Gentlemen, order please. You have seen the news so let's not waste any time. This meeting is completely unprecedented. You know that for several weeks now we have been more or less at an impasse with 'Blue Angel', with little apparent progress. Sir John Constantine" – he nodded across the table - has replaced Sir William Gore at MI6. Sir William has been taken ill – I'm afraid it's terminal and he will not be returning. Then last night, it all notched up and we are – arguably - in serious danger of catastrophe.

Since midnight I have spent hours on the telephone with the US and Russian Presidents, China, France. Israel has put its forces to the highest state of readiness. The Foreign Secretary has been talking to the EU leaders and Germany. The markets are in freefall and the media is going crazy.

Anyway, in thirty minutes time we will link across to Camp David where the President will be in session with the Directors of Homeland Security, the NSA, DIA, CIA and FBI.

The P5 will be in formal conference later today. The forum is being widened to the G20. We need the widest cooperation.

Before we link with Camp David I want us to briefly discuss the validity of the terrorist claim and establish an initial set of options under three main headings. We have to act quickly to allay public concern, stabilise the markets and, most importantly of all, physically protect our country. So, firstly, Sir John – the validity of the claim?."

"Thank you Prime Minister. The message became public at one minute after midnight 'Mecca time' as it said on the release. That was ten pm GMT and late afternoon Washington time – on Thanksgiving Day. So, we have known about it for nine hours or so. Semantic and other analysis of the text, inbuilt code words and the channels and timing of promulgation appear to confirm that the announcement is genuinely from IC, although unusually it does not use video or audio. The words '... *No agreement, No truce, No dialogue'* come straight out of the Algerian GIA manifesto. The GIA was an extremist Islamist defunct group which fought the Algerian government during their civil war in the early 1990s. Their leaders were all captured and the group supposedly destroyed, but clearly there appears to be some carryover.

The formal announcement contains one picture image. We have scanned the web and whilst there are similar pictures available, there is no exact match. Our image analysis shows that the image is genuine – there has been no manipulation at pixel level. As we might expect there is no camera metadata with the image. I have the Director of AWE online now to comment in more depth."

The touchscreen displays lit up and the link from the Atomic Weapons Establishment was live.

"Director Tweedy – Jonathan - good morning. Please explain your initial view on the image we provided earlier - over to you."

"Thank you Director. Our initial view is that this image – assuming it is not a fake - is of a '*hohlraum*', the central component in a *possible* new type of nuclear fusion configuration. It appears to be based on a design originally used in the Lawrence Livermore Laboratories in California in 2014 – for peaceful fusion power research. I said 'based on', but there are several subtle differences in shape to that of the image. The original was made of pure gold - which reflects radiation and contains it during the so-called ignition stage of nuclear fusion.

The 2014 design only briefly attained ignition. I'll try to keep it simple."

"Please do."

"Yes, well...I do need to put it into context to help explain it. A conventional fusion bomb requires a fission bomb to trigger it. A working fission bomb is not easy to produce – in itself it requires a carefully shaped conventional explosive charge to compress a plutonium or uranium core. That's tricky.

You may not remember the US losing two hydrogen bombs in Palomares in Spain – that was in 1966 They were accidentally released from a B52 bomber but when they hit the ground (one went into the sea actually) the bomb casing distorted the conventional shaped explosive charge. Phut, nothing happened except local contamination and lots of political fallout. Of course the bombs were not, technically, 'armed' anyway. To make all these stages work is very difficult – it requires specialized hydrodynamic testing – which was one of the key indicators of Iran's nuclear weapons programme – the US photographed the testing building being constructed – caught them with their pants down, so to speak.

So, there are actually three stages in a fusion bomb – conventional explosive starting a fission explosion which triggers the fusion bomb.

This new design – if it is a reality – would eliminate the first two stages and laser power would create the huge pressure and heat pulse necessary to start the fusion of a deuterium/tritium mix – these are isotopes – variations – of hydrogen. Deuterium is present in 'heavy water' – something that Germany was producing in Narvik in Norway during World War II you may know."

"Director, yes I'm sure everyone knows that." 'C' looked around the meeting table in exasperation, then back at the camera. "Please keep to the point."

"Yes, well er... sorry. A small quantity of a deuterium/ tritium mix– marble sized, in this '*hohlraum*' would be enough to trigger fusion. That's what they did in the Lawrence Livermore Laboratory – for peaceful purposes of course. In a bomb some plutonium *might* be used – it's called a sparkplug – to increase the yield. That's hypothetical of course."

"Yes, yes, you told us this at the last session. I think some of us got the gist of that, just about."

"Sorry, er…well Prime Minister, we have no idea of the size of this particular component in the image as there is no indication of scaling and the image resolution is too low to be of help – say by identifying machining marks – but this is probably deliberate. The US test configuration was less than ten millimetres long, and was not designed to test a weapons concept – just peaceful fusion 'ignition' – so they say. Up until recently we did not believe that such a design could lead to a viable weapon, but since validation of the North Korean test we have been looking hard at a variety of configurations including this one.

The power requirements were vast for the US experiment and the budget for the heating lasers alone was three point five billion dollars – there were one hundred and ninety two of them.

However, it is a big step from machining a block of gold to producing a viable nuclear weapon – as far as we know - and it would not be easy to miniaturize – unless they have come up with an alternative approach."

"Dammit man, it's your job to know. Saying that you did not believe it could form the basis of a viable weapon does not give me confidence in AWE. We know North Korea has done it."

"With all due respect Sir John, we don't know for sure that North Korea has made this design work – *and* we don't have the budget for this *and* actually, it's not my job to know. Prime Minister, my remit does not include original research – or intelligence gathering for that matter."

"Ok gentlemen, cool down. Let's get back to the issue at hand. We'll consider the other issues offline."

"Thank you Prime Minister. So, without further data all I can say is 'maybe' it could be the design basis of a viable weapon, and maybe they could construct a viable weapon. If pushed I would put the probability at less than five percent. I would go further and say that the claim of multiple weapons is not at all credible, and miniaturization for a warhead impossible.

Other than the North Korean underground tests – which we now believe to be genuine - we have no knowledge or inkling that such a weapon exists or has ever been tested, although there is the possibility that it could have been tested in an active earthquake zone. Such a test might have triggered an earthquake – or not – but no suspicions would have been raised – at least on first pass. It would be a risky way to test a weapon. An analysis of recent earthquake data in the region is being undertaken – parts of Iran are tectonically active.

So, if they have a weapon – one weapon – it may be untested. And then there are the delivery systems. The original US research – that's the bit we know about – need a large building to house all the equipment – and a massive power supply, as I said. There's no way I could see this being in a suitcase or a truck – and certainly not in a missile. I would say that it has to be a fixed installation – maybe in a building or at a push, a ship. A ship would be the most likely candidate – large enough, mobile and able to get near to a major city such as Southampton, Rotterdam or even New York. To successfully assemble and use such an untested weapon in a city would, I contend, offer a close to zero chance of succeeding. As for multiple weapons, it's just not possible – at least based on current evidence – and there's little of that - unless, of course, ships were used and even then I put the probability as zero.

"That's a brave statement, Director. Unfortunately, they have already done many things we did not think possible."

"Yes Prime Minister, I understand, but I can only give you my considered opinion as of now, supported by limited data and the work of my team – which continues."

"Why would they use such a complex – and physically large weapon? Why not a suitcase nuclear bomb that we hear about?"

"A good question, Prime Minister. There are several reasons. Firstly, a suitcase bomb is technically very complex and requires specialised components which are fairly easily traced and have strict export controls on them. Secondly, plutonium – or uranium 235 - is required. These are difficult to manufacture or obtain, and are fairly easily detectable as they are highly radioactive. The final reason may simply be one of availability of components for the triggering fission device. They knew where it was and they could simply steal it. Additional components would be easily available through normal commercial channels and without any export controls, I would expect – at least in general. It's all supposition at the moment."

"Thank you Director."

"I have nothing more to add at this time Prime Minister, except to say that our best technical people are working on this around the clock."

"I should certainly hope so. Very well, you'd better get back to your team then. Thank you. Now, let's move on."

Tweedy raised his eyebrows at the tone and words of the PM, but kept his voice level.

"Thank you Prime Minister, Director, all." The screens turned off.

"That's a lot of bloody help." This time it was the Prime Minister whose language was ripe. "Sir John, time is pressing – do you have anything else to add?"

"The ultimatum. The twentieth of December. It's not Christmas, but close. It's possible we could be looking at Christmas Day for an initial attack. Or perhaps New Year's Eve. I doubt that they would target Jerusalem – it is a Holy City for Islam too, but Paris – the French have a bad history with IC or IS - London, Rome, Berlin, New York are the obvious possibilities – perhaps too obvious."

"Moscow?"

"Perhaps, but there are many others. Our analysts are working up a list of significant dates and possible associated targets. We're factoring in the statement they made after the bombing of the *Queen Katherine*. There was a lot of ranting in there about Crusaders and Malta, so it is possible that the next target would also be of religious significance, possibly associated with the Crusades. That's the position on targets.

The name 'Sword of Allah' may be propitious. The original Sword of Allah was actually a man, Khalid ibn al-Walid, who commanded the forces of Medina under Muhammad and also the forces of Muhammad's immediate successors. He was noted for his great military prowess.

We are still trying to locate Abu ben-Zhair, who we believe is the planner behind this. We have credible evidence that he was in Malta close to the time of the attack there. He's an Algerian and we have intel which strongly points to Algeria."

"We're not worried about targets in bloody Algeria!"

"Correct, Prime Minister, but we believe that preparatory work was done there – we have hard evidence. It could be relatively easy to transport a weapon into Europe from Algeria."

The Prime Minister looked up at the plain, white-painted ceiling of the bunker and shook her head. She let her breath out very slowly and it was plainly audible in the stillness. "Anything more to add?"

"We think ben-Zhair is building a political platform to take over the IC. Certainly the centre of gravity is moving from IC in the Levant to ICIM in the Maghreb. We might expect an internal power struggle."

"You mean the 'so-called' IC – they are not a state and never will be."

"Of course Prime Minister, but a rose by any other name…"

"Keep to the bloody point!" The PM threw her paperweight at the table and it skittered across, narrowly missing the Director of MI5 and dropping into the fireplace behind him, breaking into pieces.

The PM did not apologise - sometimes a little theatre was necessary to focus the troops. Still, it was Swarovski – a bit passé now, in more ways than one. It would have to be replaced. She returned to the matter at hand.

"'C', do you have anything else to add?"

Sir John pursed his lips and shook his head, "No Prime Minister."

"No further intel at all?"

"Not as yet. GCHQ is at full stretch, as are our humint assets – worldwide."

"There has been a right royal screw-up on intel. I know it predates your time."

Sir John nodded. "In fairness, IC is extremely slippery and getting any humint is notoriously difficult. We have sent many agents in as IC converts, but the humint is relatively low grade and getting them near the high command is virtually impossible. We have lost a few too. Offering them riches on earth does not compare with what the Imams promise them in heaven."

"I'm not bloody interested in fairness or heaven when we are faced with hell on earth. We have the free world to think of and millions of lives. Ok, let's go round the table, one minute each on the validity. Chancellor, please."

The discussion was brief. Another six minutes gone.

"Alright everyone, in summary: until this is disproven, we have to assume that they have viable nuclear weapons technology, very probably the device which is missing in Iran – at least. My own inclination is towards the view that they do not have more than one weapon and that the claim of multiple weapons is a bluff. We seem to be agreed on that. If we are wrong about multiple weapons then that will not become apparent until – well, until the unthinkable happens - but we would assume that it would be one bomb first, God forbid."

There was concerted nodding around the table.

"Now, about the IC claims. Foreign Secretary – your view please."

Shami Munchetty spoke concisely and confidently, without any hint of doubt.

"Prime Minister, colleagues. Firstly, I'd just like to say that we do not agree with the suggestion that ben-Zhair is building a platform to take over the – 'so-called' – IC."

Although meant to be *sotto voce*, the comment 'No surprises there' was clearly heard around the table.

Munchetty's natural colouring was such that the blush was not obvious, though the muscles around her mouth tightened markedly as she glared at the Chancellor.

"If I may be allowed to continue without interruption PM?"

"Of course. Carry on - the rest of you keep your comments until afterwards!"

"These demands are completely preposterous. We would usually expect demands to be negotiable, but the fact that they are in the public domain and so ridiculous as a whole suggests that they would not expect us to comply. I believe that they expect to use their weapon or weapons. I will run through the demands and our initial view:

One - Recognition of IC – we think that is potentially negotiable – over a very long term, such as happened with South Vietnam.

Two - UN membership – that is potentially negotiable. This would take a long time, we would delay as long as possible in the usual ways.

Three - Freeing of all prisoners – that is potentially negotiable, some sort of exchange perhaps, though they hold few Western hostages at the moment.

Four - Removal of our forces – that is potentially negotiable.

Five - Abolition of the State of Israel – No Way. Israel will go to war over this – no question. I'm sure that the US would too. The natural inclination of Israel will be to hit Iran, and that will surely happen very soon."

"Yes, they are already mobilising their reserves."

"What about South Korea?"

"It's no secret that they have been building up their forces even more – another two divisions are being moved up to the border as we speak. They are rehearsing the shelter drills for the city populations every day and their navy and air force is at the highest threat level. We think they might try to move across the Fiftieth Parallel – the DMZ - within a few days."

"Yes, the President – US President that is – has told me that he is having great difficulty restraining them. "

So, what do you suggest, given that IC say all diplomatic channels are closed?"

"The FO has no policy suggestions at this moment – these sorts of demands are unprecedented. No-one ever closed the backchannels, not even Hitler. I have a team working on it as we speak to try and open a channel for discussion. And I have a call in to the Israeli Ambassador."

"Really?"

"Yes really, Prime Minister." The sarcasm was lost on Munchetty.

"Well Shami, your people should bloody well get their fingers out before we lose a million people somewhere – maybe here in London. I need a foreign policy position and I need it now, before I talk to Washington. And you need to be talking to someone higher than the Israeli Ambassador."

Shami Munchetty blanched – not even her sub-continental complexion was deep enough to cover the embarrassment.

"I will speak to my Permanent Secretary now for the latest update. If you will excuse me."

She stood up and left the room.

"Any other views?"

The Prime Minister was in a foul mood so the discussion was brief. The consensus was no negotiation and play for time through diplomatic channels.

"I'll sum up then, as I see it. This is a real threat and we cannot negotiate – even if they would. We have to assume that the worst will happen and prepare for a Western city to be hit. That could of course be anywhere, from Sydney to San Francisco, London to Athens. I am particularly concerned about the threat from shipping – but at least that would narrow down the target list when combined with their apparent determination to hit a target of religious significance – God forbid even Malta could be a target again!

Home Secretary – you need to increase our checks on shipping. I know you've been under pressure to increase our border patrol boat fleet because of the migrant crisis. Let's see if we can involve the Navy in some way, maybe use Fishery Patrol vessels – whatever we have."

"How do we fund this, Prime Minister?"

"Just get it done, the Chancellor will sort out budgets later. Right now we need to have a concerted plan to publish to the media so that a panic doesn't start – not everything of course – we can't let the bastards know our strategy – I mean the 'so-called' IC, not the media. Or maybe I don't.? Let's move on., next item – the Markets. Chancellor, if you please."

"Prime Minister, Right Honourable Gentlemen…"

"For fuck's sake cut the crap and get on with it!"

No one in the room – or wider Westminster for that matter – had ever heard the Prime Minister use four letter words. The silence hung.

"Yes, er, well…normally we would recommend that the London markets would stay open"

"Normally?"

"…but these are unprecedented circumstances, and it is Friday, so we can put out a holding statement to the effect that we will make an announcement on Sunday."

"And?"

"And nothing PM, that is my recommendation."

"What does the Governor of the Bank of England say?"

"As all major western markets are affected simultaneously, there is – currently – no major danger of a run on the pound. The Governor would agree with such a holding position – as would the central banks in the G20. And Monday is a Bank Holiday in the US."

The meeting continued until the scheduled link up with Camp David. By midday when the session closed, it was clear that neither the US nor the UK had any clear idea as to the immediate course of action, and a joint 'holding' press release was agreed, which focused on 'not negotiating with terrorists.'

The more vociferous press organs were demanding immediate, even nuclear, action against IC, but the informed opinion recognised that the dispersed nature of its controlling political and military bodies made this unrealistic. In many ways the IC was a 'virtual state' almost like churches had been during the communist era in Eastern Europe.

The US President was using all her weight to hold the Israeli Government in line and avoid precipitate action. The *Eshkol-Comer* memorandum of understanding made between Israel and the United States on March 10, 1965 contained Israel's written assurance - for the first time - that it would not be the first state to introduce nuclear weapons in the Middle East. Nevertheless, Israel was believed to possess nuclear weapons, but was still unaware that Iran, specifically, had been trying to circumvent the nuclear treaty. Anyway if they did know then it was unlikely that hitting Iran would solve the present crisis. Still, it would be good for votes in the forthcoming General Election to the Knesset.

Additionally, the US President was under considerable internal political and military pressure from right wing elements to undertake a pre-emptive strike against IC. The problem was that this would not prevent destruction of one of the 'infidel' western cities.

Oil prices and gold prices had tripled that morning and trading had been suspended on the major Western Exchanges as panic started to set in. 'Cyber Monday' – the next Monday after Black Friday - was being declared a Bank Holiday in most countries. It was hoped that the extra day would allow the markets to stabilise while the politicians worked out a more considered response to the announcement from IC.

*

Paris Plotting

Tariq Saqqaf had stopped in the service station on the A6 road to Paris, just outside the ring road. It was just after 5 am. The air was cold and the overnight rain had cleared. The wind blew the last of the autumn leaves into heaps against the wheels of his truck. He went to the washroom. His carryall was collected, as arranged, by a man he did not know.

Saqqaf was found two hours later. He had been pushed under his parked truck. There was a deep knife wound in his back. The knife – not found at the scene - had penetrated his heart. The dead late-autumn leaves had piled up around him in the cold early morning wind.

An experienced police team would have been able to review the service station interior video footage and recognize that the bag had changed hands, but there was simply too much data and not enough resources.

The package of semtex was moved into a lock-up garage near the La Courneuve *banlieu* just north of Paris. The *banlieu* – suburb – was a muslim ghetto.

The semtex was from the same batch that had been used on the *Queen Katherine*, purloined from one of Ghadaffi's arsenals in 2014 after Libya had fallen apart. The final package brought the total amount up to 500 kilos – half a tonne.

*

Chinese Tracking

The Chinese were twenty four hours ahead of the 'Six' team and GCHQ. In the 'Northern Wind' ops room deep under the Guoanbu building outside Wuhan, the team's data mining specialists had located and tracked the specialized cryogenics units and deep vacuum pumps which would be required for the North Korean design to be implemented by Iran – or whoever else possessed it.

At the meeting, NW1 spoke first.

"What have you found?"

NW7 - the data miner - read from his tablet.

"Seven of the cryogenics units had been ordered in the previous twelve months, and all were accounted for, bar two. One had been shipped from the manufacturer in Frankfurt, Germany, to the Department of Physics at the University of Algiers. The order on file at the makers appeared to be genuine, but hacking of the University records showed that it had not been officially ordered - or physically received, although it had been paid for. Back tracking of the payments led ultimately, via several accounts (now closed), to an Iranian bank. The other unit had been shipped to the Department of Physics at The Badji Mokhtar University – that's in Annaba, Algeria. No official order, no receipt and a similar payment history."

"Is that all?"

"No, there's more. The story is similar for two deep vacuum pumps which had been shipped from the manufacturer in Toulouse, France to the University of Algiers, Algeria – and the Department of Physics, again, Badji Mokhtar University, Annaba. Ordered and paid for, but not received. The orders did not come from the university. We tracked the header metadata of the orders and they came through the TOR II network. A dead end – although we are still trying to trace them."

NW1 looked at his team.

"Is this all you have? You need to come up with some better ideas – quickly, or you will be shovelling pig dung in the Tien Shan. What about the lasers - we have intelligence from

Pyongyang that North Korea has been buying Krypton Fluoride lasers."

There were blank faces all round. Although it was not the Chinese way to make direct eye contact, NW1 stared hard at each of them in turn. All eyes were averted.

NW2 broke the silence.

"We will get on to it right away, Comrade."

NW1 left the room without further comment.

.*

London on the Track

Ogilvy and 'C' sat at the conference table with Jonathan Tweedy on video link from Aldermaston. 'C' spoke.

"Good morning, Director. We need to establish in pretty short order how we can trace any components used in this device so that we can find it. What can you suggest?"

"Well, Sir John, at this time we still have no idea of the design of this new device, so specifying components is almost impossible. However, we would expect radioactivity. Deuterium and tritium would be used, perhaps uranium 235 and plutonium – but that would probably be shielded. The deuterium and tritium would be in relatively small quantities. Uranium 235 and plutonium are, in general, tracked worldwide and accounted for, except in some states such as Israel, North Korea, Iran, India, Pakistan and perhaps South Africa."

"That's a lot of unknowns."

"Certainly, the anti-nuclear proliferation treaties are not really worth the paper that they are written on.

Anyway, if it's a conventional fusion bomb design then the fast electrical switches - such as krytrons - used for the detonation are one obvious route, but these are on a regulated list in the US and other western countries. They require special export licences and are very carefully tracked - even India and Pakistan cannot make their own – at least, that is what we think.

There are exotic alloys and other doping materials which might be used, but again, I would expect these to be tracked as a matter of course by a variety of agencies. That's not to say that the tracking is perfect or that it cannot be circumvented, but it would probably have shown up by now. However, India and Pakistan circumvented the procedures, so it's by no means watertight. Sources are few and very closely monitored. End user certificates are needed."

"We all know how those can be fixed."

"Metals and ores are a bit different to a case of bazookas."

"We need to be sure."

"And I need you to focus on the higher probabilities."

"Such as?"

"You tell me."

"Very well. One avenue to look at – and even this is highly speculative – is high power lasers, cryogenic equipment and deep vacuum pumps. The type that *might* – and I stress *might* – be required would only be available from two or three suppliers worldwide. Most of the items are custom built anyway and capable of attaining very low temperatures and very high vacuum. I can send you a list of typical specifications and suppliers, if you wish."

"Do so, immediately."

"It should be with you in a couple of hours. Apart from that there is NBC – that's nuclear, biological and chemical protection equipment - remote handling devices and specialized machine tools for shaping these materials. However, these are much more widely available and used in many countries worldwide."

"Anything else?"

"We're continuing to brainstorm the issue, but as of now, nothing more to add. It's all a bit thin, I'm afraid."

"Right Director. Thank you for your time."

"We're putting everything we've got into solving this, you know."

"Well you need to harden it up – and quickly too! Goodbye."

Tweedy's image disappeared.

"Bloody academics! How he got that post I'll never know."

Ogilvy ignored the comment. "I'll get a team onto this right away, Sir."

"The sooner the better. Sit on Tweedy till he comes up with something more. Push him hard. I'm sure he wants this as much as we do – he sees bigger budgets and new research avenues opening up. He just doesn't see the urgency."

*

G20 Progress

The G20 taskforce set up by the UN Security Council was undertaking the huge task of analysing the possible IC targets worldwide. After The Sword of Allah Announcement, the arrogance of the Security Council had become clear to all. They recognized reality and widened the involvement of other countries.

The UK activity was typical of what was being done by most 'Christian' countries. China played its part too, although the country's secret concerns were of a different flavour.

The basic search assumptions were critical and revolved around non-portability of the weapon and a fixed installation with a minimum ground footprint of 400 square meters, with plans submitted to authorities within the previous twelve months.

Of course, this approach would be unable to detect those projects which were illegal or uninspected. In reality it made no difference. The site which ICIM had selected had been properly designed and construction had been approved as compliant by three different buildings inspectors at the various inspection stages. The inspectors had been heavily bribed or threatened, and after issuing appropriate construction stage approvals one had died in a car accident. Another had fallen in front of a train. The third had decided to retire early and visit relatives in Canada. It was noted as unusual, but there were no apparently suspicious circumstances.

The UK had identified almost sixty targets of significance. A target of significance was defined as a circle of five miles around a central location which was of religious, cultural, political or economic importance. A given circle could include many targets - for example in Paris, Rome or Washington.

Building plans and building inspectors' reports were being analysed for all ground-breaking construction and renovation activities taking place in the previous twelve months. It was a huge task, being repeated across the EU, the US, Canada and Russia.

It was more easily undertaken in some countries than others. Most modern building plans had been prepared using specialized computer-aided design software and custom search programs were quickly cobbled together. These could be used to filter those construction plans which did not meet specific parameters – for example any with a single phase electricity supply were excluded.

These were cross correlated with other factors, such as the number and type of contracting firms used for the project. Of necessity the filters were coarse, and even in the UK over 10,000 building projects warranted detailed examination.

There had been considerable argument about the assumptions – the cost of error would be huge. Most informed observers thought that the task was a waste of time, but had to be done – and quickly.

Informed participants believed that the idea of installing a complex weapon in a city building was practically impossible anyway.

The alternative, which Jonathan Tweedy of the AWE had suggested – that of using ships to carry the weapons – was also given close examination. The fleet of international merchant ships totals some 50,400 (2015). Each of those ships has a unique identification number – its IMO number (IMO is the International Maritime Organisation). This system is agreed by international treaty to minimise theft and piracy. It excludes naval vessels.

Ocean-going merchant ships are easily tracked – many actually supply this information automatically for insurance, trade and customs purposes, as well as to avoid collision with other vessels. They are also easily monitored by satellite.

An analyst pointed out that the Announcement had said 'nuclear weapons in place in several infidel cities'. This had led to debate about whether such a claim could be deliberately misleading and this line of investigation was eventually given a lower priority.

A special UN coordination team had been set up, but trying to agree on protocols, command structure and communications was, as usual in these matters, getting bogged down. There was some intelligence pooling, but what got into the pool was very limited by the self-interest of the key players. In other words, business and bureaucracy continued as usual.

*

No Negotiation

Ben-Zhair and the Inner Council of the ICIM had considered the consequences of the Announcement, at length. They had been unable to reach consensus on what the West's response would be. Under such a level of threat it would be expected that each country would seek to make its own arrangements for self-preservation, but all approaches were ignored, whatever channels they were made through.

With the realisation that there would be no diplomatic engagement, then it was expected that joint military action would be threatened, probably by NATO. However, some countries would not wish to be seen as a part of the threat and might disavow military action in the hope that such disavowal would 'get them off the hook'.

In the context this was irrelevant and would not affect targeting of the Sword of Allah. The target (and back-up) had been defined more than eighteen months previously.

The obvious actions were taken by members of the international community so that the voting public in each country could be convinced that their own government was doing everything possible to protect its citizens.

So, the United Nations passed a motion condemning the announcement made by IC as being a war crime in the level of threat and the targeting it threatened – the first time a threat had been said to be a war crime in itself. It further stated that if the so-called Islamic Caliphate wished to be considered as a state and a potential member of the UN, then it should start to behave like a state and start to follow diplomatic norms and protocols.

After much debate and a week after the Announcement became public, NATO said that all its members stood united and that it reserved the right to take pre-emptive action unless the so-called IC withdrew its threat and entered into meaningful negotiations before the deadline expired on 20th December. NATO further reserved the right to target any centres of IC government,

This last statement about targeting had taken many days to hammer out because the likelihood of high collateral damage – that is, many civilian deaths – and mostly innocent civilians at that – were likely. This in itself could be tantamount to a war crime.

The European Union issued an anodyne and pointless statement about 'working together to focus on common ground and eliminate differences of understanding in the hope that conflict and innocent deaths could be avoided".

Then on 10th December, Greece, France, Italy, Spain and Portugal publicly stated that they were prepared to enter into individual negotiation with the IC in an effort to protect their citizens and their cultural heritage. This was arguably contrary to the NATO treaty. These announcements caused uproar in the media and in diplomatic circles as NATO and the EU started to fracture internally. There had obviously been coordination between these southern European countries outside of the EU context, but their citizens could be assured that they were doing everything possible to ensure their protection, EU or not.

There was no reaction at all from the Islamic Caliphate. Ben-Zhair watched events with considerable amusement – and no surprise.

*

Site Meeting

"You are sure that we are safe?"

"Positive, Almahdi. The vault shielding is more than adequate. The monitors are showing less than 3% above background radiation. No one could suspect it – not even from outside the vault door."

"I'm worried about me first."

"As am I, but look..."

Jafa Sharifi pulled a plastic badge out of his pocket.

"This is my personal dosimeter. You see – I have not come anywhere near serious exposure in the weeks I have been here."

"Good. How confident are you that the 'Sword of Allah' will work?"

"My calculations show better than 90%, *Insha'Allah*, although this device has obviously not been tested. The vacuum chamber and cryogenic unit are all working well. We have the fuel pellet loaded and it is still within the radioactivity and temperature tolerances we require. All preassembled at the villa, as planned."

"Good. The assembly workers are buried at the villa."

"They were well over safe exposure limits and a danger to others. They were becoming ill. We did not have enough NBC equipment. They could not have passed through an airport without detection."

"Yes, Jafa, they would have been a security risk anyway. They have served Allah well – may He be praised."

"They are martyrs, certainly. Forgive me, Almahdi, but my lead technicians are asking about their wives."

"All taken care of. They are martyrs. We will all have new wives when we get to Morocco – it is being arranged at this very moment. A change of woman is good every once in a while."

"It is fortunate that there were no children, Almahdi."

"Yes, Jafa, fortunate indeed. Perhaps that was God's plan."

Jafa nodded, unaware that it had not been good fortune, just simple administration of drugs.

"Now, the other components we have, in Yanbu, what is their status Jafa?"

"Qasem Hamadani reports that they are in secure storage and stable, ready for installation, although he is only a soldier and not a scientist. He cannot truly know about such things. Nevertheless we are monitoring the container through our telemetry links to the control centre in Morocco, at Sidi Bel Abbès. The Saudis have no suspicions."

"Good. You and your team will go to Yanbu soon after you have deployed the 'Sword of Allah' to prepare for the final step in the Cause of All Causes."

"I look forward to it. Is there any news from Iran?"

"Only that Sistani is like a headless chicken. The head of NAJA has been replaced – Ashtari and his family have disappeared. I have no other news as all the important people are here with me."

Sharifi smiled and nodded in return but did not swallow the flattery. He knew that unless he was very careful he would not outlive the final weapon by many days. Still, that was nearly a year away.

"You are too kind, Almahdi."

Ben-Zhair was tiring of the religious nonsense, but he had to maintain the front at least until he had power and could quietly dispose of the stupid Imams. He saw himself as a ruler, and knew that even in the 21st century rulers had to use religion effectively to maintain power. It had been a masterstroke to name the weapon the Sword of Allah. Ben-Zhair knew the importance of symbolism and used it – religiously.

"You are sure that the radioactivity at the villa cannot be detected by satellite?"

"Yes. It is impossible, though it could be detected on the ground. But they would have to know about the farm first."

"That is not possible."

"Then we are secure. A yield of two kilotons you say?"

"A minimum – if the pellet ignites correctly. If we used the plutonium sparkplug then that would triple the yield, although it is only the small amount from our Islamic friends that we managed to hide from the UN inspectors in Iran – less than a kilo. It would flatten everything within a mile radius."

"Jafa, our target is less than half that from here - we have only one sparkplug, and we are keeping that for even greater things."

"I understand, Almahdi. I have used just enough plutonium to create contamination and a small yield increase. Just a 'sweetener', but it does increase the risk of detection."

"What is the risk of that?"

"Very small, barely above the natural background level on the street. I have checked."

"Good. *Insha'Allah*, this will be the greatest live event that the world has ever witnessed. The Sword of Allah will flatten the accursed city state. The infidels will never recover."

Abu ben-Zhair and Jafa Sharifi were drinking coffee in what would have been the staff cafeteria, three floors above Ground Zero. The main building work had been completed as far as was necessary and an opening ceremony was scheduled for January 2nd. To even the most knowledgeable observer, this was nothing more than a new bank branch, an apparent demonstration of Iran at last re-integrating into the regular commercial world. Less than ten people knew that is was a complete sham.

Jafa Sharifi continued: "The laser combining mirrors are mounted and aligned in the elevator shaft vacuum tubes. The heavy duty capacitors are in place. We have tested the krypton fluoride laser individually with the capacitors.

To store the energy to fire all the lasers at once will take over two weeks – any faster and there will be a brownout on the local power grid. That will raise questions. So, we started charging them last week - three weeks before Zero Hour. Then we only need to keep the charge topped up. We have tested all the components individually, isolated and checked all the circuits and done a complete end to end test, one laser at a time.

The control circuit is installed and has been tested. There are two control cards. You will receive the master card for arming when we weld the vault door and lock down the Ground

Zero installation for the infidel holiday, three days before Zero Hour."

"Good. And the control room?"

"As planned. Fully tested - inside a shipping container with a microwave link. It has to be within ten kilometres of Ground Zero – within that radius we can move it anywhere with the truck as long as it has a line of sight to this building. All video feeds have been tested as have the control circuits. The live video feed to the internet has been connected and tested. A good location for the control room would be overlooking the city from where we can provide a panoramic internet feed."

Sharifi opened up a Google map on his tablet and pointed. "I recommend this location, just inside the ring road. It's a park with a clear view across the airport and river to Ground Zero. You can see it from the roof here. Let me show you."

Sharifi led the way up the stairs to the rooftop exit. "The elevators have not been fitted. The shaft contains more important equipment."

Ben-Zhair agreed, although the mass of technical detail was beyond him, though the story was that the shaft contained 'leading edge energy recovery technology, and that it was healthy for staff to use stairs instead of elevators."

They walked out on to the narrow walkway about a meter wide between the tiled mansard roof and the low wall, six stories above the road.

Sharifi pointed to the north east. "There, just to the right of that office building. Here, sight along these antenna alignment marks."

Ben-Zhair stooped and sighted along the two screws protruding from the top of the wall around the roof. Behind him there was a small microwave dish mounted on an aluminium tripod.

"I see. Excellent."

"I have examined it. It is nine kilometres from here. There is parking in some trees and the microwave dish will be invisible from the access track. We have installed cameras at three other locations."

Ben-Zhair nodded. "There will be nobody about at that time, but just in case, there will be a security team with you."

"Will you not be there?"

"Of course I will."

"If there is a problem with the control room the weapon can be triggered manually through the ATM. The default firing delay is sixty minutes – enough time to get away on a scooter."

"I hope it does not come to that, *Insha'Allah*, but if it does, the honour will be yours, Jafa."

"*Insha'Allah*, it would be a great honour, but I am sure it will not come to that."

"Let us hope not."

Ben-Zhair watched Jafa's reaction and thought that he held his composure well, but he knew that Jafa was not cut out for martyrdom. He would need a backup plan – or someone to put steel in his spine. If not, he would have to put lead in his brain.

*

Paris

In the lock up near the La Courneuve *Banlieu*, Aabis Tawfiq congratulated Sawaab Nagi.

"You have done great work."

"Thank you. The registration numbers and the fleet numbers on the side match a Renault Traffic police van from the *Sixth Arondissement.* For sure it will pass on the night. You have the uniforms?"

"Yes, we have everything we need, including individual ID and weapons. I hope to have the final go-ahead in two days' time. All that then remains is assembling the device."

"Who will get the honour of detonating it?"

"That I will disclose on the day. We have two triggers connected to the detonator. A manual trigger and a timer – plus an anti-tamper trigger. They work independently. We are all honoured to be chosen for this."

"*Insha'Allah* this will hit them hard in the heart of their accursed religion."

"*Insha'Allah.* The team is ready. Have you recorded your testament?"

"Yes, it is done, I have given the file to Naadir."

"Good. Soon we will join our Brothers with Allah – may He be praised."

They left the lockup separately.

*

Early December

The coffees were on the table. Ogilvy had ordered trays of Danish pastries from the nearby artisan bakery. Food from the indoor caterer was indifferent but outside food always caused problems as it had to be scanned for bugs – and not for the vermin that might be typical of a caterer. Microbots were a real threat. This was a distinct treat and Ogilvy hoped that the sugar would help fire up some of the brightest synapses in the country.

"Right. Three hours sleep and the Danish – you should be firing on all cylinders. Let's hear your bright ideas." He scanned the tired faces, listened to the munching, watched the crumbs dropping.

"Ferries."

It was Afya again.

"We already looked at that. It's impossible to determine what was actually in a given shipping trailer. And the trailers from Tunis had destinations all over Europe. There are probably twenty thousand containers in the last month alone. We scanned all the shipping data we could locate – and those few which arrived in the UK have been opened and checked very carefully. Nothing stood out. So Afya, what's your new insight?"

"Well, there are a lot of ferry routes from North Africa – to Spain, France, Italy, even Greece. The main ferry line out of Tunis is Grimaldi. Their destinations from Tunis are Civitavecchia – that's very near Rome and Salerno – south of Rome. The Salerno ferry calls in Palermo. The next one is on Tuesday next week. The next Civitavecchia ferry sails this afternoon."

"There are commercial shippers too – freight only. What about them?"

"Well, my thinking is that any cargo that valuable would be accompanied by some sort of security, maybe subtle, but there would surely be a presence. The principals would want to keep it in sight. Containers on dedicated commercial freight lines do get misplaced in docks, and the transhipment procedure is much slower than just driving a trailer off a ferry."

"How do you know?"

"I spoke to Grimaldi earlier and booked a trailer from Tunis. It's scheduled on the three pm sailing today, direct to Civitavecchia."

Ogilvy stared at her, and the team sat up, hanging on her words.

"The driver would accompany it, and maybe a few guys as passengers."

"You need some sleep Afya."

"Hear me out, Sir."

"Very well, but get to the point."

"I'm a Muslim, as you all know. Christian history makes a big thing about the Crusades, but actually in Islamic historical tracts the Crusades do not have a very high profile. It is only the real fanatics who make a big deal about it. Read the stuff by Thomas Asbridge."

"Did you?"

"Of course Sir, two hours ago."

This woman would go far.

"Now, we know from the attack on the *Queen Katherine* that the Crusades play a big part in the minds of the planners. That is not typical mainstream Islamic thought."

"Except the radicals."

"Yes. We all saw the video and the statement from ICIM. Malta was the redoubt of the Knights of St. John *etcetera*. Therefore we need to factor in the Crusades to our target analysis."

"But what about London - the worldwide Anglican Church is based here?"

"Yes, but it was Rome which was the centre of the theological drive against Islam. Catholicism led the way. I think that Rome stands head and shoulders above any other target on our list, Sir, if you will excuse the terminology."

There was silence.

"Well, Afya, that's the most cogent argument I've heard in favour of any one target so far. And the shipping container?"

"I suggest we get our Tunis assets on that ferry to Civitavecchia today, to talk to the crew. Unfortunately we don't have any good pictures of ben-Zhair."

"True. And if they used the other ferry through Palermo to Salerno?"

"That ship is currently heading from Oran to Marseilles. We can talk to the crew - or the French DGSE or Tunisian security service can."

"No way. This stays with us. No Italians either. We have people who can pass for the DGSE. Get it organized – track down the Salerno ship, meet it in Marseilles. I'll deal with our Tunis assets and today's sailing."

"Any other new ideas?"

There was silence, but Ogilvy could feel that the mood was raised. The plates of Danish pastries were empty.

*

Ogilvy called 'C' and headed to one of the quiet rooms to explain that they had a break. 'C' was already there. Outside, it was another grey December afternoon in London. A winter gale was blowing from the west and the Thames was choppy, the sharp edge of the waves flattened by the cold driving rain. It was 3 p.m. and the street lights were already on, creating pools of light across the Embankment. It was a grim prospect. Inside, they were in an electronic cocoon, suspended physically and electronically from the outside.

"Before you start, I've just spoken to the PM. We're keeping quiet for now about Rome as the likely target. She's given us twenty four hours only. Then she speaks to the Italians and the US. That's midday UK time tomorrow. Still nothing on ben-Zhair or the other two?"

"The French say that Abdelkhader Maliani is in Nigeria trying to cement links with Boko Haram. They don't know where Mansour Bouyali is. They have some intel that he may be in Somalia with Al Shebbab, but they're not confident. I think he lacks the sophistication of ben-Zhair who studied for a Master's Degree in International Politics in Beijing. Bouyali is just a thug. We are focused on ben-Zhair – and it looks like he's on the move. We're trying to follow a tenuous trail and have a couple of agents on a ferry from Tunis to Civitavecchia, near Rome, at this moment. I'm flying our other assets from Tunis to Rome tonight – there's a bit of cleaning up to do. Tunis Station will be down to one only as we have lost a couple of people there."

"You're gambling on Rome then?"

"Yes. That's what the limited intel analysis tells us."

"Okay. Longer term my worry is that if they succeed with the Sword of Allah then someone with nous and strategic vision could weld all these people together. Then we'll see North Africa as a single political entity."

"It will never work. They are all too tribal. Arabs and Masai? Ethiopians and Ugandans? Never – just as it is impossible for the Iranians and the Arabs to work together – they are from different ethnic backgrounds."

"It's possible that Islam will over-ride their tribal differences – with the right leader."

Ogilvy looked at 'C' as if he was mad.

'C' looked back at him. His rueful smile betrayed his thoughts.

"OK, I know, Shia and Sunni will never see eye to eye. I'm just playing back some of the stupid ideas that are being floated by the PM's *special advisors*. The emphasis was heavy.

"Madness."

"Maybe, but it's a lever for us to get more resources."

"That's very cynical if I may say so, Sir."

"Whatever works, Alex. You've been in this game long enough to know that. Okay. So, we have a break you say?"

"Yes – of sorts. We have been monitoring the suppliers of the cryogenics, vacuum pump and laser suppliers. Also NBC gear – suits, breathers, scrubbers and the rest as Aldermaston recommended. One of the vacuum pump manufacturers received a request for spare nitrile 'O' rings – whatever they are - yesterday, to be shipped to Vienna, overnight courier, nine a.m. delivery. The email requesting the parts included the original equipment serial number. It matches a pump sent to the University of Algeria – one which never arrived."

"Vienna? That's not on our target list is it?"

"It is, but we think it is very low probability – and too obvious."

"Not if time is short. Vienna is what – a thousand kilometres from Rome?"

"Give or take, but there's precious little link with the Crusades. I looked it up - Duke Leopold V was at the siege of Acre, in 1191 or thereabouts. That's it."

"Hardly enough to warrant a nuke."

"Hardly."

"And the parts order itself?"

"Email. No backtrack possible. Onion Router squared."

"Payment trail?"

"Prepaid using Bitcoin."

"Bugger. Do we have anyone in Vienna?"

"Yes, but broke his leg skiing two days ago. Thin early snow, hit a rocky patch. No backup in place yet. I've got people in the air now from Berlin, but the courier's tracking data shows that the part was delivered two hours ago. We have the address."

"Traffic and security cameras?"

"None. A carefully chosen accommodation address, central Vienna."

"We should have picked this up sooner."

"Someone forgot to set a trigger on the site, so our malware did not pick it up. GCHQ tell me that the Chinese also have viral software on that supplier's system – which is how we found out about it."

"Shit. We can't afford errors like this - we'll have to take this up later. The bloody Chinese have malware everywhere. We'd better inform Austrian security so that they can chase down the detail on the shipment. We can try to get the Austrians to lock down the border."

"Already requested. We assume that the part has to be *en route* from Vienna to Rome. Too far to drive if it is a rush order. Probably another courier, though maybe a short drive in between to interrupt the data trail. "

"This doesn't sound like much of a break to me."

Ogilvy said nothing.

"Will Vienna keep the lid on this or share it with Europol?"

"We fed them a cock and bull story about the nitrile rings being used for illegal pharmaceutical manufacturing. Since we left the EU we have no formal links with Europol anyway."

"That sounds thin, but if it's all we've got, well, keep at it – the devil's in the detail and all that. Before you go, what's the latest on our contingency plans?"

"All stations on highest alert. Teams doubled up…"

"…except Vienna"

"Yes Sir. Mobile teams on standby at Northolt to provide additional backup. Plus Special Forces on standby in London and on *HMS Bulwark* – she's *en route* for Naples. *HMS Queen Elizabeth* and support ships are now on patrol in the Tyrrenhian Sea. The EU members are not keen to have our people running around on their land, even with this threat. It's even trickier now, post Brexit with visa complications. We have put some extra operatives into Paris, Berlin, Rome, Brussels, but we are thinly stretched now."

"Good. We desperately want that technology if we can get our hands on it first. The Yanks will be in there too, for sure. And if we can't get it then we have make sure no-one else gets it. I just had word that the US Sixth Fleet is being reinforced in the Eastern Med. The Israeli press is calling for an attack, although they don't seem to be agreed on a target."

"We have doubled up in Washington station, but if the device is in the US then we're unlikely to get a look-in. Here are the bullet points for your Cobra presentation."

Unusually, Ogilvy passed a handwritten sheet across the desk.

"Okay, thanks, keep this stuff off our systems – the PM is becoming very twitchy, even about Cobra. The PM will be up in arms. She's already raging after that radioactivity analysis about the Pakistani plutonium came in. The US has always been very sceptical about Pakistan, made worse by them hiding

Bin Laden. We're trying to keep the lid on it for the moment – I just hope that the Cousins can keep it away from Israel – and India, for that matter. God forbid they get hold of that intel."

Ogilvy sat and listened as 'C' unloaded his catalogue of woes. There was no-one else he could discuss this with – the position of Deputy Director was till open and Ogilvy was being lined up for it.

"The world is falling to pieces. The UN is in deadlock about what to do. China is threatening North Korea, but all the North Koreans do – metaphorically – is shrug. Japan is frantic, with the press calling for re-armament and scrapping their non-aggression treaties. Since that North Korean ballistic missile landed in their waters and the Emperor abdicated the whole area is boiling. The Israelis have recalled all Defence Force reserves. Central London is emptying and many hotels are closing until after the New Year. So much for the British stiff upper lip. The media is still behind our PM and saying that it's all a big bluff by IC, but God knows how long that editorial line will last.

The PM is refusing to move from Downing Street for Christmas, but I think we will at least get her to Chequers. Bloody fool. At least the Royal Family has gone to Sandringham. Jesus, only five days to Christmas."

"If that's their target date."

"Well it wasn't the Feast of the Immaculate Conception on the eighth."

"They did give us until the twentieth to accept their demands. So, only one day left – and then they could hit us any day. Christmas is only a guess, and they've only got to be lucky once. It was interesting to hear what the Foreign Office cooked as a response to the demands. I wasn't impressed with the early drafts - I think Munchetty is on her way out although the PM can't dump her now. Israel is making all sorts of threats about going it alone, and trying to get any concerted international agreement is impossible. As you know, our own attempts to contact IC have been fruitless. The Cousins are having no joy either. No one is. In short it's a fucking disaster. There's no way I can see that this is a bluff."

Ogilvy was startled by Sir John's expletive. Everyone was on the edge.

"Look, I've got to head for the bunker and brief Cobra. Just keep pushing, stay positive – there's an answer out there somewhere. Find it – and quickly. And don't make any plans for Christmas."

*

Six floors underground in Hainan, China, the Northern Wind team had uncovered the critical spare part shipment to Vienna, but their trail died there. They had not made the 'leap of faith' that Afya Hossein had made in London - and the British malware had locked them out of the spare parts data trail.

*

Final Announcement

Blue Angel Ops Room, SIS HQ, Vauxhall Cross, London

Ogilvy addressed the assembled team.

"I'll not stand in ceremony. I want to update you on our domestic arrangements.

Tomorrow you will report for work here at seven a.m. Bring your essentials in one bag for a week's stay. Transport will be provided to take you to our '*Blue Angel*' facility in Kent. You will work at that site until further notice. We will be in lockdown, living on site. You may tell your families and partners that you will be away on assignment for several weeks in the Home Counties, and will call them from time to time.

I shouldn't need to remind you that all details of that site are classified information. You are not alone. All teams in Vauxhall Cross are being dispersed to our out-of-town secure sites, starting later today.

This team is under particular pressure to produce results – witness the Announcement which was published a few hours ago. I need not remind you of the critical nature of this project – moving out from here is a very serious step. Any questions?"

There was a general shaking of heads. Faces were glum - the prospect of a remote Christmas and the New Year in a locked-down bunker was not cheering.

"Alright, then let's work through the so-called 'Final Announcement' It has been validated."

Their touchscreens displayed the text that ICIM had published worldwide that morning.

*

James Marinero

FINAL ANNOUNCEMENT

Issued by: Islamic Caliphate Operations Command
Dated: 20 Raby` al-Awwal 1440 A.H., 06:00 hours, Mecca time

Following our previous Announcement dated 24 Safar 1440 A.H., we note that our demands have not been met.

Therefore we will commence use of the Sword of Allah.

Nuclear weapons will be detonated in the centres of infidel cities. No warnings will be given.

There will be no negotiation. All diplomatic channels – and backchannels - are closed.

Signed: IC Operations Command

End

The meeting of the ICIM Inner Council had been fraught with argument, but ben-Zhair had eventually gained their full support. He had invoked the name of IC Operations Command, although he controlled only ICIM formally. It was a necessary risk. He noted two of the members were very shaky about the use of the weapon and he marked them down for close attention of the final kind.

There was no doubt that a major purge would be required if he was to proceed to the final step after the Sword of Allah was used. Then he would have total control, control of a level and scope undreamed of by the great conquerors of the past.

*

The Prime Minister's Director of Communications sighed in exasperation. He was no pushover and as tough with her as Bernard Ingham had been with Thatcher.

203

"Prime Minister, we just have to put out a statement. The media are clamouring, saying that the UN is a useless bunch of ditherers, the EU is worse than the WI – sorry Ma'am, that's a bit sexist."

"It certainly is! And don't call me Ma'am."

"Sorry, Prime Minister. The leader in the Times today is saying that since Brexit we have been unable to formulate a credible policy to deal with Islamist terrorism and now that the world is facing a catastrophe we are hiding behind the UN."

"I can read the bloody papers, thank you Nigel! I've seen the digest you sent me this morning. The media has the luxury of being able to pontificate about anything, but they don't have carry the responsibility."

"Yes, but…"

"Don't '*yes, but*' me!"

"Yes Prime Minister."

"And don't '*yes*' me either!"

"With the greatest of respect Prime Minister, somebody has to tell you how it is out there."

"I know, I know. Very well, draft something to the effect that we are working closely with our friends, allies and the rest of the world's peace-loving community to negate the threat to civilized order. We do not negotiate with terrorists, but efforts are underway – overtly and covertly – to eliminate this threat – if indeed it is credible."

"We did that last week, Prime Minister."

"Yes I remember, but harden it up a bit – making clear progress, intelligence operatives active in several locations in cooperation with our friends etc. Now we're out of the EU can we look again at bringing back the 'D' notice system?"

"I would strongly advise against that. Just the possibility of its re-introduction would surely get out and then the public would know that we have something to hide."

"But we don't have anything to hide."

"Then there is no need to re-introduce it."

"It's just that I think we need a bit more control over the media in these circumstances. Can we get the editors round to lunch?"

"We could, but we can't possibly invite them all. And then there is the web – sites like Guido Fawkes. They would run a mile – and damage you, for sure, possibly fatally – I mean in the political sense of course."

"Alright, let's put that aside for now."

"Very well. And the UN? You have a meeting scheduled with our Ambassador later this morning."

"UN Resolutions are a waste of time. There is no way that we can agree to these demands and the EU is in disarray since the southern members offered to agree terms with ICIM."

"I'm relying on Shami to come up with a sound policy that we can run with."

Nigel Ward rolled his eyes and took a deep breath.

"Yes Nigel, I know, don't say it. Not one of my better appointments."

"Yes Prime Minister, talent is severely limited."

"I'm going to call the US President and discuss their latest views, what progress if any they are making – and find out how close they are to the truth."

"Is there something I should know Prime Minister?"

"Nothing at all Nigel, you are fully briefed."

Ward had rarely seen the Prime Minister so touchy. The pressure was building.

*

Ground Zero, D-3

"So, we are fully operational again?"

"Yes, all critical parameters are at the required values, within tolerance. Temperatures, pressures, fuel pellet and sheath radioactivity, capacitor charge, laser alignment, mirror stability and reflectivity."

"You are sure about the pressure?"

"Absolutely. We had to change a seal in the vacuum pump, but the vacuum chamber is now down to the required level."

"It was difficult getting the replacement here at such short notice, but we have friends and brothers everywhere. What about the control unit?"

"We have tested it on location. All is well. The truck and control unit are now back in the warehouse. We will drive it back to the control site on the morning, three hours before the time that the Sword of Allah will swing at the infidels. We are ready to weld the vault door and lock down the site."

"Very well, you may give the order to seal the vault."

Jafa Sharifi dialled a number and spoke into the phone.

"It is done. The welder is at work – it will take about two hours to complete the weld. Our technicians are withdrawing. They will meet at the hotel. Only the welder remains. He will call when he has finished and we will inspect the work."

From the café across the road ben-Zhair and Sharifi watched their team come out of the Iranian bank building and drive away.

It was about ninety minutes later that the call came. They crossed the road and walked to the ATM in the windowless bank wall adjacent to the single entrance door.

The screen read:

The International Commercial Bank of Iran is sorry to announce that the facilities of this machine are currently unavailable. We apologise for any inconvenience caused.

'Why are you smiling, Almahdi?"

"I am smiling at the whole concept of the Bank. The world will think it is owned by those pigs in Iran, at least until we make our announcement. Sistani, that son of a whore in Teheran, will look a fool when the world discovers that the weapon was stolen from under his fat Persian arse."

"It is surely a touch of genius. The idea to hold an opening reception too, although I am surprised that the Iranian embassy here has not questioned it."

"Oh they have questioned it all right, but it looks genuine. The Bank has other branches in Europe. That was all arranged by Hashemi Firouzabadi, though he is in paradise now and will be unable to attend."

They laughed. "May I proceed, Almahdi?"

"Of course."

Sharifi inserted a bank card and keyed in a pin code, bringing up a master administration menu. He selected an option and keyed in another number, then extracted his card.

"The door control is enabled. You remember the numbers?"

"Yes. How could a good Muslim forget? The births of the Prophets Ibrahim, Ya'qub, Dawud. And the final one, the greatest. Muhammad. And I must use the accursed western calendar."

"Correct, without the minus sign for BC. Your turn."

They stepped to the side and ben-Zhair entered Ya'qub's year of birth into the door control pad. This man takes this religious stuff a bit too far, ben-Zhair thought, as the led flashed green and he pushed through the outer stainless steel door and then a second inner revolving door – of stainless steel.

Down in the basement, the welder was packing his gear. Ben-Zhair thought him to be a Libyan. An illegal immigrant, but part of the network, loyal and dependable. The weld was neat and still warm to the touch.

"A good job."

"Thank you. Though I haven't worked at a bank before, I think is unusual for a bank to weld its vault closed. Most people want to get in." He laughed.

Ben-Zhair pointed to the top of the vault door. "Is that a welding fault, just there?"

The welder turned to look at the door and ben-Zhair stepped swiftly behind him. His left hand clamped over the welder's mouth as his right hand drove the short knife into the base of the skull and wiggled it. Ben-Zhair stepped back quickly as the body dropped. There was little blood, and none on ben-Zhair. He turned to Sharifi, who had staggered back in surprise. "A leader must lead – and leave no loose ends."

Sharifi's complexion went white.

"Yes, for sure, Almahdi. A skilful job."

"And another martyr. One death – it is nothing compared to what the Sword of Allah will achieve. And you will make it work, Jafa!"

The magnitude of the project was now beginning to hit home, and Sharifi trembled at the thought.

He watched as ben-Zhair rifled the welder's pockets and found his keys as the body twitched and expired finally. He propped an envelope against the bottom of the door.

"What is that, Almahdi?"

"Just a message for the ungodly, Jafa. A message. The infidels may find it, and they may not – only Allah knows."

"You think that they will get in here?"

"Anything is possible. Satan is devious. Our enemies are hunting us now, for sure. But even if they get in here, they cannot stop it, can they?"

"No, Almahdi. Once we start the initiation sequence then there is nothing that can be done to stop it."

As they came out through the door, ben-Zhair nodded to Iqubal, one of his personal security team, who crossed the road and collected the welder's truck keys.

"No loose ends, Jafa, no loose ends. Come, let us finish the lockdown procedure." They moved to the ATM, ready to make the building impregnable.

Sharifi was wondering when he would be considered a loose end, but dismissed the troubling thought. His knowledge and skills were priceless, he was safe and as impregnable as the bank vault door. He held all the technical cards.

Paris

Ben-Zhair was not a gambler, but he understood probability in its broadest sense, and he understood politics.

The acts of obtaining and placing a nuclear bomb in the heart of an infidel city would in themselves bring great credit to ICIM – and attract many more faithful followers, strengthening the Caliphate and his own reputation. He would surely emerge from the shadows as the Leader recognized by all the factions. If the device failed to detonate and was discovered, then it was likely that the infidels would cover up the fact and make ICIM appear as idiots who promised everything and delivered nothing.

That is why the Paris bomb was so important. Failure in Rome – and there was a high probability of technical failure despite Jafa's calculations – would be masked by a success in Paris. Certainly, the Paris bomb was a dirty bomb – nuclear contaminants spread by conventional explosive - and the impact would not be as big as the attack on the *Queen Katherine*, but it would nevertheless be very significant. And if the two were to succeed? That was a dream of dreams for ben-Zhair.

Despite all the best communications intercept technology and decryption techniques, there is nothing that can break symbological communication. If two people agree a symbological code in advance it is impossible to decrypt the content, but it may be possible to infer the content from the results – in retrospect and usually too late. Certainly, longer messages and 'pieces of text' such as ancient Egyptian hieroglyphics can be 'decoded', particularly when they can be associated with events such as famines and floods. For the purposes of the everyday terrorist however, symbology works – provided that the symbology has been agreed in advance.

And so it did when the final call from ben-Zhair went from Rome to Paris and confirmed the go-ahead.

As the only person who knew of both devices, ben-Zhair was secure in the knowledge that any informer in a team would not know of the other device.

Assembly of the device in Paris went ahead.

*

Endgame

"'C', will you give us an update please?"

'C' glanced at the tablet in front of him, though he needed no prompting – he was living with the nightmare twenty four hours a day. Sleep was almost impossible – and it showed.

"Prime Minister, All. The trail is tenuous, but leads into Italy – that is the most probable option. All indications are that Rome is the target, although we do not dismiss Florence and Venice. Obviously, Rome and Christmas is hugely symbolic. We have four teams on the ground in Rome. They are physically quartering the city. We aim to walk every street within half a mile of a potential target. It is a huge assignment with only nine people available including some of our embassy staff – unaware of course of the true purpose though undoubtedly some will have guessed. Given the timing, we started at St. Peter's Square and are working outwards." He looked at his tablet. "I can see here as we check off the blocks. Nothing so far, and they are almost half a mile out now…"

"Prime Minister, I must protest." It was the Foreign Secretary. 'C' looked at her with irritation clear in his face, and continued, but she overrode him.

"This is madness! We will have a major incident if the Italians find out that we have a cowboy operation underway in the heart of their capital! Not only that, they can put far more bodies on the street and find this device – if it actually exists."

The PM raised his hand.

"We will deal with that if it happens, Foreign Secretary. Keep the lid on it. 'C', continue please."

"A few construction sites have been flagged and checked. We are attempting to get access to all recent building permits in Rome so that we can analyse them, but the systems in the Italian construction bureaucracy are a nightmare. They are easy to 'get into, shall we say, but poorly designed and organized along the lines of fiefdoms.

A similar quartering search is underway in London, Canterbury, York and Winchester, and the Home Secretary will be able to update us on that. We have helped the Home Office complete a review of the planning and construction data for those cities and it looks satisfactory.

Finally, in the light of the circumstances, we are moving our operations to our secure sites, at least until after the New Year. We would recommend that the Executive enacts existing plans for relocation in such emergencies. It should not be too obvious as it is Christmas after all. That's all for now. Thank you, Prime Minister."

The quartering search in Rome had started at 6 am that morning. Mary Pearce, from the trade section at the embassy, had been roped in to assist. The briefing was simple – look for any building or large vehicle that was remotely suspicious. It was assumed that a likely building would not be open for business as usual. They were each given pocket Geiger counters with unobtrusive earphones, and a specific mapping app had been loaded onto everyone's smartphone, logging the data and directing their walk. Cars, scooters, even cycles would move too quickly. Walking pace would be best. A trigger threshold was set at 3% above background radioactivity. It was a long shot. The people engaged in the survey had been told that they were gathering intelligence data on foreign agents radio transmission activity. The words Geiger counter and radiation were not mentioned during the briefing.

Mary was young, capable, enthusiastic and popular with her colleagues though some thought her flighty. Never short of a date, she ate out almost every night. One of her managers had invited her to accompany him to the opening of a new branch of an Iranian bank, on the 2nd January. As she walked down the Via dei Corridori she looked at the Iranian International Bank of Commerce and remembered the invitation. She smiled to herself and wondered what she would wear to the event. Perhaps she'd get a new outfit in the sales immediately after

Christmas. The manager was unmarried and would be a good catch, so a new outfit would be an investment. And she'd buy new underwear too – just in case.

In her pocket, the innocuous instrument spiked with a radiation count which was 2.6% above the nominal background level in the city. The data was being continuously logged and transmitted real time to a basement in the British embassy and uplinked through to AWE via satellite. Mary walked on, enjoying the cold early morning and the empty streets. By midday, the mapping was complete, and almost 200 miles of Rome's streets and alleyways had been walked.

"Foreign Secretary."

"Prime Minister, All, as you know the FO has been completely hamstrung by the policy of keeping almost all information to ourselves and not being able to discuss the latest developments with our closest European allies, so…"

"That's enough of the scene setting Shami, get on with it – we don't have time to waste!"

"Prime Minister, I must protest, I think that this is unacceptable! We cannot run British foreign policy in this way!"

"Right now I don't care what you think about our foreign policy stance. I have a country to protect. Your concern is noted, now just get on with it and give us the latest diplomatic feedback."

Munchetty sighed in acceptance – she could not win the argument with this woman.

"Very well, Prime Minister. We informed the Italians of our conclusions that Rome was a possible target, but that Venice and Florence were more likely. They say that they do not believe that it is possible. They are advising the Vatican, but expect that all Christmas arrangements will proceed as normal."

The Prime Minster held up her hand, and the Foreign Secretary paused.

"'C', are there any signs that they are taking any action?"

"No Prime Minister, although they are at the highest state of alert, in common with most European countries."

"Foreign Secretary, please continue."

"We are liaising closely with the P5, although they do not seem to have much to contribute – they are all looking inwards, except China of course."

"No surprises there then. Sorry, please continue."

"The G20 is pretty much the same."

"Have we had any feedback at all to the UN motion or the NATO announcement?"

"None at all. ICIM is completely disengaged, just as they threatened they would be."

"Hell, this really does not look like a bluff to me. They really are serious."

"We believe so, Prime Minister."

"Thank you Shami."

It was noted that the PM had used her given name a couple of times, and the experienced watchers around the table recognised that her stock was rising with the PM. She was doing a very difficult job in impossible circumstances – and the only likely outcome was extremely serious damage to the UK's diplomatic credibility if the truth became known to its allies.

"General Rushby, please update us on threat readiness."

"Prime Minister, All, the US Forces are at Defcon Two – they do not expect a conventional nuclear attack on the home territory, but the Homeland Security Advisory Service has the threat level at RED – SEVERE.

Most European states are at their highest threat levels with all police, emergency services and armed forces leave cancelled.

Here, we consider an attack very likely and that is why the threat level is 'CRITICAL'. That is the published level.

We have not changed any armed forces deployments in the Mediterranean since I last briefed you.

NATO has completed plans for a conventional retaliation, with nuclear options, but as we know, precise targeting is a major issue. These terrorists have a command structure dispersed amongst their subjugated populations and collateral damage will be huge – and by that I mean civilian casualties. That's the military aspect, but if I might just comment on the political – with a small 'p' – as it does impact our planning - we believe that if there is an atrocity of the magnitude threatened then the public will be strongly supportive of the highest level of retaliation irrespective of collateral damage. So, we are including those retaliation options."

"Thank you General. I see that you also watch the opinion polls. I have to close this meeting now. Thank you all. This is an extremely serious situation, the most serious we have faced in a generation – perhaps two. Despite the threat, the UK government will not disperse to secure locations. If we can get past New Year's Day then we should be in the clear – at least in the UK. Some critical departments will, however be dispersed. Ministers will continue to be visible in the media. Cobra meetings will continue as virtual meetings until the threat subsides.

I should wish you all a Merry Christmas, but I don't think that's appropriate in the circumstances. Our next meeting will be tomorrow, Christmas Day at the same time, unless, God forbid, there is an attack on us. "

The screens went blank.

*

Christmas Eve, 10.15 pm CET, Paris

The panel van of the *Police Nationale* – formerly the *Sûreté* – drove out of the lockup on the Avenue Louis Bleriot, near the railway line, and followed the D30 road on to the A86 across the canal. Then it picked up the A1 and headed south into the centre of Paris.

There were four men in the vehicle – two in the front and two in the rear with 500 kg of primed Semtex stacked and strapped down under a tarpaulin along with some other exotic materials. They were tense but confident. All were experienced *jihadis* and had variously fought with IC in Syria, Iraq, Libya and the Yemen several years before. They were ready for death, their videos were already with ben-Zhair's Paris controller and ready for publication. Their individual returns to France from the war zones had been very careful and taken some considerable time, staging through several countries and more than a few illegal border crossings and identities.

Three were native Frenchmen but only one was of straight European descent. The fourth man was Turkish and was of the third generation from the original *gastarbeiter* who had moved his family to Germany in the late 1950s. Their papers were genuine French passports – IC had sympathisers in the highest places in Western governments, such a great benefit of multiculturalism and post-colonial guilt. They were respected in their communities and apparent professions, now with stable families and middle-class lifestyles.

Aabis Tawfiq was driving. Traffic was light – it was well after 10 p.m. and most families were either at home, getting ready for Church or celebrating in the bars. The van moved through the 18th *Arondissement* towards the Seine.

Security was visibly increasing as they got closer to the heart of the city, but they were not stopped or challenged. The only logistical problem they had encountered was obtaining the correct model of H&K G36. There were many on the market, but only two of the version used by the *Groupes d'Intervention de la Police Nationale* were obtained. The other two G36 weapons were a close match, but distinguishable only to the trained eye. It should not matter.

"The traffic is light so we are running ahead of time. We will park and wait for fifteen minutes." Tawfiq turned into a side street near the Pompidou Centre and double parked, typical for a police vehicle. Some passers-by noticed the van and could see the four policemen inside, but few people took more than a glance. It was natural not to stare at policemen, especially in those dangerous days – and nights. They sat in silence, waiting patiently as tension built.

*

The van moved off and headed for the Pont Notre Dame.

"Three minutes. Radios on."

There was a little police chatter about a fight in a bar on the *Rue de Rivoli.*

"Two minutes."

They drove along the *Rue de la Cité* to approach Notre Dame Cathedral from the south west, passing two heavily armed policemen who acknowledged Tawiq's flash of headlights.

He turned left on to the Rue d'Arcole and flashed the headlights again. Two policemen moved the barrier aside and he drove on. At the northwest corner of Notre Dame Cathedral he drove on to the pavement and stopped.

"We are here. You know the plan. It is now fifteen minutes before midnight. I am setting the timer now for ten minutes after midnight. It will be Christmas Day and the infidels should be coming out. The anti-tamper device will be armed in two minutes. Take your positions and wait until the explosion, then take as many infidels as you can before you go to Allah - may He be praised. We will meet again in Heaven."

There was a quiet murmuring of 'Allah be praised'.

They climbed out. Tawfiq opened the rear doors and carefully checked that the small metal cashbox was in place on top of the high explosive. He plugged in the timer and gently pressed the arming button. A light came on and he exhaled slowly with relief. All was well. He was not in Heaven yet. He then locked the van and they split into pairs to head for the cathedral exits.

*

23:44 pm CET Christmas Eve, Paris

The van of the *Police Nationale* flashed its lights. Jean-Pierre Clotarde let his K&K SG36 hang by its shoulder strap as he moved the barrier to one side and let the police van through. He nodded to the driver who raised his hand in acknowledgement. He watched the van drive along the *Rue d'Arcole* and park on the pavement. The officers climbed out. One checked inside the rear door then they walked around the north tower and were lost to sight.

He replaced the barrier and walked across to his colleague, Henri Lascelles.

"Henri, did you scan the security tag on that van?"

"No, it looked genuine enough."

"Maybe I should just check. Call it in. I'm going to scan the tag."

"Okay."

Jean-Pierre headed off towards the van. Tawfiq and his team heard the radio call from Henri Lascelles to Despatch Control as Henri quoted the registration number of the van and was told to wait. Tawfiq cursed and released the safety catch on his weapon.

"Henri?"

"Here."

"I'm not picking up a security tag."

"Then back off. I'm waiting for Despatch to confirm it's ok."

"It looks genuine enough. Wait. I can see something on the floor in the rear."

"Ile Cité 3, Despatch here, come in."

"Despatch, Ile Cité 3."

"The police vehicle you wanted checked is currently near the Stade de France, I see its GPS location on my despatch screen. It has today's correct current security code. I have no vehicle showing at the coordinates you specified. Please confirm."

"Despatch, Ile Cité 3 code 9 Red NOW."

The blast took off Henri's limbs and pulped his internal organs. There was little left to bury. No trace remained of Jean-Pierre.

Then the screaming began and the shooting started as the ancient stonework of the Cathedral tumbled.

*

23.20 pm GMT, Christmas Eve, Blue Angel Ops Room, Kent

"'C', we're getting reports of an explosion and shooting at Notre Dame Cathedral in Paris during the Midnight Mass. Absolute carnage."

"I'm just watching France One now, about to call the PM."

"It might have been premature, the congregation was still inside the Cathedral."

"Unless they intended to bring it all crashing down!"

"Maybe. I'm trying to talk to the DGSE now, but…well, you can imagine. Most information is from the news channels."

"Any claims yet?"

"No, we're not hearing anything, we're monitoring all the usual sites, real time into Al-Jazeera's network, the dark web, Twitter."

"If it is ICIM they will be claiming it very soon. Casualties?"

"Too soon to tell, but half a dozen police and upwards of a hundred of the congregation. It looks like it hit the northwest corner of the cathedral – the North Tower is seriously damaged, but still standing."

"Quasimodo's Tower. They don't build them like that anymore. That probably saved lives."

"Any of our people?"

"None from Six. Sure to be some tourists in the service though."

"How did they get so close?"

"A police van. They think that there were four shooters dressed as members of the intervention force - all taken out now, although they think there could be others. Some reports of radioactivity. Our analysts are looking at the news pictures and saying it was conventional HE – but a lot of it. No simple bucolic fertilizer bomb."

"Small mercy. Sophisticated planning and logistics - it's got the prints of IC all over it. Radioactivity though – that's a real worry. Maybe a nuke gone wrong? Anyway, the Home Secretary is sending reserve police units to Westminster Abbey and Canterbury Cathedral."

"That's pointless."

"He's got to show that he's responding. Where next?"

"All roads lead to Rome."

"Still convinced?"

"Yes."

"Well we certainly didn't see Paris coming. So much for their state of emergency - years of it and still the attacks continue. I doubt that the Italians can do better."

"We're re-checking all our data. With a trawl that size something may have slipped through."

"What news from Langley?"

"Nothing. They are keeping very quiet, though we have noted they have increased personnel activity in Rome, Prague and Vienna – and of course, London – to be expected."

"Interesting. Dick Langella is not letting anything slip to me. Anyway, I've got to go and meet the PM now. I'll be hooked into our Blue Angel SMS feed."

*

Christmas Day

01:00 am GMT, Blue Angel Ops Room, Kent

Ogilvy called Tweedy who was spending Christmas at Aldermaston with most of his senior team.

"Jonathan, you've no doubt seen the news. I still think that Rome is at the top of the list. Paris was a diversion so that the Italians relax."

"It's certainly grim news from Paris."

"Have you had any more ideas?"

"Just a thin one."

"I don't care how thin it is. They're all thin. Tell me."

"The background radiation data we have for Rome is relatively poor as maps go - there is a lot of spatial variability and it's hard to separate that from natural variation with time. A quick walk is no good when radiation counts are low. We looked at the data your people collected with the trigger set at 3% above background. Background in Rome is about 0.25 microsieverts per hour. And the radiation counters that were used for the walkaround were very basic."

"Jonathan – where is this bloody double-dutch going? We're running out of time here. In case you'd forgotten, it's Christmas Day."

"Yes, well, the whole process just wasn't scientifically rigorous. There are many factors which influence the readings. We can...um… re-run the data with a lower trigger threshold level, but that might give us a lot of false positives."

"How many?"

"Depends where we set the threshold. Maybe hundreds. Still, we may be able to use a new statistical technique to dig deeper. It's all very iffy and not sufficiently rigorous. Too much noise in the data."

"For Christ's sake get on with it – it's all we've got right now."

"Very well, but it will take some time. We need to re-run repeatedly, lowering the threshold - to minimise false positives."

"You just said that, I got it the first bloody time. Can you overlay this on a map of Rome?"

"Certainly, to show the hotspots if there are any. A heatmap."

"How long will it take?"

"Three or four hours, maybe."

"Jesus Christ! Just get it done ASAP - a million lives may depend on *you*!" …and we don't want to lose the technology either…was unsaid.

Ogilvy cut the video link in frustration.

He checked the Blue Angel status screen. The operation news page was showing information from the DGSE. He opened the one report which was tagged for his security level and above. Radioactivity traces had been found at Notre Dame Cathedral and were being analysed. Intensity was low, but there was some risk to individuals. The NBC plan for the City was being executed.

He cursed as he answered the incoming call from 'C'.

"I've seen the feed. What's the latest?"

"You know as much as me then. Hang on, Sir. I'll just bring our NBC analyst into the call. Hugh – what can you tell us?"

"'C', Sir, my counterpart at DGSE has been looking at the preliminary on-site analysis. They think it's cobalt-60."

"Hang on, let me get AWE on the call."

"Jonathan, we have feedback from Paris. Cobalt-60"

"That's a relief."

"Why?"

"It's used – or was – in medical diagnostics and for commercial applications. It's dirty in the environment, but only has a half-life of 5 years."

"That's good?"

"Well, it depends on the quantity, but at least it's not a bomb, sounds like just a dirty weapon. Cobalt-60 is not natural – it has to be made in a nuclear reactor – or a fusion bomb. We should be able to trace where it came from, but it's fairly easily obtainable. In fact, in 2010 some cobalt-60 was found in two junk shops in Mumbai."

'C' shook his head in disbelief. "What do you have on the Rome survey data?"

"Nothing as yet. We're almost finished setting up the data for the next analysis run."

"Okay, let me know the instant you've got anything."

"Of course."

*

They made the gate at Tunis-Carthage airport with plenty of time to spare, after stringent security. There was no longer a proper bar in the departure lounge – alcohol had been withdrawn after the threats of IC in 2015 to target bars and tourist resorts.

"That fucking tosser, Maigret or whatever his name was. Telling me not to come back!"

"Don't worry about your boat. We'll keep an eye on her."

"She'll be stripped. The police know I was with you, and they'll find out that the 4x4 was at the scene."

"Maybe. We were out of there very quickly. They will be more concerned about finding the driver of the other car. Not only that, they don't know it was me who rented the car, so we're ok."

"Huh?"

"I'm not stupid enough to have used my Greek ID. What do you take me for – one of your Devonport dockside bimbos?"

"Ok, fair enough, sorry. I'm not used to relying on other people. Everything I have is tied up in Adèle."

"I'm not!"

Steve looked askance and smiled. Helena continued. "I understand. Anyway, change of subject. What happened to the *aperitif* and early dinner you promised."

He pointed to their fruit juice and their chicken sandwiches.

"You're not getting away with that."

"OK. Alitalia will probably have some pasta available."

"And not that either. Anyway, it will be late when we get in and we have to meet the Station people straight away."

"Why do they want us there?"

"They need all the help they can get. We're briefed in and more or less up to speed."

"Come off it, Ellie. You told me I was in this because of Maruška, because I spoke French and Arabic. I've never been to Rome and I don't speak Italian, so what's the angle?"

"I want you to hold my hand." She winked again.

"Not funny and you have a tic in your right eye. Answer the question - please."

Helena shrugged. "I'm not honestly sure. Our resources are severely stretched. You saw Jacob – clever, trained, but lacks the real experience – or he did, anyway. We have too many like him – Six has grown too fast.

If the device *is* in Rome, *if* we can locate it, we want to keep it to ourselves. We can't send the Hereford boys in – we have to do it discretely – and deniably."

"So I'm deniable?"

"Just as I am."

"I'm collecting the T-shirts."

She looked at her phone. "Meeting arrangements confirmed in Rome, 1.30 a.m. Christmas Day. We'll be met."

As they walked to the gate to have their passports checked, Helena nudged Steve's arm and he looked up at the large screen TV display, in Arabic.

"Looks like Paris, Steve. What does it say?"

"Bomb explosion at Notre Dame Cathedral, Paris. Hundreds dead."

*

The flight was on time – and full. There were no refreshments - it was just over an hour in the air. With only cabin baggage they were out through Arrivals at Fiumicino airport before 1 a.m., after a very careful inspection of their passports and landing cards.

The looked for the driver with the sign that said 'Mr & Mrs Douglas' and followed him out to the short term car park. He was plainly Italian, with a cigarette hanging out of his mouth, a black leather jacket and loafers. He looked like a very cheap gigolo.

"You were right about resources."

"Doesn't make you feel confident does it?"

He nodded and held the taxi rear door open for Helena, smiling as he did so.

Then with the car radio blaring mind-numbing disco music, he drove out from the car park.

"I'm known as Paulo. We're heading for a villa to the north of Rome. It's a temporary HQ for the next few days. We're keeping our key staff out of central Rome until the situation becomes clearer. The Ambassador has stayed though – orders from the Foreign Office."

He looked at them in the mirror as they looked at each other and laughed at his very Home Counties accent.

"Great act, er, Paulo…"

His eyes twinkled. "Whatever works, Mr and Mrs Douglas. I'm half Italian. We should be there in 20 minutes. One more thing – there's been a bomb explosion in Paris."

"We saw a news flash in Departure in Tunis just before we boarded."

"The latest we have from London is that it was conventional HE with a radioactive additive to make it dirty. Cobalt-60."

"Shit."

"Precisely. But the heat is still on here with a vengeance – we'll go straight in to a briefing – they are waiting for you."

*

02:00 a.m. CET, Christmas Day, Noel Ops Room, Villa Casalotti.

There had been a pile-up on the ring-road and it was almost 2 a.m. before the trio arrived at the villa in Casalotti. A guard opened the gate and Paulo stopped the car briefly and was then nodded through. Another guard at the front door conferred briefly with Paulo and checked their passports with a UV light. He then checked their hand luggage with a hand scanner.

They entered the villa.

Paulo asked them for their phones which he placed in a steel box in the entrance hallway as they placed their bags on a table. He then gave them each an ID tag on a strap to wear around their necks. Noel 12 and Noel 13.

Steve looked at his and whispered "Unlucky for some."

Helena glared back as Paulo put on his tag – Noel 5 - and showed them into the dining room. There were ten or eleven people seated on two sides of the ornate and highly polished mahogany dining table. All were wearing headsets. Jacob and Eli were already there and they nodded at Steve and Helena. There were a couple of other faces that Helena recognised and they acknowledged one another without smiling.

There were no tablets or computers in sight. The windows were very heavily draped and at the far end of the room was a stack of electronic equipment. There was a white noise generator hissing through speakers and a camera above a wall display at the other end of the room.

The three of them took the vacant seats.

A woman entered and the room hushed. She was in her mid-thirties, slight of build and very dark in complexion, with eyes which appeared to be black. Her black hair was worn swept back from an unusually high forehead. She was already wearing a headset.

"Right everyone. Merry Christmas. Now that's said, hopefully not for the last time, let's get on with business.

For the new arrivals, I'm known as Noel One. I'm the lead here of the Noel task force. I've just been speaking to London and updated them on progress here – which as you know has stalled. However, that is going to change. London will be providing us with a target list for us to re-check, based on the walkaround we did yesterday."

There was a groan.

"Yes, it's going to be a long day. Let's hope that we get through it in one piece.

This operation has to stay black until we are absolutely sure that there is no nuclear device here in Rome. If there is, then we want to secure the technology for the UK. That is, of course, after we have made it safe."

She looked carefully at each of the team.

"I can see that some of you are understandably nervous. We all knew when we signed up for our careers with Six that it could entail personal risk and danger.

Let me assure you that your primary objective is to *locate* a nuclear device. After that, there will be other specialists who are at present *en route*. We will then hand over to them.

We cannot be sure that we will locate a device even if there is one, but the latest intel is that Rome is the primary target and that Paris was an insurance policy for ICIM, although they haven't claimed it yet. Either way, Paris was a major blow by

ICIM or whoever, given the stringent security status in France. There will be huge political ramifications for Le Pen.

The latest I have is that the Paris device contained Cobalt-60 which is radioactive and commercially obtainable – for example by Universities and medical equipment manufacturers. On the positive side it was a basic HE device with some dirt thrown in and definitely not a fission or fusion device. It's been estimated at about a half tonne of HE.

What I'm hearing from all our channels in the Italian services is that the Italian Government is relaxing, although their security alert Level Two will continue in the absence of a direct attack. As of now, the Pope is insisting on going ahead with his Christmas blessing.

You can appreciate that this is an *extremely* delicate operation and you will have to have your wits about you. The Carabinieri will be out in huge strength, and the Italian army will be out in greater numbers than has been seen since one of *Il Duce's* parades in the 1940s.

If there's a Paris-type bomb here in Rome then I'm not worried about that – it will or will not happen and the Italians will clear up. However, we – HMG – are taking the threat of a viable nuclear device very seriously. We do think that any device as implied by ICIM announcements would have to be in a building or other large area – perhaps a disused metro line. There is solid intel to back up the claim ICIM made in their Announcement.

The G20 have been working through building projects in their major cities – a massive task that has thrown up nothing so far. All the P5 countries – plus a few others – have their own agendas. As far as we know the UK is the only country which has Rome still slotted as the prime target for use of a nuclear weapon. We do know that since March 2015 ISIS as it then was has been threatening the Pope and the Vatican very publicly.

London is still working on the walkaround survey data, and while we wait for their direction I want us to make sure that we are ready. Let's be clear – we want the technology of this device for the UK alone. Find the device and we may save many lives, but the public will never know.

Right, there's pizza and coffee coming in, and while we share it I want to throw the floor open for ideas, maybe ways in which we could infer the location of such a device.

So, let's eat and talk. By the way, 'uppers' are available if anyone is flagging."

Steve spoke first.

"I'm not really up to speed on international politics. I'm an ex-Royal Marine and have a pretty simple view of the world, so bear with me. Presumably I'm here for a reason?"

"London's orders."

"OK. First off, you just said that the Pope has been threatened. Correct me if I'm wrong, but he will be in public for the Christmas Blessing in St Peter's Square – at least, I think that's what you said?

So, the prime-time choice for time and position would be the Blessing. Lots of people to kill as well?"

There were nods around the table.

"I'm trying to think like they would think. It's not easy. What do we know about the way they operate?" Steve looked around the table. "Well?"

"Publicity and real time news feeds."

"High value targets."

"No negotiation."

"OK, let's start with real time newsfeeds. Where are their cameras, where's the data link to the cameras? That's my first point."

"Are we getting this ok?" Noel 1 spoke to a dark haired woman near the equipment rack. She nodded. "I'm tagging our data feed to Blue Angel ops back home. Carry on."

"Okay. Point two. What time is the Blessing?"

"It varies. For security reasons they do not publish a specific time."

"Right, therefore I cannot see that this would be a timed device. We don't know whether – if this is a nuclear weapon – it would be a suicide mission. I can't believe it would be, based on everything we've heard. They couldn't hide this in rucksack or under a puffa jacket. It seems to me that this is an absolutely unique event for ICIM and they would only have their experts' hands on it. Would the ICIM command want to lose their experts during the detonation? No way. The successful bomb-makers are among the most valuable assets that a terrorist organization has. Therefore there has to be a remote command link. Where's the datalink from command to device? How far away do they need to be? Is there a backup plan or link?

My final point is that if this is a nuclear device, these people would want to be outside the danger area in a command centre. They would want a good view – a panorama – to film and put out to the media – real time. A news camera in St Peter's Square would be vaporized. We need to see the bigger picture – as they do."

"Thank you for that contribution – I think we can all see why you are here. Right, you heard the man. How do we turn these ideas into action? Come on people, we need ideas."

*

01.30 am GMT, Christmas Day, Blue Angel Ops Room, Kent

"Jonathan, I've sent you a link to a meeting record, from our people in Rome."

"Right, I see it, just opening now."

"Given our assumptions about such a device, we need to know how we can prevent detonation – if we find it.

I've got people looking at the potential comms links as we speak.

What I need from you is ideas on defusing the device to prevent detonation. We've obviously got people from the armed forces that specialize in this area and they are on a plane to Rome right now, but we might not have enough time."

"Right. Generally speaking, whatever form the device takes – and I have not seen this one, even if it actually exists – physical distortion of the container would probably be enough. If there is an explosive driver such as with the conventional nuclear weapons we know, then damaging that physically would probably result in failure of the weapon. In basic terms, hitting it with a hammer would be enough, although if it's armed there *might* still be quite a large conventional explosion – depending on the design and how hardened the casing is. But with our MIRV warheads, they are hardened and can withstand considerable shock and the heat of re-entry or a high power laser weapon. You'd have to get inside the casing to physically disrupt the weapon.

In the case of this supposed ICIM weapon, if it's this new design, say, then it would be much more delicate – needing a lot of space and precise alignment of the lasers, mirrors and lenses. There would be a lot of vulnerabilities. Interrupting the laser paths would be enough, or simply damaging the mirrors. However, the mirrors and lasers are probably in a high vacuum containment system at very low temperatures – maybe stainless steel piping. Break the vacuum, damage the vacuum pumps, smash the cryogenic – that is the cooling - equipment.

Then, the lasers would as far as we know require a large power supply. That too would be a point of vulnerability. And then there is the *hohlraum* and fuel pellet - very delicate, again at low temperature and low pressure. And this is, presumably an early prototype so there would be other vulnerabilities, I'm sure. I'll give it some more thought, but my initial reaction is that if you can find the device then you can easily disrupt it – unless of course it's in a hardened container. I would guess that they are relying on stealth and would doubt that the system containment is, shall we say, weapons strength – but I could be entirely wrong. Frankly, a couple of hand grenades in the right place would have a good chance of succeeding – but don't hold me to that. One more thing – this device cannot be as small as a suitcase – and you can hold me to that."

"That's very useful. I'll get some people working on ideas so our people on the ground have some options and suitable tools and equipment."

"I'll let you know if anything else comes to mind. Now, I'd better get back to your heatmap."

Three minutes later the conversation was being replayed to the team on a BAE146 over Luxembourg, *en route* to Fiomucino airport outside Rome. The Italians would be very interested as to why a group of Englishmen were arriving in Rome so early on Christmas Day.

05.10 am GMT, Christmas Day, Blue Angel Ops Room, Kent

"Jonathan, at last. What news?"

"Alex. We've got a few radiation spikes that seem to be statistically significant. They are within the considerable limitations of the survey methodology, nevertheless I must advise caution. It's all very ropey."

"I already got that message, loud and clear."

"Yes, well, I've sent it through – your NBC man - Hugh is it? – he should have the data now."

"Good. Do you have any more on the Paris device?"

"Got to go." Ogilvy cut the line.

"Hugh!"

"Right here Sir. Look at this."

*

05.35 am CET, Noel Ops Room, Villa Casalotti

The last two hours had been spent preparing smartphone apps and radiation counters, and assembling equipment for breaking and entering, surveillance, even obtaining acetylene cutting gear. HMS *Bulwark* had anchored in the Bay of Naples to provide logistics support. *En route* she had put some gear ashore under cover of darkness near Civitavecchia. Two naval bomb disposal specialists had accompanied the equipment, although nuclear ordnance was not their speciality. Two panel vans stood in the Villa driveway, loaded ready. Several scooters had been 'borrowed' and stood ready for the team's use. Four cars stood ready. The owners would have a nasty surprise when the sun rose on Christmas morning – as would the owner of a sports shop specialising in mountaineering gear.

The team had been reconvened in the dining room, and Noel One addressed them.

"The specialist nuclear weapon defusing team from the UK is stuck in Zurich airport trying to rent a minibus to get in to Italy. All airports in Italy were closed at midnight and…"

"Lazy bastards!"

"I'll ignore that…and we don't know whether the DIS have got wind of something, so, if anything is going down in the next few hours then we're on our own – and we'll need to be extra sharp."

There was muttering around the table.

"OK, the boys from Bulwark are here with a load of gear. Designate them Noel Fourteen and Noel Fifteen." They held their hands up and responded. "Fourteen" and "Fifteen" in turn. Noel One nodded and continued.

"There's good news from London. They have narrowed down the possible locations using some sort of statistical analysis of the data we collected yesterday and an assumption that the target is the Pope – and timed to hit his Blessing in St Peter's Square today.

This all highly speculative stuff. Half a mile is thought to be the likely kill radius of the putative device and we have three radiation hotspots within half a mile of St Peter's Square, but they could be false positives. The next hotspots are more than a mile out – and there are four of those. One appears to be a University laboratory – radiation might be expected but we need to check it anyway – apparently these new counters can discriminate between the various types. It seems a hotspot could even be faulty equipment for surveying railway lines. What we need to do is check them all out in a bit more depth – radiation counts, nature of the buildings or environs.

Keep your wits about you and look for anything that is in any way out of the ordinary. You'll need to be at your assigned location for at least fifteen minutes to establish an accurate – if any – radiation count. Follow the smartphone app instructions when you get to the location – it will steer you as it logs the data – if any. Pictures as well – yes it will be dark, so watch out for carabinieri and act up as lovers – straight, gay whatever it takes. The data will be fed in here real time and straight on to London – or wherever they are hiding for the day."

There was a laugh as the mood lightened.

"Seriously, the Italian police are likely to be *very* watchful and suspicious. There again, they might have had a glass or two – there's no knowing, but they do tend to shoot first. Your tasking should be coming through now on your smartphones – and I shouldn't need to remind you to keep them on silent with your earbuds in. You should not be in any personal danger from radiation – we are talking background levels here, but just to be on the safe side, wear the dosage tags on the table in front of you, but keep them out of sight. Good luck. I expect us all back here in ninety minutes for a review. Any questions?"

"Why me and the police uniform?"

"It's the only one we could get and you are the best fit, Ten. It's your Italian paunch."

"Very funny."

"Any other complaints?" He looked around, but there was a uniform shaking of heads as the teams checked their tasking and headed for the transport.

"Ok, then get to it folks."

"Looks like we're paired up Steve."

"It works for me, but I wish you were on a plane out of here."

"Thanks for the sentiment, I feel likewise about you. You didn't ask for this crap."

"You're bloody right about that! Can you drive a scooter?"

"That's a stupid question to ask a Greek waitress! Come on, let's go. We're headed for one of the outer hotspots."

07.05 am CET, La Cinquina Bufalotta, Rome

The truck and articulated trailer rolled into the Parco dell Sabine. The sides of the truck were emblazoned with bright colours, pictures of trapeze artists, wild animals, jugglers and clowns.

The words 'Fratelli Baldacci – Circo Straordinario' stood out in bold rainbow colours.

Posters had been pasted on the sides announcing a 'New Year Circus – One Week Only!'

This was, apparently, the advance publication trailer.

Sharifi checked the position of the truck while his team pulled bush cuttings across the access track to the control site. The power generator started up and the team set about aligning the satellite dish and confirming the uplink status. The microwave antenna was adjusted so that it pointed directly across the Aeroporto di Roma -Urbe and the city, directly at its partner dish on the roof of the Iranian International Bank of Commerce on Via dei Corridori. When the signal was maximised, Sharifi announced his satisfaction with the alignment, locked the antenna and final system testing commenced.

08.30 a.m. CET, Christmas Day, Noel Ops Room, Villa Casalotti

Noel One addressed the team. "So, in summary, we have two possibles. I've discussed them with London and we are not going to focus in depth on the University site for the moment. Despite the many positive aspects – including the advanced physics department, we think that it is just too far from the Vatican – if indeed that is the target. We do need to keep our options open, so Noel Six and Seven - I want you to head out to the University now and monitor that hotspot, just in case. London is hacking their systems to find out more about the physics research programmes there. Get going."

Sunil Weeramantry and Bill Crosthwaite nodded, acknowledging the instruction and moved quickly out of the room.

The other possibility appears to be the Iranian International Bank of Commerce in the Via dei Corridori, just off St. Peter's Square."

"Christ Almighty!"

"Quite. It does seem a bit obvious. There is not much information available about it. It hasn't opened for business yet – the grand opening is in ten days' time. Apparently our Ambassador has been invited. Let's go. I will be in Mobile One with Sally - Noel Two, and Leo – Three, to coordinate events. Four, Five – you will have Mobile Three with all the equipment. The rest of the team will head out to Via dei Corridori and look at the Bank in more depth. An area this close to the Vatican is likely to be hot with Carabinieri, local police, plain clothes security - the works. Most of you will pose as DIS security people, but for those with poor Italian..." – he looked at Steve Baldwin "then you are tourists. Your cover documents are in front of you – e-IDs for those who are purportedly CISR people."

"Eight, Nine – you have Mobile Two – the Polizia van. You will put up the stealth drone two blocks out, up through the hole we've cut in the roof. It's got the location and building profiles downloaded already. Just launch and recover – it will return when its task is completed. Others – I want you to walk round the building, external security assessment, weak points – you know the score. You have the Google Earth images – they do not tell us much, but we can just make out what might be a microwave dish and a satellite dish.

If we are going in it will have to be subtle – we can't blow the doors off."

One looked around. No one laughed. The film 'The Italian Job' was unknown to most of them. Laughter was good for morale, but he wasn't having any luck. He shrugged and continued.

"We want the survey completed ASAP, but within the hour. London have tried to source the building plans for the bank, but it seems none exist. It's obvious that the original building frontage was retained, but we think everything behind that has been rebuilt. There were many contractors used in the refurb and it's proving difficult to assemble the details. Utility records are showing very high power usage over the last few weeks – strange for a building which is not yet in business. There do not appear to be any comms links at all into the building. There could be a private fibre optic link but GCHQ can find nothing. The red flags are really going up on this. Four, Five – be ready for recall into the primary target area. We have a tame Press helo available, designation Flying One. One of our guys is at the stick. We'll call him in if necessary. Hotspot One is in a flight exclusion zone, so our airborne options are limited. I think that's everything. Any questions?"

"Yes One, how are we going to stop this thing, even if we get in?"

"London is working on that right now. We hope that the bomb boys will be here in time – they are just through the tunnel and into Italy. We have a chartered helo picking them up about now. ETA three hours. Yes, I know, very tight. Yes, Eight?"

"What are we looking for with the drone?"

"Pictures initially, a live feed to London. The drone has a search pattern downloaded. Thirteen?"

"One, I suggest that we look closely at the antennae on the roof – probably microwave or laser linkage. Those links are *almost* impossible to detect outside the beam."

"OK, I'm sure London has thought of that, but it sounds like you know what to look for. When the drone goes up watch the feed on your tablet – it *might* save us some time. Noel Two will set the link up for you now. Is that all? Right, get going – you all know how important this is."

09.45 am CET, Sword of Allah Control, La Cinquina Bufalotta

In the control unit, nine kilometres from Ground Zero, Abu ben-Zhair, Jafa Sharifi and the technical team looked at the scene through the crudely cut slits in the side of the steel shipping container. At Zero Hour the shutters would be in place, and the scene would be viewed only through the cameras with filtered lenses. The inside had been sheathed in lead – only a thin layer, but deemed sufficient to absorb the expected radiation which would be fairly weak at this range.

"Ten a.m. We will now carry out our final checks." Sharifi consulted his tablet PC and looked at his technical team. As he worked through the checklist his team responded.

"Microwave link status?" – "Fully operational."

"Telemetry links?" - "Full bandwidth from Ground Zero, full bandwidth to MCC in Sid Bel Abbès. Channel hopping frequency fifty hertz, stable."

"Control circuit status?". Sharif answered this himself "Fully operational, ready for arming."

"Fuel pellet status?" - "Hohlraum temperature, stability, vacuum status and pellet radioactive emission confirmed satisfactory."

"Plutonium tracer?" - "Temperature, stability and radioactive emission confirmed within limits."

"Hydrogen Fuel Status?" - "Confirm temperature minus two eight four point three degrees K. Pressure within limits."

"Laser Combining Mirrors" – "All confirmed stable. No vibration."

"Laser alignment stability?" – "Steady, very low vibration well within tolerance. Krypton fluoride pressure stable. Pre-heating circuits operational."

"Laser temperatures?" - "All within tolerance. Number Seven close to tolerance limit. Drifting back towards optimal."

"Capacitor Charge status?"- "Fully charged. Number Three is zero point two percent below maximum. Eight hundred kilojoules available from capacitor bank. Within tolerance."

"Vacuum status?" - "Zero point five times ten to the minus twelve pascals. Within tolerance."

"Cameras?" - "All operational."

"Internet links?" - "Data rate maximum."

"Backup generator status?" - "Fully operational. Tested in the last 30 minutes."

"Well done, brothers. My software shows a 91.9% probability of success. That is as good as we can expect, but whether we will achieve ignition – and light up the hydrogen fuel - only Allah knows."

He turned to ben-Zhair and nodded. "Almahdi, all systems are operational.

Ben-Zhair stood up from his chair.

"Brothers, I have a few words to say. This has been a long and difficult road. You have worked hard. Many of our brothers have become martyrs helping us to get this far. You have all seen the news from Paris. That operation was a great success and was carried out by one of *my* teams in ICIM. The other attacks on France in the past – Charlie Hebdo, Bataclan, Nice, Lyons, Gare de L'Est – they were simple flea bites. Last night, Notre Dame was the bite of a wolf. We have not claimed it yet because there is the matter of the infidel Pope's Christmas Blessing. That will be the last that will come from that accursed church which killed so many of our ancestors. Dealing with that is your task, and I am sure that you will succeed.

Be sure that the world is now listening to us and be steadfast because there are even greater things for you to achieve – it is not yet your time to become martyrs.

For us, now, it is just a matter of waiting. We are ready to do Allah's work – may He be praised. Close the shutters."

There was a subdued chorus of 'Allah be praised'.

"Some of you may wish to pray. I will check the security perimeter and speak to our guards."

Ben-Zhair stepped outside. The morning was bright and clear. The overnight rain had cleared and he could smell the winter scents of the forest triggered by the rain and the low sun that was penetrating the olive trees. The view across to the Vatican was sharp, and there was no movement at the Aeroporto di Roma–Urbe. All flights had been stopped by the authorities as a precautionary measure. He turned on his tablet, linked by wifi to the control network and out into the world through the fibre-optic link from the bank. Using the cloned and sanitized Viber-like app, it was untraceable. His call was routed through several countries, having its metadata changed and finally linking through Afghanistan via an unmapped fibre-optic cable laid by IC to a unique communications server cluster. The conversation was brief, an approximate time given.

As the call ended he watched a fox slink through the bushes at the side of the trailer and mark its territory on a tree. He might have suspected but did not know with certainty that the fox was not the only hunter at work that morning. He smiled, then walked over and marked the tree himself.

Then he spoke to each of the six members of the security team. When he stepped back inside the trailer, he locked the door and motioned for silence.

"Brother *jihadis*, we do not know when the infidel Pope will appear on the balcony - they have not announced the exact time. It should be just before midday. Although the Sword of Allah will flatten the buildings and everything within one kilometre of ground zero, it would be best for our purposes if we detonate it when he is in plain view, in front of a worldwide audience. That will have maximum impact. So, we will have to detonate it from here when he appears. Has the Vatican released the advanced copy of the blessing text yet?"

"Not yet, but it has been issued to the press under embargo for release at eleven a.m. We obtained a copy. Here Almahdi. I have just downloaded it. They call it his *Urbi et Orbi* message."

"Good, let me read it. We must choose the best moment in the speech. Ah...here is rubbish about our brethren in Africa and Syria...Herods he calls us. Good, good, here is a mention of ICIM and also the Paris bomb last night... ah, here we are. That is perfect. I want the detonation to take place at the exact moment he ends the phrase 'Peace be with you'."

There were smiles and nods along the line of systems consoles.

"Jafa Sharifi, as Leader of The Islamic Caliphate in the Maghreb, I, Abu ben-Zhair, order you to arm The Sword of Allah."

There was a cheer.

Sharifi entered the arming code and put his thumb on the finger scanner.

"Almahdi, your thumbprint is also required."

Ben-Zhair stood next to Sharifi and placed his thumb on the second reader.

The words 'Sword of Allah Arming – Confirm Yes or No' showed on the screen.

Sharifi looked at ben-Zhair, who nodded.

"The Sword of Allah is armed, Almahdi. All that is required now is the final command sequence."

This time the cheer was loud and sustained.

The two gun shots were unmistakable. Outside.

Ben-Zhair pulled out a pistol from a holster behind his back and touched his throat mike. "What is happening Iqbal?"

"Two people walking with their dog. They are dead."

"What did they see?"

"Nothing, Almahdi. They did not pass our outer perimeter. We are hiding the bodies."

"And the dog?"

"It ran away."

"I see. Was there anyone else?"

"No, these were two old people. We will look for the car – we have the keys from the man – and conceal it."

"Good. Get it done quickly. They may be missed, but we should be clear within two or three hours – they have changed the timing of the Blessing."

"Of course. It is Allah's will for us to succeed."

The couple had been taking their grandson for a Christmas morning walk in the park to fly his new mini-drone before they returned to his parents' house to watch the Pope's Blessing and enjoy an Italian Christmas lunch.

The dog found the boy and whimpered. The six year old boy collected his drone and eventually located the concealed car. He had not been seen by the security team – but he had seen them and did not understand. His tears were silent. The car was locked. He took out his mobile phone.

*

The fine morning held its promise and warmed slowly. Ben-Zhair's Sword of Allah technical team watched through the video monitors as the crowds filled up the square. The view from cameras on the roof top of the bank at the western end of the Via dei Corridori was superb. The light was bright and the air clear. Officially said to hold 80,000 people, it was usual for the crowd in St Peter's Square to be nearer 100,000 for the Pope's Christmas Day Blessing when the weather was good.

The Christmas Eve news from Paris had shocked the Italian people. News sites across the political spectrum were more or less in tune with editorial opinion suggesting that ICIM had succeeded in Paris but their threat of full-on nuclear weapons had been shown to be a bluff. It was no more than a dirty bomb – conventional explosive spreading nuclear material – dangerous, but not catastrophic. Unfortunately the average Pierre in Paris or Giuseppe in Rome did not see it that way. Nuclear was nuclear. Period.

The Paris death toll continued to rise and was by 6 a.m. past one hundred and fifty. More than seven hundred people were undergoing treatment for radiation exposure, and five square kilometres around the Notre Dame Cathedral had been evacuated as a major incident plan was executed. The accidental early detonation and gothic strength of the cathedral had saved many more deaths.

For the religious faithful in Rome there was no doubt - if the Pope was going to show then that was good enough for them – after all, he was God's representative on Earth, wasn't he? His Christmas Day Blessing from the central loggia of Saint Peter's Basilica would go ahead as planned, but with a slight amendment – it would be sometime between 11 a.m. and 1 p.m. Usually scheduled for noon, the time window for the speech had been stretched – it was the one concession the Pope had made to his security advisors.

This lack of precise timing caused some consternation in the broadcasting networks, but there was plenty of infill with analysis of the Paris bombing. No claims had yet been made.

So, the souvenir sellers and cafés near St Peter's Square saw no difference in business to what they would expect on a normal - but unseasonably fine - Christmas morning before the Blessing.

There was some uncertainty as to the exact timing of the Blessing, but no matter, the faithful would arrive early and enjoy the atmosphere. In fact, it might even be warm enough for a gelato – ice cream would at least keep the children quiet during the wait. Waiting was good for business.

10.15 a.m. CET, Café Romano, Via dei Corridori

Steve and Helena were seated in a corner drinking coffee, listening to the radio chatter and looking at the tablet PC on the table. They had a clear view down towards St. Peter's Square.

"Great coffee."

"Yes, but it might be our last, so I'm really savouring it. You know, I once met a woman at a marina up in the Ionian. Argostoli I think it was. She and her husband had a beautiful Oyster – that's an expensive sailing yacht – must have been worth half a million quid, name of Lulu. Lulu was the boat, not her, but the description would fit her anyway. She was a lawyer in New York and they were over doing the Mediterranean, as you do. Anyway, I'm drinking Italian coffee, it's superb, and she stops by the table and says 'I can't wait to get back to New York and have a decent cup of coffee.' Go figure, as the Yanks would say."

Their earbuds crackled.

"Noel One, Eight here. The drone is up and going into the circuit. We have about ten minutes flight duration with the sigint pod and weaponry loaded."

"Roger that Eight. We have the datastream piping through now. It will do a couple of circuits above the roof and if it detects any radio emission will lock on, go into hover and monitor. Cheltenham confirm the link operational."

"Eight Standing by."

Steve and Helena watched the images in the tablet as the drone circled the Bank in the early morning light, just above the parapet, but too low to observe the satellite dish which was concealed behind a wall and aimed almost vertically.

Steve broke the silence.

"There's the microwave antenna – look just there. Yes, the drone has gone to hover and listen. It's right in the beam. That'll give the game away."

"Shit."

"Shit's right. Christmas morning and a Bank which has never opened for business. Now we've tipped off the opposition."

"Eight, One here. GCHQ confirming antenna activity – there's a lot of traffic through the antenna – forty channels they say. Encrypted - hard. Don't hold your breath they are saying.

"Blue Angel Ops are you online?"

"Blue Angel Ops here. 'C' has given go ahead for intrusive action, destroy the microwave dish."

"Noel One here. Order acknowledged."

Now the operation became much more than look and listen - they were attacking property on Italian territory.

"Right, Noel team we're going in to hit the aerial."

"Roger One. Eight here. We'll release the weapon over the antenna and then it's at your command. Confirm."

"Confirm. Drone program seven invoked."

The drone moved in towards the antenna. This was a stealth operation and big bangs were not on the cards. Less than a metre in diameter, the hi-lift drone's payload include five litres of battery acid ready for release, along with a remote controlled crawler with multi-tool to cut through the microwave guides feeding the aerial.

Steve looked at Helena. "Better pay for the coffee now – I have a funny feeling about all this technology."

*

"Jafa, we have a problem.

The two tone alarm warbled incessantly, penetrating everyone's consciousness, irritating, jolting everyone into concentration on their system dashboards.

Jafa rolled his chair back and scooted across to Sharif.

"What is it Sharif?"

"The microwave link is malfunctioning. It's intermittent, the signal level is weakening then normalizing."

"Probably one of those pigeons that they keep feeding. If so it will get cooked in that beam."

Ben-Zhair shouted. "Pigeons? By the Prophet, are you saying that a pigeon can stop the Sword of Allah?"

"No, Almahdi, I am sure it is temporary. I have taken precautions against such an event."

The alarm stopped.

"All clear now Jafa, the link is stable again. The signal strength is back to full power."

*

Blue Angel Ops Room, Kent

"Surely Alex, the Paris device can be argued to fit within the warning given in the IC announcement, but why haven't they claimed it yet?"

"There has to be more to come, Sir. If one device fails then they can still claim success. I think that we have yet to see the big one – and the Rome hotspot is looking like the site for it."

"Where are our nuclear bomb squad now?"

"Still two hours out from Rome."

"It's damned close."

"Only if they are targeting the Pope's Blessing, Sir."

"They must be – it seems obvious."

"Maybe, but we could be way off the mark."

"I know there are a hell of a lot of 'if's' in this, but somebody's got to make the call. Have you got any other ideas?"

"No, Sir. What we are doing is based on the analysis – however thin that may be."

"Well, it's not like going to war in Iraq. I've got to call the PM. I don't like the idea of egg on my face, but it would be much more preferable than being proved right."

"And then we'd still have the problem, Sir. We have a team at the hotspot now and a drone doing a rooftop survey."

"How will IC be controlling this?"

"Could be remote – just a phone code, but this would be too complex a weapon for that – just as a fully automatic timer would not be an option – at least, that's our informed guess. Much more likely to be a real time command link – even a wire."

Via dei Corridori, Rome

"Noel Eight, One here. What's happening? The video feed has gone. I'm seeing drone status 'inoperational'."

"Drone is down, One. I'm putting the camera on manual. Yes, I can see the problem. The antenna is about eight feet away. Hang on. Yes. The drone is snared in anti-pigeon netting. Sensors say it is inverted, motors off. We can't use any of the payload."

"Jesus Christ Eight! Put the backup drone up."

"We don't have another weapons pack, One."

Steve looked at Helen and shrugged.

"One, Thirteen here."

"Yes Thirteen."

"Get me up to a rooftop nearby – say within two or three blocks - with a good weapon and I'll take it out. The nearer the better. What have you got with a heavy load?"

"Hang on Thirteen, I'll find out. Noel Ten, you're the armourer, what's in the rack?"

"Thirteen, We have a Ruger Precision rifle here."

"OK One, that should do the job."

"Good. Ten, scout a suitable building, needs line of sight to the antenna."

"Roger One, just programming the search. Here we go - a few possibilities. Hotel Vaticana looks good, but they will have manned security for sure. Here, there's an insurance office block, Seguros Italiane, seven stories, I'm sending the coordinates now."

"Mobile One moving. Thirteen, meet us there."

Steve and Helena moved briskly for the scooters.

"Four, Five, prepare to move from the University."

"Four here. Roger that."

"Noel Three – look more closely at that antenna orientation – where is it pointing?"

"Roger One, just fixing the direction and elevation now from the video capture. Looks like a hillside about nine k across the city."

"Send the location vector to Noel Four."

"Done."

"Four, did you get that?"

"Yes, we're moving now. ETA – about ten thirty."

By the time Steve and Helena had arrived at the Generali Seguros Italiane building, Mobile One had parked up and was seeking and closing down the local CCTV feeds. Noel Ten was at the entrance with the alarm jammer and Jacob had the door open within seconds using the electronic lockpick. Ten re-appeared and handed a long case to Steve who ran across the lobby and up the stairs, with Helena close behind. Their earbuds gave them directions up to the top floor.

"Aghhh..." The door out on to the roof bounced Steve when he shouldered it.

Ten appeared behind them. "Hang on." He pumped the compact jack and the hydraulic arm burst the door away from its frame. Glass tinkled and crunched underfoot as they ran onto the rooftop.

Helena looked at her smartphone which locked on to the drone's transponder. She walked along the parapet wall.

"There. I can just make out the drone."

"Got it. We're a bit higher – that's good."

Steve had the case open and unfolded the stock of the weapon. He ran through the checks and fitted the hi-power scope and suppressor. Then he locked the magazine in place, stood up and looked around, appearing to sniff the air. He switched the gun to single shot and worked the bolt, chambering a round.

"Not much wind. The scope's laser says 200 yards. Right, let's get this done. Do we have any way of knowing if we do break the bugger?"

"Thirteen, One here. Our techs say they are still getting some backscatter signal from the sigint pod on the drone. It's weak, but detectable. Drone power is running out though."

"OK. One. Engaging target now."

The front of the twelve inch microwave antenna was covered with a mylar screen to keep birds, rain and snow off the central 'block' – the critical component which received and transmitted the microwaves to and from the dish itself. Steve could visualize the structure, but was guessing as he gently squeezed the trigger.

The first shot only hit the mylar cover a glancing blow but shattered it. The block remained intact. The next shot hit the block's support arm and knocked it out of alignment.

The third shot smashed the block.

"Thirteen. Backscatter signal has gone."

"One, I'll make sure anyway."

Steve had the range now. Three precision shots damaged the aluminium antenna mounting and it slowly toppled onto the roof, just as the drone control console blinked red in Mobile Two.

"Right, let's clear the scene and get back to the RV."

*

10.27 am CET, Sword of Allah Control, La Cinquina Bufalotta

The alarm was sounding incessantly. Sharif shouted.

"Jafa, the microwave link is down completely."

"Almahdi, we have a problem."

"What is it? What has gone wrong?"

"I don't know yet."

"Go to the backup system then."

"The only backup is the manual keycard at the ATM. I will turn one of our cameras to examine the antenna. That is all we can do unless we go down there. Wait - no, it's no good, the cameras are set to look out at St. Peter's Square. I cannot pan any of them enough to examine the antenna."

"Could the problem be at this end?"

Jafa looked at his comms lead technician who shook his head.

"Everything here is working as it should."

"So, we don't even know if we have power at the Bank?"

"We have power – the cameras are working."

"Then how are we getting the signal?"

"We are piggy-backed on to the city's CCTV network."

"Then point one of their cameras at the roof."

"They are too low down – they are for watching traffic and thieves."

"By all that is Holy. We have to go down there. We have no choice. Prepare to withdraw. Iqubal and Hossein will come with me. Jafa, come with me. The rest of the security team will travel with you. You know the contingency plan, where to dispose of the equipment and later the truck, before you reach Genoa."

Fifteen minutes later the truck was driving out of the park. The young boy had watched from the bushes while ben-Zhair's security team stripped the Circus signage off the truck and trailer and the technicians dismantled the microwave antenna.

His parents had received his call and were on their way to the park while a local police car headed out to investigate their report of two murders. Despite his tears the boy had the presence of mind to use his smartphone to take a picture of the truck as it left.

*

Half a mile down the road the truck passed a police car with lights flashing. The family's people carrier was not far behind. The boy's father was driving at speed, accompanied by his mother, two uncles and two aunts – plus a chuhuahua in a handbag.

The truck was headed for the autostrada and Genoa after dropping Iqbal, Jafa and ben-Zhair at the Mercedes SUV parked just down the road.

Fifteen minutes later the SUV pulled up at an auto mechanic's lockup in a dirty industrial road in the suburbs. The plastics factory opposite was closed for the holiday, and there was no sign of life at all. Hossein opened up and Ben-Zhair and Sharifi climbed on to a black Vespa scooter and pulled out.

"We meet at the Bank. You know the plan – you are to arrest us when I give the signal."

"*Aiwa, Almahdi.* May Allah protect you."

The scooter buzzed away as Iqubal drove the SUV into the lockup and pulled a tarpaulin off an Alfa Romeo saloon. It was highly polished, tuned up and in Carabinieri livery.

Iqubal and Hossein changed into Carabinieri uniforms and joked about the high leather boots, the jodhpurs and the white Sam Brownes. Dressed as such they could walk around openly with machine pistols in plain view and arrest people – or worse. Iqubal drove the car out as Hossein closed the lockup doors, then the tyres squealed as Iqubal floored the accelerator. Hossein switched on the blue lightbar and they headed for central Rome.

11 a.m. CET, Via dei Corridori

"Noel One. Four here."

"Go ahead Four."

"We're just approaching the coordinates we were given. We can see a local police car and some people gesticulating. We'll try to hook in to the police network and find out what's happening here."

"Copy that. Hold back, don't get caught up in it. Are you sure you're in the right place."

"Yes, we've checked. I'll talk to Three and re-check we got the right info."

"Three here. Yes, I can see from your trackers that you're in the right place – or at least on the right bearing."

"Six here – just listening to a police call for backup and scene of crime people. Two deaths – murder they say. Two pensioners. They have a witness – the couple's grandson. Something about a picture of a truck and a circus."

"Shit. OK, Six and Seven you monitor the situation there, keep us posted, pipe us a video clip if you can. If there's a picture, we need to hack a copy. Four, Five get down here –

Hotspot One, asap. This might have nothing to do with Blue Angel at all. The bad boys might be nearby, maybe a small error in the beam direction from here. Check around discreetly in case it's a coincidence."

"Roger that, One."

They all knew that the probability of this being a coincidence was close to zero.

*

11.10 am CET, Iranian International Bank of Commerce

Ben-Zhair watched from a seat in the café as Jafa Shafiri crossed the road to the ATM and started the manual arming process. Their scooter was parked nearby.

"Noel One, Twelve. Confirm a positive ID of ben-Zhair arriving with accomplice on a scooter. Designate targets One and Two."

"Noel One, Eight. Target Two walking to the cashpoint at the Bank. His mate has parked the scooter and gone to the Café Romana across the road.

"Roger. Mobile One approaching the bank ETA one minute. Noel team converge on targets, apprehend – no fuss, alive, load them straight into Mobile Two. Noel Twelve calls the shots, radio silence others."

"Target one now seated in the Café Romana.".

Steve's eyes met Helena's. "Ready then?" He nodded. "Always."

Ben-Zhair looked around. There were a couple of tourists on a bench – obviously engaged in a heavy discussion on this cold Christmas morning. Adulterers, obviously, else why would they be outside of their home or hotel? Wait, it seemed they had made up - they were smiling and holding hands.

There were a couple of other men in the café, one at the bar and another reading from his tablet PC. Something didn't feel right.

"Mobile One here, just approaching now. Have visual of target two at the ATM."

As ben-Zhair watched, the couple stood up and the men in the café started to move briskly towards him. A white van drove into sight obstructing his view of Jafa Sharifi, and stopped. Just then a Carabinieri patrol car pulled up and the two officers climbed out. They looked across at ben-Zhair.

"Shit! Noel team, this is One. Hold back. Carabinieri on site. Withdraw! Repeat, Withdraw!"

As Steve and Helena stood and started to move, Steve saw ben-Zhair look up then nod across at the Carabinieri.

There was a shout and the Carabinieri aimed their weapons at Sharifi.

It all happened so quickly, and then Mobile One made a u-turn, slowly.

"One, Thirteen – they are not Carabinieri – Target One is in contact with them."

"One, Eight, confirm that. Signal observed."

Sharifi was spread against the wall, then being handcuffed. Ben-Zhair stood up and walked across, apparently remonstrating with the Carabinieri. He too was pushed against the wall and handcuffed. The officers pushed them into the rear of the polizia car.

"Is it done?"

"Yes Almahdi, the Sword of Allah initiation sequence has started. Detonation cannot now be stopped."

"Then let us get out of this accursed city. We will see it all on television out at Ostia Antica."

"I always wanted to do this, Almahdi!" They jerked back in their seats as Iqubal pulled away sharply, down the Via dei Corridori and away from Ground Zero. The blue lights were flashing.

"Six, Seven, get on their tail. We're not reading any GPS transmission from the car, so it's definitely not the real deal."

"Copy that."

Two scooters buzzed away from their illegal parking spot.

"Almahdi, we are being followed."

"Lose them."

"But how can they know?"

"The devil has many ears, Jafa. He is everywhere – but he can do nothing now! Iqubal - we follow the backup plan and go to the café. We will watch the Blessing on the television. I am sure that today the prophet will allow us one beer."

"Yes Almahdi, but I would like to change out of these monkey clothes first."

"Of course, as planned."

"And I would like to get out of these handcuffs!"

"Yes, Jafa. Hussein, free our Chief Technician."

They laughed. Despite the setbacks, ben-Zhair's plans were holding together.

"Noel One. Seven. They are getting away from us."

"Blue Angel Ops, Noel One. We need any help you can get on that Carabinieri vehicle."

"Noel One, Blue Angel, Flying One is now in range."

"Noel One, Flying One. We have visual of the target vehicle just coming out of the flight exclusion area, we can follow. Silly buggers – it's the only one with the lights on. Hell, I spoke too soon. They've been turned off. Recording hi-def ident images now and tracking. I'll mark the roof."

The ultra-high definition camera on the pod under the helo was capable of resolving the details of an ant from a range of a mile, and as such its look-down images of the target police vehicle would provide exact identification down to scratches and imperfections in the paintwork – and the laser burn which the helo pod had painted on the car's roof.

"Flying One, Seven here - we have your feed, keep it coming."

"One, Twelve here. Target Two was using the ATM – the one that was out of order when we surveyed earlier. Here are my screenshots coming through now. It's in Arabic script."

Steve swore. "Thirteen here. I'm a bit rusty with written Arabic script – but it's not that. Anyone for Farsi, at a guess?

The numbers are the same – I can see a number. It looks like fifty three minutes and ten seconds – and it's counting down."

"Blue Angel Two here. I read oriental studies, never thought it would be any use. I'm seeing:

Sword of Allah
Detonation sequence initiated.
Default interval 60 minutes.
Time now 11:15 am. Time Remaining 0:53:10

Do you require another service?
Yes   No
Please retrieve your card.
Link Disconnected

"Shit Alex, where are the fucking bomb boys?"

"Noel One, Blue Angel One. About half an hour out. Maintain protocol."

"Copy that Blue Angel, sorry."

"Noel Team, Noel One here. Bomb boys are still half an hour out. Thirteen – get ready for entry. Four, are we ready yet?"

"Yes, waiting outside the *pensione.*"

"Oh fuck, here come the local rozzers. On your toes people. We don't have bloody time for this!"

The small blue Fiat cruised down the street and stopped outside the café. One of the policemen got out and went in, returning a couple of minutes later with two bottles of water.

"Four bloody minutes gone. Seven, status?"

Crosthwaite's gruff Yorkshire tones were clear. "One. Seven. Target vehicle is trying to lose us but Flying One is just feeding us the short cuts to keep up. Looks like the targets are heading for the Arab quarter."

"Ok, they may change vehicles. Stay sharp. Noel One standing by."

"Two, have you found us a suitable building yet?"

"Yes, One. There's a *pensione* in the street at the rear. Four stories plus the roof area."

"Thirteen, did you get that? Looks like we'll be using your idea after all."

"Copy that, One."

"Four, Five, Noel One here. Two is sending the address to you. Get going."

"One, Four, copy that, we're on our way."

11.20 CET Blue Angel Ops Room, Kent

"Yes, Prime Minister. That is correct. We have determined the location of the device. It is within half a mile of the Loggia at St Peter's Basilica where the Pope is about to give his Christmas Blessing. It is apparently armed and set to detonate in approximately forty five minutes – that is, five minutes after eleven, London time, when the Pope will be giving his Blessing – the precise timing is still uncertain – the time on the counter may be misleading. I cannot confirm that the device is nuclear, but I believe that is very likely. The timing is immaterial really, in or out, if this is what we think it is, then the Vatican will be flattened, along with half of Rome. Of course it could all still be a hoax – or our analysis could be wrong."

"What do you think?"

"The evidence suggests that there is a high probability of a viable device."

"And what exactly are you doing about it?"

"I am attempting to complete the mission you gave me, to obtain the technology by stealth, for the UK."

"No one ever thought it would come to this."

"With respect Prime Minister, one must be very careful what one wishes for. Beyond that, our nuclear bomb disposal experts are on their way there, but may, I fear, be too late arriving. We have a Six team on site now who are attempting to gain access to the device. They have been briefed on ways in which the device may be made inoperable."

"We have to tell the Italians."

"I am sure that the Foreign Secretary has planned for such an eventuality, but the political issues, thank goodness, are not mine to deal with."

"But the outcome will be yours to deal with, 'C'. Suggesting you were 'following orders' will not wash."

"Perhaps, Prime Minister, but the records will show what happened."

"Are you threatening me, 'C'?"

"Not at all, PM. I am here to protect the security of the UK, however that is to be done. Please excuse me - I must get back to my team."

"Wait. How long would it take, from this moment, to get the Pope away to safety?"

"I doubt that it could be done within thirty minutes, even if the Italians believed us. And then there are a hundred thousand people in the Square."

Silence.

"Hello, are you there Prime Minister?"

"Yes, I'm here. It's clearly too late. We will tell the Italians ten minutes before the *possible* detonation, along the lines that have already been agreed. Are we deniable?"

"Yes, PM, completely. The backstories are ready – a group of Islamic terrorists *etcetera*. Frankly, if goes off there will not be any traces to brush over – I will lose more than a dozen people from Six – plus people from the Navy and Aldermaston specialists."

"And I will lose British tourists and embassy staff. Hell, it's a terrifying thought, 'C'. Very well, I shall speak directly to Cobra, but I'm not telling them everything – I can't trust them all. Keep the line open."

"I'll be here Prime Minister. You will have access to the team's communications relayed real-time through to the Cobra members. We do intend to succeed, Prime Minister."

"I wish I had your faith 'C'."

"Yes Prime Minister, and the Pope's Christmas Blessing."

"And cut the feeds to Cobra."

"Of course Prime Minister, as you wish."

'C' turned off the memo app on his smartphone. It had been specially hardened against NFC and other narrow spectrum jamming – even that of the UK's jammers.

11.28 a.m. CET, A Pensione off the Via dei Corridori

"Mobile Two, are you there yet?"

"Just outside now. Four is working the plan. OK, she's calling us. We're going in."

After much banging of the *pensione* door, the old lady had opened it to see two members of the CISR – or so the ID said. Noel Four – Teresa McDougal – spoke Italian very well, albeit with a slight Glaswegian accent. She pointed to the blue Iveco panel van emblazoned with Polizia and pushed her way in, followed by Paulo - Noel Five.

"We are from *Comitato Interministeriale per la Sicurezza della Repubblica,* here is our ID."

"I have paid my taxes like a good citizen. We are closed for Christmas. Come back next week if you want to sleep with your lover."

"Shut up and listen to me old woman – we don't care about your taxes. This is a matter of State security. If you do not cooperate you and your family are going into that *polizia* van now and will be in prison until after the New Year. This is a counter-terrorism operation. There is a threat to the life of *il Papa*. It is highly secret. We don't have time to waste."

The old lady's eyes opened wide and she crossed herself. "Holy Mother of God, help Him."

"We will, and maybe the Holy Mother of God as well, but first we need your help. We will use your upper floors. Go back to the dining room, watch *il Papa's* Blessing on the TV and pray for him. Leave us alone and say nothing – or you and your family will be imprisoned for betraying State secrets. That money is compensation."

She had thought that the landlady's eyes would explode when she placed a bundle of €5,000 in €50 notes on the reception desk. "And it is tax free." The landlady grasped the bundle and waved them in, then bustled back to her family. She didn't believe in Father Christmas, but there was always a first time.

"Noel Team, One here. If we cannot get in to the building before eleven fifty then I am pulling you all out, so let's give it our best shot, shall we? We need to keep HMG clean on this."

11.29a.m. CET, Mobile One, Via dei Corridori

"Seven, One what's your status?"

"We've lost them, One. Flying One has no visual either. We're in the Arab quarter."

"OK keep at it. Flying one, keep scanning."

"Copy that, One. I have another fifty minutes fuel."

"Hang in there, team. The nuke bomb squad is about ten minutes away."

"About bloody time too."

"Pipe down, Nine, unless you've got something useful to say."

11.30 CET, St. Peter's Square

A huge cheer rang around the square as Pope Francis appeared on the Loggia, waving and smiling. He surely knew of the risk, and his Christmas message would once again attack the twisted interpretation of Islam that was prevalent and engaging the minds of the impressionable and mad, the disaffected and those with no hope in life, those who could only see war and terror as the way to improve their lot.

It was difficult for the Pontiff of such a wealthy worldwide organisation with its patent history of corruption – both moral and financial - to convince such people. He recognised reality, but still, he would be as persuasive as he could and the battle would continue as he reinforced the faith of his worldwide congregation.

He knew that many people loved him and what he stood for, but many more – too many more - felt the opposite way.

"Noel One, Flying One. We've lost the target vehicle in the Arab Market area. Continuing search with Six and Seven on the ground."

"Flying One, copy that."

11.31 a.m. CET, Pensione - Roof

"Noel Team, One here. The Pope has just appeared on the balcony of the loggia. Four, status please."

"We're up on the roof of the *pensione*. We have fired the piton into the wall of the Bank. It seems to be holding. We've put a few holes in the window opposite, but it's shatterproof. It's a hell of a swing – at least forty feet across on a line that's three stories long. Thirteen is about to launch."

"Thirteen, One. Are you sure about this?"

"Not really One, but it's what I was trained for. Is there an alternative?"

"Not in the time. Good luck."

"Thank God for the Marines."

"What was that, Four?"

"Nothing Sir, thinking aloud."

Steve attached the thin heaving line to his belt and checked the carabiner on his harness. He tested the line to the titanium piton in the bank wall.

Helena looked at him as he donned the kevlar helmet. She looked over parapet – the street was clear – and gave him the thumbs-up. Then, her lips formed in a kiss as he launched himself from the low wall around the pension rooftop.

"One, Six. We've found the target vehicle, confirm licence plate tag. It's outside a lockup. They can't be more than a few minutes ahead of us. Uploading coordinates now. Do we have any camera support?"

"Six, copy that. Blue Angel Ops, what can you give us?"

"Noel One, Cheltenham linking Mobile One to local police camera network and tag readers."

"Thanks Blue Angel Ops, Two is on it now. Mobile One standing by."

11.32 CET, Third Floor, Iranian International Bank of Commerce

Baldwin stood up and rubbed his ankle, then shrugged out of the climbing harness and untangled himself from the remnants of the vertical window blinds. He had hit the window at more than twenty miles an hour and the glass had given way immediately to his feet, although he had a hammer in his hand in case he bounced. He had taken a bump on the head against the frame but the helmet had done its work. He shook his head – he was a bit groggy. All he could remember was Helena's blown kiss. The room was empty, the ash block walls were bare.

"One, Baldwin here. I'm in. Lines pulling across now."

He tugged on the light heaving line and hauled a heavier climbing line across from the pension roof, looking for somewhere to anchor it. He hammered a couple of pitons into the wall and gave the thumbs up to Teresa and Helena. Paulo came across hand over hand in about forty five seconds. They ran to find the fire stairs and get to the ground floor.

"One, all the elevators are welded shut."

"I wonder what's in them, then? We're getting your video feed now."

Their smartphone radiation monitors started bleeping.

"Five, Thirteen. One here. We're reading increasing radiation levels on your sensors. Just above background but the trend is increasing."

"One, it's Baldwin. – we're inside the lobby now. We'd have to blow these front doors. They look like they've been designed to stop a tank. There is a vestibule as far as I can tell. All bright and shiny stainless steel doors. No sign of any door release buttons or handles. Checking the other doors now. There's no vehicle access ramp outside so no garage in the basement. There's a bit of a smell too."

"Hardly surprising, I can guess what's down there. Radiation count still increasing, but I don't know about the smell. Get down there…"

"Thanks for the reminder."

"Eleven, One. Status?"

"I've got the circuit scanner on the ATM and GCHQ are online processing the data, but I'm not optimistic – it's taking too much time. This is not regular ATM software – it's been hardened."

"OK Eleven. Work on the door access."

"Copy that but I'm getting some funny looks from the guys in café opposite."

"I'll bet. OK Eleven we'll take care of it."

"Twelve, Four. Get Mobile Two over here and park it by the bank. Ten, start patrolling. That should satisfy the spectators. We'll have to chance a police patrol."

Noel Ten appeared, in local police uniform and walked across to Jacob – Noel Eleven - at the door entry pad. They exchanged words and Noel Ten stood swinging his baton and moving on the balls of his feet while Jacob worked with the code reader and magnetic pulse probe on the door access pad.

"Ten, stop hamming it up – you look like bloody Dixon of Dock Green."

"Who's he?"

"An old London TV bobby. Before my time, but it's what they say."

"One, Eleven here. I don't think the door is alarmed. It's requesting thumbprints as well as codes. OK, we've probed the codes and pulsed them. We're scanning now. Yes there are latents on the print reader. Image lifting now and separating. Let's see what it thinks of this. Shit. 'Invalid access print' I think it says. Thank God it's in Italian and not Arabic. Two more attempts remaining. I'll increase the print image resolution. Bugger. One attempt remaining. Ok, ok I read you guys in Cheltenham. Yes, three attempts remaining, Super, great assist."

"Eleven, suppose it's linked to the detonator?"

"None of us will know if it is."

"That's some fucking comfort, Eleven."

"One, it's looking good. Maybe too easy. Ok, ok, the door is unlocking."

"Noel team, I think I'm still alive."

"Ten, One here. Get across to the café and keep the padron occupied while we get the team and the gear into the Bank."

"One, Ten. How can I do that?"

"Christ Ten, use your bloody initiative. You passed the Service entry test, so get on with it!"

"Copy that, One. I'm on my way across now."

"Noel Team, One here. All unassigned people inside now! Noel Four, withdraw from the *pensione*. Get Mobile Three to the bank and start unloading the gear. One, Two and Three standing by outside in Mobile One. Bomb boys are still stuck in traffic. Why the fuck aren't people at home on Christmas day? OK. The Pope is just starting to speak."

"Flying One, Noel Six, Seven. Noel Two here. We have images of two scooters, four hostiles leaving the street where the target vehicle was parked. It seems that the scooter licence tags are genuine. There are uniforms in sight – they must have ditched them. We're tracking through the remote roadside tag readers now, picked them up on the SP8 road, about ten minutes behind them. Downloading target images to you now. They have full helmets on. Head southwest out of the city on the SP8 route."

"Two, copy that."

"Six, Seven. Mobile One. If you locate targets do not engage, repeat do not engage. Discreet surveillance only. I am sending more support."

11.40 a.m. CET, Café Abyssinia, Ostia Antica, southwest Rome

"Why is the Pope not on the TV?"

"They don't do Christmas here, Abdul is a Muslim."

"But he sells beer?"

"Yes, to take money off the infidels, and today I think that Allah and even the Prophet might allow us to have one. But first, coffee or fruit juice?"

"Abdul, let's have the TV on, we want to see what that accursed Pope has to say about our brothers in the Levant."

Sharifi felt his smartphone vibrate. He glanced at it and his eyes widened. He nudged ben-Zhair and whispered.

"Telemetry is reporting a building intrusion, Almahdi."

"So, someone knows about the Sword of Allah?"

"It is unlikely to be casual thieves."

"Yes, but we are secure?"

"It would take them a week to disrupt the weapon. It is physically secure and the electronics are hardened. They have – what – twenty eight minutes?"

"Good, then all they have learned is the location. We already told them it was a nuclear device. Still, they may try to fly the Pope out. Maybe he has a bunker under the Vatican. Could they disarm it through the ATM?"

"Impossible. Once we took the card out the ATM disconnected itself – physically, through an electrical relay in the vault. The cable is cut. It is irreversible, no matter how clever their electronics. The design complies with all the security requirements you specified."

"Good. Look, the Pope is still speaking. All seems as normal. We will have our beers yet!"

11.45 Bank Basement Level -1

"One, Thirteen here. We're down in basement level minus one. Radiation count is well up."

"Thirteen, what do you see? Your webcam image has dropped out."

"We see what looks like a vault door, circular, steel, just like a bank vault in the movies. It seems to be welded shut. There's an envelope here against the door, and there's a body – with flies. Jesus, we need some fly killer here! I'm checking to see if the envelope is wired in any way. No, looks good. I'm opening it. It's a note in French, I think it reads 'You now know we have the technology and the capability. This is just the start. *Allahu Akhbar*'."

"Fucking joker. Thirteen, One. Send the note up here now – we need to get it away from the scene, for analysis. Can't do fly spray, sorry."

"We'll drag the body aside. It's a male – looks African, fortyish."

"Ok, Five – set up the static webcam, Eleven – sort out the video comms - we need to feed video to the bomb boys *en route*, and AWE are also online. The lads from *Bulwark* brought a laser but it will still take too long to burn through, surely?"

"Yes One, the laser is looking very doubtful given the time"

"OK. All, One here. We're down to fifteen minutes before we evacuate, thirty minutes to detonation – if the ATM is accurate."

"One, Thirteen, we're going down to level minus two now. This seems to be the lowest level. There are steel doors here. There are markings on the doors. Looks electrical."

"One, Five. Yes, markings translate 'Danger High Voltage Equipment'."

"Fuck me, as if that's a big problem right now. Sorry One."

"Ok Thirteen, AWE One are you online to confer."

"Erm.. right, AWE One here. Erm…we can see your headcam images now. If it's built in the way we think then disabling the power supply is an obvious showstopper."

"Jesus Christ AWE One, stop dithering and get on with it!"

"Erm…yes, sorry Noel One. Let's find the main power breaker. GCHQ are hacked into Rome's power control system and say that power draw through the local grid is minimal right now. I doubt that the local supply would be enough anyway. They would need to have stored energy as well – at least, if our supposition is correct."

"I can't believe that it would be that easy."

"Can you get through the doors? They can't all be welded, there must be some sort of maintenance access?"

"No go. All welded. Wait…"

"One, Five here – there's one door here with a keypad."

"Eleven, get the fuck down there now."

"Copy that one. I'm bringing a comms cable down with me. Two, have you enabled the comms repeater?

"All ready for you Eleven."

Jacob nodded grimly to Steve and Paulo as he stumbled down the last of the steps unreeling the cable and plugged in the wifi router.

"No fingerprint reader, that's good. I've got the unit in place, scanning and pulsing now. OK, here we go, door's open."

Steve wrenched the door back and he and Paulo ran into the room, and were stopped short.

"Five, Baldwin, we've got your video now. Over to AWE One."

The video image showed a room with floor to ceiling racks, double stacked with grey boxes connected by heavy cables as thick as a man's wrist. The racking was protected by heavy plastic mesh screens.

"Bloody hell! Can you focus in on one of the boxes – yes that's good. Siemens Industrial Capacitors. Ten Petafarad capacity. Ultra Fast Discharge. Christ there are hundreds of them. Amazing. Don't get too close chaps. There's huge power there – it could arc across."

In Aldermaston, the team around the table looked at AWE One, their mouths open. He was the cream of English scientific ability and propriety – and they had never before heard him swear.

"AWE One, can we literally throw a spanner in the works here?"

"I need to think about that. My guess is that they will have built in redundancy – spare capacity and a power management system. These people are far from amateurs. They will have protected this investment carefully. Any sign of power circuit breakers?"

"None. Got to be worth trying to short out these capacitors?"

"Go for it then."

"AWE One here. OK, let's look at the electric field – your smartphone should sense that. Right, I'm reading it now. It's off the scale. Stand well back."

"Is that why my hair is standing on end?"

"Could be, or maybe something else…"

"What have you brought, Fourteen?"

"Should be a crowbar in the kit – we're just fetching it down now. Give us a couple of minutes."

"Well try it anyway."

"OK, AWE One."

Fourteen turned to Steve. "The name is Lee, as in Lee Enfield. I'd like you to know, just in case I don't come out of this." Steve looked at him and nodded.

"Don't ask - my father named me after an old rifle his father had used in World War Two."

Steve shrugged. "As good a reason as any. Are you off Bulwark then?"

"Yes, a marine demolition specialist."

"I'm Steve, ex-RM myself. A jack of all trades and general shit-sweeper. Did you ever hear about a woman on Bulwark recently, a Serb?"

"Yeh, there were rumours, a bit short. Bit of trouble. Turned the ship upside down they did. I don't know a lot. Ah, here's the gear."

"Better get on with it then Lee."

"Sure, but first I've got to cut the plastic screen. Shit, it's reinforced – I think tungsten mesh core."

"One, it's Baldwin. We're pissing in the wind. Let's put a charge in to disrupt it."

"How will we know if it's worked?"

"Give me twenty minutes and I'll have a fucking answer for you."

"All, One here. Just cool down. Fourteen go ahead, use a charge. I hope they don't hear this on the street. Shit, Two's reading another police patrol approaching. Carabinieri GPS signal this time. Mobile One moving around the block. Mobile Two stay clear. Mobile Three, Status?"

"We've just parked up a block away."

"One, Fourteen, shaped charge on the mesh screen. Up the stairs lads. Fire in the hole! Seven seconds."

There was a sharp crump of sound. Out on the street, the carabinieri had stopped their car and were listening to the Pope's message on the radio. The sky was still a clear blue but the air was cool and so they sat with their windows closed. They did not feel the slight tremor through the car's low profile tyres, and the coffee cups in the café across the road barely rattled. The proprietor looked up and shrugged, surprised that the metro was still running.

"One, Baldwin. Screen is blown, apparent damage to first bank of capacitors."

"AWE One, go slowly, Thirteen. I'm monitoring check the electrical field strength. Looks just as it did before. No difference."

"Fourteen, deploying a crowbar now."

"Don't get too close before you throw the crowbar."

"There's more at stake here than me, matey."

Lee judged the distance to the capacitor terminals, the crowbar held out ahead of him in gloved hands, ready to throw as he stepped into the gap in the mesh screen.

Baldwin spoke. "Given your name, Lee, your aim should be spot on. Go for it."

Lee stepped forward. There was a flash and a sharp crack as high voltage electricity arced, then the unpleasant smell of ozone mixed with burned flesh as Lee jerked backward and dropped. The headcams flared out in the flash.

"Man down, man down."

"Noel One here. Get him out of there. Make sure there's no electrical contact with the crowbar."

"Too late One, it was like a lightning bolt."

"Noel Two here. I'm just downloading latest target location data now. We have them coming off the SR296 and north into Via Capo Due Rami ten minutes ago."

"Noel One, Flying One. We've picked them up – the bastards are walking with their helmets off, going into a café. Downloading hi-def images now. I'm close to the Fiumicino flight path and Air Traffic Control are querying my flight plan. Don't know why – they've stopped all airline traffic. Close to bingo fuel anyway."

"Flying One, Noel One. OK, RTB and refuel. Standby. Well done."

"Mobile One, Flying One, will advise when I am topped off and ready, Flying One bugging out."

"Blue Angel Ops, Mobile One. Do you have the Flying One images?"

"Yes One. Cheltenham is running recognition algorithms now."

11.47 a.m. CET, Café Abyssinia, Ostia Antica

Sharifi nudged ben-Zhair.

"Almahdi, we have monitored a brief drop in the power level."

"What could it be?"

"I'm not sure. Maybe they are trying to disrupt the capacitor bank?"

"So be it. There is nothing that we can do now. This mission is already a success after last night. But wait – there *is* something to be done."

Ben-Zhair took out his clean phone and looked across at the café padron.

"Abdul, how do you report an emergency to the police?"

"Uno, uno, tre. Quello di emergenza?"

"Niente, Niente, grazzi."

A bank robbery – that would get a police patrol on site, not that anything could be done – it was much too late for that.

11.47 a.m. CET, Via dei Corridori

"Oh fuck, we're monitoring two police car tags this time, heading this way. I see them now, Lights on, they mean business. Mobile One moving round the block. Noel Ten, make yourself scarce."

Although it was Christmas Day and the Carabinieri were on the highest alert as their cars pulled up outside the Bank and the four officers stepped out carrying their Berretta M12 sub machine guns. Although formally a part of the army, its officers are much in evidence - even apparently as traffic police.

"This is now the fourth bomb alert this morning, Beppe. The street was clear five minutes ago. Those ICIM bastards have really got things wound up."

"It all looks good to me *Tenente*. No packages, vehicles or waste bins. Nothing unusual. Check the doors."

"Doors are clear Sir, no sign of any forced entry. I can't see an entrance to a basement car park."

"We'd better look a bit closer as this call was quite specific. I'll check across the road. You check the ATM. I don't like the fact that it's an Iranian Bank. Unit thirty seven have gone to check with the *padrone* in the café over there."

His personal radio squawked.

"Yes, Thirty Seven."

"*Tenente*, the *padrone* says it has been a busy morning – he thinks because the weather is good – and one of our units was here about half an hour ago. He says they arrested two men, one of whom had been at the ATM.

"Which bloody unit was that then – I thought we were the only two units covering this sector? You'd better check with the Controller, just in case – and tell her it's all clear here. Someone has opened the Christmas *grappa* already."

"There's more. A local copper showed up and spoke to another man at the ATM. Then the copper came here and checked everyone's papers. He left a few minutes ago."

"I don't know why we're worrying then. It seems to be well covered."

"Mobile One here, just coming back round to the front door. Five minutes to extraction guys. Thank Christ those Carabinieri have buggered off – they were the real deal. Here are the nuke boys at last, thank God for that. What? OK. We've already sent the electromagnetic pulse gun down. Will the EM pulse gun disrupt the device's firing circuits through the vault wall or door?"

"AWE One here. Maybe, but they need to know where to aim it precisely. We need to get a visual probe through the door. It's too thick for x-rays.

"One, Twelve. We've got out onto the roof. There's a satellite dish hidden behind a wall. What do we do Eleven?"

"Smash the bloody thing, the LNB - low noise block - on a strut in the centre of the dish."

"Here, try this. You do the honours Twelve."

"Thanks." Helena hauled herself over the wall and attacked the satellite dish with the hammer.

"OK, that must surely be offline now."

"Twelve, One. What else do you see?"

"Elevator lift housing, the usual, and what looks like three big steel boxes."

"Headcam shots, Twelve. Get in close."

"OK, AWE One here, they look like standby generators."

"Can you see any power cables?"

"No, they must be underneath. We're forcing the access panels now. OK, we've got to the control panel of the first one."

"Yes, good, we see it on the feed. That's it, pan your headcam. Good, there's an integral fuel tank – see that red lever – yes – just there. Turn the fuel off. Same for the others."

"OK, good."

"Right Twelve, the elevator shaft - can you get in?"

"Hang on…no, no doors are welded shut."

11.48 a.m. Via dei Corridori

"All, One, two minutes to extraction, not that it matters. Nuke boys are designated Nuke One to Six. All comms through me and Nuke One."

"One, Twelve. There's another structure, looks like aircon."

"Twelve, AWE One. Get up close and let's have some cam shots. OK, good. Closer to the information plates. That's better.

Looks like it's the heat exchanger for a cryogenic unit. Maybe more than one. We need to disrupt it. Can you see any piping or power cables to disrupt?"

"No. it all seems to be heavily encased."

"OK, all we can do it cover the cooling vents – anything to raise the temperature inside."

"OK, we'll find something to block it up."

"Six, One. Just drop a fucking charge in, I'm not concerned about noise right now, but use a blast blanket anyway."

"Will do One. Fifteen seconds and counting."

"Fire in the hole!"

Just at that moment a loud cheer went up from St Peter's Square and the noise of the explosion was barely audible at street level, masked in part by the blast blanket.

11.48 a.m. CET, Café Abyssinia, Ostia Antica

Sharifi looked at ben-Zhair. There was concern in his eyes and his lips were drawn tight.

"The telemetry link to Sidi bel Abbès is down. They are on the roof for sure."

"Is there anything they can do to stop this?"

"The cryogenic heat exchanger is on the roof."

"Is that a weak point?"

"Yes, it has to have access to the open air. But it is heavily shielded – except for the vents." Sharifi consulted his smartphone. "If it is stopped completely the temperature will drift up but still be within limits for maybe twenty minutes, and then the *hohlraum*, the mirrors and lasers will not work to specification, and the vacuum pressure will increase. The fuel pellet will start fast radioactive decay. Then it will fail."

Ben-Zhair checked his watch. "Twenty minutes you say? So we have enough time then?"

"Yes, *Insha'Allah*, a few minutes."

"*Insha'Allah.*"

Via dei Corridori

"AWE One, Nuke One. What's the score?"

"Cryogenics may be down I don't know for sure. Jesus Christ!"

"What?"

"This is all guesswork – their design, everything. It's all supposition. We could be miles out."

"AWE One, Mobile One here. I hope not, or we'll be miles high, very soon. Hang in there, you're doing well man, keep the team going. What's next?"

"Nuke One, can you find a vacuum pump?

"What's a vacuum pump look like?"

"There will be big electric motors, steel cylinders, thick piping."

"Can't see anything like that. What other parts can we look to disrupt?"

"Lasers, mirrors, vacuum pump, fuel pellet. No, the pellet will be in the basement, in the vault."

"Five, Mobile One – have we got a video probe through that vault door yet?"

"One, I estimate thirty seconds."

"OK. Twelve, Roof status?"

"One, Twelve. The heat exchanger has stopped pumping out hot air."

"Great, then break through into the elevator shaft."

"Noel One, Baldwin. Starting to see a slight increase in radiation level down here."

"AWE One, Noel One – is that bad?"

"Not sure. Could be because the cryo unit is damaged. It might be good for us, it could stop ignition if the pellet starts to break down."

"And Thirteen remember your protocol!"

The reply was clearly heard across the Noel team's radio net.

"Fuck that, I can't count that high."

11.50a.m. CET, Mobile One Control

"All, One. Time's up. Prepare to evacuate."

"One, Thirteen. I'm seeing this one through."

"One, Five. Me too."

Affirmations came from every member of the team - no-one was leaving. If the device really was a nuclear bomb and worked as it should, then they would know nothing at about it. It would be the quickest and most painless of deaths.

"Noel Team, thank you. But I need to change the deployment now that we have the experts on site. Twelve, Thirteen, leave the Bank and use Mobile Two to join Six and Seven at the Target location – Café Abyssinia in Ostia Antica. ETA twenty minutes with the blues going. Coordinates downloading now."

"All, One here. Thank you. Mobile One will be outside for the duration."

11.53 Bank Basement Level-1

"Nuke One, Noel One. Status?"

"We're about half way through burning an access hole in the concrete to the vestibule. Need another seven or eight minutes at least. The pulse gun is set up and charging now. Ready for use in ninety seconds. The laser has been refocused on the inner door and has just started a burn. We don't know how thick it is. We'll try the pulse gun through the concrete before the laser's finished the burn on the door. It might work, though the stainless steel door may shield the effect and reduce the power."

"Nuke One, AWE One here. There will be a steel core to the concrete – the concrete would be too porous for a hi-vac enclosure."

"Copy that, we'll try anyway."

"Nuke One, One here. What's the score on the lower level?"

"We couldn't revive Fourteen, it was a huge shock. We can't locate the power feed to the electrified screen so we're earthing it. Then we'll try to short out the capacitors, but that's a problem – the crowbar Fourteen used melted - the current practically burned his arm off. Huge current, must have been thousands of amps. We'll put charges in place to blow the capacitor bank at zero minus thirty seconds. That will be last ditch – it will be a big bang – and it's only one bank of capacitors – at least, as far as we know. We don't have enough equipment. Or time."

"Tell me about it."

"We're drilling on of the other doors to look inside. That vacuum pump has to be somewhere. Got to go, pulse gun is charged up."

"OK. Twelve minutes everyone."

"Eleven, what's the status on the control system?"

"GCHQ are saying the ATM was definitely disconnected."

"Can they do *anything*?"

"We're running a penetration scan now – if we can at least get a response then we might be able to hack in or locate the wifi controller. It might be hard wired – fibre optic would be the most secure, in which case we haven't really got a chance – especially if the fibre is run inside the walls. Hang on One…right, great…One?"

"Still here Eleven"

"Right, One, we've cut through into the back of the ATM. What? Shit – yes One, fibre optic confirmed. It will take a while to trace the fibre run. We're just hooking up an optical transmitter to see if we can tickle it into life down the fibre."

"OK, Eleven, keep at it."

11.53 London Area

"So, 'C', what is the latest?"

The Prime Minister had closeted herself in her study at Chequers, her official country house retreat. Propped against the inkstand on front of her was the letter.

It was Shami Munchetty's letter, citing 'irreconcilable differences on grave matters of foreign policy' as the reason for her resignation. It was dated Midnight, Christmas Eve. She had not yet briefed the media, but had told the PM on the telephone that she would release the letter in time for the Boxing Day BBC radio and television breakfast time bulletins.

"Our people are actively attempting to disarm the weapon as I speak."

"Good God, man, the Pope is speaking now."

"I am well aware of that, Prime Minister."

"Is this really a credible weapon?"

"AWE believes so. The degree of planning, coordination and technology that we have seen so far is – shall I say – probably only capable of being funded and organised by a state-level entity."

"Very well. You must inform the Italian security people through your own channels."

"I will keep it as vague as possible, Prime Minister."

"On the diplomatic front, we will contact the Italian Government through the Foreign Office."

"As we agreed, we will tell them now that all indications are that the attack is focused on St Mark's in Venice, but that Rome and Florence are also possibilities."

"Exactly, that will keep the main security focus away from Rome."

"And what about our people on the ground?"

"They have refused to withdraw, and under the circumstances I am not going to press the matter."

"How long do they have?"

"Less than ten minutes."

"God be with them."

"Quite. I will be in touch as soon as I have further news."

The rich smell of the turkeys roasting in the ovens in the kitchen wing of Chequers had drifted in the still air, across the manicured lawns, penetrating the depressing mist that clung to the estate. In the circumstances it was a sickly mix and the Prime Minister almost gagged as she closed the study door behind her, and sought her family in the main drawing room, before heading to the bunker where Cobra awaited, if only virtually.

11.57 The Bank, Via Dei Corridori

"Noel One, Nuke One. We have a video probe through the vault door. There appears to be a vestibule. Increased radiation level. We see another door with a keypad about two meters away. Ambient air pressure. We could try to get through the next door from here with the laser, and – if – there's a vacuum chamber on the other side then it might be enough to stop the device."

"Nuke One. AWE One. We're looking at your video feed now. Best guess is that the vestibule is an airlock, with the inner door giving access to the vacuum chamber. We need to break through that if we can."

"Nuke One, Noel One. What about the EM pulse gun?"

"Doubtful, but we'll try both anyway. We'll start the laser burn on the next door once we have re-tuned the laser and aimed it through the hole in the first door. We have another laser cutting the concrete on the side of the vault door."

"How long will it take?"

Nuke One looked at Steve who shrugged.

"One, Five – first burn was about nine minutes."

"Shit, that's tight. Keep at it."

"Roof, One. Status?"

"We're going to use a shaped charge on the wall of the elevator lift gear. Ready to go on your order. It will be noisy."

"On my command. Ten, are you ready?"

"One, Ten, ready."

"Ok Ten, on my count three, two, one, fire."

The Bank building vibrated as the concrete of the elevator lift gear housing split open. Five blocks away, the small diversionary charge that Ten had placed against the ATM of Banco Santander exploded simultaneously.

On the Loggia of St Peter's Basilica, the Pope looked up as he heard the detonations. In a rare *ad lib* he smiled and commented on the Italians' love of fireworks. An aide approached him from the side and placed a slip of paper on his lecturn.

'Immediate and credible threat to your life. We need to evacuate you now.'

The Pope continued his Blessing without faltering, picking up the note and crumpling it, then dropping it at his feet as he looked back to the teleprompter.

"Five, what do you see, the video feed is a fog?"

"Ok the dust is clearing now. About twenty pipes running vertically down the elevator shaft. Six inches in diameter. They appear to be merged at the top end into a steel sphere with one thick pipe running down the centre. Radiation count unchanged."

"AWE One?"

"I'm guessing that they are the laser combining tubes. The pipes will be at very low pressure. We need to split them open. If of course that is the design. Probably mirrors and prisms at the top in the sphere. Maybe better to break the mirror, figuratively of course. Yes, my people here are nodding."

"OK, Roof we need to break that mirror, now, bugger the noise."

"Copy that One."

"One, Eleven. There is another counter on a panel at the back of the ATM. It is showing 'Time to Initiation Four minutes'."

"AWE One, what the hell does that mean?"

"One, maybe it is the final system status self-check, maybe the pre-warming of the laser sources. It's all a guess. Eleven, I thought you said that the ATM was disconnected."

"Yes, that's what the front panel said."

"So, we don't know whether this initiation clock is live or not?"

"No, but we've cut the power supply to the ATM – and we're not getting any joy from the fibre optic probe...and the counter is still running."

"OK. I'll get GCHQ to shut down the local power grid."

"Noel Team, One here. Local power grid shutting down in ten seconds. Acknowledge."

12.02 p.m. CET, Bank Roof

Paulo was leaning over the top of the yawning elevator shaft as he attached the small C4 charge to the sphere at the top of the pipework and started the detonator timer. There was a huge roar. He lost his grip, dislodged the explosive charge and slipped into the shaft, becoming wedged between the pipework against a supporting cross member, with one leg caught in the jagged steel of the blown doors. The leg was clearly broken – he could see one bone end protruding – and bleeding freely. He keyed his radio as he struggled, looking at the C4 charge which had lodged in metalwork supporting the pipework. He tried to kick at it, but it was just beyond the reach of his one free foot. He screamed in agony.

"One, Five here. The standby generators have started up - the fuel lines must have been dummies. I'm caught in the shaft, can't move, broken leg, bleeding. The charge is about to blow near me. It's not attached to the top unit."

"Copy that Five. Hang on, Four is on the way up."

"No, stay away, it's too late."

He kicked out desperately and barely connected with the charge, dislodging it.

Too late. The C4 charge blew half a second later as it started to fall down the elevator shaft. The pipework shook as Paulo's body was dismembered, the pieces falling down the maze of pipes, gathering speed until meeting in a heap at the bottom of the shaft.

Paulo's blood dripped over the lower sphere. The sphere contained the final mirror for steering the high powered laser beam along another high vacuum pipe, inward into the vault and onward into the *hohlraum* and the fuel pellet. There, in a trillionth of a second the huge pulse of energy would create temperatures and pressures higher than at the centre of the sun – and a fireball that would instantly consume half of Rome in just a few minutes, unless the team could damage the structure.

The laser alignment and vacuum integrity was undisturbed - the installation had been built to withstand considerable shock and vibration with the mirror and prisms mounted on springs. The alignment was unaffected – much of the energy had been dissipated as the charge was unattached when it exploded.

"Noel One, AWE. It sounds as if the Initiation sequence has started."

"Copy that AWE One."

"Noel One, Nuke One, we're getting increased electrical field readings down here. We've now got a video probe into the second welded door – it looks like the master power control room. I'm blowing the door in five seconds, ok."

"Do it!"

"Fire in the hole!"

The building trembled to a second shock as the door to the power control room was opened line a sardine tin by the strip charge.

"Nuke One, Noel one. Vault status?"

"One, the laser is still burning through the second door. We are still charging the EMP gun for a second pulse. We have no way of knowing if the first pulse worked. Electrical field levels are rising in the sub-basement."

"Cheltenham has just closed down power grid for this block. The back-up generators have started."

"They will be topping up the capacitor charge then."

"What's happening in the Power Control Room?"

"All the breakers have heavy locks on them."

"Don't waste time trying to cut them, just blow all the fucking circuit breakers."

"Copy that, we're setting charges now. Need a couple of minutes then we're ready."

"Good, I think we're nearly there, but two minutes is all you have. Noel One standing by."

"Eleven, Noel One. Status?"

"No further progress. The fibre optic probe is not producing any reaction from the ATM circuit. I've come to an end here."

"OK get up to the roof then – we may have lost Five."
"On my way."
Jacob sprinted up the stairs.

*

12.02 p.m. CET Café Abyssinia, Ostia Antica

"Are you sure we are safe here, Jafa?"

"Yes, Almahdi, from the blast certainly. The wind is blowing inland as expected, so here on the coast we are safe from any fallout and anyway we will be at sea in a few hours, will we not?"

"Certainly." Ben-Zhair checked one of his phones. "Yes, the boat is waiting in Porto Romano. It's only five minutes away, but whether we are safe from whoever has discovered the weapon, I do not know. Qasem assures me that the Press helicopter was genuine. How long now?"

"Two minutes by my timer - the Sword of Allah should now be near the end of its initiation sequence."

"Good. The let us prepare to celebrate. Abdul!"

Ben-Zhair crossed to the bar area. Please bring us four bottles of your best beer. Here, take fifty euros – you have no other customers and it is Christmas after all."

"Christmas is an infidel celebration, but I am always happy to have presents. Unfortunately not all Muslims are as devout as us and they take the opportunity to enjoy the infidel holiday."

"I'm sure that Allah will recognise your devotion Abdul."

"I hope so, but not too soon, eh?"

They laughed.

"The will of Allah is sometimes a mystery, Abdul."

"Never a truer word spoken, my friend."

"Noel One to Mobile Two, what's your status?"

"One, we're nearly at the RV with Seven and Eight in Ostia Antica. Seven and Eight have located the Targets in an Arabic café. Café Abyssinia. Under surveillance."

"OK. Noel One standing by."

"Seven, One. The café is run by an Abdul Sadeeq. No known terrorist affiliations. Noel Twelve calls the shots."

"Copy that, One. I see Mobile Two approaching. Seven standing by."

Mobile Two slowed and stopped, double parking on Via Capo Due Rami where they could see Flynn Gregory and Bill Crosthwaite - Noel Six and Seven - outside an electrical store, supposedly watching a television screen in the store window.

They crossed the road and acknowledged each other with nods then watched the screen, apparently innocuously, whilst they planned the next move.

Helena spoke. "Cheltenham confirms a match with one of the targets. Looks like it's our friend Baldacci from the ferry – aka Abu ben-Zhair."

"And the others?"

"No matches as yet."

Flynn kept his voice low. "The targets are in that café across the road."

They moved slightly and the reflection in the window became sufficiently clear to give them a good view of the café.

"Noel One, Twelve here. We're on our way in."

"OK. Good luck. One standing by."

Crosthwaite spoke quietly. "Look, he's coming to the end of the Blessing."

They glanced at the 72" ultra-high definition television screen in the window just as the Pope raised his hand, looking around at the crowd of almost 100,000 of the faithful in St Peter's Square. They did not notice the very brief lightening of the blue sky above their heads as the picture television picture went blank.

They heard a dog wail in fright and run down the street and the birds on the rooftops took flight as one in a cacophony of warning cries.

Then, they heard a cheer from the café.

Helena croaked. "No! It can't be, surely?"

"Noel Twelve here, come in One."

"Noel One, Williams here, come in One, come in One."

Helena's voice sounded hopeless and she looked at the others and shrugged.

"I thought One might react to a breach of radio protocol. Must be comms failure…or…"

They looked at Helena and said nothing, a grim realisation starting to crystallize in their consciousness. And then the ground trembled slightly under their feet as ground waves reached them, followed by a low rumbling sound and a slight pressure wave which popped their ears.

"Jesus, no it can't be!" said Bill. They looked back at the blank screen. A caption came up. *'Guasto Temporaneo'*. Flynn Gregory broke the stunned silence. "'Temporary fault' my arse. The bastards have blown it."

Then Helena, quietly, "Christine. We went through training together." They looked at her. "Noel One."

The muscles in Steve's face tautened visibly as he drew his pistol, checked it and put it back in his belt at the small of his back. "Whatever it is, we are here to do a job, whatever has happened elsewhere. Let's do it, now. Is there a back door?"

Gregory replied, his voice barely a whisper. "Yes, up an alley."

"What about the roof?"

"No idea about access – there are three floors for sure."

"Ok, you guys you take the rear entrance, with Six locating and covering the stairway. We'll go in the front. Ninety seconds, key your mike when you are in through the rear and ready to go, OK?"

"That should be enough to get in there."

"We need them alive if possible – that's very important. OK, on my mark. Go."

Crosthwaite and Gregory set off at a brisk walk, heading for the alley. The mood was grim and they wondered if they really could take prisoners.

After thirty seconds, Steve and Helena started a slow walk across the road.

"Thank you, Abdul."

Ben-Zhair nodded to Iqubal who walked across to the door as Hossein stood up and walked round behind Abdul, clamped his left hand over Abdul's mouth and pushed a knife into his back, between his ribs and into his heart, stepping smoothly back and to the side to avoid the blood. He then took the cash out of the till.

"No traces, Jafa, they will think it is a robbery."

"For sure."

"We will finish our beers and then leave. Hossein, give me the money if you will."

Iqubal pushed the bolts closed on the café door.

"Almahdi, there are people coming. A man and a woman."

The ultra-fast-acting capacitors had discharged their energy almost instantaneously, firing twenty four krypton fluoride lasers in the sub-basement of the bank. The laser beams were directed up the pipes in the escalator shaft, through prisms, their high power light combined in phase and near total vacuum at a temperature below that of liquid helium, on a highly purified mirror, bounced and reflected down through the single central pipe, meeting another mirror in a sphere next to Five's body. The mirror steered the beam into the vault, into the *hohlraum* and onto the supercooled fuel pellet.

The huge flux of laser energy raised the temperature and pressure of the helium inside the *hohlraum*, creating an enormous thermodynamic pressure wave which compressed the fuel pellet and forced the radioactive deuterium/tritium atoms to fuse, releasing a huge pulse of energy and a massive flux of neutrons. The neutrons surged outward to the small plutonium plate and the cobalt case. The neutron flux transmuted the cobalt metal instantly into radioactive cobalt-60 which would rain down on Rome in the fallout.

Ignition, fusion, instant meltdown of the Bank as the huge wave of energy surged upward and outward, flattening the historical architecture for blocks around. By the time the pulse had reached St Peter's Square, much of its energy had been dissipated in reducing building to atoms and then moving rubble at supersonic speed, with debris raining down on the crowd. Hell on earth.

"I'll go in first Steve – that will draw their attention, then you can come in after me."

"OK."

They saw one of the targets close the café door, looking up in surprise just as they approached the pavement.

"Shit."

"Eight, Thirteen. They've rumbled us. Go carefully."

"Steve – can you get through that door?"

"Unlikely. Window's best. I'll kick it when we get the signal from Eight."

Then the three clicks came over the comms and Steve put a shot through the window and kicked it in. He stood to one side, but there was no response. Then they heard shots and he kicked the last of the lower window shards. Still no shots. He took a step back and dived through the gap, rolling on the glass splinters as he fell, scanning the bar with his weapon held at arms length.

No-one.

"Clear."

Helena came rolling through the window as he pulled a table over for cover. Another shot, upstairs. Then a clunk. He peered around the table.

"Shit. Grenade."

He threw himself over Helena as the Russian F1 grenade rolled towards them.

They had only seconds…

*

"That was close, Almahdi."

"Yes Jafa, but I am always prepared. Iqubal and Hossein are the best – as are you. I choose my people carefully."

The onshore wind was creating a short choppy sea adding to the swell which had worked around the North of Corsica and down the Ligurian Sea. The Mistral had been blowing until the previous day, driving cold air down the Rhone Valley and producing a severe gale in the Western Mediterranean. The wind had changed, but the swell was still doing its work and ben-Zhair was feeling the effects as the 20 metre fishing boat drove on towards Sardinia. Give me the desert anytime, he thought.

Every morning when he shaved and examined himself critically in the mirror – at least when the opportunity to shave was possible - he said to himself 'I will re-frame the world of Islam and roll back revolutions'. That was his mantra, the mantra he had learned in Beijing.

He ran over the story again – Deb Deb, the Foreign Legion raid, his mother, his father, his education in Moscow. And then Beijing. Thousands of details, a whole life had been learned.

He now had the story word-perfect and lived it. It was his legend.

Friends and family had not seen him since his return from China. Ben-Zhair's father had been riddled with cancer and under heavy medication. The others had met accidents or premature deaths of one sort or another. The legend was protected.

The original ben-Zhair had died a quick death in a Beijing cell when as a mature graduate student he had become disillusioned with the Chinese view of the world and the plans they had for him. At first he had believed that the Islamist accommodation with the Government had been a betrayal. The Arab Spring was a surrender of Islamic control to Western consumerism, aided and abetted by the cheap technology that global businesses had shipped into those countries. The 'YouTube' revolutions some called it, but to him they were not revolutions, they were abject surrender. Then the disillusion set in. This was not what the Chinese had planned for him and so the alternative plan was enacted.

The fishing boat shuddered as it hit a larger wave and buried its bow, throwing green water aft, snapping him back to reality.

"You look a bit green, Almahdi."

"It will pass, Jafa, as must all things – even Christianity."

"Insha'Allah."

"Insha'Allah."

The plan was progressing towards its ultimate fruition and seasickness was a small price to pay. The problem was that he was now running way ahead of what the Chinese had envisaged, and there was a target on his back.

Quiet Room 3, Vauxhall Cross Christmas Night

"I've just come out of a Cobra virtual, Alex. Seems the Israelis are on the warpath. The country is now on the highest alert status."

"To be expected."

"Well it seems the FO didn't see it, despite all the signals. What a time to be without a Foreign Secretary! Anyway, update me on Rome."

"We lost almost the entire team, plus the people from AWE and Bulwark. Four of our people had been tracking the targets to Ostia Antica – that's southwest Rome, on the coast, but they are still unaccounted for. They were outside the blast and fallout area. I have people moving down there now to their last known location. It's a pretty grim toll."

"Bloody right. And that stupid Prime Minister has to live with it. That's not for repetition by the way."

"What's next?"

"Retrieval, consolidation, debriefing, data analysis – plenty to keep us going."

"And then there will be the internal inquiry, totally secret of course."

"And buried forever."

12.05 p.m. GMT, Chequers

"My God, 'C', what have we done? It's a bloody disaster!"

"We can't say that yet, Prime Minster, we don't have enough information. It's been less than an hour."

"What exactly *do* we know?"

"Very little at present. We have a Predator flying in from *HMS Queen Elizabeth* to support the Italian government's own resources. The Pope appears to be injured but safe, although there are many seriously injured still in St. Peter's Square – apart from the dead. We have lost contact with the bulk of our team and must assume the worst, although we know from our communications log that four of our people are on the trail of the perpetrators – an operation is currently underway southwest of Rome. We are trying to re-establish contact with them as I speak. It would seem that this is not a major nuclear explosion – if it was then the devastation would have been much more extensive. From what we can tell the blast radius is about three city blocks – enough to extend into St Peter's Square – as we have seen. That's about a dozen blocks totally flattened. Beyond that – well, major damage and fire."

"That sounds pretty bloody extensive to me."

"Perhaps so, PM. Nevertheless, AWE is suggesting that this is in the sub-kiloton range – but it appears to be nuclear, and a fusion device at that. This is new territory, technically speaking. As yet we do not know if any radioactivity has been released, but we must presume so. As of now, no claims have been made."

Boxing Day

08:00, Chequers

"Very well Prime Minister, I will not mention anything about the loss of our team – or even their presence - other than to report on the status of our pursuit of the perpetrators – and that is not for publication – it remains highly classified. I have briefed Tweedy accordingly to be circumspect in his report."

"I'm glad that's clear. We'll open up the links and start the meeting now."

The Prime Minister was sombre as she opened the Cobra video conference, her face was strained and her pallor, almost the pale grey of the grey fog still embracing Chequers, was apparent over the video links to all the Cobra members. In turn, the sombre faces of the Cobra attendees were clearly apparent even over the secure video links.

"Before we start, I have to announce that the Foreign Secretary has resigned her position, and the Permanent Under-Secretary is in attendance online now pending my appointment of a successor later this morning. This has not yet been announced to the media and must be kept confidential *pro tem*. Shami Munchetty will maintain this confidentiality pending my announcement later.

Now, about this atrocity in Rome. You all understand that we, the UK, at this level of government, are aware of much more detail about this technology, its deployment and this dreadful event than we have admitted – or will ever admit - even to our closest allies. No other governments, except perhaps the Chinese, are aware of these details. It is of the utmost national importance that the level of knowledge of this event remains absolutely secure, and I formally reminding you of your responsibilities in this regard and of your being absolutely bound by the Official Secrets Act. All files will be embargoed for at least a century.

I spoke this morning to the Italian President. He has confirmed that the device was nuclear in nature. There are traces of plutonium and also cobalt-60 – a persistent contaminant. You will no doubt be aware that there are at least four thousand dead – they were nearest the location of the bomb in Via dei Corridori leading into St Peter's Square – plus more than ten thousand seriously injured. Many more are being treated for exposure to radioactivity. There is a blanket of nuclear contamination over several square miles of Rome, and a radioactive plume across the Apennines and the Adriatic. All fires are now extinguished. We have offered the use of hospital facilities on *HMS Bulwark* and we have put specialist teams into place. More are on the way.

We expect that some British citizens will be among the dead and injured and a press announcement will be made to that effect. Our embassy and diplomatic staff are all safe, though being checked for radiation contamination.

There is a huge international effort being organised to help the Italian Government. You will have heard the almost universal condemnation of this atrocity. Before we move on to discuss the political implications and likely responses, Director Tweedy from Aldermaston will give us an update on what his team has been able to deduce. Director."

"Ladies and Gentlemen, our initial analysis of footage available from Rome, our own Predator and US satellite images makes it clear that the device was located in at the coordinates of what was the Iranian bank. We have reliable data from US satellites which shows an electromagnetic pulse typical of a nuclear *fusion* explosion. There is also seismograph data to support this – and we have air sample data which indicates the use of plutonium. So, we have concluded that this was most definitely a nuclear fusion device. What is surprising is that its yield appears to be less than a kiloton. A nuclear fusion weapon this small is unheard of – and not, as far as we know, technically possible.

Our airborne radiation sampling by the Predator indicates considerable cobalt-60 contamination."

"Is this the same cobalt-60 as in Paris on Christmas Eve?"

"No, Prime Minister. This cobalt-60 was produced by the bomb itself. The cobalt-60 in Paris originated from a reactor in Pakistan. This bomb was both simple and sophisticated – simple in design and sophisticated in outcome. Of course, these are just initial impressions. Our opinion could change with more data. That's all I have at the moment."

"Thank you, Director."

The link closed.

The red telephone at the Prime Minister's right hand trilled gently. "Christ Almighty, what's going on here?"

Yes, even in these advanced days hotlines still existed. There was silence as the Prime Minister raised the red handset, but she knew from her touchscreen who the caller was.

As was the norm, the touchscreen microphone was rendered mute by the hotline's near-field jammer.

"Prime Minister Jastrow."

"Yes, Prime Minister. I will not waste your time. I am calling to tell you that as I speak Israeli armed forces are undertaking a series of missions to neutralise Iranian nuclear installations and personnel. The objectives are limited and very specific. This information is not being made public yet – I am only informing our close friends and allies."

"Do I understand that you think Iran was involved in this Italian disaster?"

"There are definite indications. What does the UK know?"

"The UK has no evidence of Iranian involvement. Is there anything that we can do to assist – always assuming it is politically possible?"

"Not at present, except of course to give us all the diplomatic support possible once this news becomes public. We are not foolish enough to attempt to engineer regime change. I will leave you to your festive celebrations. *Hot a gutn tog.*"

"Goodbye for now, Prime Minister."

"Cheeky sod. 'Have a nice day" indeed. Does he think I don't understand a Yiddish insult with my background?"

The green mic light came back on and the Prime Minister recapped the conversation to the Cobra members.

"General Rushby, what's our force status in the Gulf?"

"Prime Minister, we have an Astute Class nuclear submarine on patrol outside the Straits of Hormuz. She has cruise missiles. Also, *HMS Dauntless*, a Type 45 destroyer is within twelve hours steaming range of the Strait. Of course her cruise missiles are available for immediate deployment against almost any target in Iran. We have a wing of F35 multi-role aircraft on *HMS Queen Elizabeth* along with other surface ships – off the Italian coast assisting in the rescue efforts in Rome. We can move the F35s to Akrotiri if need be. We also have a wing of Typhoons in Akrotiri, Cyprus. We have a wide range of target options programmed.

The US Sixth Fleet is on station off Israel, but we think that they will be unwilling to send these capital assets through the Suez Canal at the moment. Their Seventh Fleet is in the sea of Japan although they do have a small task force currently in the Arabian Sea."

"Thank you, General. I'm more concerned about political options right now and eliminating these ICIM bastards. With all due respect to your eminent capability, Permanent Secretary, we could do with a Foreign Secretary in post. I'll have to sort that out after lunch. I expect all of you to consider the ramifications of what you have just heard. Right, this Cobra meeting is adjourned until five pm. I need to speak immediately with the US President. General Rushby, please sit in on the call."

"Bill, get David Stallard lined up for a two p.m. call. Tell him it's national security and I need him off the back benches whatever our differences. I'm sure that the Permanent Secretary is already organising a briefing file – but double check, it is Boxing Day after all. Then I have to get the emergency meeting of the UN Security Council this evening."

*

ANNOUNCEMENT

Issued by: IC Operations Command
Dated: 26 Rabi al-Awwal 1440 A.H., 18:00 hours, Mecca time

Following our previous Announcement dated 20 Raby` al-Awwal 1440 A.H., ICIM announce that we were responsible for the nuclear bombs which were detonated in Paris and Rome. We have many more of these weapons, known as 'The Sword of Allah.' These are in place and ready to be used without warning.

We require all countries – as mentioned in the Announcement of 23 Safar 1440 A.H. – to publicly announce that they agree to the demands we have made – and to enact those demands forthwith.

Signed: IC Operations Command

End

In Algeria, ben-Zhair's Head of Security, Qasem Hamadani, had directed the team which moved swiftly to cleanse the ICIM Inner Council. It was a tightly-coordinated a strike at the precise moment that the ICIM claim of responsibility was released under ben-Zhair's instruction.

21.30 CET, Boxing Day Cagliari, Sardinia

"Well Jafa, what went wrong? The Pope is still alive."

"I do not know, Almahdi. I have looked at the news pictures. The yield was obviously less than calculated – perhaps thirty percent of what I expected. It could be that the containment area – the vault - was too deep, too well- hardened

– although I cannot believe that. It could be that the fuel pellet was insufficient and we did not achieve the energy release we calculated. I am still trying to understand the shortfall in yield. Unfortunately we do not have all the data as the telemetry failed just before ignition."

Ben-Zhair smiled. "You are too serious, Jafa. This was a great success. Yes, the Pope may be alive, but he is blind. Thousands are dead, more than ten thousand injured – and Rome is blanketed in radioactivity. The infidels now know that we have the technology and the capability – and they have no idea what is coming next. And those dogs in Iran now have Israel to worry about. We could not wish for more.

Next week we will be in Sidi Bel Abbès, preparing the final stage. Next year the Cause of all Causes will be completed and Islam will rule more than half the world.

But Jafa – remember this – we need all the yield and more for the Cause of All Causes to be a success. You cannot fail next time – we need a hundred percent."

"Yes Almahdi, I understand. One hundred percent."

Ben-Zhair's phone vibrated and he glanced at the text.

"It is done Jafar. I am now effectively the Caliph of Maghreb.

Epilogue

"This can't go to Cobra, 'C'. It's beyond Ultra."

"Obviously, Prime Minister."

"Besides you, me and Tweedy at AWE, how many of our people know the full details of the situation?"

"A baker's dozen – plus the Head of Middle East and North Africa Desk."

"Are they secure?"

"I may need to weed out one or two of the possible doubters of our actions."

"Weed out? How?"

"The way one usually deals with weeds, Prime Minister."

"Weedkiller?"

"Precisely."

"Very well. And the new Deputy Director?"

"She knows nothing – she's only been in post a few weeks. She will surely have suspicions, but nothing more."

"I understand. All Blue Angel files to be archived as Ultra Plus?"

"Yes, Prime Minister."

"Very well, let's draw a line under it."

The line dropped.

'C' could not help but be impressed. 'Hard bitch' was his view of the PM as he reviewed the files. This had been the dirtiest operation imaginable, and she had held steadfast, whatever the morality of the situation.

The people from *Bulwark* and AWE were of no consequence. But there were fourteen names from the Six team. Two sets of files. All database records re-encrypted and locked, with the key itself encrypted and locked; only paper copies accessible – and these he would personally destroy within the next two weeks. The HR files had been purged. All that was left was eight paper career summaries in one pile. Five in the other pile and one in no man's land.

Two of the team would have fatal accidents, here, in London, within a matter of days. Another two operatives were still unaccounted for. Comms analysis had shown that Elias Stone had been despatched to Ostia Antica just two minutes before detonation. His phone signal had placed him just outside the blast zone before it expired. It had been retrieved from a drain under a road. There was no body – alive or dead. The other was Flynn Gregory – Noel Six. He had been involved in the attempted capture of ben-Zhair at the Café Abyssinia. Crosthwaite's body had been recovered, but of Gregory's there had been no sign. Resources were attempting to locate Stone and Gregory, but so far their trails were dead. It had to be assumed that they were still alive – and a danger.

The others would receive commendations, posthumously and not for publication, and their cover names would go 'on the wall' – the wall that listed the names of those who had died on active service. They had been right at ground zero at the instant of detonation. Nothing remained of them, there was no doubt. The other file presented a conundrum. Designation: Noel Thirteen.

BALDWIN, STEPHEN.

Which pile should that file be put on?

'C' scanned the latest medical reports. Amnesia. The trauma of the blow to the head had caused loss of short term memory. Events prior to the Rome disaster were apparently lost. Triggering with news reports, video images and audio had not stimulated any reaction in the subject.

Baldwin's reactions were clearly those of someone with no recall of the events portrayed and the photos of people. He apparently did not know Bryan Elliott. He recognised a picture of a Greek waitress from Crete, and he recognised pictures of his boat. There was recollection of leaving Crete for Malta. There were vague recollections of the events in Malta – these would probably be recovered in full. The period after that until he had awakened in the hospital appeared to be a complete blank.

The memory loss was thought to be permanent, although one could never be absolutely sure – doctors always qualified their prognoses.

'C' locked the file in his safe. On balance Baldwin was very useful – capable, deniable and nowhere on the payroll. Provided that the amnesia lasted. At least Baldwin was not a political animal, just a simple soldier. Was it worth the risk? Ogilvy would have to pay a visit to Baldwin before the final decision. And then, he, 'C', would have to deal with Ogilvy.

And then there was Pavkovic. He shook his head, barely able to believe the report, almost a week old now. She was clever, and slippery, but beyond his control. Her nanochip was not working and she was missing on *Bulwark* or overboard. Nobody knew. The ship had been turned upside down – a particularly bad metaphor he thought.

She had escaped while being escorted to a helo for transfer to Six's private clinic. The captain was lined up for a court martial – dereliction of duty or suchlike. He hadn't had a chance.

*

The pain was like a steel band around his head. He could not move. Sounds intruded, bright light was in his eyes. It felt as if all his senses were overloaded and then, mercifully, it ended. Each time that consciousness broke through, the sensations were a little less intense. Then after three days the tidal flow of his sensations and consciousness started to abate. By day six he was sitting up in bed.

He could use the bathroom by himself though he felt very weak and unsteady on his feet. The door to his room was always locked.

The nurses and doctors had said little and refused to answer his questions, but they did at least smile – and ask him questions, questions to which he had no answer, questions like 'What is your name?', 'Where are you from?' Then they started to show him videos. A cruise liner devastated in Malta. He could remember that. Pictures - Maruška Pavkovic, Charles

Tobin, Helena – or was it Ellie? The memories came back. A villa, a firefight. Then nothing.

He watched video of the Pope's Christmas Blessing – to a point. A nuclear bomb in the centre of Rome. His shock was apparent and captured on the room's webcam which monitored him 24 hours a day.

On the seventh day he had a visitor, a face he recognized but could not put a name to.

"The medical team says you are doing well."

"I know you – you are uh…we met in…uh…"

"Don't push it Baldwin. You are making progress."

"Where am I?"

"You are in a private clinic, in Hertfordshire."

"Why?"

"You were injured."

"How?"

"I don't know. You tell me."

"I can't remember a thing."

"The doctors say that you suffered serious head trauma. Delayed concussion and slight skull fracture – apparently it would have killed most people. Everything physical appears to work well, but you have some memory loss and you may never recover your memory of the missing period. Now, there is some bad news I'm afraid."

"What bad news? What you just told me sounds bad enough."

"It's Helena actually?"

"Helena? Helena who?"

"A Greek waitress."

"Oh, yes, yes, I seem to remember something. Dancing. Greece or was it Crete?."

"She's dead."

"Is she? That's a pity, she was fun, but that was a long time ago. Crete, definitely. Oh yes – then she showed up in Malta. Real name Ellie something. Not much recall I'm afraid."

"She was killed in a car accident – in Malta. Along with Bryan Elliott. Sadly, you were the only one to survive. Came off the road at Dingli cliffs – landed on a ledge. You were very lucky." Sadder than you will ever know, thought Ogilvy, but he could now tie it all up neatly in Malta and plant a few false memories.

There was no visible reaction from Baldwin.

"Do her parents know yet?"

"She has no parents. She was an orphan, brought up by several sets of foster parents in Bristol."

"But her father worked in the British Embassy in Athens. At least, I think that's what she said. My memory's a bit patchy."

"Is that what she told you? She certainly has – or had – the gift of persuasion and a wonderful ability to play a part. No, her natural mother was a junkie, she never knew who her father was."

Steve thought about the Greek waitress he's met, who had been – so she had said – an Oxford graduate. "Is that what she told *you*?"

"That's what the records say."

"Then the records are wrong."

"No Baldwin, it's your memory that's wrong."

"We captured that Serb bitch – Maruška Pavlov - didn't we?"

"Yes that is certainly true – Pavkovic actually- and a fine job you all did. HMG is very grateful."

"For what it's worth! Anyway I need to get out of here and back to Adèle."

"Adèle who?"

"Adèle, my yacht, in Malta."

"Ah, yes. That will not be possible I'm afraid, not yet anyway, not until you are fully recuperated, the doctors sign you off – and I agree. And there is another reason. More bad news."

"What?"

"The Tunisian authorities have impounded your boat."

"What the fuck, Tunisia, why is she there? The last I can remember is...is...Malta.

"You tell me how she got there."

"I can't remember. You know more than you are letting on. You must know what has happened to me over the last few weeks. Tell me."

"We only have a vague idea of where you were and what you did."

"Tell me."

"I'll look at the files and get back to you. The last we know is that your boat was in Malta. Now she is apparently in Tabarka – a port in Tunisia. The Tunisians claim to have strong evidence and would like to arrest you – illegal entry, kidnapping, murder."

"You must be kidding!"

"Not at all. They are seeking extradition. We have told them that you are too ill to be moved – for now. Your passport is there on the side table – there is no entry stamp for Tunisia in it, so you must have been there illegally, if at all. Look, Baldwin, HMG do not want you going to Tunisia. It would cause too many problems."

"Right, I see now. Same old bloody story. Stitched up again - just like the Gate of Tears."

"Gate of Tears?"

"That job in Djibouti when you landed me right in it."

"I don't know about Djibouti – before my time I'm afraid. Look Baldwin, you were very lucky to come out of this alive. However, HMG really appreciate what you did for your country in Malta. Let it rest – the doctors say you are bound to be troubled by the memory gap but you need to learn to live with it. Anyway, HMG will make reasonable funds available to cover your work, plus expenses. Stay here and recuperate properly for a few weeks and we will sort it out. I will be in touch when the doctors are ready to sign you out. Trust me."

Ogilvy omitted to mention that the UK did not have an extradition treaty with Tunisia.

Steve glared at him as he turned and left the room then settled back on his pillows to reconcile his memories with what he had just been told by his visitor, the man he remembered from the villa. He glanced at his passport – he knew it had been doctored and that he would never be able to find the joins.

He shut his eyes and lay back, his face a mask for the video monitor in the corner of the room.

The gap in his memory was only a few hours at most. He could remember being on the line and smashing through the window of the bank, the frantic work in the bank vault, Lee getting fried and then being on the scooter with Ellie. Then, then…nothing. Ellie dead? Car crash? Bollocks. Impossible. He would discover the truth. The impounding of Adèle was news though, bad news.

He did not know that 'C' had tagged Ellie's file as one of the two for special treatment, but that his own would be returned, untagged, to the Registry in the basement of Vauxhall Cross, on Ogilvy's recommendation. For now. These files were committed to paper. One copy only.

A few days after Alex Ogilvy visited Baldwin in hospital, Ellie Williams met with Ogilvy at Leo's Lebanese Grill on Baylis Road near Waterloo Station. It was a quiet lunch hour and they chose a corner booth, each with a view of one of the exits. They ordered mezze and water.

"How's the arm?" Ogilvy nodded at Ellie's left arm in a sling."

"Much better thanks. I should have this sling off next week and then a bit of physio and I'll be as good as new. Ready for my next assignment."

"Good to hear, you did well. We have plans for you."

The waiter arrived with the mezze and drinks and the small talk stopped.

"Why did you ask for this meeting Ellie?"

"Because I know the way the service works. Rome was a seriously dirty operation – as dirty as could possibly be - and there will be a clean-up in Six as surely as night follows day. All the Noel team are dead – very convenient. Baldwin has gone MIA. Tweedy in Aldermaston must be looking over his shoulder. No doubt his team have been read the riot act and been threatened in a dozen different ways – but their knowledge was limited. And you of course – are you safe, Alex?"

"Perfectly. Unassailable you might say."

Ellie looked at him and he held her gaze steadily – but he then diverted to help himself to some falafel.

"Great mezze here, though I don't get here as often as I should. They do grilled lamb on Thursday evenings – some say they slaughter it themselves out back – they've got a halal licence. Too much information, I know, but I enjoy it."

"Cut the crap Alex! You know that if what we did gets out then it would damage HMG beyond all comprehension. We would have no friends left in Europe – and we have precious few anyway since Brexit. The damage would last for a generation – at least. The Cousins would be pissed off beyond belief and the 'special relationship' would be broken - forever. This means that HMG cannot be found out. No way. That means that both you and I are at risk, considerable risk – of the final kind. God knows how Six is going to manage the members of Cobra. They must be crapping themselves – or have they taken appropriate precautions?"

"The final stages of the op were kept very close. The idiots in Cobra don't know the half of it. Anyway, you have nothing to worry about."

"That's just the answer I would expect from someone who has already received an order about me. You will be next, as sure as shit."

Ogilvy blustered. The stolen car was waiting around the corner.

"You are as safe as houses and you'll get a commendation out of this."

"You can bet your life I'm as safe as houses. I don't know how long you think I have got, but you had better cancel any operation to neutralise me. I have taken considerable precautions and if anything happens to me then the dirty washing will be hung out to dry by Wikileaks and others. Believe me I have this covered in a dozen different ways. I just want to retire and live in peace. And I want a full pension – thirty years' worth."

Ogilvy looked up, with something close to panic in his eyes.

"Thirty years – you're not entitled."

"Wrong answer, Alex!"

He looked hard at her, then made the decision.

"Leave by the rear entrance. Now."

She looked at him.

"Goodbye Alex."

"Go find your beach Ellie."

They nodded to one another.

Ogilvy took out his smartphone and keyed the ABORT code. He had already held a similar meeting of his own with 'C'.

*

References and Further Reading

3D Printed Human Body Parts:
http://www.bbc.com/news/health-35581454

Barack Obama on terrorists and the nuclear weapons threat:
http://www.reuters.com/article/us-nuclear-summit-obama-treaty-idUSKCN0WY52M

Chinese Investment in Africa:
http://www.forbes.com/sites/riskmap/2015/07/08/chinas-investment-in-africa-the-african-perspective/#41a2a4c416e2

Chinese Quantum Communications Satellite:
https://www.newscientist.com/article/2101071-china-launches-worlds-first-quantum-communications-satellite/

Cobalt-60 Availability:
http://www.tribuneindia.com/2010/20100412/main2.htm

The Crusades: The Authoritative History of the War for the Holy Land, Dr Thomas Asbridge. Eco, 2010. ISBN 9780060787288

Davy Crockett Nuclear Weapon:
https://en.wikipedia.org/wiki/Davy_Crockett_(nuclear_device)

Drone Swarms:
http://thediplomat.com/2015/04/drone-swarms-how-the-us-navy-plans-to-fight-wars-in-2016/

Eshkol-Comer Memorandum of Understanding:
https://en.wikipedia.org/wiki/Nuclear_weapons_and_Israel

Guoanbu:
http://intellibriefs.blogspot.com/2008/03/chinese-secret-service-from-mao-to.html

Krypton Fluoride Lasers for Nuclear Fusion Implosion:
http://www.ncbi.nlm.nih.gov/pubmed/26560597

Laser Pumped Fusion Research:
http://www.scientificamerican.com/article/high-powered-lasers-deliver-fusion-energy-breakthrough/

http://www.nature.com/nature/journal/v506/n7488/full/nature1300
8.html

MI6 help Gadhafi escape:
http://www.telegraph.co.uk/news/uknews/defence/10339439/Secre
t-MI6-plot-to-help-Col-Gadhafi-escape-Libya-revealed.html

Netanyahu, Benjamin on Iranian Nuclear Deal, 2016:
http://www.reuters.com/article/us-iran-nuclear-idUSKCN0PM0CE20150714

North Korea Hydrogen Bomb Test, 2016:
http://www.bbc.co.uk/news/world-asia-17823706

North Korea Submarine Launched Ballistic Missile test 2015:
http://www.reuters.com/article/us-northkorea-missile-idUSKBN0UK02P20160106

North Korean Ballistic Missile/Satellite Launch 2016:
http://edition.cnn.com/2016/02/08/asia/north-korea-rocket-launch/

North Korean New Submarine Pens:
http://www.janes.com/article/62516/north-korea-building-new-larger-submarine-pens

Nuclear Fusion Bomb Design:
https://en.wikipedia.org/wiki/Thermonuclear_weapon

Nuclear warheads – miniature:
https://en.wikipedia.org/wiki/Davy_Crockett_(nuclear_device)

Plutonium in Seawater off the Algerian Coast:
https://www.researchgate.net/publication/26501974_Plutonium_Isotopes_Concentration_in_Seawater_along_the_Algerian_Coast

Plutonium in Seawater:
http://www.sciencedirect.com/science/article/pii/S0265931X10002705

Protector Drone:
http://www.janes.com/article/55008/uk-to-double-top-end-uav-fleet-with-new-protector-platform

Remote detection of radiation using lasers:
http://physicsworld.com/cws/article/news/2016/mar/24/nuclear-contraband-could-be-spotted-using-laser-pulses

*

Author's Notes

It is August 2016 and as I have been writing the final chapters of this second book of The Maghreb Trilogy, the UK, Europe and the world have been witnessing events of huge historical importance.

The UK has voted to exit from the EU, resulting in a new British Prime Minister – the second female to hold the post. London is expecting ISIS sponsored terrorist attacks. Currency and equity markets have been in turmoil.

France is under continual terrorist attack and is at war with ISIS. Russia is eyeing European instability and Putin is calculating his chance of more land-grabbing after his annexation of the Crimea.

Turkey has been subject to an attempted Armed Forces coup and the President has taken unprecedented powers which amount almost to dictatorship, with mass arrests of opponents. The country's secular status appears to be in doubt.

The complex war in Syria has intensified, ISIS is arguably extending its grip on the Levant, and the US is bombing Libya.

In the Far East, the dispute over the Spratly Islands in the South China Sea has intensified following the decision by the Permanent Court of Arbitration in favour of the Philippines. China lost on every count and has announced that it rejects the decision.

In the UK, the decision to proceed with construction of the Hinckley 'C' nuclear power station has been delayed, partly it is thought, because of the new Prime Minister's concern about Chinese involvement in strategic UK infrastructure.

And just today, another North Korean ballistic missile test has been announced and the missile landed in Japanese waters.

In the build up to the US Presidential Election, the final candidates are an experienced female politician and an outlandish entrepreneur who has been described as 'mentally unstable' (http://talkingpointsmemo.com/livewire/ruben-gallego-trump-mentally-unstable) .

All this has happened within the last two months. And, of course, North Korean nuclear bomb and missiles tests are real.

If I had written these events into a novel as fiction the conjunction of circumstances would have been ridiculed as completely fanciful. Well, that's the privilege of an author – and, as they say, 'truth is stranger than fiction'. 'Sword of Allah' takes many of these events and facts and presents a tale which is potentially possible.

Although this book is a work of fiction, it is not beyond a stretch of the imagination – after all 9/11 took years to plan and organise. I have shamelessly embellished the facts and the political, military, scientific and technical aspects to develop a story which I hope you have found to be engaging, entertaining and informative – that, after all, was my purpose. And yes, some names have been changed to protect the innocent.

The framework of facts and actual events is available to you, the reader, in the References and Further Reading section.

A final point I would emphasise: The nuclear *weapon* technology involving lasers and a '*hohlraum*' is speculative, but the peaceful fusion research based on that design concept, at Lawrence Livermore Laboratories, is a fact, and the prime directive of the Laboratory is to enhance US national security. Should we fear for the future?

Finally, my thanks to Rosy Jensen for her critical eye, invaluable support and critiques during the writing of this book.

James Marinero
Portugal, August 3, 2016
james@jamesmarinero.com
Facebook: facebook.com/james.marinero

P.S. An online review of this book would be very much appreciated. Good or bad, your opinion can help me to improve what I deliver to you, the reader. Or, just email me your review.

About the Author

James Marinero grew up in West Wales and has at various times been a chef, a milkman, maths lecturer and private tutor. He spent over 30 years in IT as a consultant and project manager and ran his own computer business for several years.

He has been passionately involved with boats and the sea for over fifty years and is now achieving a lifelong ambition to write novels and entertain readers. He spends much of his writing time on his boat, which he has sailed extensively in the Atlantic and as far as Brazil. He is a qualified open water diver.

During his various careers he has worked in the Middle East, Russia, Scandinavia, the US, Kazakhstan and much of Europe. His wide educational background includes degrees in Physics, Oceanography and Business.

His personal interests, career, education and travel background have equipped him well to write adventure and techno-thriller novels.

When he is not on his boat he lives on the Hampshire coast.

The Magreb Trilogy

Sicilian Channel
Sword of Allah
Cause of All Causes (coming soon)

SICILIAN CHANNEL

Steve Baldwin, ex- Royal Marine, had sailed from Suez to Crete in search of the quiet life, still licking his wounds after a disastrous Red Sea mission and British Government treachery.

He tangles with Helena, a Greek waitress with a mysterious background. All is not what it seems and an agent tries to trap him into yet more dirty work. He is deniable and to avoid their clutches he leaves the island - only to find Helena waiting with bad news when he gets to Malta.

Islamist terrorism is spreading across the Sicilian Channel from the Maghreb into the soft underbelly of Europe – and Malta, with its Crusader history, is a key target. Abu ben-Zhair, the Islamist master planner, is upping the terrorism stakes.

Then, Baldwin's loyalty to his country is severely tested when he is coerced into the pursuit of a psychopathic female assassin – Maruška Pavkovic – with whom he shares some painful, bloody history. Can he ever escape these two clever, dangerous and demanding women – one of whom he has been ordered to kill?

Available from all good bookstores and online in all formats and via James's website: www.jamesmarinero.com

GATE OF TEARS

An up-to-the-minute (and beyond) thriller setting a ruthless psychopathic Serbian female terrorist against an ex-Royal Marine and an Australian gold mining oligarch.

Set in the context of the politically volatile Red Sea region and reflecting the revolutionary changes sweeping the region, political expediency with high level betrayal in Government and the Intelligence Services culminates in naval and aerial confrontation between NATO and Israel on one side, and China and the Yemen on the other.

Alaska to Australia, Britain to Djibouti, this is an illuminating look at Chinese Superpower ambitions - their worldwide Golden Shield Intelligence Program - humint, elint and cyberwar, together with their nuclear-powered blue water naval ambitions.

Available from all good bookstores and online in all formats and via James's website: www.jamesmarinero.com

Non-fiction by James Marinero

SUSAN'S BROTHER

In 1957, at the age of 9, Susan's brother was in an adult unit – a unit treating very seriously ill mental patients. In 1985, Susan's brother took delivery of an Aston Martin DBS.

The intervening 28 years hold a remarkable story about a man who grew and prospered as a successful engineering professional, but started out as a dyslexic 'slow starter', abused and unwanted by his parents and sister.

This is based on a true history, a history that gives hope, a history that demonstrates how simple acts of kindness by friends and neighbours can help someone overcome tremendous handicaps, identity denial and family abuse to become a success both as a person and a parent.

There is also a message about those who learn to abuse as children and continue that abuse into adulthood with their own children, and also about those in the extended family who turn a blind eye out of a misplaced sense of family loyalty.

This book has some dark moments, but it is a book written to uplift, as it was related to James, by Susan's brother.

Available from all good bookstores and online in all formats and via James's website: www.jamesmarinero.com